PENGUIN BOOKS

AFTERLIFE

Praise for the Parallon series:

'Full of twists, immaculately researched, it is very exciting and unpredictable' *Independent on Sunday*

'It's a great ride with evocative settings and intense emotion'
SFX (4 stars)

'WOW . . . that rare gem of a book that I can't stop thinking about and will read again and again . . . Outstanding! It's ten times better than *Twilight*' Waterstones, Cardiff

'Vivid . . . captivating and passionate'
London and South East Libraries

'It's a page-turning intellectual teen read that ANY adult would enjoy. Open the page, open your mind and go with the flow. TIP TOP TERRIFIC!' Waterstones, Thanet

'I enjoyed this book because of the strong characters and the fresh . . .

DEE SHULMAN has a degree in English from York University and went on to study Illustration at Harrow School of Art. She has written and/or illustrated about fifty books, but the Parallon trilogy is her first series for teenagers, which is surprising considering she lives on a campus with about 760 of them.

parallonbooks.com
deeshulman.com

AFTERLIFE

DEE SHULMAN

Book 3 in the Parallon series

PENGUIN BOOKS

PENGUIN BOOKS

Published by the Penguin Group
Penguin Books Ltd, 80 Strand, London WC2R ORL, England
Penguin Group (USA) Inc., 375 Hudson Street, New York, New York 10014, USA
Penguin Group (Canada), 90 Eglinton Avenue East, Suite 700, Toronto, Ontario,
Canada M4P 2Y3 (a division of Pearson Penguin Canada Inc.)
Penguin Ireland, 25 St Stephen's Green, Dublin 2, Ireland (a division of Penguin Books Ltd)
Penguin Group (Australia), 707 Collins Street, Melbourne, Victoria 3008, Australia
(a division of Pearson Australia Group Pty Ltd)
Penguin Books India Pvt Ltd, 11 Community Centre,
Panchsheel Park, New Delhi – 110 017, India
Penguin Group (NZ), 67 Apollo Drive, Rosedale, Auckland 0632, New Zealand
(a division of Pearson New Zealand Ltd)
Penguin Books (South Africa) (Pty) Ltd, Block D, Rosebank Office Park,
181 Jan Smuts Avenue, Parktown North, Gauteng 2193, South Africa

Penguin Books Ltd, Registered Offices: 80 Strand, London WC2R ORL, England

www.penguin.com

First published 2014
001

Set in 10.5/15.5 pt Sabon MT
Typeset by Jouve (UK), Milton Keynes
Printed in Great Britain by Clays Ltd, St Ives plc

British Library Cataloguing in Publication Data
A CIP catalogue record for this book is available from the British Library

ISBN: 978-0-141-34028-9

www.greenpenguin.co.uk

MIX
Paper from
responsible sources
FSC   FSC® C018179
www.fsc.org

Penguin Books is committed to a sustainable
future for our business, our readers and our planet.
This book is made from Forest Stewardship
Council™ certified paper.

For Max

So Far in the Parallon Trilogy . . .

Book 1 *Fever*

London AD 2012: After two expulsions, orphaned sixteen-year-old rebel misfit **Eva Koretsky** unexpectedly wins a place at St Magdalene's School for the highly gifted. There she finally makes some friends, joins a band (the Astronauts) and gets to play with the school's new electron microscope. When virologist Professor Ambrose shows her some unusual slides, she can't resist exploring further, and inadvertently becomes infected by a deadly virus. Defying all medical prediction, Eva survives, but is severely weakened and plagued by vivid nightmares.

Londinium AD 152: When eighteen-year-old gladiator **Sethos Leontis** is dangerously injured in the arena, he is taken to the house of his patrons to recover. There, he falls in love with Livia, their adopted daughter. But she is betrothed to Cassius, the ruthless Londinium procurator. Seth and Livia plan to flee, but Cassius and his guards intercept them. Seth is forced to watch Cassius cutting Livia's throat before they turn on him.

*

Parallon: Seth wakes up miraculously healed in a shimmering world where he has the power to invent his own environment. But he is alone – and Parallon without Livia is an empty prison. When he discovers the vortex, a fiercely guarded time corridor, and survives the experience, he becomes the reluctant protégé of Zackary, the vortex's mysterious guardian. Meanwhile, fellow slave Matthias has arrived in Parallon and, as more and more people follow, Seth discovers that all the inhabitants are connected by a devastating fever. Zackary finally agrees to help Seth track the fever by sending him through the vortex to begin research in the formidably equipped St Magdalene's School.

London AD 2013: Seth walks into the St Mag's biology lab and finds himself face to face with Livia. Except she calls herself Eva. And she doesn't know him.

When Eva sees Seth for the first time, some buried memory is triggered, but she doesn't trust it, especially as his presence seems to be exacerbating her nightmares, and his touch is almost overwhelming. Despite every effort to avoid him, she continues to be magnetically drawn to him, until she can resist no longer. He finally convinces her that she somehow shares a past with Livia and helps her remember their passion, and Cassius's vicious revenge.

But the rediscovery of their love is marred by the knowledge that Seth believes he carries a deadly virus, and one kiss from him could kill her. Having already lost her in one life, Seth decides, to Eva's dismay, that he is not prepared to take that risk.

The rift this causes almost breaks them both, and finally

unable to hold back any longer, Eva reaches up to kiss him, determined that wherever their love takes her it is a place she wants to go . . .

Book 2 *Delirium*

London AD 2013: Eva survives the kiss, but her health is deteriorating fast. She and Seth begin a desperate search to find out about the virus, both aware that her time is short. Despite all her computer-hacking skills, Eva cannot find a source. She is sure the mysterious Professor Ambrose holds the key, but she can't uncover his whereabouts. Meanwhile, Seth's blood-sampling experiments have revealed that his blood is 100 per cent lethal to every teenager at St Magdalene's. Teachers appear less susceptible, proving that there is an age correlation.

TV news journalist Jennifer Linden is investigating a series of mysterious disappearances and forms a reluctant alliance with DI Nick Mullard, the detective heading the investigation. When the Astronauts' record producer is arrested as a murder suspect for one of the disappeared, Eva comes into direct contact with Nick and Jen. Seth catches Eva just as she's about to tell Nick about Parallon. Though Seth prevents her from speaking, he feels completely betrayed. They argue and she watches in despair as he heads away into the storm. When he fails to return, Eva believes he has left her forever.

Parallon: The Romans, under the ruthless magister (aka Cassius), have taken over, transforming Parallon into a tyrannical Roman state, boasting a huge arena for endless gladiatorial battles. Determined to avoid slavery a second time, Matthias shows the

Romans the vortex, which they greedily appropriate in order to acquire an army of vicious soldiers.

London AD 2043: Worried about the way the escalating traffic is affecting the vortex's stability, Zackary sends Seth into the future to locate astrophysicist Louis Engelmann, an expert in wormholes and dark matter. While there, Seth, increasingly suspicious of Zackary and his motives, sneaks into Zack's lab and discovers the Parallon files – a digital environmental simulation, uncannily similar to the physical world of Parallon. But before he can find out more, Seth gets caught, and in his struggle to escape, accidentally infects Engelmann's colleague, Lauren Baxter, with the virus. Finding herself in Parallon, it becomes Lauren's unenviable task to try and repair the extremely unstable vortex.

London AD 2013: Matthias has been sent by Cassius to find Seth and bring him back to Parallon. Assuming he's with Eva in 2013, he unwittingly leads Cassius right to her. Seth arrives too late to prevent Cassius's death blow, and desperately tries to infect Eva with his own blood. As her body slowly disappears, Seth realizes that she will arrive unguarded into the hostile world of Parallon. He has to reach her before Cassius does . . .

Significant Characters from Books 1 and 2

London AD *2012/13*

Eva Koretsky, misfit, genius hacker, singer and guitarist with the Astronauts

Sethos Leontis, originally first-century AD gladiator slave in Londinium, travels to London 2013 via a time corridor

Astrid Rettfar, bass player and band leader of the Astronauts

Rob Wilmer, in love with Eva, plays keys in the Astronauts

Sadie Bekant, drummer in the Astronauts

Rose Marley, school matron

Dr Crispin (aka The Crisp), headmaster of St Magdalene's

Professor Ambrose, visiting pathogen virologist

Jennifer Linden, TV journalist, Channel 7 News

Nick Mullard, London City Detective Inspector (in a relationship with Jen Linden)

Brodie Covington, MI5 operative, former colleague and friend of Nick Mullard

Theo Mendez, indie record producer

Londinium AD 152

Domitus and Flavia Natalis, adopted parents of Livia

Sabina, Cassius's house-slave (helped with Seth and Livia's escape attempt)

Vibia, Natalis house-slave (helped with Seth and Livia's escape attempt)

London AD 2043

Professor Louis Engelmann, astrophysicist, former mentor to Zackary

Lauren Baxter, astrophysicist, colleague of Engelmann

Anton Trepov, doctor and friend of Zackary

Rana Shah, Zackary's intern

Parallon

Cassius Malchus, the magister, formerly Londinium procurator and husband to the missing Livia

Otho, one of Cassius's elite guard

Rufus, one of Cassius's elite guard

Pontius, one of Cassius's elite guard

Matthias, formerly Seth's best friend and fellow slave

Georgia, one of Matthias's girlfriends

Clare, friend of Georgia, in love with Seth

Elena Galanis, a café waitress whom Matthias inadvertently infected in 2013 London and brought over to Parallon

Winston Grey, a motorcyclist whom Matthias inadvertently infected in 2013 London and brought over to Parallon

Zackary, enigmatic figure who lives near the river and the vortex

Prologue

Zackary's Lab, London

15 November AD 2044

'No!' Zackary stared at the cage in horror. How could this be happening to him now? He thought he'd finally cracked this thing. In fact he was so sure this time that he'd virtually written his Nobel Prize acceptance speech.

So what the hell was happening to that rat? It was definitely sick. He glanced across at the others. They were all fine. Well – better than fine, actually. Their memory function was now off the scale. They could navigate even the most complex mazes with 100 per cent accuracy. And they could do it fast. On the multiple T-maze trial, each rat had completed the course in less than nine seconds. Their knowledge didn't have to be learned and memorized any more. It was embedded.

He'd created super-rats, which meant he was on the verge of step two: creating super-humans. Once his Memory Data Transfer program was operational it would change the world. Implanted memory would not only serve as a powerful medical remedy for dementia, stroke and brain trauma, but more significantly could eliminate the requirement for virtually all education.

Instant knowledge.

No more need for schools, universities or internships, ever. And although world recognition would be his primary reward, Zackary had no doubt that his twenty-three patents would be worth billions.

He glanced uneasily across at the sick rat. It was now lying on the floor of its cage, shuddering.

This wasn't the first time he'd had to deal with viral transmutation. The damned Tachyovirus had nearly finished him. One tiny code anomaly inserted directly into the hippocampus had killed 112 rats. But he'd eliminated Tachyo. He'd rewritten all the maze code, and ceased using the hippocampus implants. The direct receptor transmissions had been working like a dream. Until this last transmission. So how could it have caused such a reaction? He'd only incorporated one additional data stream: the preliminary human memory program. There shouldn't have been any glitch with it though. He'd used exactly the same direct receptor system as before.

This had to be an anomaly. The rat had to be suffering from some totally unrelated ailment.

But in his heart Zackary knew how unlikely that was. He peered into the cage. No. This looked nothing like Tachyo. It was way more virulent. The rat had started sickening within moments of transmission.

He knew he couldn't move on to trialling the other rats, let alone the human subjects he'd lined up, until he'd checked out the damn animal. He'd have to take a blood sample and eliminate any possible connection with the data transmission. So he pulled on a pair of latex gloves, unsealed a syringe and lifted the rat out of the glass cage to examine it. He couldn't believe how fast its health was deteriorating. It was now bleeding from its mouth and nose. Sighing, he inserted the syringe. The rat jerked violently, swung its head round and viciously bit his hand.

'Christ!' hissed Zack, frowning as he watched two small beads of blood oozing through the latex. 'Useless bloody gloves,' he cursed.

He gripped the rat's mouth shut to prevent any further attack, continued drawing blood until the syringe was full, then placed the shaking animal back inside its cage. It shuddered for a few seconds and then went still. Dead still. Zackary checked its pulse. There wasn't one.

He peeled off the gloves and threw them in the incinerator, cleaned his hand with an antiseptic wipe and took the blood sample across to his EPQ-scope. Pipetting a drop of rat blood on to a slide, he clipped the slide into place, set the record mode, then keyed in the magnification and watched the monitor.

'What the hell?' he breathed, instantly recognizing the spiky thread-like structures. But there were too many. They were everywhere: wriggling across the screen, invading the T-cells, multiplying faster than he could conceive. Tachyo had never proliferated this fast. There had to be something wrong with the EPQ-scope. He was just about to recalibrate, when he realized the screen had gone completely blank.

'I knew it. Damn malfunction!' sighed Zackary, more than a bit relieved.

He restarted the EPQ-scope and pulled out another slide,

then turned to the syringe to collect a second blood sample. The syringe was empty. Could he have taken out two syringes? He frowned. Where the hell was the rat-blood sample? He started banging around the lab looking for it. No sign of it at all. Cursing, he picked up the empty syringe to draw a second sample, and watched in dismay as it slipped through his shaking fingers. He stood blinking at the floor for a few moments, wondering why it appeared so blurry.

The recording, he suddenly remembered. He could slow down the recording of the first sample and see what was going on.

Zackary increased the magnification so that he could focus on one unique T-cell. Then he slowed down the playback time by 100. But it was still too fast to follow, so he slowed it down by 500. This time he saw everything: individual spiky threads worming into the central T-cell cavity, then splitting over and over until the cell was so bloated it burst. Only it didn't splatter everywhere – it just disappeared, leaving a completely empty screen.

Zackary snorted. Matter couldn't simply dematerialize. He played the recording again. And again. He banged his fist on the table and stood up. His legs felt shaky. He felt queasy. Thirsty. He needed water. As he moved across to the sink he glanced over to the sick rat.

The cage was empty.

Zackary swayed for a moment, gaping. How could it have escaped? It was dead . . . and the door was still clip-locked shut. Nonetheless his eyes swept around the room looking for an escaped dead rat. He stumbled across the floor to his monitor screen, slumping down in front of it.

He had to look over the transmission data again. If Tachyo was back he needed to find it and eliminate it. Right now. He was hosting a meeting later that day with the five competing tech companies. He'd guaranteed them watertight results.

God, it was hot in here. He lurched over to the window to let in some air, then sat back down at his screen, moving straight to the Parallon simulation. This was the data transmission he'd been trialling on the sick rat. He started scrolling through the code, comparing sequence strings, looking for anomalies. He scrolled through screen after screen, page after page, and was about to abandon it when he spotted something . . . a repeating code sequence jumping line by line up the screen, overwriting and replacing the original code. With each line the process speeded up, moving faster and faster up the screen, devouring years of Zackary's painstaking programming.

He blinked at the screen in horror. He had no doubt that he was watching a Tachyo-hydra: a super-virus that proliferated as he watched, and was now aggressively wiping out all his data – his world-changing data. And it wasn't going to stop until there was nothing left.

He began frantically trying to power off the computer, knowing that it was the only way to freeze the virus, but he'd programmed in a power-source override system which would take him at least twenty minutes to disarm. He glanced back at the screen. He didn't have twenty minutes. He didn't have twenty seconds. The virus had now devoured its way through 426,788 screens of data. Only six left. He stared at the screen in defeat, watching the sweat of his past and the dreams of his future evaporate.

And he had just transmitted that virus directly into the brain of a rat – and the rat had been as powerless to defend itself from the infection as his computer had been. It had skipped right across the organic component in the synthesized brain receptor at the most devastating pace.

He stared at the screen. The Parallon file – the summation of seven years' work – had only three lines of code left . . . He scrubbed his eyes. This had to be a nightmare. The screen was swimming. The whole room was spinning. He tried to stand up, he needed to adjust the thermostat, it felt like a furnace in here, but he couldn't seem to locate his legs. Why was the floor hovering at that strange angle? Why was he shivering in a pool of vomit? Why had the room gone so dark? Why was everything fading to nothing?

1

Lost

I opened my eyes and found myself staring up at a cloudless, velvety black sky. I blinked, mesmerized, as always, by the awesome pattern of stars scattered across the universe. But for some reason the view didn't fill me with the usual sense of tranquillity. Cold fear was coursing through me and I couldn't remember why.

I jerked my eyes away from the sky and looked around. I was lying on my back on hard pavement, in the middle of a dark, empty street. Unfamiliar buildings loomed over me. And I was completely alone.

My heart was pounding in my chest. I jumped to my feet . . . What was I doing here? I had to remember. Sounds. I could hear sounds. Marching feet. I shuddered . . . I knew those sounds . . . Roman soldiers . . . Guards . . .

Oh God, not Londinium. Please not Londinium. I stared wildly around me, my heart sinking: even in the murky moonlight there was no mistaking the marble columns, the uniform, ordered Roman buildings, straight paved roads. Swallowing the mounting panic, I glanced down at my clothes and frowned. In all my visions of myself in Londinium I was wearing long, fine tunics. But this time I was dressed in jeans, trainers and a white T-shirt . . . covered in blood.

Whose blood? Mine?

Suddenly memory crashed into me . . . Cassius. He'd ambushed me. Again.

How had the most feared Roman procurator managed to find his way into my world? He'd caught me outside a London rock venue!

Matthias! I hissed as the fragments fitted together. Matthias was how. Seth's treacherous friend had led Cassius straight to me.

And Cassius wanted me dead. I had felt his hands round my throat. I had seen death in his eyes. Yet here I was. Alive.

How had I escaped? And how the hell had I ended up in Londinium again? I hit my head in frustration. I just couldn't remember.

Tramp. Tramp. Tramp. The soldiers were getting closer. Were they coming for me? Was Cassius with them?

I started running – I didn't care where I went as long as I got away from them.

Staying close to the buildings, skimming through shadowy columned peristyles, keeping my steps light and soundless, I moved on and on, not once daring to stop. And my legs carried me easily. Running felt effortless, natural. Like it always used to. How was I managing to run this hard, this long, this fast? I'd been too weak to do much more than crawl for months. Was I dreaming? Had I fallen into one of my strange visions again? Would I wake up in hospital?

Or never wake up?

I stopped dead . . . I could feel my heart thud, hear my

8

panting breaths, feel my pulse race. This felt real. I leaned against a column and shut my eyes, relishing the cool stone at my back. Stretching my arms above my head, I skimmed my fingertips slowly along the ridged surface. My body felt so good. Like new. Like it didn't have a virus raging through it, crippling every cell.

I couldn't suppress the shiver of pleasure. It had been so long since I'd felt this way. Truthfully, the last time I felt this fit, I'd been too damned fixated on other stuff to notice . . . fighting with Mum and my stepdad, or running away from Downley Comprehensive . . . Now that old life didn't feel like it belonged to me any more. Even St Mag's felt weirdly remote. But that was good. I couldn't let myself think about St Mag's – not yet. I had to stay focused.

My eyes scoured the street. I'd chosen a useless place to stop. Even when I craned round the column I could barely see to the end of the road. I needed to get higher up if I was going to be able to find out where I was, or where the soldiers were headed.

Cautiously, I crept out of my hiding place and edged along the buildings to the end of the street. But this road proved as dark and deserted as the one I was leaving. The moon's feeble light barely touched the vertical columns and porticoes, which loomed like pallid ghosts in the night.

I stood for a moment wavering. I could hear sounds, though it was hard to locate their source. I held my breath, ears straining. There they were again . . . Definitely movement . . . rustling. I hurried quickly on, looking neither right nor left, until the bright flames flickering from two marble urns stopped me in my tracks. I felt a sudden wave of familiarity. They were flanking a pair of huge carved doors. Some part of my brain knew this place, could name it . . . the Temple of Jupiter. My heart was pounding again. I'd been here. Without thinking, I quickly skirted round the side of the temple, knowing that as soon as I'd edged my way to the back of the building I'd find . . . our meadow. I stood in silence, inhaling sharply as the scent of grass suddenly pushed me back to another time – a snatched moment with the boy I loved: I could taste him, feel the warmth of his arms round me, hear the urgent words he was whispering . . . to me, to Livia.

But as I looked for the heavy oak tree, our treasured meeting place, the momentary brightness of my memory was eclipsed by the ominous darkness that now shrouded everything. The warmth of the meadow evaporated, and I was staring at huge sinister shadows and looming hostile shapes.

Get a grip! It's only bushes and trees!

But my body was ignoring my brain's commands and began retreating towards the entrance of the temple. Maybe I could hide inside? I pushed hard on the doors. They were locked tight. I leaned against them in frustration. I wanted to pound my fist against the wood, but knew how stupid that would be. So, reluctantly, I turned away and squinted along the street. My stomach lurched. I was on very familiar ground here. Way too familiar. Just a stone's throw from the gaudy palace where Cassius had held me captive. I could even make out the silhouettes of the monstrous golden eagles that marked the building's grand entrance. I turned to go back, but the sound of the approaching soldiers forced me to veer on to a small unfamiliar side street. It was pitch-dark, but my legs remained steady as I crept relentlessly forward until I was rewarded with the glimmer of moonlight ahead. I rushed towards the light, but when I reached the end of the road, I froze.

Oh God. The forum. It was bigger than I remembered. And in my memory it was always daytime. Always filled with people. And noise. And . . . Seth. My treacherous mind conjured an image of him, a heavy wool cloak draped over his injured shoulder; his clear blue eyes burning into me.

A wave of misery and loss suddenly rocked me. How had I let him in again? Thank God Astrid wasn't here to catch that moment of weakness. She'd worked relentlessly over the months since Seth stormed away to help keep him out of my head.

But it wasn't fear of Astrid's wrath that forced my brain back to my present crisis. It was the sound of marching footsteps . . . terrifyingly close.

I was now standing frozen in the middle of the forum, like I'd deliberately placed myself there for target practice. I gazed frantically around. There was absolutely no cover here. I had to move. Fast. There was a road on the far side. Could I make it across before they saw me? I had never sprinted so hard, my own footfalls and heartbeat thundering in my ears, drowning out all other sound. I'd just about reached the road, and was on the point of ducking behind a low wall, when I felt a hand suddenly pressing against my mouth, and an arm banding across my chest.

2

Company

Parallon

'Thank you, Zeus,' gasped Seth as he staggered out of the river on to the bank. Hunching over, he tried to catch his breath. It was dark, but there was enough moonlight for him to to be able to make out the numerous injuries his journey through the vortex had caused. He was pretty sure he had cracked a few ribs this time too. But the pain didn't bother him, especially as he could already feel the healing taking place, reassuring him that he had arrived in Parallon.

'I should be thanking Lauren Baxter not Zeus for my safe passage,' he thought ruefully, as a wave of sickening guilt washed over him. Lauren had probably just saved his life, and all he'd done to deserve it was ruin hers. She'd had a great career at NASA until he'd destroyed it by infecting her with his lethal virus. Now she was trapped under savage Roman rule in Parallon, spending every waking hour trying to stabilize the vortex. If it wasn't for her, he'd be either flailing around in a hell of dark matter or . . . dead.

But he didn't have time right now to indulge in either guilt or gratitude. He had to get moving; his position by the water was too exposed. Crouching low, he ran silently towards the deep shadow of buildings. Within minutes he was nearing Zackary's house, but he wasn't stopping. He needed to hurry north, to the place where Eva would have arrived – before anyone else got to her.

He heard the guards long before he saw them. Patrols didn't move stealthily. Their function was to assert power and instil fear; so they didn't hide. Which meant they were easy to circumvent. Keeping to the shadows, Seth moved quietly past them, but his eyes continued to scan the streets warily. The guards would not be his only enemies. If Cassius was controlling Parallon in the same way he had Londinium, it was unlikely he'd operate without a network of secret police: men who knew how to move silently. Seth had been ambushed by them before, and he wasn't about to make the same mistake again.

Desperate to get to Eva, he moved fast but carefully, all senses on high alert. Which was how he heard a distant figure pounding heavily in his direction. Who travelled so recklessly through this dangerous Roman prison? He shut his eyes briefly.

Please don't let it be Eva.

His stomach twisted with anxiety. She would have no idea where she was, or what kind of hell she'd landed in. Immediately Seth headed towards the sound. As soon as he was close, he let out a snort of disbelief, and hauled the idiot he recognized off the road and into a doorway. 'Matthias! Do you want to guarantee every Parallon guard knows you're back?'

'Seth!' beamed Matt, ignoring his censure. 'I was trying to find you!'

'Lucky I found you first,' hissed Seth, rolling his eyes. 'You'd better hide out here while I look for Eva.'

'No way, man. I'm coming with you,' argued Matthias.

'You're not. I intend to travel *undetected*.'

'I'll keep quiet!'

Seth shook his head and pushed Matt back into the doorway. 'Wait here quietly, brother, until I get back.'

Matthias gazed up into those clear blue eyes and nodded mutely. His heart swelled with happiness. Seth was here. His world was back in balance.

3
Aftermath

Camden Town, London

12 July AD 2013

Rob was staring blankly down at the blood-stained clothes at his feet.

'Christ, Rob, the police are here.'

He heard the words, but they didn't penetrate his dazed brain. He was too confused. The last half-hour had effectively wiped out all coherent thought.

'Rob, the police are here,' Astrid repeated urgently.

'The police?' he echoed stupidly. Astrid was pointing towards the two sets of flashing lights at the end of the street.

Rob frowned. He was having a problem focusing. All he could do was look down at the blood. Eva's blood.

'Guys! We've got to get rid of Eva's stuff.'

'What?' he rasped, suddenly alert, suddenly aware of another woman – the woman now reaching purposefully towards Eva's clothes. His hand shot out, grabbing her shoulder and forcing her away before he was even conscious of his own fury. 'Don't you dare!' he snarled. 'Don't you dare touch Eva's things.'

'So you want the police to find them, do you?' the woman snorted impatiently.

Rob stared at her in disbelief. 'Who the hell *are* you?' he choked. 'Astrid, do you know who this woman is? Because I bloody don't.'

'This *woman* has a name,' hissed the stranger. 'Jennifer Linden. And I'd really appreciate it if you addressed me by it in future.'

'I'll bear it in mind,' he growled, fixing her with a burning gaze. 'Now perhaps you and your name could just get lost. Because there is no way we are going to get rid of anything of Eva's.'

He crouched down and ran a tender finger along the blood-soaked white T-shirt, his shoulders shuddering.

'You clearly weren't paying attention,' Jen snapped. 'Because if you were you would probably have noticed that a couple of minutes ago your friend, Eva, disappeared into thin air.' She paused to stare at Rob and Astrid ferociously. 'So, forgive me for asking, but how exactly were you intending to explain that small detail to the police and ambulance crew heading this way?'

Rob clenched and unclenched his fists. He was struggling to hold it together, let alone argue. He hadn't drunk or smoked anything that could possibly account for the nightmare he was now stuck inside. What the hell was going on? One minute they were playing the best gig of their lives and being offered an American tour; the next, their singer, the girl he loved, lay dying on the pavement. Then that bastard, Seth – the same bastard who had abandoned her weeks ago – was attacking her with a knife! And when he'd tried to stop the maniac, this Jennifer bloody Linden woman, and that weird Matthias guy, had held him back. So he'd been watching with impotent rage when the impossible happened: Eva Koretsky stopped breathing . . . and then literally disappeared. And instead of pulling the knife on Seth and making him pay, he had stood there gawping while Seth charged off into the night muttering something about getting to Eva before Cassius could.

Rob wasn't stupid, yet he was having a hell of a problem working out what in God's name was going on. He gazed imploringly at Astrid, but she was staring down at the bloodstained pavement looking as dazed as he felt.

Jen Linden's eyes were fixed on the three policemen emerging from their cars. She quickly pulled Astrid and Rob into the shadows behind a parked van. The police flashed their torches into the street, giving a cursory glance around.

'Probably a hoax call. We should head back to the Underworld,' one muttered to the other.

'Aw, really? I hate that place. Rock venues always bring on my migraine.'

'You're such a pussy, Trev! But we've got no choice. That's where the call-out came from. Better do some witness checks there just in case.'

Jennifer's mouth twitched. 'Good luck with that,' she muttered under her breath. They'd have a job getting a coherent statement from anyone there. It was dark, loud and totally rammed. Suddenly her mobile vibrated in her pocket. She winced when she noticed one of the policemen had a phone to his ear. Damn. She hadn't thought to block her number when she'd dialled 999 earlier. Who'd have guessed the response teams would be so efficient? Praying the PC was too far away to hear the faint buzz, she held her breath until her phone went silent and the police continued on their way.

'Look, guys,' she breathed to the frozen pair beside her. 'They might well come back, and if we get caught standing over the remains – I mean, the – er – stuff Eva left behind, the police are going to come up with the wrong conclusion. Those blood-stained clothes aren't going to help them catch the monster who did this to her. They are just going to implicate us . . . We *have* to get rid of them.'

Astrid and Rob just stared blankly back at her, which she decided to take as tacit acquiescence. Slipping from behind the van towards the clothes, she paused momentarily to gaze down at the grim way they retained the shape and position of Eva's body. Exactly as Nick's had. Her thoughts shifted involuntarily back to that awful hospital bed . . . the frantic team of doctors . . . Nick's motionless body . . . No – she couldn't let her mind take her there. She snatched up the clothes and tossed them straight into the wheelie bin she'd crouched behind earlier.

There was still blood all over the ground, but she was pretty sure the gathering rainclouds would rectify that situation before the police decided to come back.

'Right,' Jen hissed, 'we need to get you two back to your people at the Underworld without being spotted by the police.'

She reached for her phone, hoping the map app would offer a circuitous route to the venue.

'Damn.' The screen was flashing with a voicemail alert. 'Looks like I'll have to come up with something viable to tell the cops,' she muttered, homing in on their satellite position. 'OK, we can cut through behind the tube station, and get to the venue that way,' she grunted. 'Let's go.'

A few minutes later Rob and Astrid stood dazedly at the back entrance to the Underworld.

'You two look completely shell-shocked,' murmured Jen, feeling an unexpected wave of empathy. She had, after all, been a total wreck herself when Nick had disappeared. But she couldn't get sentimental. There was too much at stake. And too many unanswered questions. Especially about this evening.

'That guy – Seth . . . who exactly is he?' Jen asked.

'I thought *you* had all the answers,' snapped Rob.

Astrid shook her head at Rob and sighed. 'Basically Seth is – was – the love of Eva's life.'

'Hmmm – well, it certainly looked like he reciprocated,' mused Jen.

'Oh yeah? He *walked out* on her,' contradicted Rob icily, 'and broke her heart.'

'When did he walk out?'

'Months ago.'

Jen frowned. 'How'd they meet?'

'School. He was in our year.'

'You're kidding, right? No way is that guy a school kid. He's army, SAS . . . I dunno. You can't have *not* noticed the way he's built . . . the way he moves.'

Rob bristled. 'He was at our school –'

'Until he wasn't,' hissed Jen. 'So how long was he at your school?'

'He arrived the term after Eva.'

'That really helps.'

'Seth started at St Mag's in January,' clarified Astrid. 'And disappeared in May.'

'So where'd he go?'

Astrid and Rob shrugged.

'Weren't you curious?'

'We were doing everything in our power to try and stop Eva thinking about him. She was a total mess. The last thing we were going to do was speculate about where he'd gone.'

'So what was he doing back tonight?'

Neither of them answered. The question hung in the air.

'Did Eva ever mention a man called Cassius?'

'The guy that Seth went after?'

Jen nodded grimly. 'Cassius was the psycho that killed her.'

'What happened, Jennifer?' choked Rob.

'By the time I got there, she was already on the ground. But I saw him. Huge. Terrifying. And when that Matthias guy and I tried to stop him, he seemed kind of triumphant . . . gloating. He lifted her limp body, and tore into it with that huge knife . . .'

'Why?'

'Apparently it was a message for Seth.'

'*What*?'

Jen shrugged. 'He really hates Seth.'

'So – definitely not a random psycho.'

'Oh no. The way he attacked her was . . . personal. Sick.'

'Did Matt know him?'

Jen nodded. 'Definitely. So did Seth.'

'Jeez,' whistled Astrid, biting her lip.

'So. Eva never mentioned Cassius?'

They shook their heads.

'How well did you two know her?' asked Jen quietly.

They blinked back at her.

'Aren't you guys like – best friends?'

'What are you getting at?' growled Astrid.

'Well, didn't she tell you *anything*?'

Astrid's jaw twitched, and Jen shifted back defensively. 'OK – whatever. We need to stay in touch,' she continued. 'I don't know if Seth'll turn up again, but if he does, you have to ring me. Immediately. Any time. I really need to talk to him. Now, give me your phones.'

Rob's eyes widened, waiting for Astrid to erupt. Nobody pushed Astrid around. But she said nothing at all. Just handed over her phone.

A few minutes later, Jen had updated all three contact lists, and was shoving open the stage door. 'Let's just hear it one more time,' she whispered.

'Hear what?' asked Rob.

'Your *story*!' snorted Jen impatiently.

Rob rolled his eyes. 'Seth came back and persuaded Eva to run away with him – to Greece.'

'Rob, you have to get this right. You will be questioned hard. The disappearance of a pair of teenagers will not go down well. St Magdalene's security will be scrutinized. And the press might start sniffing around once they get any kind of love angle going. Which means you will be asked a lot of questions about Eva and Seth . . . So – did you have any idea she was planning to run away with him?'

'She wasn't –'

Jen looked exasperated. 'We can't let them suspect anything other than elopement. So – *as her best friends* – it's better if you *had a feeling* she was keeping something from you.'

Rob's fists clenched white, but he remained silent. Jen sighed. 'Look – I'm sorry you two had to get involved in this. It's big, it's messy and it's very scary. Probably the less you know about it the better.'

Astrid's eyes flashed. 'I have just watched one of my best friends bleed out on the pavement, Jennifer,' she hissed vehemently. 'I have no idea what is going on, or what this big, scary mess is, but don't you dare tell me the less I know about it the better. And if you expect me to betray Eva by pretending she didn't just get viciously attacked, but skipped blithely off into the sunset, then you don't know me at all!'

Jennifer pressed her fingers between her brows and massaged the skin. Astrid had just reminded her how incandescent she herself had been when the MI5 guy had told her to lie about Nick's death.

'Astrid, the last thing I want is for you to betray Eva,' she said finally, her voice husky. 'But think about it. Eva clearly didn't want you to get involved in this either.'

Astrid stood silently for a moment, biting her lip. Then she took a deep breath and nodded reluctantly. 'So, do you think she died because she knew too much?'

Jen didn't think so. Eva's death looked way more personal. But Astrid didn't need to hear that. 'Maybe,' she answered.

Her eyes drifted momentarily towards a movement near the front of the building. She craned round to see more. It looked like the police were heading in their direction.

'You'd better get inside,' she urged. 'Try to say nothing at all until Eva is missed.'

'That's going to be dead easy with Theo and his American guys,' Astrid muttered.

Jen raised her eyebrows.

'Yeah, OK, I'll come up with something,' growled Astrid. 'You coming then, Rob?'

Rob moved robotically towards the door.

'By the way,' Jen said suddenly, 'I don't suppose Eva ever mentioned Parallon to you, did she?'

They both looked blankly back at her.

'Just a thought,' she sighed, turning and walking away.

4

Reunion

How many times did I have to get ambushed before I started paying attention? Here I was again: an iron grip round my chest and a hand across my mouth. Memories of the last time flooded my head . . . Seth and I about to board a boat to freedom . . . Roman guards . . . paralysing fear . . . Cassius. I swallowed convulsively as images of his vicious face slid into my consciousness. *No!* I couldn't let him take me. I bit down hard on the hand at my mouth and struggled furiously to wrench myself free.

'For Christ's sake, do you *want* them to hear you?' a voice hissed in my ear, as I was unceremoniously dragged down behind the low wall.

He was speaking English. Not Latin.

A pulse throbbed in my neck. Not a Roman guard then.

I wasn't stupid enough to want to bring the guards rushing over, but neither could I assume that my captor was a friend simply because he wanted to avoid them too. And I wasn't a big fan of the whole hand-over-mouth, arms-round-chest thing either. Definitely didn't help pile on the trust. It wasn't doing great things for my breath control either. I continued to struggle . . . quietly.

'If I uncover your mouth, will you promise not to scream?' he rasped, as I chewed mercilessly at his hand.

I nodded. He slowly released my mouth and loosened his grip on my chest. As soon as I was free I swung round to look at him.

'*Pro-Professor Ambrose?*' I gasped.

After all this time. All this searching. The man responsible for infecting me with the virus was finally right in front of me. And, despite the millions of questions I had for him, I couldn't think of one word to say. I just gaped.

And he looked equally stunned. He was staring at me like I was a ghost.

'Come on,' he murmured finally. 'Let's try and get you back to my place before they clap you in chains.'

'Y-you've got a place? In L-Londinium?'

He blinked at me like *I* was the crazy one. 'This isn't Londinium, Eva.'

'B-but –' I gestured wildly round at the Roman buildings.

'Shhh,' he hissed, touching a finger to my lips. 'We'll talk as soon as we're safe. Come.'

'Why the hell should I come with you! You're the one –'

His hand clapped over my mouth again, and his furious features practically touched mine. 'Eva! If you stay here they will catch you and torture you. Now I promise you, whatever misconception you have of me right now, I have no intention of doing you any harm. I never did.'

I narrowed my eyes at him. Yeah, right.

He narrowed his back and hissed, 'Are you going to come quietly or am I going to have to gag you?'

Despite the threat, there was something about the slight

quirk of his mouth as he said those words that relaxed me a bit. For some reason it was an expression that felt strangely familiar and comforting. I huffed out a breath, rolled my eyes and let him guide me silently through an endless succession of colonnades and streets. From time to time he would pause, touch me lightly on the shoulder in warning, then pull me quickly behind a pillar or wall until another patrol of guards passed by. They seemed to be circuiting constantly.

What was happening here? It looked so much like the Londinium I remembered, yet the constant military presence felt way more sinister. Almost like I'd landed in the middle of a war zone.

'Nearly there,' breathed Professor Ambrose, pulling me firmly towards a doorway. I suddenly realized that we were right by the river. I froze. Just ahead of me was the exact spot Seth and I had been ambushed that fateful night when Cassius had forced me to watch my beautiful gladiator being beaten and tortured. My heart began pounding and I jerked sharply away. 'Where are you taking me?' I demanded, my eyes searching frantically for a place to run to.

Professor Ambrose grabbed my shoulders. 'What the hell's happened to you, Eva? You never used to be this –'

I pulled out of his grasp. 'You don't know me!' I hissed, my voice shaking with tension.

'Let me get you inside before they circuit again,' he sighed. 'I promise you'll be safe there.'

'Safe with *you*?'

He didn't answer, just held tight on to my hand and pulled me to the doorway. Swinging open a pair of heavy wooden

26

doors, he revealed a second door with a keypad entry code. This second door triggered another memory.

I'd been here before.

I was beginning to feel lightheaded and tried to slow my breathing as he dragged me up a staircase into a big room. A room I knew.

'Oh God, where the hell am I?'

'Don't you remember *anything*?' asked Professor Ambrose, pressing me down on to the sofa, and squatting down opposite me. He took my hands and tried to hold my gaze. 'Focus, Eva.'

I pulled away from him, burying my face in my hands. I was shaking.

He stood up and rubbed my back gently.

I stiffened. 'Don't touch me,' I snapped.

He sighed, dropped his hands, and moved away from the sofa. 'Would you like a drink? Coffee? Tea? Wine?'

I lifted my head to find him watching me, a tentative smile hovering on his lips. A smile that I . . . recognized.

'It's coming back, isn't it?' he whispered.

I looked around the room: Glass coffee table, white sofa . . . shelves of books.

'We're in your library?' I said uncertainly.

He nodded and smiled. 'You spent months exploring this library . . .'

I turned back to him sharply. His penetrating dark eyes looked so familiar. My eyes skimmed over his sharp cheekbones, the uncompromising mouth, the strong narrow jaw. But his cheeks seemed gaunter. His hair was greying and there was a network of faint lines around his eyes.

'What the hell happened to you, Professor? You look older. Way older . . .'

He flinched. 'A lot has happened since I saw you last . . .'

I shook my head, pulled myself out of the sofa and began pacing. It couldn't be more than six months since Ambrose came to St Mag's, but he appeared at least fifteen years older. I swallowed hard. Waves of jumbled images were beginning to tumble round my head.

'Where are we?'

'Parallon, of course.'

'Parallon!' I gasped. 'Seth's Parallon . . .'

'*Seth's* Parallon?' he sneered.

'Seth told me about this place . . .'

'Sethos Leontis, the gladiator?'

I frowned. Why did he sound so hostile? I backed cautiously away.

'This was *my* Parallon, Eva. Not Seth's. I brought you here myself.'

I felt myself begin to sway. What was he saying? I shook my head.

'Eva, I don't know what happened to you in Londinium –'

'You mean London, Professor –'

He shook his head, 'No, Eva, Londinium. The Romans –'

'W-What do you know about the Romans?' I choked, grabbing on to the back of the sofa for support.

Professor Ambrose started moving towards me, his hands held up in a gesture of submission. 'Eva – I –'

But he never got to finish that sentence because the door suddenly flew open and two people burst into the room . . . Matthias and . . . *Seth*.

'Talk of the devil!' hissed Ambrose.

Seth stood by the door completely motionless, his clear blue eyes fixed on mine.

'Eva . . .' he breathed.

I stared back at him, unable to believe that I was really seeing him again. And he looked just the same . . . *my* Seth . . . only – he wasn't mine any more. He'd walked out on me. Or rather – *run* out. The bleak memory of that awful night suddenly filled my head, until all I could see was the empty quad as I sat in the pelting rain, waiting and waiting for him to return. I closed my eyes. I had to get control.

'Eva, are you OK?'

I could hear him moving in my direction. My eyes snapped open. 'I'm fine,' I said quickly, unable to look away.

He instantly stopped moving, and we stared warily at each other. I suddenly noticed he looked like a shipwreck survivor – his clothes were all ripped and soaking, and he was covered in cuts and bruises.

'Seth, you're hurt –'

He shook his head and smiled. 'No, Eva. Nothing could hurt me now.'

'Very glad to hear that, Leontis,' snapped Professor Ambrose. 'But, as you're dripping Thames water all over my floor, the same can't be said for my parquet. I would very much appreciate a costume change.'

Although Seth's eyes remained fixed on me, his expression changed to one of barely suppressed fury. And almost before the fleeting expression had shifted, his ripped clothing had been replaced by a fresh pair of jeans and black T-shirt.

I had just witnessed the *Parallon effect* Seth had once told me about – the Intention–Creation principle. He had literally just willed his clean dry clothes into existence. And witnessing this weird phenomenon was somehow triggering memories of my own . . . I purposefully looked down at my bloodstained T-shirt, then watched in awe as I willed myself into a favourite hoodie.

Professor Ambrose chuckled. 'It's coming back to you, isn't it, Eva? Which hopefully means you will remember just how much I hate it when you wear that dreary, shapeless stuff . . .'

I gasped in shock as my comfy hoodie and jeans suddenly dissolved into a seriously uncool knee-length navy dress.

'What the –'

Before I could finish that sentence, Seth was standing with his hands raised between Ambrose and me. 'Don't you dare mess with Eva. She's –'

'She's what?' snapped the professor. 'If you think you –'

'*Stop!*' I yelled, pulling Seth back and glaring at Ambrose. I was about to say more, when my eyes registered a small movement by the door. Matthias. Hovering uncomfortably. '*You!*' I choked. 'How could you come here with Seth after what you did?'

Matthias bit his lip and shook his head. 'No – I –'

'Don't try and deny it, Matthias,' I whispered. 'Cassius told me.'

'Cassius told you *what*, Eva?' asked Seth in a chillingly quiet voice.

I clasped my hands together because they had begun to shake, and took a deep, unsteady breath. 'It was Matthias who led Cassius to London.'

'Matt?' demanded Seth, gazing at him in horror.

Matthias was shaking his head wildly. 'It wasn't like that, Seth – I had no choice . . . He took hostages – I didn't know what to do –'

'But you took Cassius straight to Eva?'

'No! I promise I didn't know he was following me – I just came to London to find you, Seth –'

'*For Cassius!*' I spat. 'Seth, you have to get away! Cassius knows you're alive and he wants you. Badly. He doesn't know where you are yet, but he won't give up until he does!'

Seth stared at me in disbelief. 'What are you saying, Eva?'

I frowned. How much clearer did I have to be?

'You have to leave –'

'Eva, I'm not going anywhere. You say Cassius wants me badly. Well, I want him more. It's time to end this.'

'No, Seth!' I gasped. 'You can't fight Cassius! He'll –'

'You're wasting your time, Eva,' snorted Ambrose. 'I'm assuming you know what Seth is . . .'

'What do you mean?' I snapped.

'He's a brawler! A gladiator! Fighting is the only thing he knows. He wouldn't know *how* to turn away from a fight, however hopeless the odds. And I can assure you, the odds are hopeless.'

'Well, someone has to fight him,' said Seth. 'Look around you! You've seen what he's done: Parallon's been turned into a prison. A Roman prison.'

'The soldiers and guards . . . they're all C-Cassius's men?' I croaked.

'Everything belongs to Cassius now,' hissed Seth. 'The soldiers, the guards, the slaves, the roads, the buildings . . .'

'And we're lucky enough to have with us tonight the skilful architect of this glorious new world!' sneered Ambrose, his eyes fixed on Matthias.

Seth frowned in confusion. 'What do you mean?'

Ambrose's eyes hardened, but didn't move. 'I've watched this man strutting from building to building, glorying in his handiwork . . .'

'Matt?' gasped Seth. 'Y-you turned Parallon into . . . this?'

'I was obeying orders, Seth! I had no choice.'

Seth stared at Matt in bewilderment. 'Cassius's orders?'

Matt squirmed.

'Matthias, what have you done?'

'Seth, I swear working with him was my only option – I couldn't be a slave, Seth. Not again.'

'What about the others?'

'Others?' stalled Matt.

'Your friends – at the house – Georgia, Clare, Elena . . .'

Matt didn't answer immediately. He was blinking down at his hands. At last he looked up, his face white. 'C-Cassius took them . . . to fight in the arena.'

'*What?*'

'He said he would make them fight in the arena until I brought you to him.'

'You were going to *trade* Seth for them?' I gasped, staring at Matt in horror. '*That's* what you were doing in London?'

'I-I thought Seth would be able to come up with a better plan . . . I just didn't know what to do!'

For a moment nobody spoke.

'It was the right thing to do, Matt,' said Seth at last.

'No!' I cried. 'Have you any idea how much Cassius hates Seth, Matthias?'

'Why exactly does Cassius hate him, Eva?' interjected Ambrose.

The room went silent. I stared at the table, but couldn't bring myself to answer. 'Long story,' I sighed, turning away.

Ambrose strode towards me and grabbed my shoulders. 'I've got all the time in the world,' he said quietly.

'Get your hands off her, Zackary!' snarled Seth, striding over and prising Ambrose's hands away.

'Zackary?' I frowned. '*Y-you're* Seth's Zackary? The man who showed him the vortex?'

Ambrose rolled his eyes. 'Well, I certainly wouldn't call myself Seth's, but yes, of course I'm Zackary. Professor Zackary Ambrose.'

I heard Seth release a slow breath as another piece of the puzzle slotted into place.

'But, Eva,' sighed Ambrose, 'you already knew my name.'

I shook my head slowly. *Did I?*

I glanced up into those dark impenetrable eyes. They were fixed on mine, and in a moment of blinding clarity I was suddenly absolutely certain that there hadn't been thousands of missing puzzle pieces. Just one. And he was standing right in front of me.

5

Stand-off

Parallon

'Start talking, Zackary,' demanded Seth. 'My patience isn't infinite.'

Professor Ambrose chuckled without humour. 'What a surprise that is,' he mocked. 'And I expected so much more from a *gladiator*. Very well, let's talk.'

Despite the palpable hostility in the room, Ambrose smiled broadly at me and pressed me on to one of the cream sofas. Then he lowered himself casually on to the sofa opposite. Seth, who had been smouldering in the middle of the room, strode over to sit down next to me. His shocking physical presence still had the power to double my heart rate. I edged away a little and could have sworn I heard his breath catch when I moved.

Matthias, who had remained hovering by the door since my bitter attack, now moved towards us until he was standing beside Seth, a hand on his shoulder. It was both a gesture of solidarity and gentle restraint. I glanced up at him and was shaken by the expression on his face. He was looking down at Seth with such fierce love that my stomach twisted uncomfortably.

Ambrose heaved a sigh. 'I have *some* answers, Sethos. But not all. There are clearly things I know nothing of.' He looked from Seth to me with narrowed eyes.

'What is Eva to you?' asked Seth furiously.

Ambrose shrugged. 'Wine, anyone?' A bottle of red and a bunch of stemmed glasses materialized on the low table in front of him. He didn't wait for us to respond before pouring our drinks and silently handing us each a glass. I was grateful for the physical distraction, frankly. Seth's burning presence next to me was becoming overwhelming.

We sat in silence, waiting for Ambrose to speak. He languorously swilled the wine around in his glass, slowly inhaled the scent, then took a long, leisurely sip. Seth shifted his weight impatiently.

'Zackary!' he hissed. 'We're all –'

'I had brought a few people over to Parallon before Eva,' began Ambrose, as though Seth hadn't spoken. 'And all but one had been very specifically chosen . . .'

'Chosen?' I repeated stupidly.

Ambrose sipped his wine, and fixed his intense gaze on me. 'You *know* all this, Eva,' he said quietly. 'I told you all this.'

I chewed my thumbnail anxiously. His words were achingly familiar.

'And then I chose you . . .'

My breathing hitched. 'You didn't choose me. You tried to kill me.'

Ambrose was shaking his head. 'As soon as you started asking those smartass questions in that school biology lab, I knew I had to bring you here. You were just so . . .' he swallowed, '. . . so bright . . . so alive . . . so curious. But for the first time ever, I felt qualms. You were still very young, I couldn't quite bring myself to – to infect you. So I gambled. I gambled on your curiosity. I left the virus with you. It felt more honourable that way – your decision, so to speak.'

'*My* decision?' I gasped. 'I had no idea what I was touching. How could I?'

He shrugged. 'You're a scientist, Eva. You needed answers, didn't you? You didn't care about the consequences . . . That's because you're just like me.'

'Eva is nothing like you!' shouted Seth, jumping to his feet and rearing towards Ambrose venomously.

Matt grabbed Seth's shoulders, holding him still. 'Sit down, brother,' he murmured soothingly. 'We need to hear what he has to say.'

Seth stood for a moment longer, tensing his fists, while he regained control. Then he slowly sat down.

'So what went wrong?' I asked quietly. 'Why didn't I die?'

Ambrose stared at me in bewilderment. 'What do you mean, Eva? You did die. You came straight to Parallon.'

'No,' I argued, my voice tight. 'I got the virus. Nearly died. And then I recovered. Sort of.'

'Eva, look around you. You know this place. You came here. You must remember it.'

I gazed around the room. I couldn't deny it. I had been here before. I knew that if I walked out of the door and turned left I would find the kitchen. And if I took the stairs to the next floor I would find . . . my bedroom.

My bedroom.

I had lived here.

I swallowed. 'Your lab is downstairs,' I said huskily.

All eyes turned to me: Seth's filled with confusion; Matt's unreadable. Ambrose just looked kind of relieved.

'Zackary –'

The moment of tension was broken when a tall, blonde, attractive woman suddenly burst into the room.

Ambrose smiled. 'Lauren! Excellent timing. Do come and meet my – er – guests . . .'

The woman moved cautiously towards us.

'Seth, of course, you already know. And this is Matthias, and over here is Eva. Eva Koretsky. Do join us for a glass of wine.'

Her eyes shifted between us as she sat on the sofa next to Ambrose and took the proffered glass. 'I feel I'm intruding,' she murmured warily.

Seth laughed hollowly. 'No, Lauren. Zackary did all the intruding a long time ago.'

Lauren frowned at his tone, and her eyes flashed from Seth to Ambrose.

Seth cleared his throat. 'Zackary?' he prompted.

Ambrose closed his eyes briefly and nodded. 'So . . .' he said finally. 'I gave Eva the virus and when she arrived in Parallon, I brought her to my house.'

'To live with you?' asked Seth quietly.

Ambrose nodded. 'To live with me.'

I kept my eyes on Ambrose, but I could feel Seth staring at me. I could hear him swallow. I could feel the sofa tremble. I could practically hear his brain ticking.

'You – and Eva . . . ?' he choked.

'*Don't be crazy, Seth!*' I hissed, not daring to look at either of them. But Seth wasn't the only crazy one here. I was totally freaking out. I mean, why the hell didn't I remember any of this? My heart was thudding, my hands shaking. I reached for my glass of wine and slopped it towards my mouth. Ambrose leaned across the table and put a hand on my arm.

'Hey, calm down, Eva,' he soothed. 'You never used to be quite this jumpy! You trusted me! You were my perfect little protégée until . . .'

'Until w-what?'

He sighed. 'Until I messed up.'

We waited, while Ambrose poured himself another glass of wine. 'When I first brought you here, Eva, you were a damned spitfire; furious with me for infecting you with the virus, and stomping around like a sullen brat. You even tried to run away a couple of times.'

I felt Seth shift his weight next to me as he hissed out a breath. I didn't dare look at him.

'But despite your obvious hostility I could tell you were intrigued by the place. So I proposed a deal.'

'What kind of deal?' snarled Seth, jumping up with barely contained rage.

'Get a grip, gladiator, for God's sake,' hissed Ambrose. 'What the hell do you take me for?'

Seth remained standing, while Ambrose continued. 'I agreed to teach Eva anything and everything she wanted to know, as long as she accepted my timescale; and in return she promised to give Parallon a chance.'

Seth's eyes darted to mine. I was chewing nervously on my lip.

'After a year or two –' Ambrose continued.

'*A year or two?*' I gasped.

Ambrose nodded. 'I think so. It's so hard to gauge time here. Anyway, after a year you'd pretty well assimilated. You'd read virtually everything in my library. I'd taken you into the lab a few times. I'd even started telling you a bit about my life before Parallon . . .'

I gazed at him dubiously. 'And then?' I prompted.

'And then I let you talk me into doing something really stupid.'

I blinked.

Ambrose took a deep breath. 'I'd made a careless mistake . . . which you thought you could sort out. And – and I let you try.'

'What kind of mistake?' I asked.

His jaw twitched as he glanced around the room. His mistakes clearly weren't topics he enjoyed discussing.

'I'd inadvertently brought someone to Parallon. Someone I really didn't want here.' He ran a hand through his hair.

I bit my lip. I was getting a very bad feeling. My eyes flicked instinctively to Seth's. He was watching me, his expression unreadable. Dragging my gaze away, I looked back at Ambrose whose eyes were also fixed on me. I waited for him to continue. But he didn't. Instead he stood up, sauntered over to the bookshelf and picked out a book. Then he returned and dropped it in my lap.

I glanced down at it, and my eyes began to swim. I didn't need to open it. It was so damned familiar I knew every page.

'My Latin conversation book,' I breathed.

Ambrose smiled, sat down on the sofa opposite me and sipped his wine. He was watching me. And waiting. Waiting for the memories to flood my brain.

6

Recovered Memories

Parallon Past

Professor Ambrose was frowning at me. As usual.

'What?' I asked, rolling my eyes. I put down the book and sighed. 'It's not that hard!'

'English is an excellent language – and one we both speak well. This one, on the other hand, was dead nearly 2,000 years before you were born. And not without reason, I might add. So why on earth would you want to have conversations *in Latin*?'

I shrugged. 'It's fun?' I suggested lamely.

He shook his head. 'No, it isn't fun. Microbiology is fun. Flying a plane is fun. Latin conversation isn't. Where does this weird interest in Latin come from, Eva?'

'You can probably blame Shakespeare, Professor.'

'Please stop calling me Professor, Eva. You know my name.'

He'd told me his name hundreds of times: Zackary. But it felt too informal to call him that.

'I read *Julius Caesar* when I was a kid. Then I got into Roman history. Latin just came after that.'

'Lord, were your parents on some kind of hot-housing mission?' he laughed.

My parents? No way was I going there.

I deflected. 'Nah. Nothing like that. I – I just had a lot of free time.'

He steepled his fingers under his chin and gazed at me. 'Why are you so attracted to the Romans, Eva? They're a brutal lot.'

I rolled my eyes again. 'Duh. Yeah, they were brutal – but they were also brilliant . . . And Latin is so – well – cool.'

Ambrose was biting his lip. 'You certainly have an aptitude for it. I wouldn't be surprised if you could actually pass for a Roman!'

'Shame we can't test that particular theory,' I sniggered.

'Actually . . . we can,' he responded quietly.

I stopped laughing, and narrowed my eyes at him. 'Why do you do that, Professor?'

He raised his eyebrows. 'Do what?'

'That whole cryptic thing. You know I hate it!'

His mouth quirked. 'Nothing cryptic about my last statement.'

'Course not! OK – so – let's go find a couple of Romans for a bit of Latin conversation, shall we?' I snorted, getting to my feet and waiting with my arms folded.

'There's only one Roman in Parallon,' murmured Ambrose, staring up at me. 'And he's the last person I'd want you to have a conversation with.'

'What?' I gulped.

Ambrose was looking vaguely uneasy.

'Professor, are you seriously telling me we-we've got an actual ancient Roman living here?'

'Eva, sit down. I want to talk to you . . .'

I reluctantly sat down again. His voice had an ominous quietness.

'. . . I want to talk to you about Parallon.'

My head shot up.

Finally!

Although Ambrose had honoured our deal, and been a tireless, generous teacher, happy to talk to me about anything from Solid Angle Definition to fresco painting in Renaissance Italy, he had remained extremely resistant to any conversations about Parallon itself.

And there was so much about the place I just didn't get.

I knew that it seemed to operate under different physical laws. Time passed; we could measure it; but nothing seemed to be marked by it. Nothing aged or died. And objects clearly didn't possess an equivalent molecular structure to those on Earth. Obviously anything that could be *willed* into or out of existence had to obey different laws of matter, and I had hundreds of questions on the subject that he hadn't answered yet.

I got the impression Ambrose had lived in Parallon for ages. I also knew he'd found a way of travelling back to our world. After all – that's how I met him in London. But whenever I asked him how he got there, he just shook his head, and said, as he did about all things Parallon: 'All in good time, Eva.'

Yet suddenly he was opening up! I glanced across at him. His expression was tense.

'As you know, Eva,' he began uneasily, 'you aren't the only person I've ever brought here.'

I nodded. Although I'd hardly encountered anybody else, Ambrose had told me there were several others. But being

42

a total social misfit I'd been in no particular hurry to check out the rest of the Parallon gang.

'When I learned I could leave Parallon and return to our world,' Ambrose went on, 'I was a bit like a kid in a sweet shop. Over-enthusiastic. Especially when I discovered the elasticity of time. Occasionally, when somebody particularly interested me,' he looked pointedly in my direction, 'I brought them back to Parallon.'

'Using the virus,' I breathed.

He nodded, and looked at me defiantly. 'I was extremely particular, Eva. We are talking a *handful* of people from the entire compass of time.'

His eyes dropped to his lap and he fidgeted with a thread on his shirt.

I waited.

'Only, unfortunately, on one occasion, I infected a man in error . . .'

'Who?'

'A Roman. In Londinium.'

'Why was he an error?'

'He was vicious and brutal. And now he is here . . . I don't want people like that in Parallon.'

'There are vicious and brutal people everywhere, Professor.'

'Not here,' he said firmly.

'What has he done?'

Ambrose shook his head. 'Not much – yet. I just know what he's capable of.'

'How?'

'Because I saw him in action in Londinium.'

'You actually visited Roman London?' I gasped in awe.

'Yes, I actually visited Roman London, Eva,' he intoned, rolling his eyes.

'Can *I* go?' I whispered.

'Absolutely not,' he snapped.

'Why?'

'Were you not listening when I mentioned the savage and brutal part?'

'Our history is full of savage and brutal, Professor –'

'But we don't have to go and look for it!'

'*You* went. So it wasn't too savage and brutal for you.'

'I'm older and wiser . . .'

'My Latin is way better than yours.'

'Latin conversation doesn't get you very far when a bloody great brute of a man is throwing you on to his bed.'

My eyes widened.

'All I'm saying, Eva, is that women there are a lot more vulnerable than men.'

'Roman women were pretty powerful, comparatively . . .'

'Not girls of your age! Enough now. Let's go for a walk.'

But I nagged away at it. For days.

'The Roman, Professor. You have to tell me what happened.'

'No, I don't. Now please just let it go.'

'What if I bump into him here? I need to know what to expect.'

That got his attention.

'You see someone in a Roman tunic – you walk in the other direction.'

'Who *is* this guy?'

Ambrose gazed at me for a moment, then sighed deeply. 'He was some kind of guard. I made his acquaintance in Londinium when I was unfortunate enough to witness him disciplining a couple of street-sellers.'

'What kind of disciplining?'

'Eva, you don't want to know.'

'So how did this guard end up here?'

'I accidentally got in the way.'

'Accidentally?'

'Definitely accidentally. When the violence erupted I was trying to get the hell out of there. I got spotted. This guy didn't like people walking away from his particular brand of entertainment.'

'So what did he do?'

'He hit me across the face. Drew blood.'

Ambrose shrugged as if that was the end of the story. And I guess for the Roman it was.

'Is there any way of getting him out of here?'

'Too risky.'

'Why?'

'Eva, you're an exceptionally bright girl. You tell me.'

I groaned. He was always doing that – making me work for my answers.

'OK – so if Parallon is some kind of alternative universe . . .'

He raised his eyebrows. With Ambrose, that could mean anything. I shrugged and ploughed on.

'. . . it means you have to be using a – a wormhole to travel to and from our world?'

I glanced nervously across at him. I caught the twitch of a smile. That gave me the confidence to go a bit further. 'So why can't you take the Roman through the wormhole and dump him back in Londinium?'

'Pretty good reasoning, Eva. Apart from the last section.'

'You mean the dumping bit doesn't work?'

He shook his head. 'I love the idea of dumping him back in Londinium. Especially because if I took him back to his own time, there's a high chance he'd get trapped there . . .'

'Trapped?'

'Unless you travel through the vortex with a clear destination, your cells are hard-wired to return to their point of origin . . . the time of your death. Definitely not a good place to end up. It is where you are molecularly at your weakest, physically insubstantial and with no muscle or oxygenated blood to sustain you. If anyone was unlucky or stupid enough to find themselves there, the chances of them making it out again would be very slim.'

'Cool! So there's your solution. We dump the Roman in the vortex!'

Ambrose shook his head. 'Can't risk it.'

'Why not?'

'Because I happen to know someone who survived.'

I stared at him for a moment. Then realization dawned. '*You* . . . Of course! How else would you know?'

He nodded. 'Fortunately, I hadn't even got out of the vortex when I realized what was happening. Only someone immensely powerful would be able to compete on a molecular level once they were tackling air and gravity.'

'So it's very unlikely your Roman guard would make it back then.'

'The odds are good, but not good enough. I can't risk exposing the wormhole to him. Not a man like that. A time corridor between two worlds would offer him almost infinite power.'

Ambrose wasn't going to cave. I had to let it go. But I carried on thinking about it for days and days . . . Until I came up with another plan: an awesome one.

'Professor, you don't happen to remember the date of your meeting with that Roman guard?'

'Sometime in January AD 153.'

'So – supposing someone arrived in Londinium at a point in time before that, and managed to change the circumstances so that the guard wouldn't be around in January AD 153 to meet you . . .'

Professor Ambrose gazed at me for a few minutes. 'Potentially even more risky given the danger of creating a time anomaly.'

'I really don't think –'

'Clearly!' snorted Ambrose, rolling his eyes. 'Eva, you know enough about causal effects not to make reckless suggestions. Even a slight event-shift could set off a devastating chain reaction.'

'What about the hefty time anomaly you already created by infecting the guard in the first place?' I spluttered. 'I'm only offering a possible way to repair it.'

Ambrose narrowed his eyes at me in warning. He didn't like it when I got sassy. But – hey – I was right, and I could tell he was kind of considering my idea.

Neither of us mentioned my awesome plan for about two weeks. In fact I'd almost given up on it, when suddenly Ambrose came storming into the library, fury emanating from every pore.

'Professor?'

'For Christ's sake, Eva, my name is Zackary!' he shouted, striding into the kitchen and noisily attacking the coffee machine.

I sat at the table trying to focus on the book I'd been reading. Ambrose could be pretty volatile at times, and this was clearly one of those times. I had discovered that my instinctive strategy – get the hell out of the line of fire – didn't work well. He always got worse when I ran out on him. So I'd learned to sit the moods out.

When two mugs of coffee slammed on to the table and Ambrose flung himself into a chair opposite me, I cautiously looked up.

'OK, Eva – we're going to discuss your plan,' he said tightly.

I bit my lip. Did he mean the Londinium plan?

'What's happened?'

He held his mug in both hands and stared down at the contents. 'I want that bastard out of Parallon.'

'What did he do?'

Ambrose shook his head. 'You don't need to know, Eva. But the truth is I think you will probably be safer in Londinium at the moment than you would be here, which is why I'm prepared to consider the plan.'

'But won't he be in Londinium too?' I whispered.

'Yes, but he won't be immortal there,' hissed Ambrose. 'And if we play it right, you won't ever have to go near him.'

A few days later, Ambrose and I were shivering in wet Roman garments on the bank of the River Thamesis. The year: AD 152.

7

A Simple Plan

'You went with Zackary to Londinium?' Seth hissed, gazing at me like I'd grown two heads.

My throat felt thick as I tried to swallow. I nodded, my eyes darting around the room. Ambrose was sitting opposite me, kind of smirking. Matthias was looking totally bewildered, and the slightly scary Lauren just sat frowning into her wine glass.

'How could I have forgotten so much?' I murmured, staring wildly back at Seth.

He leaned across the sofa towards me and put a finger out to brush back some hair from my forehead, and then stopped, pulling his hand away, like I was something poisonous.

'So, what happened when you got to Londinium?' Seth asked through gritted teeth. He drained his glass, and roughly grabbed the bottle for a refill. At no point did he try and look at me again.

I opened my mouth to tell him, but my throat had completely seized. I bit my lip hard, frantically trying to still the horrible quiver that indicated tears were gathering.

Ambrose cleared his throat. 'Perhaps I'll carry on from here, shall I, Eva?'

I nodded mutely.

'As soon as we arrived in Londinium I took Eva to meet a woman called Tavinia Agrippa –'

'Flavia's best friend,' I gasped. 'I remember her!'

At the mention of my adopted mother's name, I felt Seth freeze beside me.

Ambrose glanced at him quizzically, but continued. 'I'd met Tavinia at a banquet on my previous visit, where after only two glasses of wine she'd become appallingly indiscreet, and told me how worried her childless friend Flavia was, because her husband, Domitus, was threatening to divorce her in favour of a fertile woman. It took very little *persuasion* to convince Tavinia – and then Domitus and Flavia – that their troubles would be over if they adopted my beautiful young protégée . . . Livia.' Ambrose waved his hand casually towards me.

'It was a perfect plan. Flavia and Domitus were delighted with the transaction. Their adopted daughter's Latin conversation was articulate and witty, as was her Greek. Eva's guitar skills made her an accomplished kithara player, and she sang like . . . an angel. She was the consummate asset, and they were completely smitten.'

'But *why*, Zackary?' croaked Seth. 'Why would you put Eva in that situation? What were you hoping to gain?'

'Pretty straightforward really . . . Domitus was a close associate of the procurator – Cassius Malchus . . .'

My own shudder at the mention of Cassius's name was completely eclipsed by the furious hiss that erupted from Seth. Ambrose'e eyes flashed to mine uneasily as he continued.

'And it was one of Cassius's elite guards – a big bastard called Pontius – whom I'd inadvertently brought across to Parallon. I was pretty sure that with her charm and skills alone, Eva would be compelling, but with the added bonus of the time-amp factor –'

'The what?' interrupted Lauren, mystified.

I rolled my eyes and glanced at Seth. He was – after all – the master of time-amp. But Seth just lifted his glass to his lips, leaned back in his chair and continued his impassive gaze at Ambrose.

Matthias cleared his throat. 'When we travel through the vortex, certain characteristics get – well – amplified . . . The further away you get from your own time, the more powerful and controllable that amplification becomes. So if you are naturally charming or persuasive, you will be more so.'

Lauren nodded slowly. Then her eyes flitted across to Seth. 'Yep,' she said, 'I think I know exactly what you're talking about.'

A muscle in Seth's jaw twitched, but otherwise he remained unresponsive.

'Anyway, with her particular gifts,' continued Ambrose, 'I was pretty sure that Eva would find it easy to persuade Cassius that Pontius had behaved inappropriately in some way, and have him removed from service. That way, Pontius would be far away when I arrived eight months later. Simple.'

'So in coming up with your *simple* plan, Zackary, it never occurred to you that by pushing Eva directly into the path of Cassius, the most sadistic psychopath in the whole of Londinium, she might be in any kind of danger?' roared Seth.

Ambrose paled and swallowed. 'Eva promised me she would head straight back to Parallon if anything went wrong,' he whispered. 'You gave me your word, Eva!' he accused huskily, leaning across the coffee table to grab my hand. But Seth threw himself between us.

'Don't you dare touch her, Zackary. You and your spectacularly *simple* plan got Eva's throat cut!'

There was a heavy silence.

I took a deep breath. 'Actually, it was *my* spectacularly simple plan, Seth,' I said, holding his gaze with mine. 'And – and I don't regret any of it.'

'*What?*' he gasped.

'If I hadn't gone to Londinium, I-I would never have met y–'

But I was too humiliated to finish that sentence. I quickly stood and walked out of the room, up the stairs and into the bathroom. As soon as I made it through the door, I turned the lock and leaned my head against the cool tiles. Only then did I allow the tears to fall.

8

Doubts

Parallon

Seth stood up and slammed out of the room. He needed to hit something, someone . . . and the list of worthy recipients was growing fast.

Although Cassius was indelibly at the top of the list, Zackary was definitely a close second. The man had just freely admitted that he'd taken Eva to Londinium, placed her in terrible danger and then left her there alone. Of all Zack's sins, and there were clearly many, this one was unforgiveable. Seth wanted to pummel the man into oblivion.

But right now he had to go after Eva. Talk to her. She had hardly looked at him since he'd arrived. Why? And she wasn't wearing the ring he'd given her – the ring she never took off. Could Cassius have taken it, or . . . did it mean something else? What the hell had happened since he last saw her? It had only been a few days.

And then he remembered . . . for Eva it had been much longer. But still . . . why did she seem so cold? He cursed Zackary again. This was all *his* fault too. Not only had he convinced Seth to go on the kamikaze mission into the future, he'd also sworn that Seth would be back before Eva noticed he'd gone. Seth's jaw tensed in misery. How well he'd been played. But surely he hadn't been gone so long that Eva had stopped loving him?

He needed to talk to her. Right now.

He climbed the stairs two at a time and began swinging open random doors . . . three bedrooms and a study. All empty. Only one door left to try. He turned the handle. Locked.

'Eva!' he shouted, hammering with his fist. There was a small movement inside. 'Eva?' he whispered. 'Please open the door.'

He thought he heard her crying. 'Please, Eva!' he implored.

'G-go away, Seth!' she croaked.

'I can't,' he whispered. 'Please don't make me leave.'

He heard her hollow laugh. 'You already did that. Months ago.'

'Eva, I never –'

'There's nothing to say, Seth. I'm sorry; I-I'll be OK in a minute. I just need some time to – to get my head round everything.'

'Please just open the door, Eva! Together we can –'

'*Together?*' she choked.

Seth rattled the door handle in frustration.

'Stop, Seth! Please don't do this.'

'Do what, Eva? What am I doing?'

He stood with his palms flat against the door and waited for her to answer. But there was no response.

'Eva?' he whispered again. He pressed his forehead to the door, willing it open, but Eva's will was stronger, and the door remained resolutely shut. At last, he squatted down on the floor outside and leaned his head against the wall.

Flexing his shoulders, he tried to take some good deep breaths. His body hummed with excess adrenaline. If he didn't get his mind off the girl in the bathroom refusing to talk to him, he was going to smash the damned door to pieces. And that wouldn't go down well with anyone.

You are a gladiator. Your body is a machine that you control.

He replayed his mantra over and over in his head, until his fists gradually unlocked and his muscles relaxed. But the moment he released the tension, his mind skipped free, and began sifting through the latest revelations.

When he thought about it, it seemed kind of obvious that Zackary should turn out to be the elusive Ambrose. Zackary was ubiquitous . . . literally everywhere. And wherever he went, bad things followed. He'd never trusted the man.

But Eva did.

She'd spent months at St Mag's hating and relentlessly pursuing Ambrose, but now that she recognized him, she seemed totally comfortable with him. And the Eva he knew trusted nobody . . . So why would she trust the man who had infected her with the virus, brought her to Parallon, then abandoned her in Londinium?

OK, so she hadn't exactly been dragged to Londinium, she'd wanted to go. And it sounded like Zackary hadn't forced her to present herself as Livia, she'd willingly played the role.

He had to face it. The Livia he'd fallen in love with in Londinium wasn't real. She was a 21st-century girl on a mission for Zackary. And she'd been an excellent actress – a worthy protégée for Zack.

So where did the act begin and end? What had really happened between the two of them in the blue room of the

Natalis house? Had she ever genuinely cared for him? Was anything about their love true? Livia had been his reason and his purpose for so long now he didn't know who he was without her. He had torn himself apart over her; endured years of emptiness for her; travelled across time and fought against death for her.

He buried his face in his hands.

He knew he was lost when he felt his shoulders shudder. Sethos the Corinthian did not weep. He was a man who abhorred weakness, a man afraid of nothing. So where was that man now?

9

Power

Cassius's Palace, Parallon

'I want the gladiator,' bellowed Cassius, thumping his fist on his marble-topped desk.

'Yes, magister,' responded Otho. All three of his elite guard were standing on the other side of his desk, wearing matching expressions of deference. They kept their heads bowed and their eyes downcast.

'A-and in the meantime, master . . . are we to c-continue training for the expansion?'

'Of course. Once we have Parallon entirely secure we will begin the invasion beyond.'

'A-and the dangers of the river corridor?'

Cassius's jaw tightened. 'I do not wish to hear any more cowardly concerns about the corridor. If it claims a few more soldiers, so be it. Soldiers are expendable and replaceable.'

'But, magister, we are losing *many* men in the corridor. *Trained* soldiers —'

'Be careful, Otho. Insubordination is treason,' hissed Cassius quietly. 'I had assumed the loyalty of my elite guard was beyond reproach.'

'It is, of course, master,' rasped Otho, bowing low.

'Good. Now I do not wish to hear another word of the corridor. Make some burnt offerings to Jupiter and Neptune, then bring in some more of those decent prison recruits. They have the right attitude.'

'You mean the Belmarsh convicts, magister?'

'Exactly.'

'Magister,' said Pontius quietly. 'Once we have made the offerings, I believe we will be ready to begin the expansion of your empire. Parallon could not be more secure. We have complete control of the streets and buildings. All gatherings have been forbidden, allowing no opportunity for broad communication. No citizen is permitted to travel in numbers greater than two, and we have a full curfew at sundown. Our network of spies is now huge. Nothing will get past them. Any slave with even the smallest hint of spirit or defiance is taken care of in the arena, where he will remain injured, underfed and exhausted.'

Pontius ended his speech with a small bow, so he missed the fleeting frown of displeasure crossing the magister's face.

'Pontius,' Cassius said in a dangerously soft voice. 'Parallon is secure when *I* say it is secure. And we will commence our invasion when I say we are ready. I hope that is clear.'

'Of course, magister,' answered Pontius, 'I only —'

'Silence,' hissed Cassius. 'We have digressed too long. I called this meeting for one reason, and one alone. The gladiator. I want him. Why has he not been found?'

'Y-you are certain he is in Parallon, magister?' asked Rufus.

'He will be here to avenge his whore the moment he hears I killed her. And we have to be ready to welcome him.'

'I am sure he won't be able to slip past an army of two thousand men, magister,' smirked Rufus.

Cassius narrowed his eyes. 'You'd better make sure he doesn't.'

10

Rebellion

Parallon

Marching feet. It was a sound my subconscious instantly recognized . . . and feared. I was out of bed and crouched behind a chair before I'd even registered I was awake.

The sunlight was so bright it made my eyes water. I squinted against it, trying to make sense of my surroundings: embroidered duvet cover, large oak desk, familiar overflowing bookcases . . . my room . . . at Professor Ambrose's.

How did I get here?

Instantly last night's revelations came crashing to the front of my brain and I winced. Professor Ambrose was Seth's famous Zackary; the love of my life couldn't stand the sight of me; and Cassius, with the help of a huge Roman army, was now controlling Parallon.

The thundering sound of marching gradually receded. They must have passed right under my window. Holding myself tight against the walls, I edged my way round the room and peeked out.

There were hundreds of them. Where the hell were they going? As I craned my head round to follow their path, my attention was suddenly diverted by another sound: raised voices. Seth and Ambrose were arguing downstairs.

I willed myself into a pair of jeans and T-shirt and followed the shouting into the library. The first person I saw was Lauren, leaning against the bookshelves, her expression wary. Her gaze was fixed on Seth and Ambrose, who were facing each other, their postures oozing aggression. Matthias stood next to Seth with his arms folded.

Neither noticed me, so I waited uncertainly by the door.

'– it's the *only* way!' Seth was snarling.

'Of course you'd say that. Fighting is your solution for everything!' spat Ambrose.

'For God's sake, Zackary, you think you can *talk* the Romans out of here? Parallon has been invaded and annexed by one of the most successful armies of all time. It was a stealth attack, and *nobody* had a clue how to fight back. You are all living under a tyrannical dictatorship, which isn't going to go away. Neither will it get any better. It is time to do something: time to retaliate. So we need to gather everyone willing to fight back.'

'And how can you possibly think you'd stand a chance against the legions of vicious thugs Cassius has been assembling?'

'By uniting everyone. Matt says there are hundreds of people hiding in basements and attics. We spread the word; then begin training and organizing them. We have infinite resources in Parallon –'

'So, Seth the noble gladiator is going to form his little gladiator army, and make sure everyone is equipped with his very own net and trident! Yes, that'll definitely do the trick!' sneered Ambrose.

'*I'm not a fool, Zack!* I understand combat. Not just the

sick, forced duelling of the arena. Of course gladiatorial weapons would be totally useless in a war. And I know we can't match Cassius with his hordes of trained soldiers, but they don't have all the advantages. His troops will have been trained to use swords, shields, catapults, bolts and slings, because those are the weapons the Romans understand. But we don't have to fight like with like. We could train our people to use weapons the Romans have never seen. I didn't spend my whole stay in London wasting time in the school biology lab –'

Wasting time? Is that how he saw it? Is that how he saw us? I must have made some kind of choking sound, because Seth's eyes darted in my direction, but that was his only acknowledgement of my presence. '– I also learned how to shoot.'

'Oh, well done, Sethos. A bit of archery – a couple of bows and arrows should really sort them out.'

'Not *bows and arrows*, Zackary,' hissed Seth through gritted teeth. 'I could string and shoot a bow when I was five. I'm talking about firearms: assault rifles, pistols, machine guns . . .'

I gasped. 'You learned to shoot guns at St Mag's?'

Professor Ambrose's head jerked towards me in surprise. 'Eva!' he smiled. 'I didn't notice you arrive!' But I didn't respond. My eyes were trained on Seth. Waiting for him to answer me.

He refused all eye contact, but lifted his chin defiantly. 'I'm a gladiator, Eva. Physical prowess is my currency. I may have been ripped from the arena, but I never gave up training. Every day in Parallon, I trained a little harder, even when Matthias begged me to stop. But when I arrived in London, I realized there were other ways to fight . . . weapons I'd never seen. I did some research. I joined the rifle team –'

'You never told me.'

'You hate guns,' he muttered. 'I respected that.' He took a deep breath. 'But I needed to know I could protect you – us – wherever we were –'

What?

'Clearly did a great job of that then, didn't you!' hissed Ambrose, moving over to me. 'We were just about to have some breakfast, Eva. Come and join us. Did you sleep well?'

I nodded mutely, my eyes darting between Seth and Ambrose nervously.

'Hey, it's fine!' smirked Ambrose. 'The gladiator and I have a healthy – though somewhat volatile – understanding.' He lightly touched my elbow, and led me over to the dining table. At some point during the argument, Lauren had morphed from her rabbit-in-headlights position by the bookshelf to serene kitchen goddess, because she was now carrying in a tray of five mugs and a steaming jug of coffee.

'I really don't understand why you insist we *brew* the coffee, Zackary,' she sighed. 'The whole point of Parallon is that we don't have to bother.'

'Where's the fun in that?' he laughed. 'Anyway, it doesn't taste nearly so good without that glorious brewing aroma.' He closed his eyes and sniffed appreciatively. 'I've done clinical trials!'

'I bet you have,' snorted Lauren.

Ambrose pulled out a chair and gestured for me to sit. Matthias placed a tray of cut fruit, yoghurts and flatbreads on to the table, and we all chewed our way through it as though we were oblivious to the silent animosity simmering between Seth and Ambrose.

After about ten minutes of unadulterated awkwardness, Seth stood up.

'OK, Matt, we'd better get going.'

Matt looked momentarily terrified and answered in Greek, 'Y-you want to start recruiting right now?'

'And then training,' Seth replied, pulling out a street plan. 'You're absolutely certain the Romans know nothing about your building?'

Matt shook his head. 'It's well outside the original Londinium boundaries, and the Romans are vague about the geography beyond the old city walls. I built it ages ago. You remember how much Georgia and Clare liked dancing – we used it for our bigger parties. When the Romans arrived, I just re-fronted it and left the interior untouched.'

'And it will be easy to convert to a training ground?'

'We just need to soundproof it, and . . . maybe create a couple of tunnelled entrances – ideally from inside other buildings. That way there would be no observable activity on the outside.'

Seth nodded approvingly. 'So, are you joining us, Zackary?' he asked, cocking his head to one side.

Ambrose didn't even bother to answer. He just turned on his heel and strode from the room muttering furiously about bloody suicide missions.

Seth stared after him for a moment, and then looked purposefully down at his jeans. Seconds later he was wearing a Roman tunic, sandals and a large woollen cloak. And, just like that, my Londinium Sethos was standing before me. The sight of him literally took my breath away. His eyes suddenly met mine, and if I hadn't known better I might have misinterpreted the look he gave me for . . . No. It could only have been nostalgia.

By the time I'd torn my eyes away, Matthias was also dressed like a Roman, and rolling up the map.

I stood up quickly. 'Should I be wearing a tunic or a dress?' I asked.

Seth glanced at me and frowned. 'What do you mean?'

'For the training – will I draw more or less attention if I'm dressed as a girl or a guy?'

Seth blinked at me. '*You're* not coming, Eva.'

'What?'

'You can't seriously imagine I would let you fight!'

'Why not?'

'You know why. Don't be ridiculous.'

'You think it's ridiculous that I want to fight? I know I'm not nearly as strong as you, but I'm sure there's stuff I could do. I'm a fast learner, and you need everyone you can g–'

'I don't need *you*, Eva! Now just drop it.'

'No way. If you're going, I'm going.'

'*No!*' he bellowed. 'You're staying here with Lauren and Zackary. And you will not leave this building. For anything. Do you understand? I can't train soldiers and be constantly worrying about your safety. I need you here, out of harm's way.'

'Why the hell would you be worrying about my safety? There's no reason I should be any worse at it than any of the other new trainees. I'm not sick any more.'

'That isn't what I meant . . .'

'So what did you mean? That it's OK for *you* to go out and

risk your life in Cassius's territory, but not for me? That's not reasonable, Seth! In any case – you don't get to tell me what to do.'

Seth stared at me, his face a mask of bewilderment. I stood rigidly in front of him, my fists clenched, my shoulders tight. I really wasn't going to give way here, and I meant every word. I'd been weak and vulnerable, and let Cassius fatally overpower me twice. I *had* to learn how to fight him.

Matthias hovered beside Seth, his eyes moving uneasily between us.

At last Seth took a deep breath and strode wearily towards the door.

Yes! I crowed inwardly, following closely behind. But as soon as he stepped on to the landing he stopped and shouted.

'*Zackary!*'

I frowned. *What the hell?*

A moment later, the lab door opened and Zackary appeared at the bottom of the stairs. Seth was already leaning over the banisters. 'I think I may have finally found something we'll both agree on.'

'I very much doubt it,' answered Zackary icily.

Seth shrugged. 'OK, well try this then. Eva wants to come out with Matt and me to train.'

'*What?*' Zackary roared. 'No bloody way, Eva! We've only just got you back!'

I'd spent years without one single person giving a damn where I went or what I did, and suddenly there were two Neanderthals blocking me like a couple of belligerent prison guards. My veins were positively pulsing with outrage.

'For God's sake, this is Parallon! What's the worst that can happen? I get injured? So – I'll heal. Why the hell are you being so dictatorial?'

Ambrose closed his eyes for a moment in the way teachers do when you've said something exceptionally stupid and they're trying not to explode. Then his expression softened slightly.

'Eva, Cassius has guards and spies everywhere. By simply walking through this door, you are putting your life at a risk. Which is why – whatever the reason – I'd stop you leaving the building. However, *this* plan –' he shook his head in exasperation – 'is *suicidal*. As would be the case with any scheme requiring hundreds of people to converge onto one meeting place . . . Because within a matter of hours the entire Roman army will be storming it.'

'You're wrong, Zackary,' snapped Matt. 'Anyone who's avoided Roman attention this long will have worked out how to move around unnoticed. So as long as each one of us is meticulously careful, the Romans shouldn't find out about it.'

I couldn't believe Matt was actually defending my position, and was just about to flash him a grateful smile when he turned to me.

'But, Eva, you've only been in Roman Parallon a day, so you don't know your way around yet, and you're too damned noticeable to go very long undetected.'

'I can travel with you –'

He shook his head. 'You can't, Eva. The guards will instantly arrest any group of three or more. If you were to get captured, you'd be putting the whole rebellion in jeopardy.'

'How could me getting arrested possibly do that?'

'Because,' he answered coolly, 'Seth would be forced to stop doing whatever he was doing to come and rescue you.'

That shut me up.

I'd been totally outmanoeuvred. How could I selfishly insist on putting the entire plan at risk? I glanced at Seth's face, but he refused to look in my direction.

Moments later he and Matt were descending the stairs, while I watched in frozen silence. Then, just as he reached the front door, Seth turned and looked up.

'Eva,' he said huskily. 'Please don't leave this house. Not for anything. You're safe here.'

I wanted to say I didn't give a damn about my safety; all I wanted was to be with him. But I didn't say anything. I just stood mutely at the top of the stairs as he turned away and walked out of the door.

11

Blog

Shoreditch, London

4 September AD 2013

Jennifer Linden rubbed her eyes and looked at her watch. 1.00 a.m. She really should put the laptop away and go to bed. Her boss, Amanda, would be so on her case in the morning. She stomped over to her tiny kitchen to make some coffee. She knew she wasn't going to bed. She had her blog to finish. Not to mention completing the day's final European rainfall stats for Amanda.

It was just her luck that Amanda's big story – the whole escalating climate change thing – had become a damn world preoccupation. And since Amanda (and consequently her trusty slave) had been the first to highlight the trend with reams of impeccable statistics and data, they were now the go-to news team. Which meant Jen had virtually zero personal time or space to dedicate to her own obsession.

So she had to use borrowed time and space. Time she should have been devoting to other stuff . . . like sleeping.

Sighing deeply, she started banging open cupboard doors. Where the hell was the coffee? Her life could have been so much easier if she'd managed to get hold of Brodie Covington, Nick's MI5 contact. She'd given up trying to phone him. Whatever number she called from, he didn't pick up. She'd even bribed her mate Darren, the best IT nerd at the newsroom, to try and find an address for the guy, but MI5 protected their people well, and he'd drawn a blank.

Darren had managed to help her out with a couple of other things, though . . . like accessing the police file on Eva Koretsky. Jen had been gobsmacked.

'Yep – your seventeen-year-old schoolgirl runaway has got a pretty impressive police record!' he'd smirked.

'Why, what'd she do?'

'Class A hacker. And according to this statement from her mother, she started her life of crime when she was about five years old!'

He'd sounded so admiring that Jen had found herself snapping out an unexpectedly bitchy response. 'Well, maybe I'd have had more luck if I'd got child-genius Koretsky to find Brodie Covington then.'

Darren had just shrugged. 'Probably,' he'd agreed, without rancour.

'Bingo,' smiled Jen, discovering the coffee tin behind a massive pile of washing-up. She wiped off a stray dollop of soy sauce, unscrewed the lid and groaned with pleasure. Coffee was just about the only thing she ever remembered to buy, probably because she literally couldn't function without it.

As the machine hissed consolingly, she contemplated the last paragraph of this evening's blog.

She'd written her first blog about two months earlier. Well, 'blog' was perhaps an over-complimentary definition – drunken rant would have been more accurate. At the time, her sense of loss and outrage had been so overwhelming that she'd been just about ready to throw everything in: her job, her flat, her life. They all seemed so pointless when the thing that filled her brain, the thing that she thought everyone should be talking about and dealing with, was totally off-limits. The police wouldn't touch it. MI5 had effectively gagged her, and she knew that she'd blown her credibility with the newsroom long ago. So she had started her own anonymous web-rant: listing names of the disappeared, and dating and mapping last-known sightings. She'd managed to get photos of quite a number, and the illness symptoms of several, as well as links to newspaper articles. The only two people she never named were Nick Mullard and Eva Koretsky. Nick, because she was still too raw, and would rather chew off her own hand than allow him to become a statistic; and Eva because she'd given the damn girl her word that she wouldn't betray her.

Gradually, over the weeks, the public response had increased. She'd reached the point where her weekly blog now got over 10,000 hits, as well as hundreds of comments . . . most of which were posted by wack-jobs unfortunately. But nonetheless Jen sifted through every response meticulously.

Tonight, for the first time, she'd decided to mention Ambrose. Ambrose was a name Eva had put her way. Eva had clearly exhaustively trawled the internet for any references to him, so Jen decided this was about the only way to go.

She was just typing the final sentence when her door buzzer sounded. Frowning, she looked at her watch. 2.45 a.m.

Who the hell came visiting at this time? Had to be a drunken error. She ignored it. The buzzer went again. And again.

Eventually she marched over to the intercom and snarled, 'Wrong bell! This is flat seven.'

'Jennifer?'

She started. 'Who is this?'

'Just open the bloody door, Jen, it's Brodie Covington.'

She pressed the door release, and a minute later she and Brodie were glowering at each other across her living room.

'So, what on earth do you think you're doing?' he hissed.

Jennifer stared in disbelief. 'What the hell's that supposed to mean? You're the one who's just barged into my flat in the middle of the night!'

'OK, then. Let's try and put this simply . . . What is it you don't get about the words *leave it alone*?'

'Nobody tells me what to do! Not even MI-bloody-5!'

'Great epitaph, Jen. So you'd rather write a stupid crank-blog than stay alive?'

Her jaw dropped. 'How do you know about my blog?'

'I work for MI5, for Christ's sake. You're a national security threat. I know everything there is to know about you.'

'W-what?'

'And I can't go on protecting you forever,' he added wearily, slumping on to the sofa.

Jen's legs shook slightly as she sat down on the rocking chair opposite him. 'What do you mean?' she whispered.

Brodie ran his hands through his hair. 'Jennifer, you've got to let these disappearances go. We don't know what we're dealing with . . . we've got special ops guys from the US and Europe, counter-terrorist teams and a whole host of paranormal experts working on it . . . so, *please*, the last thing we need is a national panic. Nothing you can do or say is going to

72

improve this situation. As a reporter you could do infinite harm . . .'

'Come on –'

'Jennifer, the only reason I'm here is because Nick was my friend. I owe him. And I couldn't let anything happen to you because of that. But I'm begging you, for your own safety, for the good of the country, let us do our jobs.'

Jennifer stared at Brodie for a few seconds, and then nodded slowly. 'OK, then,' she exhaled, throwing her hands up in resignation. 'I'll let it go.'

Brodie smiled with relief. 'Thank God,' he muttered. 'You were becoming one of my biggest headaches!'

'Good to know I haven't lost my touch,' she smirked.

Brodie pulled himself off the sofa and stretched. 'Maybe now we can both get some sleep,' he sighed.

As she watched him walk towards the door, Jen suddenly jumped out of her chair.

'Brodie, wait.'

He turned.

'I know where they all end up.'

'Who?'

'The disappeared.'

Brodie cocked his head to one side, waiting.

'It's a place called Parallon, and –'

'Where the hell's that?' he interrupted.

Jen took a deep breath. 'You can only go there if you've got the virus.'

Brodie stared at her.

'I don't know whether Nick was targeted or if he was just caught in the crossfire, but I think that the Belmarsh prisoners were specifically targeted. Along with hundreds of other people.'

'There aren't hundreds . . .'

Jen raised her eyebrows and moved across to her laptop. Pulling out a memory stick, she bit her bottom lip and whispered, 'It could be millions, Brodie.'

'Do you think we could miss millions of disappearances!' he scoffed. 'We're talking a handful at most.'

She shook her head. 'These terrorists aren't constrained by time, Brodie. They can travel anywhere. Past or future.'

Brodie gaped at her in stunned silence.

'Here. This is everything I've managed to access . . . names, dates, times.'

'If this is just the stuff you've been blogging – I've already got it.'

She shook her head. 'I've only blogged about disappearances over the last couple of years. This is my full database.'

Brodie was staring at her. 'So – if what you're telling me has any substance . . . what do you think they're after?'

Jennifer paused. Should she share a speculation she'd been avoiding even thinking about for weeks?

What did she have to lose?

'I think they may be building an army.'

The idea of an army that could move about in time, amassing indefinite numbers, exponentially expanding every time it killed someone, was unimaginable. Jen tried to suppress her shiver of fear.

'Take it,' she croaked, placing the memory stick into Brodie's hand and watching as his fingers curled round it. He stood for a moment in silence. Then started backing slowly towards the door.

'Oh – and, Brodie, look out for a man named Ambrose. Pretty sure he's a big player in all this.'

Brodie nodded distractedly and pulled out a notebook.

'And if a guy by the name of Cassius comes your way, head straight in the opposite direction.'

Brodie frowned, then scribbled both names in his book. Before he closed it, he glanced up at Jen, narrowed his eyes and murmured, 'Was there something else you wanted to share?'

How did he know? Jen had been considering mentioning Seth and Eva, but had stopped herself. She trusted Brodie, but some weird sense of loyalty silenced her.

'Nothing else,' she mumbled.

'OK then.' Brodie hesitated in front of her, his shoulders taut. 'Well, I'd better get going. Do me a favour, Jen. Unless you decide you want a job at MI5, please try and forget we ever met.'

'Already forgotten,' she smiled weakly.

'You did good, Jen,' he said quietly. Then, holding the memory stick up in a salute, he opened the door and headed down the stairs.

Jennifer stood at her fourth-floor window, watching Brodie Covington's tiny silhouette get into his car and drive away. She couldn't help noticing the two-car convoy that pulled out and followed him. She prayed that they were on his side.

So was that it? Was her brush with MI5 and disappearing bodies and alternative universes finally over?

Jennifer leaned her head against the window and released a shaky breath. For the first time since she'd lost Nick, she felt something inside her loosen. The solitary, lonely weight of responsibility she'd been carting around for months had unexpectedly lifted. Yet nothing had changed. The bodies were still missing. The fear of an unfathomable war was still terrifyingly real.

But it was somebody else's problem now. She'd handed on the baton. Perhaps she could finally get some sleep.

But by the time she was lying under her duvet, clicking off her bedside lamp, she found herself struggling against an aching emptiness . . . an uneasy feeling that her tenuous connection with Nick was finally broken.

12

Gentle Persuasion

Cassius's Palace, Parallon

'The magister will see you now,' announced the broad red-headed guard known as Otho.

'M-me?' stammered a youth, looking desperately around the other reluctant faces lining the lobby. They all averted their eyes, so the boy stepped hesitantly forward. The guard pushed a heavy curtain across the imposing archway and led the shaking youth along the glistening mosaic floor towards the large desk at the far end of the room. Behind it sat the magister, Cassius Malchus, flanked by two further guards.

As he approached, the terrified visitor fell to his knees and whispered in Latin, 'Hail, noble Cassius, I salute you.'

He had practised that phrase a hundred times on the journey to the palace, knowing he couldn't afford to get it wrong. But he was praying that the big guard following him would be able to translate anything the magister said back, because that one sentence was where his Latin began and ended.

Cassius snapped out an incomprehensible instruction in Latin, but before the boy vomited in fear, Otho hauled him to his feet. 'The magister wishes you to state your name and report. I will translate.'

'M-my name is T-Truman,' began the youth. 'And I'm af-afraid I h-have n-nothing to report.'

'*Nothing?*' hissed Otho.

'I-I'm s-sorry.' Truman gazed down at his feet, cursing the heat in his cheeks.

Otho roughly grabbed his chin and examined his face dispassionately. 'You're lying,' he spat, jerking the boy's head so hard, he screeched in pain. 'I suggest you amend your report.'

Truman swallowed convulsively, his eyes darting hopelessly back to the doorway.

'*Speak!*' bellowed Otho.

'I-I d-did hear a r-rumour –' Truman finally mumbled, gnawing the inside of his cheek.

'A rumour of what?' snarled Otho impatiently.

'A – a rumour that – that – the g-gladiator you seek . . .'

Otho struck him across the back of his head. '*Speak, damn you!*'

'. . . S-Sethos L-Leontis . . . h-has returned.'

Truman wasn't prepared for the speed of the reaction. Cassius was suddenly out from behind his desk and looming over him.

'*Where is he?*' he thundered, grabbing the boy's hair and wrenching his chin up.

Truman's eyes widened in terror. 'I d-don't know . . .'

Cassius continued to hold fast to Truman's hair. His hooded eyes were fixed on the boy's face and didn't miss the slight muscle tremor along his left cheek – or the small strained movement in his throat as he tried to swallow.

'What are you concealing?' the magister whispered, bringing his face so close that Truman lost the power to breathe.

'*What. Are. You. Concealing?*' repeated Cassius, his eyes merciless. 'Speak, before I rip out your tongue!'

Truman tried to look away, but those eyes held him, owned him, controlled him. 'Th-the –'

Cassius was not a patient man. 'Pontius,' he said quietly.

'Of course, magister,' responded the guard, picking up the long, heavy black cane lying casually across Cassius's desk. A moment later Truman was screaming in agony on the floor as searing heat ripped across his shoulders.

'Another ten strikes should loosen his tongue,' smiled Cassius, regarding the writhing figure in front of him.

Truman reached his threshold at five. As the pain and fear spun through his skull, he finally accepted that resistance was futile – he didn't stand a chance against the Romans. None of them did.

'P-please,' he howled, his face wet with snot and tears. 'I'll t-tell you . . .'

Pontius threw the cane to the ground and kicked him. 'On your feet, you pathetic runt,' he snarled, pulling Truman off the floor by the hair.

Truman reluctantly lifted his eyes to find the magister regarding him with a cold, reptilian stillness. He drew a deep shuddering breath.

'Th-the people are s-saying that th-the gladiator is p-preparing an army!'

Pontius's grip on Truman was suddenly gone and he fell back, landing in a sprawling heap on the ground. The pain as his raw skin collided with the mosaic floor was so intense, he nearly puked his guts up, and was too stunned by his own miserable condition to notice the powerful impact his statement had had on his oppressors. He closed his eyes, desperate to ease the dizziness, and prayed with every fibre of his being that they were finished with him.

The next thing he knew he was being shoved roughly back into the lobby, uncomfortably aware of the terror-filled eyes staring at his bleeding, broken body.

Had they heard his screams? *Had they heard his betrayal?* Truman kept his eyes to the ground as Otho propelled him towards the front door.

'From now on, you will be vigilant,' Otho hissed. 'Blend in. Get yourself enlisted. You will find out where they're training, how many, and when the planned attack is. The magister will see you in a week.'

Truman nodded mutely.

'And, Truman –' Otho's hot breath burned the back of his neck – 'if you do anything to try and evade us again, you will wish you had never been born.'

13

Codes

Parallon

'Zackary, we need to talk,' said Lauren quietly.

We had just finished eating breakfast and Ambrose was striding towards the door, about to head off to his lab. 'Not now, Lauren,' he muttered impatiently. 'I've got a lot to do.'

'God, Professor, that is so rude,' I snapped before my brain caught up with my mouth. The prof didn't take kindly to insurrection. But, hey, I was itching for a fight.

I'd been stuck in his house for three weeks now, avoiding or being avoided by everyone except Ambrose himself. So I guess it was kind of idiotic to start a fight with the one person talking to me. But I was so wired.

Maybe wired wasn't exactly the right word. Frustrated? Heartbroken? Lonely? Bereft? You name it, I was feeling it. I missed my life. I missed St Mag's. I missed my friends – Astrid, Sadie, Rob. But most of all I missed Seth. Weird, huh! I mean, I'd endured all those months without him at St Mag's, but having him here – so close yet so distant – was torture. For the past three weeks he'd been going off every morning to train his rebel army and had hardly spoken two words to me. In fact he was avoiding all eye contact. It was tearing me apart. And to add insult to injury, he was still refusing to let me train with him. From what I'd picked up, there were hundreds of people now enlisted. He wasn't refusing to train any of *them*. I got that he couldn't bear to have me there, and that he didn't think I was good enough to be a useful soldier, but it was a pretty harsh punishment to deny me the chance to learn how to defend myself. And I felt so vulnerable here. Armed enemy soldiers were passing by the window every fifteen minutes. The whole thing was driving me insane.

To be fair, Ambrose had been doing his best to find stuff to distract me with, either in the library or his lab – but that's exactly what it felt like he was doing: distracting me. Babysitting.

But he definitely wasn't babysitting right now. He was standing by the door glowering while Lauren sat at the table frowning nervously between us. I grinned apologetically as he finally sighed and strode back to the table.

'What do you want to talk to me about, Lauren?' he asked with a sarcastically sweet smile.

'The vortex,' she answered icily.

Ambrose pulled out a chair and sat down wearily. 'I thought you had it covered.'

'And I thought you were cleverer than that, Zackary,' she hissed back. 'Engelmann led me to believe you were some sort of genius. But if you were, you wouldn't just assume that blasting a bunch of electromagnetic waves at an unstable wormhole was going to *cover* it.'

Ambrose held her gaze. 'Astrophysics isn't my field,' he responded. 'Which is why I sent Seth to talk to Engelmann.'

What? Not another damn thing in Seth's life I knew nothing about. 'Who's Engelmann?' I asked.

Ambrose sighed. 'Engelmann is a NASA physicist I knew. In my time.'

'And your time was . . . ?' I prompted. As ever, I was out of the loop. Ambrose was so cagey about his life before Parallon.

'I – er – ended there on 15 November 2044,' he said quietly.

Hmmm. 2044. I guess that made sense. I'd seen some of the advanced technology in his lab.

'So what did Engelmann suggest we do about the vortex?' I asked.

Lauren gave me a hard stare, 'Look, Eva, I'm sure you're a sweet kid, and I know you're bored hanging around all day while your crush is off playing soldiers, but this is grown-up science –'

Before I could respond to the multiple insults Lauren was chucking my way, Ambrose interrupted.

'I wouldn't underestimate the *kid* if I were you, Lauren. Her mind is the sharpest I've ever encountered . . . apart from my own, of course!'

Lauren's eyes narrowed. 'Whatever,' she said, without glancing my way. 'OK then – let me tell it to you straight. We have a negative density overload. I've blasted the thing with as much ramped electromagnetic radiation as the generators can produce, but its impact is waning. I've been doing my best to reformulate the composition in the hope of counteracting it, but either my maths is faulty, or the negative density parameters are too expanded, or I'm missing something crucial . . . Whatever the reason, the formula isn't working. I can't work out how to reliably stabilize it. The most I can manage is a temporary fix. Which means the wormhole is extremely volatile.'

'Too dangerous to use?' Ambrose asked.

'I certainly wouldn't want to risk it,' she shrugged. 'Especially as any activity inside it will only undermine the stability further.'

'So there's no way out of Parallon?' I whispered. The possibility of escape had been sustaining me for the past three weeks.

'If only that was the worst of it, Eva . . .'

Ambrose and Lauren exchanged tense glances.

My eyes moved nervously between them.

'You'd better tell her, Lauren,' sighed Ambrose.

'She doesn't need to know. It's not going to help anyone telling *her* –'

'Telling me what?' I growled.

Ambrose turned to me wearily. 'The instability in the wormhole could have significantly more serious implications . . .'

'What kind of implications?' I whispered.

'The black hole kind,' he muttered reluctantly.

'*What?*' I exploded, shaking my head. 'But that's not possible! Wormholes can't transform into black holes – it's supposed to go the other way round –'

'Normally, Eva,' agreed Ambrose. 'But Parallon appears to be having an inversion effect on the data projections.'

I stared at them both in horror, willing them to tell me they were joking. Neither uttered a word.

'So how long do we have?' I finally rasped.

Lauren sighed. 'Look, Eva, Ambrose is talking worst-case scenario here.'

'Presumably neither world could survive a transformation like that?' I croaked.

It wasn't really a question.

'We shouldn't despair yet,' said Lauren briskly. 'I'm working on this. There has to be a way to get the vortex stabilized . . . It's just such a complex equation . . .'

'So if you manage to balance the density and stabilize it, the whole black-hole thing goes away?' I demanded.

Lauren cocked her head to one side. 'As I said, Eva, the black hole really is a worst-case scenario –'

'Well, what's the best case?'

'Obviously, to fix the vortex and return it to the completely stable corridor it once was.'

'Any realistic hope of that?' I asked.

She shook her head. 'I gave up on best case weeks ago. Unfortunately, the longer the vortex is unstable, the worse the fallout.'

'Fallout?'

'Reverberations. Broader meteorological effects – on climate, land masses . . .'

'Here – or Earth?'

'Most likely to be there, as the physical world here doesn't seem to conform to causal dynamics in the same way.'

'So what will happen?' I whispered.

Lauren shrugged. 'May have already started . . . extreme weather, disruptions to the Earth's surface, earthquakes, volcanic eruptions . . . you name it, baby.' Lauren leaned back in her chair, folded her arms and gazed at us impassively.

A horrible vision of my friends at St Mag's being crushed by an earthquake suddenly flashed through my head.

'*God, no!*' I gasped.

'That's worst-case scenario, Eva,' Lauren repeated.

'C-can I take a look at the work you've been doing?' I asked tentatively.

Lauren's head jerked back in disbelief, but Ambrose put a hand on her shoulder and said simply, 'Great idea, Eva. Lauren, show the kid your data.'

Lauren was not happy. She could hardly bring herself to speak to me, let alone share all her painstaking research. But Ambrose was virtually ordering her to collaborate. With a mutinous huff she shoved her tablet over and watched in stony silence as I began scrolling through screen after screen, trying to make sense of the rows of figures.

Although I kind of hated Ambrose for forcing this, my discomfort with Lauren was completely eclipsed by the shock and horror of her revelations. After reluctantly bringing me up to speed on each equation premise, Lauren finally strode off to fix herself a coffee. The bliss of her sudden absence made me realize how hard it had been to focus with her huffing impatiently down my neck, so I created myself a replica tablet and copied all her data files on to it. Then, leaving her tablet on the dining table, I headed off to carry on working in my room.

After several days meticulously analysing her formulae, checking her multiple number strings and exploring all her various radiation stats, I had to concede that there wasn't anything wrong with her maths. All the equations checked out and all the calculations were accurately premised, so hypothetically the electromagnetic pulses should have been providing the exact density balance to restore the wormhole's stability.

But they clearly weren't working.

Yet Lauren was continuing on the same trajectory: checking and rechecking the same calculations, then repeating the conclusions over and over.

But given the desperateness of the situation, why wasn't she moving on? Looking for another angle? As a hacker I'd learned early that if you came to a dead end you had to cut your losses quickly and try different doors. When you couldn't get in one way, you went for an alternative route. Well-guarded digital gateways were time-sensitive, so unless you acted instantly you'd miss your chance to skip through spyware ambushes and would find yourself locked out.

As soon as I worked out that Lauren's data was good but ultimately ineffective, I started to consider why. The wormhole was somehow defying all the equations – equations based on layer upon layer of sound, provable maths. Maths that started with funadamental, unshakeable premises like $E-mc^2$.

But what if such equations didn't apply to the world of Parallon? Matter and form certainly didn't obey the same laws of physics as they did on Earth. So why should we expect the equations to comply?

Great. So now I had to try and construct a damn theory of relativity able to support both Parallon and Earth. Oh – and without the benefit of being bloody Einstein.

But . . . I did have something that Einstein didn't have.

Ambrose's lab.

Ambrose would have had a coronary if he'd twigged I'd worked out how to get into it without him. I kind of blamed him for guarding the place so jealously. Anyone trying to keep me out of something automatically made me want it more.

So it became a matter of pride for me to crack his door and computer access codes. The doorway was fairly straightforward – a long symbol sequence on a wall keypad, which Ambrose always tried to mask with his body when he keyed in. With a bit of conversational distraction I could catch him keying two consecutive digits per visit, always counting the beeps to place them into his twenty-one symbol sequence.

I'd assumed the computer itself would be horribly protected and it would take me weeks of stolen moments to get inside, but when Ambrose left me in his lab for ten minutes one day to go and speak to Lauren, I discovered that he had virtually no protection on it at all. Just a universal voice-touch activation lock.

I couldn't wait to get inside it. It wasn't simply the additional computing speed and power I craved. It was access to Ambrose's work. I'd seen glimpses of programs that I was desperate to check out . . . And from the little hints he'd dropped, I was pretty sure Ambrose knew a hell of a lot more about Parallon than he was currently prepared to reveal. And though it was a massive longshot, maybe – just maybe – I would find the key to the vortex there.

14

Secrets and Lies

Astrid's Bedroom, St Mag's, London

8.00 p.m., 7 October AD *2013*

'Can I come in, Astrid?' called Sadie from the corridor outside.

Astrid was standing by the window, watching the rain smash against the glass with relentless power. The storm showed no sign of abating.

'Sure,' she answered tonelessly.

Sadie walked in and slumped on to the bed. 'Theo called again,' she murmured.

Astrid didn't bother to turn round, just ran her finger through the condensation distractedly.

'Astrid – I'm getting sick of telling him we haven't heard from her. And he's getting pretty sick of it too.'

'He'll give up eventually,' shrugged Astrid, leaning her forehead against the glass.

'I don't want him to give up. And I can't believe you do either. The band meant everything to you!'

'It's over, Sadie. I told you that in July. Eva's not coming back.'

Sadie stared at her friend in disbelief. 'For God's sake, Astrid, *talk* to me!'

'There's nothing to talk about,' sighed Astrid, turning to face the room and leaning heavily against the window frame.

'You must have heard something from her!' Sadie persisted.

'Do you honestly think I wouldn't have told you if Eva had been in touch?'

Sadie stared at her friend and shook her head. 'What the hell happened that night at the Underworld, Astrid? Why won't you tell me?'

'I *have* told you,' intoned Astrid, rolling her eyes. 'Seth and Eva ran off together.'

'I know that's the story you told the police –'

'That's *all* I know.'

Sadie's eyes narrowed. Then she picked up her phone and started tapping out a number.

'I'm off to the library,' sighed Astrid, reaching for her jacket on the back of the door. But Sadie's hand shot out and gripped Astrid's shoulder, holding on tight as she waited for the call to connect. 'Rob? Yeah, cool. Hey – could you meet Astrid and me in practice room three? Like – now? Per-lease! Come on, Rob – a little rain won't kill you! For Christ's sake – just man up . . . or borrow an umbrella! Five minutes? Great.'

'It's a total deluge out there!' gasped Rob, slamming the door behind him and ineptly trying to shake rain off the hoodie he was wearing. The jacket was completely soaked through, so his only option was to peel himself out of it. Muttering a string of profanities, he threw it against the wall, flopped down at the keyboard and fixed Sadie with a stony gaze. 'So what the hell is this about, Sades?' he demanded.

'*That*, Rob, is precisely what I'd like to know,' she hissed from her perch behind the drum kit.

Rob stared at her in confusion. Running a finger lightly up and down the black notes, his eyes shifted from Sadie to Astrid.

Astrid refused to return the eye contact. Instead she squatted down on the floor and picked at a thread on her jeans.

'*Enough!*' exploded Sadie. 'It's time to tell me what's going on! You and Astrid have been zombie-ing round the place like someone just *died* –'

'W-what?' gulped Rob, shooting a panicky glance at Astrid.

'I don't know what you're talking about, Sadie,' snorted Astrid. 'We're just bombed cos the record deal's fallen through.'

'Yeah, I totally get that, Astrid. I feel the same way . . . But . . . I dunno – there's something definitely not right here. I mean – I know Eva was never really into the whole fame and fortune thing, and Theo got on her nerves, but she was buzzed by the music. I know she wasn't faking it . . . And I just don't think she'd run out on us like that. Completely. Without a word. I mean, to be honest, she didn't look fit enough to run anywhere that night. By the time we finished playing she could barely crawl. So why the hell would she suddenly decide to run away?'

'She went with Seth –'

'Yeah – so you keep saying. And I know she was – like – totally in love with the guy, but he abandoned her months ago. And broke her heart. I mean, Eva wasn't an idiot. Would she really take off with him? I mean, *really*?'

'We – er – figured Seth must have been in touch with her.

You know – secretly,' murmured Rob, twisting his hands disconsolately.

Sadie stared at him. 'Rob, the three of us spent virtually every waking hour with her when Seth left. She was bereft – practically catatonic. We would have *known* if he'd contacted her . . .'

Rob and Astrid continued to stare down at their laps.

'. . . and Eva was hardly the eloping type. And she didn't need to *elope* with Seth to spend time with him. The two of them were brilliant at getting round school rules. Besides, she loved it here. She loved the work. I mean, she was completely obsessed with science. And classics. And maths. And art. And music. *Our* music. I just don't think she would have given it all up for a guy that clearly didn't give a sh–'

'For what it's worth, I think he did love her . . .' muttered Astrid.

'Yeah, whatever,' snarled Sadie. 'Look, the police and her parents may have bought the whole eloping story, and for some reason so did the Crisp, but *I* don't. So, Astrid, spit it out. Why'd she really walk out on us?'

Astrid stood up, strode over to the bass guitar, heaved it carefully off its stand, adjusted the strap and swung it over her shoulder. Then she plugged it into the amp and switched on. Rob, whose upper body had been slumped across the lid of the keyboard, immediately sat up and flipped the power switch on. Then he cocked his head expectantly.

But Sadie didn't move. She sat with her arms folded, staring at them both till Astrid finally took a deep breath and said, 'Eva had no other choice, babe.'

'What the hell does that mean?' snorted Sadie.

'Nothing. Everything. I don't know, Sades. But please – can we just drop it now and play some music?'

Sadie hovered over her sticks, unable to choose between throwing them across the room and beating the hell out of the kit in front of her. She was furious . . . Furious that Astrid expected her to buy into a totally lame story . . . And even more furious that they didn't trust her with the truth.

She was also scared. She'd never seen Astrid so shell-shocked. Something bad went down that night at the Underworld, and she needed to find out what.

But right now Astrid was playing the opening riff to 'Psycho Stalker' and Rob was punching out his eerie sustained chords. She looked at their faces, and for the first time in ages they looked calm, anchored. Like they used to. Her heart flipped and her fingers tightened round the sticks.

'Please, Sadie?' mouthed Astrid.

Sadie shook her head. 'Oh, for God's sake,' she sighed finally. 'You win! Let's play the damned song . . . but don't you dare pull that third bar rhythm change or I'm out the damned door.'

15

Interrogation

Cassius's Palace, Parallon

Even at the furthest end of the corridor, the screams of pain were piercing. But Cassius, striding ahead of his elite guard, appeared oblivious. As they passed through the narrow, heavily guarded passageway and neared the solid iron door, the screams grew louder, now clearly underscored by low keening and wracking moans.

The four huge guards at the doorway bowed low the moment they glimpsed the magister and his retinue, and they had already heaved the door open by the time Cassius reached it.

Impassively he surveyed the scene of bloody carnage before him. Two half-dead men hung from chains, their skin completely flayed, broken bones jutting through gaping gashes. Littering the floor, a groaning mass of bloody bodies was presided over by six torturers brandishing his preferred instruments: whips, scourges, curved knives, one even jauntily wielded an axe.

'Well?' asked Cassius, fixing each torturer in turn with his penetrating gaze.

They shuffled uncomfortably.

Finally one cleared his throat. 'Er – we still have nothing, magister.' His eyes remained fixed on the ground in front of him.

'*Nothing?*' thundered Cassius.

'I-I'm sorry, magister. Nobody has said one word about the rebel army.'

Cassius glanced around in disgust. 'Get rid of them,' he muttered, kicking one of the broken, bloody bodies at his feet. 'And clean up this mess.' His lip curled in distaste at the blood and gore now smeared across his sandalled foot.

'This place stinks,' he snapped, striding purposefully from the room. Pontius, Otho and Rufus followed swiftly behind him, and they maintained the pace all the way to Cassius's office.

'How many still to question?' demanded Cassius.

Otho walked quickly over to the strongbox, unlocked it, then rifled efficiently through the documents inside until he pulled out the one he sought. For a moment he stared down at the long list of names. Then he cleared his throat.

'Magister, that was the final group.'

When the silence became unbearable, Pontius spoke. 'So far, Truman is the only one to speak of the rebel army. Perhaps *he* is the one lying?'

Cassius ran a thumb back and forth across his jaw, his eyes resting on one of his large bird murals.

'Magister,' ventured Rufus, 'they've been torturing spies for weeks. Not one has yielded *anything*! And, in truth, how likely is the story? Could any one of the weak, flaccid inhabitants of this world ever be turned into a soldier? And what kind of man would have the power to transform such pathetic specimens

into an army? That worthless gladiator slave? I don't think so.'
Rufus began to laugh, but the sound died in his throat when
Cassius turned from his mural and regarded him coldly.

'Only a stupid man would underestimate the Greek, Rufus,'
murmured Cassius. 'Leontis is here, I can feel him . . . And I
intend to flush him out. How many in our army, Pontius?'

'Three and a half thousand men, magister.'

'And are they fighting like Romans yet?'

'I am overseeing the training myself.'

Cassius nodded. 'I need you elsewhere now, Pontius. From
this day, you three – and only you three – will be responsible
for the interrogation of captives, prisoners and spies. I want an
escalation of road patrols. We need to be bringing in more
citizens for questioning. Make house calls. Arrest women. They
break quicker. Nothing will slip past you. Is that clear?'

The elite guard nodded.

'You are relieved of all other duties. Otho, see to it that your
work is redistributed. That is all. You may leave.'

Pontius, Otho and Rufus bowed and strode quickly away.

Cassius continued to contemplate the intricate mural in front
of him. But he was no longer seeing birds. He was seeing a
young retiarius striding proudly into the arena. 'I am going to
find you, Sethos Leontis,' he hissed, 'and when I do, you will
wish with all your heart that you had died with your whore in
Londinium.'

16

Duty and Love

Parallon

My opportunities to get into Ambrose's lab alone were painfully few. I had resorted to short, very tense forays in the middle of the night because somehow Seth had convinced Ambrose and Lauren that they had to watch me continuously when he wasn't around. Which was ironic really, considering Seth could hardly bring himself to look at me at all when he was here.

What I didn't get was why he was so paranoid that Cassius was still out to get *me* when it was clear to everyone that he was out to get *Seth*. Cassius had publicly declared it, for God's sake. And for the last six weeks Seth had been putting himself at risk of getting caught every day from dawn till night when he went off to train his troops. OK – he was a brilliant fighter, but it would only take one person exiting the training ground carelessly, one indiscreet recruit, one infiltrating spy . . . and Cassius's entire army would be storming the training ground and crushing the resistance.

I glared gloomily out of the window into the dark night. Worrying about Seth all day was bad enough, but I also had a damn vortex to worry about – and its potential effect on the future of my whole world. And this evening I had been banking on some quality time in the lab, because Ambrose was finally out for a few hours. But Lauren had been sticking to me like glue. And it was definitely not friendship or love keeping her close. Although she and I had established an uneasy truce, she clearly didn't like or trust me. So her closeness was obviously a directive from Seth or Ambrose. And it was driving me crazy. Especially as I felt like I might be on the verge of a breakthrough.

The more time I spent on Ambrose's computer the less I felt I knew the man, but the more I understood Parallon. In fact, I now firmly believed that his hard drive probably contained just about all the information I needed. I had found what looked like encrypted fragments of an entire virtual Parallon prototype. This was not necessarily significant in itself – with the right software any half-decent programmer could construct a virtual world – but why would Ambrose construct a virtual Parallon on his computer when he already had the real Parallon outside his front door? It made no sense. Not for someone as innovative as he was. And why encrypt it?

Obviously the fragment I was most interested in finding was the one containing the river code . . . Because maybe – just maybe –

'Eva! Will you please stop pacing!' snorted Lauren from her perch on the sofa.

I stopped.

She uncurled herself and stood up. 'Why don't you put some food together, while I nip out to do a quick check on the generators.'

'Sure,' I muttered, suddenly hungry. 'Pizza OK?'

'Zackary won't eat pizza,' Lauren reminded me pointedly.

'Do you think they'll be back soon?'

'I would think so. Ambrose said the fights normally last about three hours.'

Ambrose was making one of his obligatory appearances at the arena. Very few people went to watch the gladiators voluntarily – they were ordered to go. Nightly. Absences were registered instantly and swiftly punished. When the Romans first seized power, they took a census of everyone in Parallon – everyone they could lay their hands on. Although a number of people managed to slip through the net, Ambrose wasn't one of them. But he had found a way of playing the system by sharing his identity with one of the *unlisted*. Now the two of them took turns at the arena. The arrangement served them both: Ambrose had more freedom, and the friend had an official ID when he got stopped on the street.

'Make the food, Eva. I'm sure they'll be back any minute,' said Lauren, as she headed for the door.

I moved over to the window, scouring the street for a glimpse of anyone. The guards were moving towards the end of the road, but of course I saw no sign of the others. I shivered. God, I needed to get busy before the adrenalin pushed me over the edge.

'Lauren, be careful,' I called. 'The guards are still close.'

'I do this every night, Eva. I think I can manage!'

I heard the front door close. Lauren would be gone for exactly fifteen minutes. Did that give me time to get anything done in the lab?

Hell, yeah.

But I'd barely reached the third step down when Ambrose appeared at the front door.

'You're back!'

He grinned up at me, but looked tired and kind of bleak.

'Everything OK?' I asked.

'Just hungry,' he smiled. 'Are the boys –'

I shook my head. 'Not yet.'

'Where's Lauren?'

'She just went to do the generators.'

'She wasn't supposed to leave you –'

I snorted angrily. 'For God's sake, Professor, I'm not a kid!'

He shrugged. 'What do you say to fajitas?' he asked, heading over to the dining table.

Ambrose was good with food. Way better than me. I'd discovered that you couldn't create effectively in Parallon without understanding the thing you created. And just about the only food I understood was pizza. Which is why I rarely got asked to do dinner.

'Mmm, smells good!' called Lauren from the bottom of the stairs. 'Zackary must be back!'

I rolled my eyes as she bounded into the room.

'How's the vortex holding up, Lauren?' asked Ambrose quietly.

She nodded. 'It's hanging on in there. I'm just about keeping it under control with the night generators. Obviously it won't hold forever.'

'What if you pulsed during the day as well?' I asked. I needed more time.

'Too dangerous,' said Ambrose. 'The patrols would –'

'Can someone give me a hand?' Seth's husky voice suddenly interrupted from the bottom of the stairs.

I was out of the room and flying down the steps two at a time before I'd even registered he was home. 'Seth, are you OK?'

Seth glanced up at me in surprise. 'Of course I am.'

Matt, on the other hand, looked far from OK. He had one arm slung over Seth's shoulder, the other hanging limply at his side. One of his legs seemed to be injured as well. Seth was heaving him through the hallway.

I moved forward to help, but Seth instantly froze.

'Zack can help me,' he said tightly.

I backed away, stung. Ambrose was still making his way downstairs.

'What happened?' he asked.

Seth shook his head and grinned. 'It's nothing serious – just Matt getting over-enthusiastic in training. He wasn't ready to –'

'– take on a gladiator,' rasped Matthias, chuckling weakly.

'You shouldn't have attacked me from behind, Matt!' accused Seth. 'My instincts are too ingrained.'

Ambrose moved to Matt's other side, and slipped his shoulder under his injured arm. Matt groaned and muttered as the three of them stumbled upstairs. I followed slowly behind, unable to take my eyes off Seth's strong shoulders as they shifted under Matt's weight.

Seth laid Matt out on one of the sofas and Ambrose checked him over. 'You'll be as good as new in less than an hour I should think,' he smirked.

'Hurts like hell,' grimaced Matt.

'That'll teach you to mess with our resident hero!' scoffed Ambrose.

I could feel Seth's annoyance from across the room.

I helped Matt sit up and brought him some food, and then went to join the others at the table. The conversation was more stilted than ever. Matt was the one we all relied on to keep it light, and without him the atmosphere between Seth and Ambrose positively crackled. I had been hungry earlier, but now I could hardly swallow. During the whole meal Seth didn't look at me once.

Afterwards, Seth took the plates out to the kitchen and announced he was going to get cleaned up and head to bed. I watched as he walked wearily out of the room, every part of me longing to follow him. It wasn't until I heard the gentle click of his door closing that I unfroze and dragged myself across to the sofas to join the others.

'. . . I wouldn't be surprised if they started doing house-to-house raids,' Matt was saying. 'They've doubled the patrols, and the guards are definitely more aggressive with their stop-and-searches. No question Cassius has got wind of the resistance. We've had to stagger our training arrival times, and now have twenty-one different tunnel entrances.'

'The arena fights have got more sadistic too,' muttered Ambrose. 'No longer content to have a winner and loser, they've added the delightful feature of ritual mutilation to ratchet up the humiliation of defeat. Sick bastards.'

I swallowed back the bile. 'So – how are Seth's soldiers shaping up, Matt?' I asked.

Matthias smiled weakly. 'Quite well. Seth now has them all trained to use knives, handguns and assault rifles. As soon as the bulk of them mastered *still* targets, he rigged up damned *moving* ones. Zeus, the man is merciless!' he chuckled.

'Matt, are there any girls training, or is it just guys?' I asked quietly.

Matt rubbed his newly healed leg disconsolately and refused to return my gaze.

I had my answer.

'Well, I think I'm about ready to turn in,' yawned Ambrose, standing up and stretching.

'Yeah, I think I'm going to head off too,' said Lauren, picking up her tablet. 'Hope you're back to full health in the morning Matthias!'

'I'm practically there already,' grinned Matt. 'But I think I'll play invalid a little longer and sleep here tonight.'

'Enjoy it while you can,' I laughed, creating a pile of blankets and a pillow for him. Then I moved across to the shelves for a book to take to bed with me.

'Er – Eva . . .'

I turned. 'Yeah, Matt?'

'You do understand why he's making you stay here?'

'Sure. He doesn't want me around.'

'You can't seriously believe that's the reason?'

'Oh, please, Matt! Seth can hardly fake basic civility now. He can barely bring himself to look at me.'

'That's complete rubbish. It's *you* playing all the games. And what I really don't understand is why. Why are you treating him like this, Eva?'

I just spluttered incoherently. *What?*

'Was it always a game for you? Did you never care about him?'

'What the hell are you talking about, Matt?' I choked.

'He's loved you so long, so completely, it has practically consumed him. And for most of that time I've hated you – for distracting him . . . for taking him . . . for destroying him. It all made me so angry. But you were his everything. He lived for you. Would have died for you. I watched it, over and over: in Londinium, in Parallon, in London –'

I blinked at him and shook my head. 'I thought so once,' I whispered, 'but Seth gave up on me in London months ago. Ran as far and as fast as he could.'

Matt was frowning in denial.

'Hey, it's OK, Matt. I get it. He got over me. I don't blame him.'

'You're so wrong, Eva. I saw him with you in London six weeks ago. When you were lying on the ground, bleeding to death . . .'

'You must be mixing up your timelines, Matt. Seth wasn't there. He hadn't been in London for ages . . .'

'Eva, we were *both* there – Seth and me.'

'I remember *everything* about that night, Matt. How it began – at the Underworld – and how it finished. With just Cassius and me. Nobody else.'

'So how do you think you ended up *here*, Eva?'

I frowned. 'Th-the virus . . .' I answered uneasily. I had to admit this had been a niggling question at the back of my mind – because I'd been pretty sure I didn't have any active virus in my blood. 'I guess – Cassius . . . Cassius must have infected me.' I shuddered. The thought of any of Cassius's blood in my veins made me want to vomit.

Matthias shook his head. 'It wasn't Cassius, Eva. It was Seth. He got to you just in time. He gave you his blood – held you – watched over you . . . until you disappeared.'

'I *disappeared*?'

'That's how the virus plays out, Eva – you didn't know that either?'

I frowned. Yes . . . I did know. Jennifer Linden had described that happening to Nick. And I'd seen the slides in the lab. It just felt too weird to think about.

'As soon as your body was gone, Seth headed straight for the vortex. He was desperate to get to you before Cassius did.'

'He followed me here?'

'He would follow you to hell, Eva.'

'That may have been true once,' I sighed. 'But not any more.'

'Zeus, Eva! What aren't you seeing here? He orbits you. And yet you walk around like a walled island, oblivious. Tell me – did you ever love him?'

I gaped at Matt. 'I've *always* loved him! I wish to God I could switch it off – it's killing me. But I can't.'

'So why in Apollo's name do you act like you hate him?'

'Are you crazy, Matt? It's him that hates *me*.'

'Believe me, Eva, Seth doesn't hate you. Every morning he leaves this house with two ideals – duty and love: the first propels him to the training ground so that he can teach the people of Parallon to finally stand up for themselves, but the second is what drives him to survive long enough to return to you each night.'

'No –'

'I wish he *had* stopped loving you. He'd be stronger without you. You've always made him vulnerable. And never more than now . . . His uncertainty about you is distracting him. And his survival – Parallon's survival – depends on him staying focused. Which is the only reason I'm talking to you about it. You've got to sort things out with Seth, or you will jeopardize this war.'

I lay awake for ages, trying to think calmly about what Matt had told me. But I had my own mini war raging inside my head. One side was desperate to believe that Seth still cared, and was searching for all sorts of teeny bits of evidence to support that theory: the few times I'd caught him staring at me; his fury every time Ambrose was near . . . But on the opposing side was the fact that he had walked away without a word, leaving me alone for months.

Matt had accused me of freezing Seth out. Which I guess was sort of true. Seth had tried to talk to me on that first night. And I hadn't let him. Of course I hadn't. I needed to keep myself safe – I was still so raw and I couldn't bear to hear his excuses.

Did he still want to talk to me?

Matt seemed to think so, but did Matt genuinely have any idea what was going through Seth's head? He'd known Seth a long time, but he had managed to completely mess up his own friendship, so was he such a great adviser? And I couldn't quite get a handle on his agenda. I thought he cared about Seth – sometimes it seemed like maybe he even cared too much. But was there something else going on with him? I hadn't forgotten that he was the guy who'd led Cassius straight to me. Was his plan to get rid of me? Could he still be working for Cassius? Was he intending to hand Seth and the rebels over? How could Seth trust him after so much betrayal?

And then my anger at Seth started brewing again. He was perfectly happy to trust Matt: to take *him* off to train; to teach *him* how to defend himself . . . But not me. No. he was shutting me out just as much as I was doing it to him.

And there was a war brewing. The Romans were going to start house-to-house searches and I hadn't the faintest idea how to fight them. How the hell was I supposed to construct a new theory of relativity, terrified that at any moment the Romans were going to bash down my door?

But Matt *was* right about one thing. I did have to fix things with Seth. And for that to happen, Seth was going to have to stop shutting me out; and I was going to have to grow the hell up, find some strength and claim my life back. I couldn't let anybody else control it again. Ambrose had done it. Cassius had done it. Now I was allowing Seth to do it. I had been living by their rules for too long. It was time to make some of my own.

17

Promise

Parallon

I didn't sleep at all. At 4.30 a.m. I tiptoed down Ambrose's creaky stairs and eased the front door open. I had spent the last hour peering through my window, checking the guards patrolling outside. They had just moved to the next street, which gave me at least ten minutes to find a good spot to hide. I quickly chose a shadowy nook just behind one of the columns supporting the corniced entrance to Ambrose's house. Within a few minutes I was shivering. I had hastily slipped on a simple Roman dress, and was now seriously regretting its flimsiness. But even before the regret was fully formed, a soft woollen cloak was wrapped round my shoulders. It was such a shock I nearly shrieked. Would I ever get used to this weird place?

The guards were circuiting again, so I pressed my body hard against the cold marble and waited in the shadows. I remained there silently watching as they completed their second circuit, until finally I heard the sound I'd been waiting for – Seth whispering on the other side of the great wooden door: 'Are you ready, brother? We have to leave right now.'

Seconds later he and Matthias silently emerged from the

building and slipped quickly across the exposed section of road into the shadowy peristyle opposite. Damn, I wasn't expecting that. I couldn't cross the road after them; they would see me. So I had to follow them from my side. I managed to keep pace pretty well for some time until I encountered a totally open stretch of building, with no columned cover or arches to hide behind. I stood against the final column and tried to work out what to do. I was at a T-junction. My side of the road continued straight on. But Seth and Matt were already rounding a corner and heading away from me as quickly and silently as cats. I was about to lose sight of them completely. The only way I could continue this pursuit was to cross over. And it was the worst place to cross – I would be visible from three directions. So, best-case scenario – Seth and Matt would see me; worst-case scenario – the Romans would. The patrol was due in about two minutes, so if I didn't move now, I'd be caught wherever I stood. My heart was pounding hard as I sprinted across the road and plunged into the shadow of the doorway opposite. I leaned against the wooden panels, took a deep breath, then peered round the portico to see where Seth and Matt had got to. I could see no sign of them.

I took one last glance behind me, then edged round the corner, heading in the direction I'd last seen them. I tried to move quickly but quietly, tried to edge along buildings, under arches, between columns, exactly as they had done, all the time keeping my eyes trained ahead, determined to catch any movement that would betray them.

The sky was just beginning to lighten as I neared the end of the street. I had no idea which direction to turn now, as there were three alternatives: left, right, straight on. I squinted ahead. Was that the forum? Surely they wouldn't choose to go that way – it was probably the most exposed area in Parallon. I'd discovered that on my first night back. That left me with two options. I edged my way to the left to check out the lie of the land . . . A straight, empty road with plenty of columns and arches to hide behind – but also, unfortunately, the distinct sound of several marching feet. I turned to the right. It was clearly the safest choice, but I couldn't get a clear view from where I was crouching. I'd need to cross the road. Which was kind of risky, given the guards were heading this way. But if I was going to move, the sooner I did it the better. I was just on the point of leaping across, when a hand shot across my mouth and I was pulled firmly into the doorway behind me.

Before I got the chance to bite the hand or struggle out of its iron grip, I heard a sharp intake of breath. And my heart began thudding in a completely different way. I knew whose body I was rammed against. I would know this man anywhere: his scent, his skin, his touch; not to mention the energy that pulsed between us like a current.

'Eva?' he hissed. 'What the hell are you doing here?'

His hand dropped from my mouth, and he pulled me round to face him. Oh God. I hadn't been this close to him for months. It felt so . . . right. But it wasn't. The expression on his face made that perfectly clear. He was blazing with fury.

Well, so was I. I pulled myself out of his arms and started pummelling his chest. And once I started I couldn't stop. Tears rolled down my face and my shoulders shook as I hit him and hit him.

And he just stood there taking it, his arms at his sides.

'Eva,' he finally whispered.

I lifted my face to his and I felt him shudder; his arms were suddenly round me and he was kissing me, across my wet cheeks, along my neck. And then his tongue was licking away my tears, his fingers clenched round my hair, like he would never let me go. My fists uncurled on his chest, my palms flattened against the fabric of his tunic. I could feel his heavy thudding heartbeat, I could feel his warm skin, his taut muscles, his rumbling tension. Then his lips touched mine, softly, tentatively, questioningly. And my mouth instinctively opened for him, granting him access. The heat of the connection literally exploded through me, completely shattering the frozen wall I'd carefully constructed, releasing all the pain and desolation . . . and love. We were locked together, his breath inside me, mine inside him, panting, clinging to each other, drinking each other, needing each other.

Matthias coughed. We jerked, instantly crashing back to the here and now. Stumbling apart, we both fought for control as we faced Matthias. But as soon as I released my grip on Seth the feeling of loss was so sharp that my eyes darted to his in panic. He was gazing back at me with an expression of such need that all we could do was move back against each other. When Seth's hands locked round mine, I shut my eyes at the instant relief. God, I had missed this. Him. So much. He had taken half of me, the best of me, with him when he left.

'Why are you here, Eva?' whispered Matthias urgently.

'I needed to be with you . . . to be part of this. I – I have to learn to fight.'

'No, you don't,' interjected Seth. 'You absolutely don't.'

'I *do*, Seth! You are away from dawn to night. We are alone – Ambrose, Lauren and me. We are vulnerable. Not one of us can protect ourself. I need to learn this. And it's wrong that you should try to prevent me.'

'We've been through this before, Eva! I can't build and train an army if I'm constantly watching you, worrying about you getting injured –'

'Well – *don't*! I'll keep away from you. Someone else can teach me. But please don't shut me out, Seth. I have to be able to defend myself next time Cassius –'

'There won't be a next time with Cassius, Eva!' Seth snarled.

'How do you know that?'

'Because I'm going to kill him.'

'And what if he gets to me before you do?'

'He won't.'

'He might –'

'I'll protect you.'

'Seth! I want to protect myself. And the others. Anyway – you're away *all day*. You aren't protecting us –'

'The house is fortified. And I've asked Zackary –'

'Are you kidding? You've got *Professor Ambrose* guarding us? He's a scientist, not a bodyguard! Don't you think I am capable of learning this stuff?'

'Of course you're capable. I'm just not prepared to put you in the line of fire – which is what training would mean.'

'I'm already in the line of fire! The Romans are ruthless and Cassius *hates* me. As soon as he realizes I'm here he'll come for me. Please don't make me face him helpless again.'

'Why do you think I'm keeping you safely in the house? It's too dangerous for you to walk these streets, to rub shoulders with every Parallon inhabitant. Any one of the people I'm training could be a spy, or become one. Cassius is capable of torturing even the most loyal person into betrayal.'

Both our eyes flicked to Matthias, who stared at the ground uncomfortably.

'Yes, I can see there are risks, Seth, but –'

'Eva, at Zackary's you're safe. Cassius isn't looking for you. He believes you're dead. Nobody knows you're here. The moment you expose yourself your life is at risk. And you're too precious to me for –'

'Seth – you're precious to me, but I let you face danger each day. Because I know that's what you need to do. I don't want to be a prisoner in that house any more. It doesn't make me feel safe, it just makes me feel alone and vulnerable. I'd rather live with a bit of danger than not live at all.'

Seth had dropped my hands some time ago. Now his fists clenched as he clearly struggled for control.

'I've got a suggestion,' said Matt quietly.

We both turned to him sceptically. 'How about – instead of bringing Eva to the training arena, which is pretty wild and unpredictable – we could use the upper floor at Ambrose's house to teach her some defensive moves . . . in the evenings, or before we leave in the morning.'

We both gaped at Matt, absorbing his words. His suggestion was a major compromise on what I'd been looking for, but I could live with it. I really didn't want to distract Seth or jeopardize his work, and neither did I want to attract any Roman attention – I had no burning need to wander the Parallon streets. I glanced at Seth. He hadn't dismissed the idea either. Suddenly his eyes met mine. His beautiful clear blue eyes. My heart stuttered.

'All right,' he breathed finally. 'We'll start tonight.'

His eyes were locked on mine, and I felt the corners of my mouth turn up. 'Thank you!' I whispered.

Something in the hold of his shoulders relaxed, and his mouth was suddenly smiling back at me. I couldn't help it, I felt myself being magnetically drawn back into his arms. I buried my head in his chest and inhaled deeply. I suddenly knew we could do it. We were strong enough. We were meant to be together – two halves of a whole. We didn't function well apart. I noticed with surprise that the leaden desolation I'd been lugging around with me for months had evaporated. I felt alive again.

I wanted to hold on to him; drag him home with me now, stay there for ever and never let him out of my sight again.

But I couldn't. He had a war to plan, an army to prepare. And I had a wormhole to recover.

'You'd better get going, then,' I smiled, reaching up and kissing him briefly on the mouth. 'I'll see you tonight.'

Reluctantly, I pulled away from his warm orbit, and turned to start heading back, but Seth's hand caught my arm.

'Eva, I'll walk you home.'

My heart leaped at the prospect of a few more minutes with him. But then I glanced at Matt. He looked horrified.

'No, Seth,' I sighed, 'I've already made you late. I'll be fine.'

'Eva, I can't let you go alone. Please –'

'She'll be careful, Seth,' interrupted Matt firmly. 'She hasn't got far to go – and we have a very small window of time left now to get into our training tunnel. There are nine hundred raw recruits waiting for your guidance. You cannot let them down.'

Seth stared at me for a few more moments, then pulled me

back towards him, grabbed my chin between his hands and kissed me fiercely. 'Stay in the shadows. Keep away from the patrols. Watch for movement in windows and doorways – there are spies everywhere. Any eyes could be Cassius's eyes. If anything happened to you, Eva, I –'

I stopped his words by pressing my lips hard against his. I pulled his head closer and ran my hands through his hair. 'That goes for you too,' I whispered. 'I love you, Seth. Stay safe.' Then I pulled away, swallowing hard. 'Now go and kick some ass!'

Seth smiled. His hand held on to mine for a brief moment, and then he released me.

'I'll watch you till you're past the next building,' he murmured. 'And then we'll go.'

I smiled and turned away, wishing I could speed up time. It was too long to wait till Seth returned home to me.

18

Challenge

Parallon

'Come on, man, let's move,' hissed Matt, tugging his friend's arm. But Seth was immobile, his eyes trained on Eva as she moved away from them. Though his feet were firmly planted, every atom of his body was reaching out to follow her. He groaned. She was taking that feeling of completeness away with her, and he couldn't bear the idea of being apart from her again. The further she moved away the more unbearable it became.

'We're going to be late, Seth,' warned Matthias.

Seth nodded, but couldn't shake his uneasiness. He didn't want Eva moving through Parallon by herself. His fear for her safety was suffocating, and the impulse to go after her, overwhelming.

'*This* is the reason you can't have her anywhere near you, Seth! When she's around you completely lose focus. Now *let her go.* You'll see her tonight.'

But Seth refused to stop watching until she had moved through the furthest peristyle and had disappeared into the shadows.

'Something feels wrong, Matt,' Seth persisted. 'I – I –'

'Apollo's blood, Seth, pull it together. You've got a damn

army waiting for you. Eva's fine. You saw the way she moves, fast and sure. Nobody will catch her.'

'*We* caught her,' argued Seth. 'I knew she was behind us almost immediately.'

'That's because your hearing is keener than a wolf's. And you and Eva have this strange connection. I didn't know she was there. Nobody else will hear her, I promise. Now come *on*!'

'May the gods grant that you're right, Matthias!' Seth murmured, then turned his head and braced himself for the day ahead.

He grappled all morning with his uneasiness, but Matthias watched him like a hawk, reminding him that he had a crucial job to finish. So he pushed himself on, forcing himself to concentrate, whether he was instructing combat fitness, overseeing target practice or supervising the resistance to interrogation sessions. Although his troops were developing discipline, most still lacked strength and stamina. Without these qualities they wouldn't stand a chance in a protracted fight, so he decided to spend that afternoon working on their endurance.

Half an hour into the session one of the recruits, a large heavily tattooed guy, flopped down on the floor and refused to continue. 'No, man! No way am I doing one more bloody press-up.'

'Get up,' said Seth quietly.

Matthias glanced at his friend. He knew that tone. It spelled danger. He prayed the lazy recruit would get up and do the damn exercise, or he was going to regret it.

Unfortunately, the recruit didn't move. 'Look, man, I've been here since dawn working my ass off. I'm not doing any more of your stupid army gam–'

Before he'd finished the sentence, he felt himself being heaved off the ground by the collar and pulled to his feet.

'You think this is a game?' demanded Seth, now standing threateningly close. 'Is that why I've never seen you do more than *play* at it? I'm sorry, but we have no use for *children* in this army. We need soldiers. We need men and women who can fight, who can watch each other's backs, who can stand up to a battalion of ruthless, meticulously trained Roman legionaries. Have you ever seen the Romans fight? As a legion they unite to become one huge, savage killing machine, made up of individuals without fear. These men are trained to beat a fellow soldier to death for falling asleep on his watch, and to march forty miles in full armour, with back-breakingly heavy packs. They are men who do not fall until they are dead.'

The room had gone quiet. All the other training groups had begun to gather round.

Aware suddenly of the silence around him, Seth's eyes flicked across the training ground. At that moment the recruit suddenly willed a knife into his hand.

'You don't get to tell me what to do!' he snarled.

Seth cocked his head. 'Are you threatening me?'

'Put the knife away, man,' warned Matthias.

The recruit ignored him and lunged.

With barely any visible movement, Seth had grabbed the knife, hurled it into the centre of a target over ten metres away, and slammed the recruit to the floor in a headlock.

Ignoring the ripple of gasps erupting around the training arena, he hauled the man to his feet.

'Go home,' he said quietly. 'You can't help us fight this war.'

The recruit moved slowly towards the door. His fury had

been replaced by bewilderment. He'd grown up on the streets, one of the toughest kids on the block. Nobody had ever got close enough to disarm him before. And he was way heavier than Leontis, so how had the guy managed to tackle him to the floor without any effort?

Matthias moved over to him. Recognizing the disbelief on the recruit's face, he murmured, 'This wasn't about wielding power or punishment. Sethos was trying to teach you stamina and strength, because without them we don't stand a chance. And not only did you cave physically, you questioned his judgement and his leadership. A soldier without loyalty or humility is of no use.'

'That's –'

'There is a reason Seth is leading this army,' continued Matthias. '*Nobody* can fight like he does. Nobody can strategize like he can. He is the only man capable of freeing Parallon from the Romans.' He slapped the recruit on the back, and began walking him to the door. '*Truman!*' he called.

A terrified-looking youth who'd been leaning against a wall watching them, hurried quickly over.

'Y-yes, sir?' he stammered.

'Would you escort this man from the building.'

Truman nodded, and put his hand on to the recruit's elbow.

'Be careful as you leave,' added Matt, holding both of them with a steady gaze. 'If anyone reveals this army to Cassius, his betrayal will be committing all the people of Parallon to a dark eternity of tyranny.'

Truman dropped his eyes to the ground and led the recruit away.

19

Distraction

Parallon

I crept through the shadows, scanning every corner, window and doorway for guards or spies. But instead of feeling fearful and trapped, I felt strangely free. The tightness that I'd been carrying around in my chest for months had unravelled and I could breathe again.

In just a few hours, Seth would be home. There was so much we needed to say to each other, so much to work out, to apologize for, but deep down I knew that whatever happened now, whatever our future held, we would face it together.

I peered through the half-light towards the buildings ahead. I could see Ambrose's place from here. I just had to wait for this patrol to pass and I'd be able to make the quick dash across the exposed part of the road to his house. But the guards had barely marched past the building when the door opened quietly and Lauren slipped out.

What the hell was she doing, leaving right now? The guards were way too close. Her expression was really tense, and she was carrying her tablet and heading for the river, so clearly she was on vortex business. But my alarm at her recklessness suddenly turned to panic when I realized she hadn't changed her clothes. Instead of Roman dress, she was wearing a white shirt and jeans.

Had she completely forgotten where she was?

Could I create her a Roman cloak to shove over her shoulders from this distance? Before I'd finished asking myself that question, I caught a sudden movement from one of the patrolling guards. His head had jerked round and his gaze was now fixed on her disappearing figure. My stomach lurched as his hand reached out and touched his partner's shoulder. They immediately diverted from the path they were on to go after her.

Oh God! She was dressed wrong; she spoke no Latin . . . and she was an *unlisted*. She absolutely couldn't get caught. Especially as she was the only person keeping the vortex marginally stable.

What could I do? I had to help her.

In the heat of the moment, the only thing I could think of was distraction – to shift their attention from her. But did that mean I had to divert it to me? That idea definitely sucked.

Maybe if Seth had taught me some tactics I'd have been able to think of a brilliant way to stop them following her, but what did a geeky girl know about cool military moves? All I could come up with were three totally crap ideas: flirt with them (no way); feign injury (but then what?); throw stones at their backs (yeah, and get them really pissed off).

Then suddenly I remembered a PC game I used to play where you were given a power and a curse. If you played it right and chose the right power you'd win. Most kids chose high-impact weapons and tried to fight their way through, but my favourite was the smoke launcher. It didn't cause injury, but by smogging up everything your getaway was invisible and you skipped straight to the next level.

I willed a smoke launcher into each of my hands and threw them hard. With a loud crack they hit the ground just behind the Romans, prompting Lauren and the two guards to turn round. I just caught Lauren's eyes widening in horror as she took in the scene behind her, then thankfully she broke instantly into a run. The guards had managed to get a pretty decent look at me just before the smoke started billowing all around us, but I was already sprinting in the opposite direction. I couldn't see anything, but I could hear their heavy footfalls setting off behind me. Luckily, I didn't need vision to know the layout of the roads in this section because I'd spent so long looking out of Ambrose's library window. I knew that halfway along the street there was a small temple. That's where I headed.

As I neared, I could just make out the double-arched doorway. Temple doors were usually unlocked during daylight, but the relief was almost overwhelming when I pushed at the latch and the doors creaked open. I closed them quickly behind me and moved into the cool, dark interior, clinging on to a column to catch my breath. Sooner than I expected I heard the heavy footsteps of the guards' approach outside. They slowed when they got near the door, and I froze silently in place. After a couple of moments they continued past. I stayed leaning against the column, closed my eyes and breathed out a shaky sigh of relief.

'Lauren, you so owe me,' I muttered under my breath.

I hated to admit it, but I was pretty freaked out after that run, so I rested against the pillar for a few moments more.

When I felt ready to face the streets again, I opened my

eyes . . . directly on to the solid chests and smirking faces of a second pair of Roman soldiers.

What the hell? Had they been lying in wait or was this random bad luck?

'Who were you running from, my sweet?' one of them demanded in Latin, grabbing my wrist painfully between his fingers.

Random bad luck, then.

I stammered incoherently, unable to think of a single plausible story.

'Just tell him why you were running,' said the other one, glancing warily at the way his partner's hand was gripping me.

But I was all out of ideas.

'What's your name?'

Another impossible question. I stood mutely before them.

'Ah! An unregistered!' The first guard grinned, pulling my chin roughly between his fingers and lifting my head to face him. 'By Hades,' he hissed between his teeth. 'She's a peach. Hmmm. I know exactly where she's going now.' He pulled me roughly towards him.

The second guard instantly wrestled me out of his grasp. 'Do you want to get flogged, man?' he snarled. 'You can't sample the goods – not before the elite guard.' His eyes flicked to mine for a moment. 'Let's just do our job and get her to the holding area. They'll probably pass her on to us when they've had their fill.'

'Lucius, man – if we bring this woman to the holding area, the prison guards will take one look at her and grab the first bite. *They* won't resist, you know they won't. So why in the name of Jupiter should we? Come on, if we're quick no one will know, and we can both get our fill before anyone else! Look at her – she's sweet as honey.' He leered down at me, licking his lips, then slapped a rough hand over my mouth and began dragging me through the temple towards an alcoved area at the back. I struggled against his hands, nightmare memories of my time in Londinium with Cassius flaring in my brain. But the moment he slammed me up against the sharp edges of an altar, the other guard drew his knife.

'Let her go, Titus,' he snarled, 'or I will report you to Pontius myself. His orders are unequivocal. We take all prisoners straight to the holding area.'

For a few moments Titus held me against the altar, his body heaving with fury. Suddenly his hand lashed out and slapped me hard across the face. Then he dragged me back across the temple, out through the doors into the light. I had been reprieved.

As they led me through the eerily empty streets, I did my best to memorize the route. I had to believe I would get out of this situation somehow, and the only way to do that was to keep my brain busy, keep thinking. But when the huge columned walls of the arena suddenly loomed in front of me, my spirits began to sink. It was still barely dawn, so there was no braying crowd: the arena was deathly quiet, but I knew that in a matter of hours it would be filled with blood and screams and shouting.

'Where are you taking me?' I asked huskily.

Lucius glanced across at me and pointed. 'The arena holding area. All prisoners are taken there to be categorized and questioned. But a girl looking like you is unlikely to end up wasted in the arena,' he said quietly. I couldn't tell whether he was trying to comfort or alarm me, but his words filled me with foreboding.

Just before handing me over, Lucius pulled the hood of my cloak well over my hair and face, then leaned close to my ear and murmured, 'I've done all I can now. Keep your head down or this will turn into a feeding frenzy.'

And then he was gone.

20

Hell

Arena Holding Area, Parallon

Nick Mullard was crouched against a mildewed wall in the dank basement of the gladiator holding area. He was watching the doorway. He'd been monitoring it for weeks: charting guard-changes, official visits, prisoner drop-offs.

Not one day had passed since his arrival in Parallon when he didn't reflect on Winston Grey's first greeting: 'Welcome to hell.'

At the time he'd assumed the guy was just being flippant, but when, only hours later, he and Winston had been dragged from the villa, clapped in chains and then forced to get pummelled nightly in the arena, Nick had to acknowledge that Winston wasn't kidding. He had indeed landed in hell.

But then, he was no stranger to hell. He'd been there before. A lifetime ago.

His first hell had been different: he'd chosen it. Afghanistan. He'd put himself through the gruelling SAS training and approached his mission with a sense of purpose and quiet confidence. He'd thought he was prepared. He knew he could withstand heat, thirst, exhaustion, pain, fear and even torture.

But what he hadn't expected was the bleak, overwhelming sense of powerlessness, as one by one his team got blown apart by landmines or rocket attacks. His training hadn't prepared him for that particular brand of hell. And here he was again. Feeling powerless.

He couldn't see the sky from his shadowy corner, but he could tell by the light seeping under the crack in the door that it was early morning. He probably had eight hours before getting dragged into the arena for the routine bloodbath.

Most of the other gladiators gave him a wide berth, because he was one of the fighters nobody wanted to go up against. Despite the fact that he'd shattered his right leg in Afghanistan, he was still one of the best in the barracks. He was slower than he had been, a little clumsier, but he was strong, and his relentless training had taught him perseverance. And in the arena, that was the greatest asset.

He heard the stirrings of the other prisoners as they began to wake and glanced across at the still-sleeping body of Clare, curled in a tight ball next to Georgia. His jaw clenched in fury. Clare was the girl who had taken him in when he first arrived in Parallon. He'd been shell-shocked and bewildered, and she had risked her own life and that of her friends to hide him. But she was so fragile, nearly broken by this monstrous nightmare she'd found herself in. Thank God she had Georgia. His eyes flicked to Georgia's arm as it lay protectively across Clare's back.

He couldn't see Winston from over here. Winston would be lying in a filthy heap with the rest of the *unhealing* in the furthest dankest corner of the cellar. Winston was beyond help now. He'd made himself unreachable. The only thing his mind was able to consistently focus on was holding on to the pain and injury. All his energy went into countermanding the Parallon effect. It was his only way to rebel against the nightly arena hammerings. Because weeks ago he had admitted to himself that he was no longer able to attack people for no good reason.

The arena fighting didn't touch Nick the way it did the others. He had no problem dehumanizing his adversary. Probably because it was what he'd been trained to do. Especially knowing that whatever injury he inflicted, his opponents would be healed the next day.

The girls were beginning to wake. He watched Elena move away from the others to create a bowl of soapy water to wash in. She looked up and saw him watching her, smirked, and created an opaque curtain to block him out. She was playing with fire. If the guards saw the soap, water or curtain, she would be beaten. Creation was absolutely forbidden by slaves.

Nick smiled. Elena Galanis, the girl whose disappearance from London had set him on this inexorable path to Parallon, turned out to be just about the only woman in this dungeon who knew how to fight. She was genuinely tough. A born survivor. For weeks now he had been trying to work out how they could pool their resources, how to blast out of this prison and lead the pitiful inhabitants to safety. But despite many whispered conversations, he had no real picture of the layout of Parallon, since he'd been either crouched behind blankets in a kitchen or imprisoned in this basement since he'd been here. He didn't even know what was on the other side of these walls. Were there others who could join them? His training had taught him that if he was to plan a successful breakout, he needed intel. And despite meticulously questioning every new prisoner thrown down the stairs, only one of them had ever suggested that there might be allies on the outside.

'I've heard rumours of a Greek warrior who is raising an army against Cassius. But it's probably just some desperate fantasy,' the last guy had choked between post-torture retches.

A flurry of movement at the door and a cry of pain brought Nick back to the present. He jumped to his feet as a girl was unceremoniously flung down the stairs. He caught her just before she crashed on to the stone floor.

She was shaking and bleeding, but conscious.

'Come and sit down over here,' he said, as he helped her to stumble across to his little patch of territory in the corner. She slid down the wall on to the floor and put her face in her hands.

'How could I have let this happen?' she kept moaning to herself.

'Hey. Look around you. This happened to all of us. We *all* let it happen,' he murmured bitterly.

She froze suddenly, then threw down the hood of her cloak and turned her bruised face to his, her eyes widening with recognition. '*DI Mullard?*' she gasped.

Nick gazed at her face in disbelief as his two worlds suddenly came crashing together.

'Jesus, Eva – Eva Koretsky!' he choked. 'What the hell are you doing here?'

21

Disclosure

Arena Holding Area, Parallon

The situation wasn't exactly funny. I had been beaten and thrown into a deep dungeon. But, for some reason, seeing Nick Mullard's bewildered expression made me start to laugh. And instead of treating me like a nut-job and pushing me away, he just held on to my shoulders while the laughter shuddered through me . . . until tears began to fall, and I found I was sobbing. What the hell? I was totally losing it here. But Mullard just wrapped his arms round me and waited until I calmed down.

'Do you want to talk about it, Eva?' he whispered finally.

I took a deep sniff, shook my head and gratefully grabbed the tissue he passed me. 'Don't let the guards see that,' he muttered.

'Why not?' I asked.

'Creation is forbidden,' he shrugged, glancing around the dank space. 'Otherwise we might have decorated a bit,' he added with a wry smile.

I tried to smile back, and then followed his eyes. What I saw made me think of one of those Bosch paintings of hell. Dark, dripping walls alive with flickering shadows cast by flaming torches fixed at regular intervals along their surface. Each torch cast its own dim circle of light on to the filthy, beaten bodies writhing below.

'God,' I breathed shakily. 'We've got to get out of here.'

Nick Mullard's head shot up and he stared at me. 'Do you know, Eva, you're the first person thrown down those stairs I've heard say that.'

'You've got to be joking. Surely everyone wants to get out of here?'

He shook his head. 'By the time most of them arrive they've already lost all hope.'

I glanced around at the barely moving bodies and tried to breathe normally, but a sudden movement at the door above the stairs instantly set my panic button. 'I-I've really got to get out of here, DI Mullard –' I gasped urgently.

'Eva, please – my name's Nick,' he muttered. 'I am not a DI here. And – what are you afraid of – apart from the obvious?' he asked, waving his hand around the horrific prison.

I cowered against the wall and pulled my hood firmly over my face, my eyes fixed on the door above me. 'The – the moment Cassius finds out I'm here, my life will be over . . . and . . .' I thought of Matthias's warning.

'And – what?'

'. . . the rebellion could be jeopardized.'

'Rebellion? What the hell do you mean?'

I turned to face him. He had a right to know. 'Seth's building an army,' I said finally.

Nick leaned against the wall and closed his eyes. 'Thank God,' he murmured.

Then he frowned. 'So this Seth – who is he? All I've heard is a garbled rumour about some heroic Greek warrior.' He laughed wryly.

I bit my lip. 'A-actually – you met Seth . . . in London . . .' I said, feeling my cheeks heat up. For the first time I was grateful for the lack of light in here. That particular meeting had not gone well.

Nick Mullard was watching me, his eyes narrowing as he flipped through his internal filing system. His face suddenly registered the moment. 'Starbucks? The guy who stormed in and hauled you away?'

I nodded reluctantly.

'Impossible, Eva – he was just a kid! He couldn't lead an army!'

'No, Nick, Seth's not a kid. And people – follow him.'

'So where'd he learn to fight?' Nick asked sceptically.

I shrugged. 'The arena mainly.'

Nick stared at me for a moment, and then frowned. 'Christ, he's not the *famous gladiator* the magister is offering a reward for is he?'

I felt my body go rigid. Of course I knew Cassius was looking for Seth – Matthias had been sent to London to find him – but the fact that even the prisoners down here knew, and there was a price on his head, meant that it was literally only a matter of time.

I licked my lips nervously and nodded.

'So what's his plan?' Nick asked.

'I really don't know. He never told me,' I answered bitterly.

'In that case how could you possibly put the whole thing at risk?'

I stared down at my hands. 'B-because when Seth finds out I've been taken –'

Nick's head jerked up, understanding dawning. He was nodding. 'That figures. And the magister knows what you mean to Seth, so he can use you as bait?'

'I think he'd probably give it a go. That's what he was going to do last time.'

'*Last time?* How far does this go back, Eva?'

'About two thousand years,' I smiled weakly. 'Though the last time I met Cassius I told him Seth didn't care about me any more.'

'And he believed you?'

'I think so. I believed it, so I was fairly convincing. Anyway, Cassius probably hates *me* even more than he hates Seth.'

'Why would he hate you?'

'Because when I was his . . . I tried to escape.'

'What do you mean – *his*?'

I paused, then swallowed hard. 'I was m-married to him.'

'Christ!'

'And I tried to run away with Seth.' I shrugged stiffly. 'Cassius managed to stop me though.'

'How?'

'He cut my throat.'

'Jesus, Eva! How'd you survive that?'

I found myself absently skimming a finger along the line the knife had sliced.

'I didn't survive it. That was the first time Cassius killed me . . .' I sighed.

Nick was staring at me in confusion. 'I think I may need a bit more than that, Eva.'

I nodded. This was going to take a while.

22

Crime and Punishment

Arena Holding Area, Parallon

Nick Mullard was running both hands through his hair, frowning. He hadn't said one word since I'd confessed my whole damn story. I was seriously regretting it.

'Maybe I –'

'Eva,' he interrupted. 'This is absolutely the worst place for you to be right now. We've got to –'

Another movement at the top of the steps had me jolting round anxiously. Was I about to face the *categorization*?

'Is this it?' I gasped urgently. 'Are they coming for me?'

'Don't think so,' he answered. 'Probably just a guard change. The categorization crew normally arrive around midday, which gives you about four hours.'

My eyes darted wildly around the pit. 'Is there any way to avoid it? An escape route? Somewhere to hide?'

Nick looked at his hands uncomfortably. 'The Romans keep a numerical register of us all. If a prisoner goes missing . . . everyone gets punished.'

I nodded slowly and leaned back against the wall. Perfect.

There was no way I could let everyone take a beating for me. I was totally trapped.

'Who's this then?' rasped a voice near my face.

An unsmiling girl about my age was now squatting in front of us. Her blonde hair hung in lank clumps, and there was a patch of dried blood on her cheek.

'Georgia, this is Eva,' said Nick. 'She just got here.'

Georgia was frowning at me. Suddenly she moved forward and pushed the hood off my face. Her eyes widened. 'God, it's *you*! It's really you! I never believed you actually existed . . . But what's with the fake name?'

What the hell?

'My name is Eva, but – whatever . . .' I muttered, pulling the hood back into position. This chick was weird. And now she was shaking her head. 'I've seen the notebooks, Livia. They're full of drawings. You couldn't be anyone else.'

I felt the blood drain from my face. 'What drawings?' I whispered.

'Seth's drawings, obviously,' she frowned.

'He did drawings? Have the Romans seen them?'

'Hey, chill out!' she murmured. 'The only person around here you really have to worry about is Clare.'

'Who's Clare?'

'The girl heading this way.'

'And why do I have to worry about her?' I asked as a small weary figure approached.

'Because she's hated you *forever*.'

Great. Another one to add to my collection. 'Why?'

Georgia rolled her eyes. 'Because forever is just about how long she's been in love with Seth . . . Oh hey, Clare!'

'What's that about Seth?' the girl demanded warily, her eyes shifting between us. 'Is it t-true, then? Has he really come back?' Her eyes were casting around the dungeon hopefully.

I hid my face under my hood, trying to make myself invisible, but my movement seemed to have the opposite effect. Immediately the girl was peering down at me. 'You don't need to hide from *us*, you know,' she smiled.

'Hey, Clare, let's go and check on Winston,' said Georgia quickly, jumping to her feet and trying to steer her away.

'I've just been over there,' Clare sighed, settling on the floor next to me. 'No change. So tell me, what's all this about Se–'

A loud clattering at the top of the stairs made me jump.

'Hey, relax, newbie, it's only room service,' murmured Georgia, patting my shoulder.

We watched as four cowering house-slaves carried in heavy wooden trays filled with greyish loaves of bread and earthenware jugs. They placed them carefully in the middle of the floor and stood aside as people from every corner of the dungeon converged on the food, hauling it desperately back into the shadows.

I couldn't believe it. This was Parallon. They could eat what they wanted, when they wanted. Why were they buying into this dry bread and water deal? I watched in bewilderment as Nick leaped across to grab us all a loaf to share, along with a jug of water. He tore me off a lump. It was coarse, very tough and pretty well unchewable. I shrugged and transformed my piece into a soft white roll and cheese.

Nick's eyes narrowed and he shook his head.

'What?' I smirked, taking a large bite. It had been hours since I last ate.

'You haven't seen the punishments, Eva,' he answered quietly, transforming my bread back to its original form.

I frowned at him, my stomach clenching. Actually, he was wrong. I *had* seen and *received* plenty of Cassius's punishments, incarcerated in his palace in Londinium. Images of his bedchamber swam before my eyes: the chains attached to the wooden bed frame, the leather belt held between his fists, the knife at his hip . . .

'Eva?' Nick was leaning over me. 'Are you OK?'

My heart was pounding. I took deep breaths. He held a cup of water to my lips. I shook my head. I couldn't swallow anything. I leaned back against the wall with my eyes closed, waiting for my body to settle. There was a reason my brain tried to shut down when memories of my time with Cassius bubbled up. Some memories were meant to stay buried.

'Hey, is the new girl all right?' I felt a hand gently pulling at my hood.

'Oh my God – I don't believe it. It's . . . her! *Livia!*'

I opened my eyes wearily. Clare's shocked face was inches from mine.

I sighed. Clearly arguing about my name wasn't going to make this go away.

She slumped down next to me. 'So, i-is he back?'

I glanced at her warily. 'Seth?'

She rolled her eyes.

I nodded.

'With *you*?'

I felt a sudden furious wave of possessiveness, and I wanted to hit her for even questioning it.

But she was glaring at me, waiting for me to speak.

'Do you see him here with me?' I snapped, wishing to God he *was* right now.

Instead of backing the hell off, her face just loomed closer, and she was fixing me with blazing eyes. 'Why did you leave him, Livia?' she hissed. 'You completely broke him.'

'You think *I* left *him*?' I choked. 'You think I could ever leave Seth? He is my li–'

I couldn't tell her what he was to me. So I shut my eyes and leaned back against the wall. I was fighting for control.

'This army Seth's training –' said Nick suddenly, cutting through the atmosphere bristling between Clare and me.

I glanced across at him. 'Yeah?'

'How many troops?'

'About nine hundred, I think.'

Nick looked around the basement speculatively. 'I think we could add to their number . . .'

I sat forward, desperate to go with the subject change. 'I'm listening.'

'There are at least forty reasonably able-bodied gladiator slaves here. I may even persuade some of the *unhealing* to join us. This could be exactly what they need: a real purpose. Now that I know there are people on the outside we can work with, I have to start prepping everyone. I'll begin training tonight.'

'In here? What about the guards?'

'I think I can get round them,' he murmured thoughtfully. 'Eva, do you have any idea how long we've got?'

'I think they intend to strike in a few days. B-but . . . that could all change now . . .'

Nick's eyes caught mine. 'You mean Seth won't wait once he finds out you've been taken?'

I shrugged apologetically, praying Seth wouldn't do anything reckless.

23

Manoeuvre

Training Ground, Parallon

Seth stood against a wall with his arms folded, trying to concentrate. He wanted to get home. He couldn't stand to be apart from her for another moment. But he couldn't leave here yet. He needed his army ready. It was only a matter of time before the Romans would torture the rebellion rumours into hard facts, and then Cassius would be primed to attack.

'Are you ready to start the manoeuvre?' asked Matt, striding over.

Seth nodded and narrowed his eyes at the scene he faced. He had expanded the operation below ground, and had created a two-kilometre training zone, decked out as a simulated Parallon street. He scanned the environment in front of him, and although he could see no sign of a soldier, he knew that behind doors, columns and archways one team would be strategically positioned to defend the replica temple to his left, while the other was easing into an attack formation to capture it. The fight for possession would go on until nobody was left standing if that was what was required. And that was a real possibility, because today they would be using live ammo.

'I still think you're crazy, man,' sighed Matt. 'What the hell is wrong with plastic bullets? They still get the hit; they still go down; and you'll still be able to select the genuine soldiers from the passengers. So why do you need to do this?'

'This exercise isn't for *me*, Matthias.'

'Well, it sure as hell can't be for them, Seth!'

'It won't kill them –'

'It won't kill them, but if they get hit they'll be in agony for hours. Is a simulation worth that? You're not just getting a bit sadistic in your old age?'

Seth turned on Matthias furiously. 'Sadistic?' he hissed. 'Zeus, I thought you, of all people, knew me better than that.'

'Hey, man, relax – I didn't mean –'

'You never do, do you Matthias?' sighed Seth, moving away to his observation deck. He hadn't thought he needed to explain his actions to Matt, and he didn't intend to now. But he did have a very good reason for conducting this battle exercise with live ammo. He knew better than anyone that it was only when you were actually fighting for your life that winning became the imperative. When you knew that one lapse of concentration, one badly aimed strike, one clumsy move could end with you in a pool of blood, face down in the sand – only then did you realize that winning meant the difference between survival and death.

Seth cast his eyes over the silent scene before him, lifted his hand and gave the signal for the manoeuvre to begin.

24

Categorization

Arena Holding Area, Parallon

The categorization was due in half an hour. I had no idea what would happen then. OK – I had several ideas about what could happen then, and I wasn't exactly gagging for any of them. There were no good options when it came to the Romans. So for the sake of my mental well-being, I decided it would be healthier to stop thinking about it altogether. Unfortunately, I had limited distractions. Nick had got to work as soon as the breakfast remains had been taken. He had very little time to covertly recruit allies and build a fighting team, with an entire prison to get round before the day's games started. And that left me stuck between Clare's baleful looks and Georgia's news-from-outside interrogation – which of course I failed at dismally, having been stuck in Ambrose's isolation tank for the past six weeks.

So I tried to zone out from the girls to watch Nick as he skirted from one bedraggled group to another. And pretty soon I became aware that I was witnessing something else: a strange physical transformation sweeping through the prison in his wake. Shoulders began to straighten; eyes danced; spines grew taller and chests broadened. The atmosphere in the room shifted from one of abject misery to one of taut energy. I glanced at the guards at the top of the stairs. Would it be obvious to them too?

My eyes anxiously scanned the room. Now Nick was squatting next to a girl in the middle of a set of hardcore sit-ups. She was listening to him, nodding thoughtfully, but refusing to compromise one moment of her workout.

After a couple minutes, he leaned in close to breathe something in her ear, and as he straightened, his eye caught mine, and with a tiny movement of his head indicated I should join them.

I pulled my hood down over my face, and moved cautiously over.

'Elena Galanis!' I gasped. The missing girl: the person who had inadvertently wreaked total havoc with my life, was staring back at me.

'Do I know you?' she frowned.

I shook my head and smiled ruefully. 'No, you don't. And to be honest, with my track record, that can only be a good thing!'

Suddenly the entire basement went deathly silent, and the heavy vibration of several pairs of feet thundering down the steps froze me in position.

It was time.

My mouth went dry, and I felt Nick's hand tighten on my shoulder.

'Christ,' he said. 'The elite guard are here.'

I swung round to see Pontius, Rufus and Otho following four guards into the basement. My heart began pounding. If they were overseeing the categorization there would be no way

I could get through it incognito. My mind began to spin, but Nick was still talking.

'Do they know you, Eva?' he frowned, pulling my hood further down my face.

I tried to swallow, and managed a stiff nod.

I felt him heave a deep breath. 'Whatever happens,' he whispered into my ear, 'whatever they do to you, remember this is Parallon. You will heal. And Seth will come for you.'

Then he moved swiftly with Elena towards the centre of the floor where people were beginning to form lines, and they both slipped into place.

The elite guard were now standing on a platform near the steps, impassively watching. Another guard, holding a large ledger, began moving along the lines of prisoners, counting and registering names.

I shrank back against the wall, hoping against hope that the elite guard had come on different business, when Otho lifted his cold grey eyes and cleared his throat.

'Categorization prisoners here,' he announced, gesturing to the area of space immediately under the platform. Terrified figures began shuffling obediently towards the platform. I had to follow them, but despite my brain's desperate instructions, my legs were refusing to cooperate. I simply couldn't move.

Suddenly Nick Mullard was by my side, easing me forward and steering me towards the platform.

'*Get back in line, slave!*' bellowed the nearest guard, and instantly Nick was being thrown against a wall and lashed with a heavy leather strap.

'*Stop!*' I screamed, hurling myself between the guard and

him, but Nick pushed me away, hissing, 'For Christ's sake, Eva, get down to the platform before it's too late!'

I stumbled away and forced my shaking legs towards the elite guard; the only sounds in the room were my uneven footsteps, the sharp whistles and cracks of leather against skin, and Nick's involuntary groans.

I finally came to a stop when I reached the others waiting to be categorized. They were standing with their heads bowed, cowering. I took my place behind them. I was the only girl, the only one trying to hide under a hood. As if hiding was an option now. The incident with Nick, and my humiliating stumble down to the platform, had nixed that. If I'd worn harlot red and ridden through the place on a white unicorn I couldn't have drawn more attention. Now every single eye in the room was fixed on me.

'So,' growled Pontius in Latin. 'What have we here?'

I could feel the physical relief of the guys in front of me as they realized I was the one he was homing in on. I kept my eyes to the ground. Only a miracle was going to save me now.

It clearly wasn't God's day for miracles. Pontius stepped off the platform and came to a stop inches away from me. 'Kneel in the presence of your master,' he snarled.

I immediately fell to my knees.

'Mmmm. She understands Latin?' he said softly, menacingly. 'This just gets better and better.' He licked his lips. 'Let's see if she has any other assets, shall we?'

With one swipe he tore off my cloak and threw it across the room. I kept my eyes trained down and folded my arms round my body. I was trying not to shake.

'Nice,' he hissed, running a finger down the back of my neck. 'Sw-e-e-e-t.'

I did my best to conceal a shudder of disgust. The next moment I felt his fingers in my hair. He was coiling it slowly, deliberately round his hand. When he had gathered its full length he jerked his hand forcefully back, pulling my head up hard. Instantly I was staring into his shocked face.

'*Livia!*' he hissed.

I closed my eyes.

'Well, well, well. Won't the magister be pleased.'

25

Surrender

Training Ground, Parallon

Although it was well after dark by the time the attack force took the temple, Seth wasn't happy. The defenders had surrendered, which was the last thing he'd expected or trained them for. Surrender was an alien concept to him – it was cowardly, dishonourable and weak. You couldn't build a successful army out of men who surrendered.

He moved away from the manoeuvre aftermath and paced. For the first time since he'd taken on the task of training this army he felt defeated. How had he ever thought he could turn them into soldiers capable of taking back Parallon? These people hadn't changed. They still caved under pressure. Which meant they were totally unreliable.

'Well, at least we can go home now, I'm starving,' grinned Matthias, moving across to slap him on the shoulder.

Seth reeled round and stared at him. 'Matthias, do you understand nothing about combat?' he snarled.

'W-what do you mean, brother?' answered Matt uneasily.

'We've just watched half our army throw down their weapons

and give up – and you ask me what I mean? Were you here today?'

'Yes, I was here, Seth,' muttered Matt, 'I have just taken thirty-five soldiers off to the medical wing with wounds that would have killed them if they weren't in Parallon.'

'In the name of Zeus, Matthias, this is a *war*! What the hell do you expect? Have you lost track of what's at stake here? Oh no – I was forgetting,' he went on bitterly, 'capitulation is what you do, isn't it? Anything rather than stand up and fight . . . You were one of the first ones to let the Romans in. Isn't that so, Matt?'

'I'm sorry we can't all be heroes, Seth,' retorted Matthias. 'Some of us choose survival.'

'*Survival?*' roared Seth. 'You call *this* survival? Well, you'd better hang on to your survival, because I'm through.'

'No, wait, Seth,' cried Matthias. 'We need you.'

'I can't help you any more.'

Seth started striding towards the door when three of his officers barred his path.

'Let me pass,' he commanded.

'Matthias is right, Leontis,' argued Joe Kennedy, one of Seth's most trusted men. 'Nobody can lead this army but you.'

'This isn't an army, Kennedy. Well-trained troops don't capitulate. Soldiers that surrender after a few hours of assault are not soldiers I would want on my side. Who can trust them? Their fear is more powerful than their cause. For us to win this war it *has* to be the other way round.'

'Not everyone wanted to surrender,' persisted Kennedy.

Seth took a deep breath and nodded. His officer was gently reminding him that he couldn't blame the whole team for dutifully obeying orders: orders they would have received from their commander – a man Seth had appointed himself.

'Where is Perchik?' sighed Seth.

Kennedy glanced over to the corner, where Officer Perchik was chatting with some of the temple team. 'Stay here, I'll bring him over,' said Kennedy, moving swiftly off to fetch him.

'Er – I'll just go and check on the injured,' muttered Matthias, heading in the opposite direction. Seth nodded absently and watched as Perchik paced towards him.

'Sir?' he said, as he reached Seth. 'You wanted to speak to me?'

Seth said nothing for a moment, just continued watching him. He had initially considered him a talented and able fighter. 'How do you think that exercise went, Perchik?' he asked quietly.

Perchik licked his lips. 'Well, obviously I would have preferred it if we'd held on to the temple, but when I got word that the outer court was breached and at least twenty of our people were down, I knew I had to pull out before any more of them got hurt.'

Seth nodded slowly. 'Perchik, do you remember the premise I gave you before we started the simulation?'

Perchik blinked, and tried to recall Seth's words.

'Y-e-s . . . you said that we were guarding the keys to the city . . . and that if we allowed anyone to get through our defences, the city would be lost; all our families would be lost; we would be lost . . . And there would be nobody left to fight for us.'

'That just about sums up it up – good. And yet after five and a half hours, what did you do?'

Perchik averted his eyes.

'I'll tell you, then. You lost it all. You opened the door and let them take you, your family and your city.'

'I had no choice. We had so many injured.'

'You lost twenty-three soldiers, Perchik. Twenty-three *temporarily* wounded soldiers!'

'I was trying to be responsible.'

'You gave up on your own war. Was that responsible?'

'But that wasn't a *war*! We were playing a *game* . . . against our own people. I wouldn't have made that decision if the Romans were really attacking.'

'Oh no?' sighed Seth bitterly. 'You made that decision last time.'

'W-what do you mean?'

'Why do you think we're here, Perchik?'

Perchik frowned and shrugged.

'We're here because you already gave the Romans the key to the city! I was just hoping I'd be able to train you to try and get it back . . .'

'And we will . . .'

Seth shook his head. 'I said something else to you before we started the exercise, do you remember?'

Perchik gazed down at his feet and squirmed.

'I said I expected you to fight for your city till the last man went down.'

Perchik nodded. 'I-I just assumed you were talking hypothetically,' he mumbled.

'*Hypothetically?*' bellowed Seth. 'If we were fighting a hypothetical war, maybe I would have been talking hypothetically. But we're not. This is real. This is your one and only chance to reclaim Parallon, and if your performance this afternoon was any indication of how fit you are for the job, we can all just give up now.'

Seth moved across to the door. He was wasting his time. He needed to get out of there.

But once more his way was barred. This time his entire army had gathered round him. One man moved forward. Seth recognized him immediately as Brandon, the man he'd chosen to lead the attack.

'Don't make assumptions about everyone, Leontis,' Brandon began. 'Some of us *have* changed. I was full of fear until you arrived in Parallon and taught us a different way. I admit I'd allowed myself to be cowed and enslaved by the Romans. But that's not me any more. I would never have let my troops give up today. I was determined to get the keys to the city back. I would have walked my guys through fire to get those keys. And I'm pretty certain they would have followed me.'

Seth glanced across the sea of weary faces and finally saw what he'd been looking for over the past six weeks: commitment, determination and grim desperation.

And he felt chastened. He had almost abandoned them.

'You're right, Brandon, I'm sorry. You commanded a highly disciplined force today and fought bravely. I am proud to call you brother.' Then he clasped Brandon's hand and raised it in the air. 'The victors,' he shouted, and Brandon's team cheered long and hard.

'And as for the defenders,' continued Seth, 'let that be the last surrender I ever witness! Now, go home! Travel safely, eat, drink and rest. Tomorrow, we will prepare our attack on the Romans.'

26

Fear

Cassius's Palace, Parallon

I was in a dimly lit cell. No window. No sound. There was a thin mattress on the floor in the corner. And that was about it. Just four stone walls and a locked door. Not even a line of scrawled graffiti to distract me.

I had no idea how long I'd been here. Three hours, maybe four? For a while I toyed with the idea of making the place comfortable. I could easily give myself a decent bed, a delicious meal, a library of books. And a part of me really wanted to see how they would handle that when they came to get me and saw all that forbidden creation. But the truth was I was too scared.

Pathetic really. Especially as I knew that whatever I did, however perfect my behaviour, it wouldn't make any difference. I was going to get punished . . . Cassius got off on hurting people. Especially me. And he'd want to hurt me a whole lot more for turning up here alive, when I was supposed to be well and truly dead. I just didn't particularly want to give him any more reasons to make the punishment heavier.

I hated to think of myself as pathetic – I would have way preferred defiant. And I'd never had a problem with defiance until I met Cassius. But I guess standing up to your stepdad or your head teacher wasn't in quite the same league as defying a tyrannical sadist.

I shivered. I couldn't believe I was about to face him again. And nothing had changed. I felt just as terrified. Just as weak. Just as powerless.

And I was pretty sure this waiting was part of the torture. Cassius was always good at mind games. He liked messing with people's heads almost as much as their bodies.

My pulse was racing again. Deep breaths.

My mind began to flail. Panic was setting in. I wanted to get out of here.

I ran to the door. There was no handle. Of course. It was bolted on the other side. I pushed against it, but there was no movement in it at all. My heart was thumping. The room suddenly felt airless, smaller. Were the walls closing in? Yes, they were. Oh God! I started banging on the door with my fists. I couldn't breathe.

'*Let me out!*' I howled hoarsely. '*Let me out!*'

27

Taken

Zackary's House, Parallon

'Eva?' called Seth as soon as he heard Matt click the front door closed behind them. They were home late. His longing to see her was bordering on pain, and he couldn't wait a moment longer. He bounded straight up the stairs to the library and peered in.

Lauren was staring wildly at them, wringing her hands nervously.

Seth felt his body freeze. 'Where is she?'

Lauren stammered. 'Sh-she never came back. Z-Zackary's out looking for her.'

'What happened, Lauren?'

'I-I was careless . . . nearly got caught leaving the house . . . E-Eva was leading the guards away f-from me —'

'When?' he croaked.

Lauren swallowed hard. 'She's been gone since dawn.'

All the misgivings Seth had been feeling throughout the day came crashing back. And now the thing he feared most, the *only* thing he truly feared, had happened. She had been taken.

He had failed the girl he loved *again*.

'Seth, brother, where are you going?' shouted Matthias as Seth sprinted back down the stairs.

'Where do you think?' Seth hissed, pulling open the front door.

'Don't be a fool!' gasped Matt, trying to drag Seth back into the house. 'You can't just walk into the holding area and carry her out – the place is guarded day and night.'

'Take your hands off me, Matt,' snarled Seth, swinging into the fresh night air.

'Seth – listen to me –'

'I listened to you this morning, Matthias . . .' Seth snapped. 'That was the last time it'll ever happen.'

Matthias felt a stab of misery at the comment. Seth *had* listened to him that morning. Finally. And Matt had been congratulating himself all day that he'd got Seth to walk away from Eva and come with him. At last, Seth had shifted his focus from the massive distraction that girl represented. And now she was about to completely derail Seth and the rebellion. Which was exactly what he'd been working so hard to prevent.

'What are you going to do, Seth? Get *yourself* caught too?' challenged Matthias, following Seth through the door.

'Get away from me, Matthias. Before you bring every damn guard in Parallon down on my back.'

'What do you think is going to happen when you start banging on the door of the holding area, demanding your girlfriend back? They're going to fling the door open for you and send her out? Think about this, man!'

Seth suddenly came to a stop inside the doorway of the building they were passing.

'Matthias, tell me something. Were you ever my friend?'

'Always, Seth,' choked Matt. 'How can you ask?'

'How many times have you betrayed me, Matt?'

'How many times have I saved you?' he countered. 'I never meant to betray you. You are my brother. I love you.'

'But you don't love Eva.'

Matthias stared at the ground. 'What I don't love is the way she comes first.'

'She does come first. She is my centre.' He touched his heart. 'She lives here, Matt . . . And if anything happens to her . . .'

Matt flinched at the fierce pain in his friend's eyes.

'So what's your plan, Seth?' he muttered.

'I'm going to find a way into the holding area and get her out.'

'I told you – the door is guard–'

'Matthias, do you think I'm a fool? I won't be using the *door*. This is *Parallon*.'

28

Insurrection

Arena Holding Area, Parallon

Nick Mullard pulled himself slowly off the thin layer of bedding, his head spinning. His back was on fire. He closed his eyes, trying to absorb the pain. Christ, how long had the flogging gone on? He couldn't remember it stopping.

The holding area was eerily quiet. He opened his eyes and glanced over to the doorway. No daylight coming through. Had he lost the whole day? What the hell was the time? He needed to get himself upright – he had a unit to train.

'*Nick, lie down!*'

He turned his head. Georgia was squatting next to him, her hand pressing on to his shoulder. 'Leave it for tonight. You need to heal.'

'Let go, Georgia,' he winced, shaking her off and pulling himself to his feet. 'This thing is going to blow and we need to be ready. What time is it?'

Georgia didn't answer. She was too busy trying not to stare at him, her cheeks flushed. Nick frowned, and looked down.

'Oops,' he smirked. Clearly the tunic he'd been wearing before the beating had been stripped off at some point. He sighed. His back, buttocks and legs were still burning, and he didn't relish the weight of a tunic against his raw skin.

'It's OK, Nick, I've got it covered,' grinned Georgia, and before he'd had a chance to protest, a thin loin-cloth hung from his hips. It wasn't unfamiliar – he'd played retiarius in the arena a few times, and this was all he wore there.

'Does the job, I guess,' he shrugged. So are you going to answer my question?'

Georgia glanced at the doorway. 'The last arena show finished about two hours ago. So it must be nearly midnight.'

'Perfect. Well – are you coming or not?'

Her eyes widened. 'We're really doing this?' she gasped, standing up.

Nick created two body-shaped mounds on the floor where they'd been lying, and moved silently towards the next mattress. He shook the shoulder of the prone figure, and realized immediately that he was trying to wake up a bolster. He grinned. His instructions had been followed. Glancing at all the other prone shapes on the floor, he hoped that the same applied to them. Certainly nobody stirred as he and Georgia made their stealthy way to the back of the holding area – the masked-off section that marked out the territory of the *unhealing*: their meeting place.

A flickering light illuminated the gathering. Something in Nick's chest stirred as the light caught fifty pairs of eyes blinking expectantly towards him.

He had just opened his mouth to speak when a series of cracking sounds on the floor to his left had him instantly in a defensive pose, his right hand wielding a large knife and his body poised to fight.

29

Contact

Arena Holding Area, Parallon

Two calloused hands gripped the sides of the hole now gaping in the ground next to Nick. The hands were instantly followed by a pair of muscled arms, a head covered in dark, wavy hair, powerful shoulders, and finally the undeniable body of an athlete.

'Oh my God, *Seth*!' gasped Clare, rushing towards him.

'Be quiet, Clare,' hissed Georgia, also dashing over to greet him.

Seth stood for a moment, bathed in the flickering torchlight, frowning in bewilderment at the sea of faces around him. It took him only a couple of moments though to register the hostile stance of the man wielding a knife towards him.

He instantly adapted his own pose, flexing his knees, loosely angling the handle of a dagger now nestling against his palm.

'*You!*' he breathed, suddenly recognizing the man before him: the man who had caused the terrible, tearing rift between him and Eva.

Nick Mullard sheathed his knife, and relaxed his pose. Although he had no idea about the devastating part he'd played in Eva and Seth's relationship, he recognized sexual jealousy when he saw it. He'd seen it in this man's eyes the last time they'd met. It had riled him. But he didn't want to fight Seth this time. They were on the same side.

'She said you'd come,' said Nick.

'Where is she?' growled Seth, also sheathing his knife as his eyes scanned the room.

Nick was grudgingly impressed. Eva had told him the boy was good, and Nick was beginning to believe her. Not only had Seth got here fast, he'd done it virtually soundlessly, and chosen the ideal landing spot. Had Eva been here, it would have been the perfect rescue plan.

But she wasn't here, and it was his unfortunate task to break the news.

'They took her at around midday,' he murmured.

Seth clenched his fists fiercely. 'Do you know where?'

Nick shook his head. 'I'm sorry.'

'Did you see who came for her?'

Seth caught the flicker of anguish as it passed over Nick's face and instantly understood. He closed his eyes for a brief moment. 'Cassius?' he rasped.

'As good as . . . The elite guard.'

'A-and they knew her,' Seth intoned hopelessly. It wasn't a question.

Nick sighed. 'They knew her,' he confirmed.

Seth stood like a man of stone for several moments, unable to unfreeze his brain.

Guilt and self-recrimination were the first emotions to wake up, once his numbness cleared, but he didn't have time for them. He was vaguely aware of Nick talking to him.

'It wasn't the usual categorization,' Nick was saying.

'Normally it's instant . . . gladiator, house-slave or, in the case of the attractive ones, bed–'

'*Enough!*' hissed Seth furiously.

'But maybe the fact that they recognized her could be an advantage . . .'

'You have no idea, do you?' said Seth wearily.

'Eva told me –'

'She told you who she was? What she is to Cassius?' Seth spluttered.

Nick nodded uncomfortably.

'And yet you're saying she could be *at an advantage*?' snarled Seth. 'Are you completely *deranged*? Because if you were in any way sane you would know how much danger she's in.'

'Seth, you have to understand that looking the way Eva does, there was never going to be a good option for her,' said Nick quietly.

Seth was finding it difficult to breathe.

'So at least this way – there will only be one man . . .'

'Cassius Malchus isn't a man,' said Seth, turning to leave.

'Seth, Seth! Don't go!' gasped Clare, clutching on to his cloak.

Seth twisted away from her but she held on fast. 'Seth, please don't go. Look around! We need you so much!'

Seth stopped moving for a minute and took a deep breath. Then he turned. 'I know, Clare,' he said. 'And I'm working on it, believe me. But right now Eva needs me more.'

'Is it true, then? Are you really building an army?'

Seth's eyes swept the room uneasily. He never discussed his plans openly. There were too many spies. But the sea of hopeful battered faces was almost too much for him.

'I'm going to help you,' he said finally. 'I give you my word.'

He turned to go again, but this time Nick grabbed his shoulder.

'I need to speak to you, Seth. Can you spare a moment?'

Seth ran a hand through his hair. Hadn't this guy already said enough?

Nick was not a man who begged. He could see Seth wanted to be anywhere but here, but there was no way he could let him go yet. They had a war to plan. And if begging got the job done, he'd damn well beg.

'Please?' he said.

Sighing, Seth turned back once more and prepared to hear him out.

30

Defiance

A Cell, Cassius's Palace

I was rolled into a tight ball on the floor, shaking. The walls had moved in so close that each side touched me. Like a coffin. Even the ceiling had closed in. I was fighting for air, fighting to remain conscious. Fighting to remember my name.

How long had I been here? I had no idea.

What kind of prison was this?

I tried to play Nick's words in my head: *Whatever they do to you . . .*

Did he know they would do *this*? Did he know they would find my worst fear and use it? How had they done that?

Whatever they do to you . . . Whatever they do to you . . .

Weren't there other words? Good words. Words to cling on to. Why couldn't I remember them? At the first nudge from the invading walls I couldn't remember anything as the dark, paralysing fear enveloped me.

A cacophony of sound: fast, heavy pulse; gasping breaths; rattling of keys . . . a door unlocking.

'*What the hell?*' a rough voice rasped.

Suddenly I could feel air around me again – the ceiling was

no longer rammed against my shoulder, it was moving away from me. The walls were retreating. I took a stuttering breath and tried to move my head. Sweat glued my hair to my neck. I couldn't stop shaking.

A light hand on my shoulder. I flinched.

'What happened here?' asked a voice.

Was he talking to me? I tried to move my lips, but they weren't responding.

'Don't think this was the magister's work,' said a second voice. 'Probably fear. Dangerous to be claustrophobic in a Parallon cell. Give her a second.'

'Christ – look at her. We can't take her to the magister in this state. He'll flog us. We'd better get her cleaned up.'

'We don't have time. What part of *immediately* didn't you get?'

'No choice, man. If he thinks we touched her –'

'Shit . . . you're right. Hey, Livia – can you hear me?'

Breathe. In. Out. In. Out.

I opened my eyes. My head was still buried in my arms. My joints felt cemented in place. A hand on my shoulder.

'Hey, take it easy. We're just going to pick you up off the floor.'

I was being firmly lifted. The shivering was slowing down.

I swayed on my feet as a pair of arms held me steady. Suddenly my cloak was pulled off, and I was standing in just my thin tunic, hair plastered to my forehead, my arms clutched tight round my chest. I lifted my eyes. Two guards, in Cassius's familiar livery, stared down at me. They were both broad-shouldered and had clearly been chosen for their physical strength, but they didn't have the malevolent aura of the elite guard. Maybe they hadn't been with Cassius long enough.

'So *you* are the famous Lady Livia.'

I glanced between them, frowning. Oh God, I couldn't be Livia again. I closed my eyes and tried to find some strength. But it had entirely deserted me.

'Do you know what a shower is, Livia?' whispered one of the guards in English. So they weren't Roman.

I nodded.

'Watch the door, Jake,' he murmured, and seconds later he'd installed a small cubicle in the corner of the cell.

'Are you crazy, Samuel?' rasped the other guard.

'Just make it fast, Livia,' shower guard urged, handing me a towel.

I stepped just inside the door, pulled off my dress and ducked under the jet. It was like finding heaven after hell. I needed to wash the sweat out of my hair, and the moment the thought occurred, a bottle of my favourite pomegranate shampoo appeared in my hand. I sighed, poured some into my palm and began massaging it into my hair.

'Hurry, Livia,' hissed Samuel. 'The magister is not a patient man.'

My brief moment of bliss was over. I turned off the jet, grabbed the towel and tried to prepare my thoughts. I was about to face Cassius and I needed to focus. Whatever happened I had to remember that he couldn't kill me. But he could hurt me. He would hurt me.

I took a deep breath. I had to handle this. I had completely lost it in the cell – I couldn't let it happen again. Cassius wanted to break me and he could not know how close I was.

I dressed myself in a simple soft white robe and sandals, then did my best to coil my hair into the style I'd worn in Londinium.

When I could avoid it no longer, I walked out of the steamy sanctuary of the shower back into the cell.

The guards were leaning against the wall opposite when I emerged. They instantly straightened, their eyes widening in surprise. I guess it was a bit of a transformation from gibbering wreck, but I wished they would stop staring.

Samuel moved suddenly from me to the shower, and a moment later it had disappeared. I took a couple of deep breaths as they led me from the cell.

'Will I be coming back here?' I asked.

'Our orders were simply to take you to the magister.'

The only people who ever had any insight into Cassius's business were his elite guard. And even they were only afforded selected information. Cassius did not share. The thought of him sharing actually made my mouth twitch for a moment. And the fact that I'd nearly smiled suddenly filled me with a weird sense of power. If Cassius could make me laugh, how could he possibly break me?

I lifted my chin and walked steadily between the two guards, along a narrow, torch-lit corridor, and through an atrium that could have been beautiful if it hadn't been marred by a huge statue of Cassius throned on a dais behind the fountain. As my eyes reluctantly followed the idealized portrait up towards his glittering golden crown of laurel, I glimpsed the sky above. It was dark. How long had I been here? Unfortunately it seemed Cassius wasn't big on clocks. He was still clearly stuck around AD 152 judging by all the wall hangings, murals and intricate floor mosaics.

We were moving swiftly down a wide, heavily guarded corridor into a large, semi-circular antechamber. When we arrived at a pair of carved wooden doors, two fully armed soldiers crossed their swords to bar our way.

'We bring the Lady Livia,' announced Samuel.

The soldiers nodded and heaved the doors open. We were ushered forward into a huge, dazzling room.

Mirrors and glazed windows stretched the entire length of one wall and torches filled the spaces in between. If my stomach hadn't felt like a hard rock had taken up residence in there I might have found the effect spectacular. But it would only have been a fleeting sensation. Because windows, mirrors and candlelight were the last things I was thinking about the next moment, when I found myself face to face with Cassius Malchus and his elite guard.

Cassius was staring at me in furious disbelief. 'So it is true,' he murmured quietly. 'My beautiful whore-wife still lives.'

'Magister,' breathed my two guards, immediately prostrating themselves on the floor.

I knew better than to remain standing, so I knelt behind them, my head bowed.

'*Get up,*' snarled Cassius. I wasn't sure who exactly he was talking to, so I hazarded a quick glance up to his face. His eyes were black beads of fury.

Not good. I had seen that look before.

I started stumbling to my feet.

'Not you,' he hissed. 'I want you on your knees, watching.'

My heart sank. Watching what?

Otho and Pontius casually strode over to my two guards and hauled them to their feet.

'Why did you keep the magister waiting?' demanded Otho in a menacingly quiet voice.

'I'm so sorry, magister, we –' Samuel, the guard who had created my shower, allowed his eyes to flick to mine for a moment, then he swallowed and continued, 'w-we went to the – er – wrong cell.'

Oh God, he was covering for me. Cassius would punish him twice as hard for that little rebellion: he could smell a lie even before it was uttered.

One small eye movement between Cassius and Pontius, and my two guards were instantly chained to one of the central columns and their tunics ripped from their backs.

'Pontius, I think the scourge would be a suitable way to remind my retinue that I expect punctuality and honesty.'

Moments later, their howls of pain were ricocheting off the marble walls.

I screwed up my eyes to try and stop the tears. Cassius was watching me as Pontius struck the guards over and over again. It was to punish me as much as them, because he knew how much I hated his beatings – and these guards were being beaten for their kindness to me.

'Stop!' I screamed, throwing myself between Pontius and their bleeding bodies. The scourge caught me squarely across the back of my ribs and the pain was so intense it knocked the air from my lungs. Before I could find my breath, another strike sliced across my arm and shoulder. Unable to hold myself upright, I slid down the column, covering my head with my arms as I prepared for the next blow. When it didn't come, I glanced up.

Cassius had grabbed the scourge out of Pontius's hand and looked about ready to hit him with it. *'Nobody strikes my wife but me!'* he roared.

I was curled round the column, my white dress now scored with bloody gashes, staring down at the marble floor, waiting for Cassius's next move. For a few moments he was completely still. I could see his sandalled feet, but little else.

'So, Livia, are you going to tell me why you defy me at every turn?'

'Nobody defied you, Cassius,' I croaked. 'Not even your guards defied you. When they came for me, I was a mess and – I-I wanted to be properly dressed for you so I made them wait.'

It was the truth. Sort of.

'And why didn't they tell me that?'

I glanced at the bleeding guards. 'I think because they didn't want to dishonour you by admitting the mess your wife was in when they came for me.'

It was a risky strategy, but if it meant ending their torment it was worth it.

Unfortunately, Otho had other ideas. 'Magister – I wouldn't trust this wo–'

'When I need your council, Otho, I will ask for it. You may take the guards back to their quarters and grant them salves. They will return to duties in the morning. Pontius and Rufus, I wish to be alone with *my wife*.'

My heart started to pound. Being alone with Cassius was never a good idea. Especially when I had made him angry. He was staring at me like he wanted to tear me apart.

'Get up,' he said, his eyes fixed on my ripped dress and dishevelled hair. 'Regrettably, Pontius has thwarted your grooming efforts.' He stalked around me. 'But I do like the dress modifications,' he added, stroking his fingers along my back.

I recoiled and his hand instantly shifted to slap me hard across the face. I staggered backwards.

'Still so defiant, Livia,' he breathed, his mouth suddenly hard against mine, both hands pinning my arms against my body.

I closed my eyes. I knew what was coming. When I was in Londinium, when I was trapped in that palace-prison with Cassius in his bedchamber, when nobody answered my screams for mercy, I eventually found a way to escape; to disappear; to blank out. And here in Parallon, in this new palace, as soon as I felt his hot breath against my skin, I was gone – far from that great marbled room – to a place he could never reach me . . . beside Seth – the scent of grass and wild summer flowers, sunshine beating down on our backs, no sound but our laughter and birdsong . . . a place where I was warm, happy and safe.

31

Announcement

Parallon

Matthias waited in Seth's newly created tunnel underneath the arena holding area. He strained to hear what was going on above, but Seth had filled in the opening the moment he'd climbed through it. The floors were of solid stone and he could hear nothing.

Seth had told him not to follow, but Matt couldn't let him go off on this crazy rescue mission without somebody at his back. This whole Eva thing was turning into one major distraction for everyone, and the sooner Seth hauled her out of here and got back to the campaign the better. He was surprised it was taking so long. The plan wasn't complicated: retrieve Eva and get the hell out.

They've probably left by a different exit, he suddenly realized. *I'd better get going. I'm no good to anyone down here.* It didn't take long to reach the tunnel entrance inside the Temple of Minerva. He hauled himself quickly up into its shadowy interior and, casting one last hopeful look behind him, hurried towards the temple's huge front doors. And then he stopped. He could hear footsteps outside, marching footsteps. The usual patrol – or were these reinforcements?

Had the plan failed?

The footsteps came to a stop right outside the temple. Matthias ducked behind the altar. He could hear a murmured conversation. A laugh. Hammering . . . more laughter . . . and finally the sound of retreating steps. He let out a deep breath, but remained crouched in position long after the footsteps had receded. Then, before he could change his mind, he darted across the marble floor, through the pronaos and edged on to the steps outside.

His eyes scanned the empty streets around him. No sign of the patrol now, thank the gods. He squared his shoulders and started down the steps towards the street below, allowing himself one final glance back towards the temple interior – one last check for Seth and Eva. If he hadn't turned to make that final check he would never have seen the pair of framed notices now nailed to the columns at the temple entrance.

An icy chill ran down his spine when he moved closer to read:

TO ALL CITIZENS OF PARALLON

MAGISTER CASSIUS MALCHUS
REQUIRES THE PLEASURE OF YOUR COMPANY
IN THE ARENA
AT NOON TOMORROW
TO CELEBRATE THE
RETURN OF
HIS WIFE,
THE LADY LIVIA.

Matthias stared at the notice for several seconds. Then he turned on his heel and ran.

32

Development

Zackary's House, Parallon

'*Seth!* You're back!' gasped Matthias, hauling him quickly through Zackary's front door. 'Thank the gods! What the hell happened to you? I've been going out of my mind!'

But Seth didn't answer. He was sprinting up the stairs and heading for his bedroom. Matthias followed, desperately trying to gauge his mood. Had he seen the announcement? Did he know Cassius had Eva?

'You've been gone practically all night. It must be nearly dawn,' Matt yawned, sitting on the edge of Seth's bed. He watched as Seth unselfconsciously stripped off his tunic, threw it across a chair and headed for the bathroom.

'Are you going to be ready to leave in ten minutes, Matt?' Seth called.

'Where are we going?' asked Matt guardedly.

'The training ground.'

'O-K . . .' said Matthias slowly. Surely Seth hadn't just given up on Eva? Should he mention the notice? How could he keep it from Seth?

Seth strode out of the shower, a towel tied loosely on his

hips, his hair dripping small rivulets of water down his neck. Even after all this time, Seth's physical beauty took Matt's breath away: his strong profile, the easy ripple of his muscles as he pulled the towel across his chest to dry his skin. But despite his distraction, Matt knew he had to speak.

'Seth – there's been a development . . .' he began.

Seth cocked his head to one side. 'What kind of development?' he asked, throwing the damp towel across a chair. A moment later he was wearing a fresh tunic and fastening a knife belt.

'C-Cassius has posted up an announce—'

Seth hauled a cloak round his shoulders and stood by the door. 'Are you coming, Matt?'

'Seth?'

'I've seen the notice, Matt,' Seth said, moving quickly down the stairs. 'I need to talk to Lauren before we go. Have you spoken to her or Zack since you've been back?'

Matthias nodded.

'So Zackary knows what's happened to Eva?'

Matt bit the inside of his mouth. 'He knows.'

Matt didn't particularly want to mention that Zackary was in a homicidal rage. With Seth. Whom he blamed for everything.

It was probably just as well Seth was leaving the house before Zackary got up. Not because Zack's anger stood any chance against the fighting machine that was Sethos Leontis, but because Seth probably didn't need Zackary to remind him that Eva was now incarcerated with a vicious sadist who knew everything there was to know about torture, and who had already tried to kill her twice.

33

Purpose

Arena Holding Area, Parallon

Twenty-four hours ago, the only thing Nick Mullard had known about the magister was that he was the despotic psychopath who'd managed to turn Parallon into a living hell.

But finding out about Eva's history with him, and that she'd been forced to marry the bastard – well, that had made him want to throw up. So Seth's manic desperation about her wasn't difficult to understand.

Still, nobody was going to achieve anything by being reckless. And last night he had been surprised to discover that, despite his desperation, Sethos Leontis was possibly the most controlled fighter he had ever encountered. And he had met a few. You didn't survive army, SAS and Afghanistan without doing that. So within about an hour of meeting the guy, he had been forced to admit that he was probably a damn fine leader. Which had raised his optimism level by about a hundred per cent. But as it had started close to zero, there had been a bit of a way to go.

Before Seth left, he and Nick had constructed the loosest of plans. But they had been forced to completely restructure them when Seth had burst back through the tunnel fifteen minutes later brandishing Cassius's notice.

For a while they had both simply stared at it, reeling at the speed with which the game had changed.

'Is there any possibility,' asked Nick, 'that Cassius's entire motivation is exactly as stated . . . to use the arena for a public gloating . . . to make sure everyone – especially you – knows that Eva – Livia – whatever he calls her – is his again?'

Seth shook his head and laughed bitterly. 'If it was any other man, I might consider it,' he sighed. 'But Cassius isn't a man – he's a monster. Why would he gloat about the return of the girl he thought he'd killed twice over? I assure you his purpose will be darker.'

'To flush you out?'

'At the very least.'

'Because he wants you to fight in the arena?'

'He enjoys my ability to entertain – yes – but he'll also want to humiliate me . . . own me . . . make me suffer . . . He'll want to publicly punish me for stealing her away from him, and punish Livia for defying and betraying him. And where better than the arena? The perfect setting for a tyrant to wield his power in a grand public punishment.

'But . . . we must also consider that it is his way of trying to flush out the rebellion . . .'

Nick nodded as the full import of that scenario sank in.

Cassius was now calling the shots. Assuming he knew of Seth's involvement in the rebellion, he now held a priceless hostage and bargaining tool. Which meant he had been able to dictate the time and place of battle. They had completely lost the element of surprise. Their only option now was to try to plan a two-pronged failsafe strategy.

Yeah, right.

Nick was preparing for battle with a broken, demoralized team, and Seth with a barely trained army of volunteers. And they were going up against a vicious cohort of legionaries led by one of the most devious bastards in the history of the world.

He'd never faced worse odds. But hell – what choice did he have?

34

Presentation

A Cell in Cassius's Palace, Parallon

Pain. Familiar pain. Inside and out. I was floating on it, enclosed by it, trying to cast adrift from it, but something was pulling me back . . . a voice.

'Livia – can you hear me?'

I pushed it away. I didn't like that name: Livia . . . it meant torture and fear and –

'Please, Livia . . . She's not responding.'

'Are you surprised? Look what he did to her.'

'But if we don't get her ready, he'll flog us again!'

'Look – you go and make sure the handmaids have her costume and jewellery set out properly, while I prepare some oils and salves. She's still so banged up – he's left her no time to heal.'

I was drifting again . . . warm water . . . fluttering movement . . . soft mutterings . . .

'Livia, this might sting a little, but it will –'

Jerked back to consciousness, I sat up with hard, panting breaths tearing through my aching throat. *Aghh*. Shooting pain everywhere . . . my brain suddenly flooded with dark memories.

There were hands on my skin. I instantly shrank back, only to find myself trapped against a cold stone wall. I opened my eyes, staring wildly around.

'Hey, it's OK. I'm not going to hurt you, I just need to –'

I stilled and tried to focus on the face in front of me, a face I recognized – the shower guard from yesterday . . . Samuel.

I peered at him. When I'd last seen him he'd been covered in blood and was being dragged out of Cassius's hall. Now he looked fine. Thank God. I stared at his unmarked face. He was smiling. I tried to smile back, but my mouth wasn't working yet, so, embarrassed, I glanced down at the bowl sitting on the bed between us: it was filled with bloody water. I frowned. I thought he was healed. Then he dipped the bloody cloth he was holding into the water, wrung it out, and gently leaned towards me. I flinched away.

'What are you doing?' I gasped, as he softly dabbed at my shoulder. I closed my eyes, instantly remembering the injury – the cracking pain as Cassius threw me against his carved desk.

Don't think about it. Push it away. Go back to the meadow with Seth.

But I couldn't zone out. Every shift of the wet cloth across the patchwork of bruises and cuts covering my body threw me back to the moment each one was made. I couldn't bear it. I grabbed the cloth from the guard. 'Thanks, I can take it from here,' I rasped.

What the hell was wrong with my voice? A rhetorical question . . . I knew. My throat was raw from the hours of hopeless screaming . . . Pain did that. It made you scream. Even when there was no point. When you knew nobody would come. Screaming was just a reflex. Like crying when you peeled an onion. You couldn't help it. Even though every fibre of your body didn't want to scream. Didn't want to see Cassius's eyes darken with pleasure at every sound he wrenched from you.

I quickly washed away the blood, wishing Samuel would leave instead of staring at my bruises with such obvious distaste. But guards were guards were guards. They never gave you privacy.

'Clean,' I said finally, dumping the cloth in the blood-red water and pulling myself to my feet. He gently pressed me back on the mattress, and handed me a jar.

'This will help with the bruising,' he murmured.

'No, it's fine, I'll be healed soon.'

'And it will help with the pain,' he added firmly. I sighed and started rubbing the ointment into my skin. He was right – it did help.

'Thank you,' I whispered shakily. I had never encountered any kindness from Cassius's guards in Londinium. It was so unexpected that for some reason it made me feel weaker. My lip began trembling, and I had to bite down hard on it to stop myself crying.

Stay tough, Eva. You won't get through this otherwise.

Samuel cleared his throat and gestured to the handmaids standing at the cell door. 'Cassius wants you dressed like a queen today.'

I frowned. That could only mean one thing. He wanted to present me to someone. I touched the healing cut on my cheek in surprise. In Londinium he had usually tried to avoid injuring my face and hands when he had plans for me the following day. I was the original trophy wife and had to look my best.

'We can use make-up on that if it concerns you,' said one of the handmaids at the door. She was moving tentatively towards me, carrying a pile of shimmering garments in her arms.

'Who am I to meet?' I whispered.

Samuel, my guard, shuffled uncomfortably. My stomach twisted.

'The whole of Parallon,' he said finally.

'My God,' I breathed in horror, my mind flailing to play catch-up. 'He's made an announcement?'

Samuel nodded.

'Where?'

'The arena . . .'

I exhaled sharply. Of course – where else?

'. . . at noon today – in two hours.'

I stood in frozen horror. What was Cassius up to? Why make such a public declaration of ownership? Apart from the big powerfest, what was he hoping to gain? Seth? Try to use me to bait him? No. He couldn't. I'd told him Seth didn't love me any more. He believed me. I prayed he believed me . . . because if he knew that I was the one thing that made Seth vulnerable, he would play him ruthlessly. But if it wasn't about Seth and me, what else could it be about? Some sort of declaration of war?

Dammit. Cassius held all the power again. Even if I wasn't to be used as bait, I had somehow become the catalyst. By being caught I had taken away Seth's only advantage: the element of surprise. If Cassius was declaring war, it was now on his terms and he would be playing to win.

The rebellion, Parallon's one chance at life and liberty, was in jeopardy. And I was to blame.

35
Control

The Arena, Parallon

'I feel defenceless coming here with no weapon at all, Seth,' murmured Matthias.

'This is Parallon, Matthias. We can call our weapons when the time comes. You know the plan.'

'We're just so vulnerable without anything.'

'Shhh, we're moving.'

For the past hour, they had been queuing against the curved columned perimeter of the arena, along with every other Parallon citizen. One by one they shuffled forward, drawing ever closer to the guarded turnstile. Seth was banking on getting through using Zack's ID, so he was praying they hadn't put out a description of him. Behind him, Matthias's tension was palpably mounting.

Seth had considered wearing a hooded cloak in case he was recognized, but had quickly discarded that idea when he realized nobody was wearing cloaks. He had no choice. He simply had to get through without arousing suspicion.

'Halt,' commanded the guard in Latin as he reached the turnstile.

Keeping his features impassive, Seth turned towards him.

'Name?' the guard barked.

'Zackary Ambrose,' answered Seth, casually moving his arms behind his back to conceal his gladiatorial tattoo. He didn't know if this guard came from Londinium, but he couldn't afford to take that risk. The tattoo would be an instant identifier. Fortunately, the guard noticed nothing, and proceeded to pat down Seth's tunic, checking for concealed weapons.

'Go to aisle seven,' he commanded finally.

Seth exhaled slowly and, resisting the impulse to turn and check on Matthias's progress, continued to follow the orderly queue of people through the huge, buzzing auditorium to the bank of tiered seating the guard had indicated. He needed to sit as close to the arena floor as possible, so when he spotted a gap just about big enough for two on the third tier, he squeezed his way as casually as he could down through the crowd towards it. He was just edging along the row when he felt a small touch on his elbow.

'Right behind you, brother,' Matthias murmured.

Seth nodded, but didn't turn his head. It was imperative they drew no attention to themselves.

Once they were seated Seth glanced across at Matthias's hands clenched on his lap. They were shaking slightly. He winced. Matt wasn't made for war . . . even though he bore some responsibility for bringing it to Parallon. But he couldn't think about that now. He had to concentrate on what lay ahead, on keeping himself focused until it was time to act. And he absolutely couldn't allow himself to think about Eva, or what Cassius might have done to her.

Although his expression did not change, his fists flexed. His chest tightened. He had to control the rage. Taking deep breaths, he reminded himself again why he was here; what was at stake and how many people depended on him. At last his muscles began to ease. He was back in control and it was time to take stock. He glanced around the crowded auditorium. The building was massive – much bigger and more decorative than the Londinium arena. And it was virtually full. Yet despite the size of the audience, the atmosphere was surprisingly subdued; people's expressions were tense. He had expected the same exuberant excitement of a Londinium arena audience, where the blood and violence of the gladiatorial games was anticipated with raucous delight. Perhaps it had something to do with the number of soldiers and guards. Zeus, the place was teeming with them; they lined every wall and every aisle.

So – Cassius had made his first move; his proclamation of power. There was no doubt about it: he had a formidable force behind him. Seth surreptitiously scanned the arena, trying to roughly calculate their number . . . It had to be about three thousand. His nine hundred troops could not compete. But he had always known that.

As his eyes continued to sweep the auditorium, one of the soldiers guarding his aisle glanced across at him. He instantly dropped his gaze. He needed to stay invisible.

Even with his head down, Seth could not mistake the whispered anxiety building around him. Although Parallonians were used to their compulsory visits to the arena, this 'celebration' was something else, and nobody had any idea what to expect.

Matthias straightened, and Seth looked up. The last stragglers were being herded towards their seats and a deathly hush settled over the crowd. Seth's muscles tightened and his eyes shifted to the great empty circle of sand below him. It was pristine. Smoothed and raked and ready.

Suddenly a clash of cymbals and an ominous drumming announced the procession marching into the arena. Seth's jaw tensed. At least five hundred more soldiers moved in stunning synchronization, circling the arena until they formed a complete ring around the circumference. As the circle closed, they came to a perfect stop, and turned to face out into the auditorium.

Next came the liveried guards, around twenty of them bearing a large silk-covered dais, which they carried into the centre of the sand. When it had been carefully placed, they stepped away from the platform and flanked it.

Seth's knuckles whitened when the next group strolled arrogantly into the centre: Cassius's elite guard. The three of them strode towards the dais, climbed on to the steps, then turned to face a final group of liveried guards carrying an ornate litter.

Seth and Matt were close enough to make out the intricate golden bird and leaf carvings decorating the frame. The litter was placed on the dais, the curtains were opened and Cassius Malchus stepped out in full regalia: a heavy white toga bordered with purple silk, and a golden laurel crown circling his head. He stood in the centre of the dais, and surveyed the auditorium.

'Easy, brother,' murmured Matt, glancing at his friend, whose muscles were flexing dangerously.

'Hail, magister,' boomed the guards.

'Hail, magister,' repeated the huge auditorium in a single voice.

A small smile flickered across Cassius's face. Then he clapped his hands for silence, and nodded towards his elite guard. They signalled to the soldiers standing by a large wooden door and the drummers started beating out a slow rhythm as a small detachment of guards emerged. In the centre of the unit he could just make out a girl in a glittering gown, wearing a long veil of flame red.

As the group reached the dais, the girl stepped forward and the elite guard escorted her on to the platform beside Cassius. Seth held his breath as she stood, head bowed, hands clasped before her.

The drummers stopped beating and the silence in the arena was deathly.

'Welcome, citizens of Parallon,' Cassius intoned in a loud clear voice. 'As you know, we are gathered here today to celebrate the recent arrival of my wife, Livia.'

He turned to the figure next to him, and gestured to Pontius, who stepped up behind her and flicked away the veil.

Seth gasped. She looked exquisite. Her thick black hair was woven with pearls and golden leaves, and coiled and twisted into an intricate pattern down her back. She wore a shimmering gown of palest gold, flecked with glittering thread and heavy with pearls. Both wrists were enclosed – *manacled* – in jewelled bangles, and even from his seat three rows back, Seth could see glinting on the third finger of her left hand the large golden wedding ring. He couldn't suppress the hiss of anger. His ring was supposed to be there. He glanced at her face. Her cheeks were flushed and her lips parted in discomfort as she stared at the sand in front of her. And then he caught sight of something that transformed his anger into rage: the faint discoloration on her cheekbone.

Seth's fists clenched and a savage shudder ripped through his body. Matthias instantly put a steadying hand on his back.

'Be still, brother,' he warned.

Seth tried to swallow. How could he remain still; sit here impotently, while that bastard –

'Not yet, Seth,' soothed Matthias.

Seth glanced at the guards and soldiers, and took a deep, steadying breath. Matt was right. He had to wait. He had to follow the plan; his own plan . . . to hold off until everyone was filing out of the arena, a time when there would be the fewest civilians and the guards would be at their most distracted. The only thing he would achieve if he moved now would be to get himself captured. He settled stiffly back into his seat and stared at the girl on the platform. His girl. The girl he would literally do anything for.

Cassius was striding around her. 'Beautiful, isn't she?' he taunted, running a finger down her exposed neck and along her shoulder.

'I imagine there are many of you who would like to touch my lovely bride?' he smiled, gazing out at the audience.

Nobody dared move.

'What – *nobody*?' he gasped. 'Your magister's beautiful bride is standing here, sweet and luscious in her garments of gold, and nobody wants to touch her?'

The audience squirmed uncomfortably.

'What's he playing at?' muttered Matthias.

Seth couldn't answer. He was having difficulty breathing. Just seeing Cassius's hand on Eva's skin was killing him.

'I always consider it an act of gross ingratitude to turn down a gift,' continued Cassius, 'stupid, even.' His voice dropped ominously as his hand circled Eva's breast: 'Especially a gift from your magister.'

'I would like to touch her, magister,' grunted one of the guards nearest the dais.

Cassius's head turned in surprise. Then he nodded. 'Anybody else?'

Several hands around the auditorium rose tentatively.

'All right,' Cassius declared. 'Form a line.'

The elite guard stepped down from the dais and began to organize a queue of men.

Seth's eyes were trained on Eva. She was still staring at the ground, her shoulders taut. But he could see she was shaking.

'Matt – I can't –'

'Peace, brother,' Matthias urged. 'Cassius is playing a *game*. And we don't know the rules yet.'

'Citizens,' smiled Cassius, 'these men here have freely stated they wish to touch my lovely bride. Bring them forward.'

The elite guard and five soldiers escorted the line to the centre of the arena.

Cassius gestured to the first man – the guard.

'Go – taste my Livia,' murmured Cassius, his eyes hooded.

The guard smirked happily and jumped on to the platform. He reached out his hand greedily, but before she had even had a chance to flinch, there was a furious growl, a flash of silver, and Cassius was swinging a heavy curved sword. In a ghastly spray of blood the man's hand was severed clean from his wrist. He screamed and fell backwards.

'Flog them all,' ordered Cassius, gesturing to the line of now terrified men. As they were hauled out of the arena by a unit of guards, Cassius moved slowly towards his bride.

'*Nobody touches what is mine!*' he bellowed, his eyes burning into her, though she kept her head bowed, her hands clasped before her.

'Nobody but me,' he added, plucking a coiled strand of her hair and running it through his fingers.

The arena was silent. Suspended in time. Waiting. Cassius lifted his head to the audience and smiled, a dark sinister curve of the mouth.

'Livia knows that, don't you, my sweet?' He grabbed her chin between his fingers and forced her head up. 'Livia knows exactly what happens to anyone who touches what is mine . . . What happens to them, my love?'

She blinked into his face, her eyes wide with fear.

Seth's body jerked forward.

Matthias pulled him back. 'Wait!' he hissed.

'What happens to them, my love?' repeated Cassius. 'What happens to the man who touches what is mine?'

'H-he is punished,' she croaked.

'Correct.' Cassius nodded. 'And what happens to my wife, Livia? My *sullied* wife. What should a wronged husband do with her?'

Seth shook off Matt's arm, his breath burning his chest. He was fighting for control.

'Hold on, Seth,' hissed Matthias, regaining purchase and pushing down hard on to his friend's shoulder. 'This is a trap. Cassius is trying to rile you.'

Seth was panting with unused adrenalin. The veins in his neck stood proud, his body shuddered with the effort of remaining still. He couldn't hold on. Eva needed him.

She was staring up at Cassius.

'Well, Livia? I am becoming impatient. What does the husband do with the ruined wife?'

'He does whatever he sees fit,' she answered finally.

Cassius laughed. 'Yes, he does,' he agreed, grabbing her neck and kissing her mouth with such force she staggered backwards. The guards standing behind caught her and held her upright. Cassius turned slowly and stood away from her so that everyone could see the blood now running down her chin.

'People of Parallon,' he proclaimed with a feral smile. 'It is time to sit back and enjoy watching me behave as I *see fit*.' Then he snarled, turned and savagely ripped Eva's dress in two, throwing the pieces violently across the floor, sending hundreds of pearls scattering through the sand.

'*Eva!*' roared Seth, flying from his seat.

Her head jerked up, her eyes wild. '*Seth, no!*' she screamed. '*Get out of here!*'

'In the name of Zeus, Seth,' begged Matthias behind him. 'This is not the plan!'

Seth could no sooner follow the plan at this point than stop breathing. He was tied to the girl out there on the dais; the girl who was about to be publicly brutalized by a vicious sadist. And nothing would stop him going to her now.

36

Insurrection

The Arena, Parallon

I stood shivering in the arena, my dress ripped off me, too humiliated to look up from the sand, knowing only too well what lay ahead. I had been barely conscious last night when Cassius finally finished with me. And I knew what I was about to face here would be worse. Because this time Cassius wouldn't just be using me for his own gratification, this time I was to be a public announcement: a display of power, a sadistic taunt.

And I had been praying Seth wouldn't be here to witness it, because the only thing worse than what I was about to face was the idea of him having to watch it. The time Cassius had forced me to watch as he kicked and butchered Seth in Londinium was the worst torture I'd ever endured. And Seth was a fighter, so finding himself helpless would be intolerable. I looked around the massive auditorium. It was heaving with soldiers and guards. Seth's entire army stood no chance in this arena. There were literally thousands of Cassius's men. I only prayed the rebels would never be reckless or desperate enough to take them on.

And then I heard Seth's voice. His lone battle cry.

I lifted my eyes and there he was, running straight towards me, right past the thousands of soldiers as though they didn't count, as though I was the only person there. And in that instant my heart overflowed with love for him. Impossible love. And unbearable pain. Because I knew in that moment we were both lost.

As soon as Seth's feet hit the sand, soldiers and guards converged on him. He disappeared inside them like an ant devoured. I could see nothing, but I could hear. Shouts and groans and the sounds of clunking armour echoed across the eerily still arena. A few moments later the mass of bodies surged forward until they reached the dais. There, the soldiers parted and I watched in horror as they dragged Seth up on to the platform and threw him at Cassius's feet.

In that short time they had transformed him from a warrior into a broken, bleeding prisoner. He lay sprawled across the white silk, his blood soaking the fabric around him into a halo of red.

'*Seth*,' I sobbed, throwing myself beside him. I had just reached out my fingers to touch his bruised face, when my head was jerked backwards, a hand grabbing harshly into my hair, wrenching me to my feet.

'Get him off my dais,' snarled Cassius to his guards, who began dragging him away.

'*Seth!*' I screamed, fighting and biting the arms that bound me, desperate to get to him, twisting against the grip of my captors.

Seth's head lifted and his eyes flickered open, immediately finding mine. And in that moment of connection, all the things we needed to say to each other were said: all the longing and regrets and promises. And I knew I wasn't staring into the face of a broken man. I was looking at a man blazing with a wild and terrible fury.

His eyes flashed over me, and suddenly I was dressed in a pair of cargo pants, trainers, a black T-shirt and padded vest. All the heavy gold jewellery was gone and instead of Cassius's gaudy ring, Seth's twisted silver knot of Heracles nestled on my third finger. I was blinking down at it, when a large curved knife appeared in my hand.

And then I heard the gunshot.

My eyes darted in terror back to Seth. He was pulling away from the guards who'd been holding him, his right arm now free and wielding a black handgun. The shot had clearly been his, because one of his guards was now hopping and screaming with pain. The other guards tightened their grip, but despite the fact that he was still being manhandled, Seth managed to fire a second round behind him – this time hitting another of his captors in the thigh. With this guard down, Seth's feet succeeded in getting purchase on the sand and he pulled himself free.

Firing the gun into the air, he shouted, 'People of Parallon! The time has come to choose your side. Continue to live in terror as slaves to the Romans or fight for your freedom –'

'*Seize him!*' roared Cassius furiously, pulling a dagger from his belt.

'*Look out, Seth!*' I screamed as the dagger flew towards him. Seth dodged to the side and the dagger landed in the throat of the guard behind him, who gasped and sank instantly to the ground. Oblivious, Seth was already aiming his gun at Cassius, but before he could pull the trigger, Cassius grabbed me and pushed me in front of him.

'*You coward!*' shouted Seth, 'You would use a woman to shield you?'

'Not *any* woman. *Your whore!*' hissed Cassius. 'Is she really worth all *this*?'

'She is worth everything!'

Soldiers were converging on Seth, blocking my view of him. I struggled hopelessly against Cassius's arms, but now his elite guard had joined him, forming a ring around me. I screamed Seth's name, but my voice was instantly stopped by Cassius's hand over my mouth.

'*Eva – be creative! Use –*' yelled Seth, his voice suddenly drowned out by a huge surging roar. The arena had erupted into total chaos – the auditorium was writhing with struggling bodies, shouts and cries filling the air. Several of the Roman soldiers and guards heading our way were being stopped and attacked by troops in 21st-century battledress wielding rifles. My heart leaped. Seth's army was here!

But before I could get any sense of how they were faring, the elite guard were pushing Cassius and me away from the fray, onto the arena floor and through the arched wooden doors into the large shadowy antechamber where I'd been held earlier.

'I think we should move to the cellars below, magister. The rebels have powerful weapons, and we cannot risk a street ambush,' growled Otho in Latin.

Cassius, casting his eyes around, nodded and started dragging me towards the small door on the opposite wall. The elite guard followed right behind us, through the narrow torch-lit corridor and down a dark stone staircase. But we had barely reached the bottom step when the door at the end of the passageway swung open and a dark roaring crowd surged towards us.

'Merda,' spat Cassius, pulling me like a shield directly in front of him. He'd stopped moving forward, but he was clearly standing his ground. The elite guard tried to pull us back for a retreat, but Cassius held firm.

'They are nothing but slave scum,' he murmured. 'They may outnumber us, but they cannot match us.'

I couldn't believe his confidence. He stood facing a large hostile crowd with complete equanimity. Then he held out a hand. 'Stop!' he roared.

The crowd slowed but didn't stop. And as they neared I could see that it was Nick Mullard leading them. So he had successfully persuaded the gladiator prisoners to fight. He moved deliberately nearer, his head held high, the others right behind him.

'Let the girl go, Cassius. It's over,' he said quietly.

'*Seize him!*' yelled Cassius furiously.

The elite guard moved instantly forward, but Nick raised his gun. 'If you come any closer I will shoot.'

'If you touch my guards, this whore will wish she'd never been born!' answered Cassius, pulling my head back, grabbing the knife from my hand and pressing the blade hard against my neck.

Oh God, I was here *again*: about to have my throat cut by Cassius. I closed my eyes in defeat – and then I remembered he couldn't kill me. Not here in Parallon. Yesterday he had spent hour after hour torturing me, but I was completely recovered now. I would survive this. I opened my eyes, feeling stronger, ready. But Nick was hesitating.

The knife at my throat pushed through the skin. I could feel the heat of the blade, the blood on my neck.

'Nick, do it!' I gasped. 'Shoot them.'

37

Operation Minotaur

Arena Cellars, Parallon

Cassius's knife was ripping through Eva's neck; she was passing out. The only way to be sure of stopping him was to shoot him between the eyes . . . immediately. But Seth's entire plan would fail if Nick shot Cassius through the head. And anyway, Cassius was nicely shielded by Eva, so the chances of getting a clean shot were slight. He decided to go for distraction. Shifting his focus slightly, he smoothly squeezed the trigger, and the next moment his bullet was ripping through Cassius's ear. The magister roared with pain. His hands went slack, the knife slipped through his fingers and Eva crumpled to the ground.

Otho and Pontius moved immediately to pull Cassius back towards the stairs, while Rufus went for Eva. But Nick darted forward and had his pistol trained at Rufus's chest before he could reach her.

'I wouldn't get any closer if I were you,' hissed Nick.

Rufus snarled defiantly, a long sword instantly appearing in his hand. But Nick was quicker. His second bullet had blown a hole right through Rufus's sword arm, before he'd even had a chance to lunge. Howling in shock, the guard dropped his weapon and stumbled after the magister. Nick swept Eva up in his arms and turned to his waiting company.

'Follow me!' he bellowed, as he carried her up the staircase.

Bursting into the daylight he stalled momentarily, shocked by the sudden brightness and deafening clamour. But seconds later he was searching the writhing, clashing bodies for Seth. It didn't take him long. The man was like a tornado, whipping through guards and soldiers with lethal precision. By the time Nick caught up with him, Seth was in hand-to-hand combat with two Roman soldiers.

'*Operation Minotaur is go, Seth!*' he shouted.

Seth didn't turn his head, just smiled grimly, kicked out his left foot, unbalancing one soldier, feinting to the right and burying the knife he was holding into the second. Then his eyes found Nick and instantly widened in horror when he saw he was carrying Eva's limp, bleeding body.

'This is Parallon,' shouted Nick over the clamour of gunfire and clashing of weapons. 'She'll be OK. We must proceed as planned.'

Seth nodded stiffly, gestured towards an exit with a slight movement of his head, then spun round to slice through the Roman guard he had temporarily brought down.

Keeping his weapon cocked, Nick glanced wildly back towards his troops. He made brief eye contact with Elena, who gave him a mock salute and hurled herself into the chaos of fighting on the sand. She was now in command of his team.

Nick started moving in the opposite direction, heading for the exit Seth had indicated. He gently turned Eva's face into his chest so that she wouldn't be recognized – he couldn't afford her identity to attract attention. Then he started pushing through the throng of battling opponents. It was mayhem.

The previous night, he and Seth had talked about the most effective weapons to rapidly terminate conflict – grenades, bombs, missiles – but had decided they would be too messy and imprecise. They didn't want to risk their own soldiers. So they were reduced to small arms: assault and sniper rifles, pistols and close-combat knives. Nick prayed Seth had trained his unit to fire with reasonable accuracy, because he was never going to make it across to that exit if their snipers weren't good shots. As a precaution he created combat helmets for Eva and himself, and moved forward in a low crouch, constantly turning 360-degree circles to check his back. Encumbered as he was, it wasn't easy to mount a great defence, but any Roman soldier moving in on him was rewarded with a bullet. He would have given anything for the comfort of having someone at his back, especially as it looked as though some of the Roman soldiers had abandoned their traditional hardware and had moved on to guns themselves. He and Seth had been hoping that most of the Roman soldiers would be unfamiliar with 21st-century weapons, but they'd known it was unlikely all Cassius's men came from Londinium. Unfortunately, some of them looked pretty adept with their firearms.

He was almost at the gate when he saw a pair of Roman guards hurtling towards him. He raised his pistol, but they put their hands up.

'Don't shoot,' one of them shouted.

Nick held his gun steady and said, 'Let us pass.'

'Is that the Lady Livia?' one whispered in perfect English.

Nick's eyes narrowed, and his fingers tightened on the trigger.

'We want to help you –' said the other, 'join you.'

Nick cocked his head on one side. 'And I should trust you – why?'

The first guard reached a finger over to touch Eva's hair. Nick instantly swatted his hand away with his gun.

'Livia sacrificed herself to protect us,' hissed the guard. 'She didn't have to – she hardly knew us. Sh-she stood up to him. That sadistic bastard . . . Just a girl . . . It's time we did the same.'

'Are there other guards like you?' murmured Nick.

'Look around you.'

Nick frowned, suddenly noticing that soldiers in 21st-century battledress were now seriously outnumbering the guards in Cassius's livery. They had jumped ship.

For the first time in a long while, Nick felt the corners of his mouth turn up. Then he stared at the guards thoughtfully. 'OK,' he said finally, exchanging his gun for a knife. 'Don't change your clothes – stay in those uniforms, and . . . look like you're fighting me.' They instantly complied, and as a group they edged towards the doorway. Nick took a fleeting glance behind him, and when he caught sight of the pockets of movement rippling in his direction, he sighed in relief.

Operation Minotaur was underway.

38

Battle

Arena, Parallon

A roaring noise filled my head. Was it coming from inside or out? A volley of gunshots; the clash of armour and swords; grunts; shouting. I was being dragged, no, carried. I could hear choking. Someone was hurt, I needed to help, but it was so dark.

'Nearly there, Eva,' a breathless voice whispered in my ear. A voice I knew, but couldn't place. I tried to answer, but my mouth felt too far away.

'We're clear. But we've got to get out of here. And I need you conscious. Can you open your eyes?'

I struggled to move. Something was pressing hard against my neck. A hand?

I tried to jerk away from the pressure, but it jerked with me. I opened my eyes in panic.

Nick Mullard was staring down at me. 'Hold still, Eva, or it won't heal.'

I blinked; tried to locate myself. Behind him – bright sunshine . . . We were no longer in a basement corridor. How had we got out?

'I'm going to lay you down for a few minutes, Eva,' he whispered.

I squinted up at him, trying to piece together what was happening. His face was glistening with sweat under a military helmet. I could feel heat radiating off him. He'd been running. I glanced around. I was lying on the riverbank. Surely it wasn't safe to be out in broad daylight? And the moment the thought was formed I saw two uniformed guards wearing Cassius's livery running this way. Nick hadn't seen. He was still leaning over me.

Nick! Watch out!

Those were the words I opened my mouth to say. Unfortunately, a horrible painful croak was all that came out.

The pressure on my neck increased. Nick was pressing a bloodied wad of padding in place.

'Don't try and talk yet, Eva.'

He still hadn't spotted the guards. My agitation grew. I had to tell him. 'Behind you!' I wheezed.

He turned, but instead of jumping up defensively, he raised an arm in greeting.

I was about to freak out. Why was Nick working with Cassius's men? And then I saw who they were . . . Samuel and Jake – the palace guards who'd helped me. They'd joined our side. I raised my hand to greet them, but Nick grabbed my fingers and placed them over the wadding on my neck.

'Keep pressing here, Eva,' he said, then stood up and hurried towards the two men. They spoke in murmured undertones – the guards trying to catch their breath and gesturing towards the direction they'd come from. Nick appeared to be giving them urgent instructions, glancing frequently in my direction. I had a feeling that whatever they were talking about concerned me and I needed to hear it. I tried to sit up. Sharp stabbing pain shot through my neck. I lay back again, nervously lifting the blood-soaked wadding, and running my fingers lightly along the thick, deep gash. Cassius had surpassed himself. He'd probably sliced right through my vocal chords. Simple cuts and bruises didn't take long to heal in Parallon, but this could take a while. I took a deep breath and sat up. The movement jarred, but didn't make me sick or dizzy, so I was just about to announce my recovery to Nick when my eye caught movement in the distance. I squinted. At first it looked like a wave of grey and red, but as the sound of pounding feet and clanking armour carried towards me I was in no doubt. A Roman legion was heading right this way.

Not good.

'Nick,' I croaked.

'Eva, I told you not to –' he began, with a disapproving frown on his face. Then he caught my terrified expression and turned to the direction I was gazing.

'*Christ*,' he hissed. 'That was fast! We're out of time . . . Eva, do you know how to find the vortex?'

'What's the plan, Nick?'

'We have to lure Cassius and his men out of Parallon. It's the only way to get rid of them permanently.'

He was right. It was the only viable way to win Parallon back. Except that the vortex was about as stable as a leaf in a storm. Such a huge exodus might create enough negative density to set off a black hole. A potential catastrophe for both worlds. Could we risk it? I pulled myself to my feet. Nick took my elbow and we started jogging towards the spot.

'What the –' I gasped when we arrived. There were three columned sentry posts ranged round it.

'Oh God,' I murmured, walking nervously towards them. Had the Romans set up guards on the vortex? A moment later I was sighing with relief. Tucked inside the buildings stood Lauren's pulsing generators. So she was risking day-blasting now. Did that mean that the instability had increased?

'Is this it?' asked Nick sceptically.

I nodded.

'OK, thanks. Now I need to get you to Zackary's house. Seth's orders.'

'I don't take orders from Seth, Nick,' I whispered huskily. 'Or from you.'

Proud words. Only problem was the delivery – which was more of a wheezy croak than a proclamation. I pressed on to my throbbing neck. God, I needed this cut healed – like, now. I wasn't prepared to think about how well an injury would stand up to a trip through a volatile vortex. Because there was no way they were going without me.

'This isn't a game, Eva. It's a fight to the death. You've got no combat training. Plus you're a catalyst. For both Cassius and Seth. The only way your presence could possibly add to this mission –'

I looked up hopefully.

'– would be to make us more vulnerable.'

Great. Just what I wanted to be: a liability. I sighed. 'Message received,' I muttered, instantly regretting the effect on my throat.

Nick nodded, and beckoned our two guards. 'How much do either of you know about guns?' he asked.

Samuel grimaced. 'How do you think we ended up in Belmarsh?'

'Oh Christ,' muttered Nick, blanching.

I understood his reaction. Jen Linden had told me that Nick had been infected while investigating the virus at that prison.

'Eva,' he murmured, drawing me away from the two guards. 'There's no way I can trust these two. I'm going to have to –'

'They've already proved we can trust them, Nick,' I argued huskily.

'Do you have any idea what kind of people end up in Belmarsh?' he hissed.

I glanced over at them and shook my head. 'I don't know what they did to get there, but they defied Cassius to protect me yesterday, and they are with us, not him, now,' I shrugged.

'That may have more to do with you than with the cause,' he muttered, gazing at the smooth dark water, trying to look convinced. Finally he turned back to Samuel and Jake.

'OK, you two, time to prove yourselves worthy of the rebel army.' Instantly their Roman dress transformed into 21st-century combat gear, complete with body armour, helmets and assault rifles.

They stared down at themselves and grinned, while Nick seriously upgraded his own equipment. He was suddenly bulked out with hundeds of rounds of ammo, an assault rifle, a shotgun, a knife, a pistol, and a huge pack strapped to his back.

'You can't possibly be planning a ride through the vortex carrying that lot?' I gasped.

He shrugged. 'There won't be any handy humvees around

when we get to the other side, so we have to take everything we'll need.'

'Where are you heading?'

Nick's eyes widened and he shrugged. This was clearly something they hadn't discussed.

'You do know you can't go back to your own time, right?'

He stared at me like I was speaking Vulcan.

'When the hell did you and Seth work out this fantastic plan?'

'The night you were taken. We didn't have much time then . . . and it looks like we're totally out of time now,' he added, glancing back at the road. The mass of soldiers was getting closer.

'Nick,' I said urgently, 'when you jump, you have to be really precise in your intentions. Concentrate on a date – but make sure it's not one on your own lifespan. Your body can't manifest in your own time and you risk getting trapped there.'

'So whatever time you come from – that's the one to avoid?'

I nodded.

'OK – so we pick a time we can all make. How do we get the Romans to follow us to the same date?'

'As long as their intention is to follow you, they should arrive on the same time trajectory.'

At least that was the principle.

I did my best to sound confident but I wasn't. Far from it. They were about to head off to an unknown destination using a highly unstable wormhole. The chances of them making it out alive were virtually zero.

39

Bait

Arena, Parallon

'Pontius has spotted me,' murmured Seth to Kennedy. They were fighting back to back, taking on Roman soldier after soldier. 'Check Matt's standing by.'

'I'm on it,' breathed Kennedy, melting away. Seth continued to fight, aware that a few metres away, Pontius was in urgent conference with Cassius and the other elite guards.

Despite the fact that Seth was now fighting off four Roman soldiers, he was still deliberately choreographing the moves, gradually edging himself towards the exit Nick had recently carried Eva through. And he couldn't suppress the almost imperceptible twitch of a smile when he noted that Cassius and his men were creeping his way. Just as he'd hoped. But it was way too soon to celebrate.

Out of the corner of his eye he watched Matthias's stealthy approach. Although his friend held a pistol in one hand and a knife in the other, Seth knew that Matt would probably have avoided any actual combat. He loathed fighting.

Now, Matt, he urged silently. The guards were getting almost too close, and he needed a head start.

Moments later, Matthias ran towards him. 'Seth,' he yelled in Latin. 'Mullard's managed to save Livia. He's taking her down to the river.'

Seth flinched, sure Matt had overdone it – it sounded so damn obvious to him. But the die was now cast. The game was on. Kennedy and Brandon were instantly at his side, and took over his fight while he and Matt ran straight for the exit.

As soon as they'd cleared the arena, Seth looked over his shoulder. His glance couldn't fail to see that Cassius had taken the bait. He and his elite guard and a troop of Romans were now following them. Perfect.

'I'll run on ahead to hook up with Mullard, Matt, and you just make sure they keep you in their sights.'

Seth pulled away from Matthias and started running in earnest. He had been the fastest sprinter in Corinth until the Romans had come and ripped him away. Since then, although he still kept himself at peak fitness, he rarely allowed himself to sprint, considering stamina a more necessary skill. But nothing came more naturally to him than speed.

It wasn't long before the river was glittering before him. He scanned the bank for Mullard. And then he saw *her*. His beautiful girl. His Eva. To his immense relief she was no longer unconscious. In fact, she was standing. But . . . *What the hell?* Mullard appeared to be dabbing her neck. When Seth had glimpsed her in the arena, he'd noticed blood, though no specific injury, but as he approached her now, it looked like her neck was bleeding. Surely any injury sustained in the arena should be pretty well healed by now? How badly was she hurt? And what in Apollo's name was she still doing here? His instructions had been absolutely specific. Whoever reached Eva first would see her safely to Zack's house. Why was she still with Mullard?

He had to get her away from here before Cassius saw her. The last thing they needed was the magister diverted from the chase – and there was no diversion more potent than Eva. He ran harder. Desperate to reach her.

Eva and Mullard were standing right at the vortex site. Now that he was so close, Seth couldn't suppress his shudder of unease. The last time he had travelled through the vortex he'd barely made it back alive. No amount of combat injury or torture competed with the hammering he'd taken then. And he didn't particularly relish the prospect of a re-run . . . or the idea of inflicting it on Matt and Nick. But he had no choice. He prayed Lauren had augmented the electromagnetic pulsing as he had asked her to last night. Were those weird sentry structures what he hoped they were?

He could see no sign of Lauren, but now, standing just a few metres away, was his entire reason for living.

'*Eva!*'

She was running towards him. And at that moment the vortex, the Romans, the war and all the evils in his life were instantly eclipsed.

'Oh, baby,' he groaned as she buried her face into his chest.

He closed his eyes, wanting to prolong this, to stay here and forget everything else. But, unfortunately, everything else would very soon be crashing towards them on thundering feet.

'Eva, I need to get you to Zack's house. Matt's leading Cassius this way –'

'They're already here, Seth,' Eva gulped, pointing.

Seth turned to see Matt waving frantically as Cassius and his soldiers gained ground behind him.

Damn. From this distance Cassius would have a clear view of Eva. There was no way he could get her away safely now.

Seth ran a hand through his hair, looking wildly around for other options.

'Seth.'

The word was spoken so softly he almost didn't catch it above the approaching shouts and footfalls of the soldiers.

'Eva?' He moved his ear to her mouth.

'To use the vortex as a corridor for this many people is going to put a huge pressure on the negative density . . .'

The speech was too long for her throat. She began swallowing convulsively.

Seth's eyes homed in on her injury. 'Did Cassius do this?' he snarled, touching her throat gently and offering her a newly created cup of water. She coughed and blood spattered her lips.

'God, I'm sorry, that was gross,' she croaked, wiping her mouth on her sleeve. 'Listen to me, Seth . . . The vortex is already unstable –'

'I know, sweetheart. That's why I don't want you with us.'

'I belong with you, Seth,' she rasped. 'If I had to stay in Parallon without you –'

She didn't need to finish the sentence. He understood. He felt the same way. But still he absolutely couldn't bear the thought of her being tossed like a rag doll around the vortex.

And if they made it through – what then?

She'd be stuck in the middle of a bloody urban war, without the luxury of the Parallon healing mechanism. And she was already injured. He was certain that the Parallon healing effect didn't work once they were inside the vortex.

'Seth, let's move!' panted Matt, barrelling towards them.

'Christ,' hissed Nick. 'We've gotta do this now. Eva, you have to get out of here.'

'We've left it too late,' said Seth bleakly. 'Eva's going to have to come with us.'

40

Choices

River, Parallon

Seth stood on the side of the river and pulled Eva in to his waist. He was frantically reassessing the plan. Her presence changed everything. His previous objective – to rid Parallon of Cassius and Roman rule whatever the cost – was suddenly inadequate. He now had to find a way to keep himself alive long enough to get Eva safely back. And the vortex was as dangerous an enemy as Cassius.

So . . . assuming they didn't all get smashed to pieces inside, where was his best destination? Where the hell could he lead them to gain the most advantage? It was a difficult decision . . . the further he went into the future, the more physically and psychically powerful the Romans would be, which would give them a distinct advantage over 21st-century Nick and Eva. Yet they would be at a cultural disadvantage. The buildings and the technology would be alien and potentially unnerving . . . not to mention the absence of Latin.

Seth narrowed his eyes as he considered Cassius and the battalion of soldiers heading straight his way. His own little party was going to be physically overwhelmed whatever happened. He decided he would have to take the cultural advantage. He glanced across at the equipment Nick had prepared himself with, and replicated it, adding a couple of strong curved knives to his arsenal. Then he looked down at his beautiful girl.

'Eva, have you ever held a gun?' he asked.

She shook her head. 'Maybe if someone had let me *train* . . .' she muttered.

He felt the pressure of her accusation deep in his gut. She had been right all along. In trying to protect her, he had left her defenceless and vulnerable. He couldn't give her a gun then, it was more likely to be used against her than by her. Instead he handed her a canister of pepper spray and a couple of small retractable knives – easily overlooked by arrogant soldiers, but potentially lethal.

'I'm hoping you won't need to use a knife, Eva, but if anything happens to me, hold the handle firmly and go deliberately for an exposed, unexpected place – eye, back of knee, inside of wrist. Don't even think about trying to kill anyone. Just concentrate on not letting go of the knife, and doing enough to get away. I'll do everything in my power to stay close.'

Before she could refute or challenge him, he kissed her hard on the mouth and turned to Matt, Nick and their two new companions.

'I'm heading for a time I've visited before – 2043. I will be concentrating on the date. You will be focusing on staying with me. However bad it gets in the vortex – and it could be really bad – keep my name in your head and repeat it over and over. But – and this is really important – if you arrive on the other side and you look down at your hands and they are transparent, *don't* get out of the water. It will mean you've found yourself back in your own time where you will be powerless and unable to survive. In that case, you're going to have to return to the vortex and head back to Parallon.'

'So what about that lot, Seth?' murmured Matt, nodding his head towards the soldiers thundering towards them. 'If they follow us to 2043 – how are we supposed to fight all of them off? There are hundreds of them.'

'It's really unlikely they'll all make it – the vortex isn't stable enough, and their destination intentions will probably be muddled. Some will die in the water, some will end up in the wrong time. But we have to kill any of them that do make it. We can't let a single one of Cassius's men survive and return to Parallon. Our primary targets, though, are Cassius and his elite guards. Any questions?'

Nobody spoke.

'Let's do this then,' exhaled Seth, slowing his breathing and clearing his mind. He moved his arm from about Eva's shoulders and took her hand.

'Hold on tight, baby,' he whispered. Then he cast his eyes around at his troop, nodded once, and they all jumped.

41

Release

Vortex

I held tight to Seth's hand, shut my eyes and desperately willed the water to be warm. And it was. So for a few moments I felt like I'd accidentally slipped back into one of my rare perfect dreams . . . splashing in tropical waters with Seth by my side . . .

But of course we weren't in some perfect dream, and we weren't alone. Matt, Nick, Samuel and Jake were treading water right beside us.

'So – what happens now?' asked Nick, frowning across the flat surface of the water dubiously.

'We –' began Seth, but at that moment the slight current that had been playing round my legs suddenly intensified, and Seth's hand tightened fiercely round mine. Just before I shut my eyes to brace myself I took one last look at the riverbank and caught a final glimpse of Cassius snarling down at us. It was a snapshot moment, one that swirled inside my head as I was dragged inexorably downwards, sucked into the depths of the river, as powerless to resist as an ant in a whirlpool.

But I had my anchor.

Seth.

His hand clasped round mine – a tight defiance against the swirling water raging against us: vast, overwhelming, elemental rage. It was grabbing us. Pulling so hard. So tight. My lungs, ribs, throat, eyelids, all compressed. Impossible to breathe. And the pain. Churning, wracking pain . . . my head twisting from my neck, my arms wrenching from my shoulders, weights like trucks smashing into me . . . throwing me, tossing me. I tried so hard to hold on. All my focus on that one point. My hand in his.

But I lost my grip. I lost my grip on his hand. And he was gone.

Seth was gone. Seth. My Seth. I couldn't reach him. My mind begged for him, screamed for him, but he had been swallowed into the churning maelstrom. I clawed and fought for him until there was nothing left to fight with. The pain and the noise and the fear gnawed away at the only thing I had left of him . . . his name.

I still had his name. Tucked safely inside. I held on to it so hard. Protecting it. Guarding it.

But there was so much noise. Screaming. Shouting. Roaring. People? Water?

The noise wasn't just outside me, it was everywhere. Inside my bones. My muscles. My head. My mind was slipping open. Fingers of acid flame were driving into it, pulling it apart. Too much pain. Too much noise.

Oh God. Make it stop.

I needed to hold it closed. There was something precious in there; something I was clinging on to.

But I was having a problem remembering what it was. Darkness was seeping in. I just . . . I just couldn't hold it back any more.

And it felt good to let go.

42

Storm

Hunched against the howling wind, Jennifer Linden took one last wistful look at the OB van and slammed the door shut behind her. Kishoor was already battling his way through the pelting rain with the camera equipment.

'It's a bloody joke,' she muttered, trying to fasten her hood. The wind whipped it instantly off her head, and it thrashed around her ears in a wild, hellish dance.

Jen bit her lip. A year ago, she would have given anything for this opportunity, this second chance to prove herself in front of the camera. But that was before. Before her world imploded. Now, her old ambition, her obsessional attention to detail, her desperate drive to uncover truths just seemed stupid and childish.

It took fifteen minutes of battling against the wind before Jen and Kishoor were positioned as near to the river as the police would permit. Then, doing their best to stay vertical, they had to wait for an eternity to get the broadcast go-ahead from Hugo at the studio.

Suddenly her headphones crackled. 'Jen, don't just stand

there, for Chrissake! Take the mic and *say* something – anything. Nobody gives a damn what it is,' hissed Hugo through the buzzing headset.

What the hell? Cursing furiously under her breath, Jen cast an agitated glance towards Kishoor, who was doing everything in his power to hold the camera steady.

She just had to stay focused. She was the one Hugo had tasked to do this broadcast, and although she knew the main reason was because there was nobody else around, she had to prove she could do it. So gripping hard on to the microphone, Jen took a deep breath, counted to three and began.

'I'm standing here at Greenwich, as close to the banks of the river as I can get.' She hesitated a moment. She couldn't see the camera properly because the rain was plastering her hair in her eyes. Cautiously, she took one hand off the drenched, slippery mic so that she could push the offending clump back. 'Behind me, you can see the preparations for the major repair work on the Thames Barrier.' Rain dripped from her nose. She tried shaking it off. 'Number 10 has confirmed that construction workers can't wait until the weather eases, as meteorologists are forecasting even higher water levels. The barrier was built thirty-five years ago to withstand nine thousand tonnes of water. Nobody could have predicted the unprecedented levels it is now defending against. With these new terrifying weather fronts, engineers are desperately trying to come up with a design for raising the barrier to withstand far greater swells of water. General flood damage across London is now so extensive that costs of repairs are running into the billions. But that is nothing compared with the catastrophe we face if they can't raise the barrier height in time.

'The most vulnerable dwellings have been evacuated, and high-ground shelters are being designat–' Jen's eyes suddenly widened as a huge piece of sheet metal came flying towards her. Kishoor threw out an arm, shoving her down to the ground, throwing himself and the camera kit down after her. As they lay panting in a swirling pool of debris, Jen watched the missile crash into the lamp post behind them.

She glanced across at the camera. At least the recording light was off. She was fairly certain the *Channel 7 News* audience could do better than live footage of her and Kishoor flailing on the ground. But she really didn't care. Neither did Kishoor. He was more worried about the cracked lens and his bleeding elbow.

'I'm so sick of all this, Jen,' he gasped. 'I wish we lived somewhere else.' Jen nodded her agreement. What had happened to the good old dependable British weather? Lately it had developed into one of the most extreme, unstable climates in the world.

But who the hell was she to talk about stability? After all, her whole universe had pitched completely out of kilter months ago, when two people had defied all physical laws and disappeared before her eyes. She knew now that there was no such thing as a predictable universe, and a deep sense of foreboding made her fear that the worst was yet to come.

43

Carnage

River Thames, London

Light. Crashing slashes of light were bouncing against his eyelids, pushing Seth back to consciousness. But everything felt wrong. The pain – *that* he recognized. His body was used to the pain. But this churning bed of water, the hammering torrent on his face . . . was he still trapped inside the vortex? He groaned. How much longer must he endure this? A violent resounding crash forced him to open his eyes and blink. Jagged streaks of white light crossing a black sky filled his vision. Was that lightning? The brightness was so dazzling he had to shut his eyes, but they instantly jerked open again at a sudden booming crash of thunder. He shuddered. He was lying in a swell of freezing, churning water, lashed by pelting rain, in the middle of the wildest electric storm he had ever encountered.

But at least it meant he'd survived the vortex, he thought wearily.

And then he jolted awake properly. He wasn't supposed to be here alone. Not this time. Eva was with him. He started flailing about frantically in the water. Where was she?

It was so dark that the tossing water was ink black. Oh God, please let her be here. He couldn't lose her. Not again.

But he *had* lost her, he remembered bleakly. He had lost his grip on her hand. Let her go. His heart started pounding as total panic flooded through his veins.

'Eva!' he began shouting, as he swam in frantic circles, desperation completely obliterating the terrible pain and weariness in his limbs.

Coughing. He could hear someone coughing; some frenzied thrashing.

He ploughed through the choppy water towards the movement, and as he did so became aware of more thrashing on his other side . . . And then a beam of light.

'Seth, is that you?'

'Nick?'

The light was bobbing its way towards him, its beam casting around the water, and now settling on the thrashing figure Seth had been making for.

Matthias.

Nick reached him at the same time. 'Can't believe we made it,' panted Nick. 'When you said the vortex would be bad, Seth –'

'Have you seen the others?' interrupted Seth, his eyes scanning desperately about him.

'Samuel and Jake are through. Jake's pretty messed up – Sam's helping him to the riverbank.' Nick's voice dropped. 'Eva?'

Seth swallowed. 'Matt, can you make it to the bank?' he rasped.

Matt nodded weakly and started pushing towards the blurry lights at the water's edge.

'Any idea if we've hit the right time, Seth?' murmured Nick as he squinted after Matt.

'Hard to see anything much – but looks like 21st-century buildings – and you don't appear to be too transparent, so I'm guessing we're not far off,' answered Seth distractedly, his eyes completely focused on combing the surface of the water.

The rest of the group had made it. Surely she would be here?

'Take this,' muttered Nick, handing Seth his torch. 'I'm going to try building a camp; get some of this stuff dried out. Be careful, Seth, Cassius's men weren't far behind us.'

'Do you reckon you can make it on to the bridge?' Seth nodded. 'It'll give you a clear view of the river and pretty good cover when the Romans arrive.'

Nick squinted towards the looming dark shape in the sky. 'What about you, Seth? You'll be completely exposed in the middle of the river,' he warned. 'And if you stay out here much longer you'll get hypothermia.'

'I'll be OK,' responded Seth, beginning to move back towards the place he'd surfaced. And then he felt it: a great shifting beneath him, as though a huge water demon was waking up. Nick's eyes widened, and he began swimming as fast as he could for the bank.

But Seth wasn't going to swim away. He couldn't. Somewhere down there Eva was struggling to get free, and he would wait for her. A sudden surge of pressure from the centre of the water erupted in a volcanic blast, throwing Seth backwards so powerfully, he was smashed hard against the water surface, briefly blacking out.

When he opened his eyes, bodies were being tossed everywhere like flotsam and jetsam; human detritus. Some were motionless, some flopping about like dying fish, some groaning; one or two were dragging themselves towards the shore.

The Romans had arrived.

But Seth wasn't leaving. He shone Nick's torch around, checking face after face, desperately suppressing the fear that was now clutching his gut.

Had the vortex claimed her?

He frantically checked again, aware that of the hundreds of Romans who'd followed them into the vortex there were no more than thirty here. And most of these looked dead.

Eva! Where the hell are you, baby?

His brain was starting to cloud, but despite the internal fog, Seth was aware that he'd seen no sign of Cassius or the elite guard. Had the vortex claimed them too? Zeus! Was Eva's sacrifice the price?

The torch beam started to shake. Seth looked down at his hand. He could no longer feel it. He tried to move his fingers, but they were rigid. A part of his brain recognized that his body was seizing up. The water was too cold. He needed to get out of it. But the despairing part couldn't quite give a damn.

And then the surface ahead of him appeared to shudder. Seth stilled and watched as two more figures were tossed to the surface. His heart stopped when he saw long black hair whipping through the waves. He charged through the water like a machine, his eyes fixed on her motionless form, neither daring to hope, nor to give up hope. When he reached her, she was lying on her back, her face streaked with blood. Clamped round her left wrist was a large hand: the unmistakable bejewelled hand of Cassius Malchus.

The bile that instantly rose to his throat made Seth roar. He could not bear to see that monster so close to his girl. His motionless girl.

Eva's eyes were shut. Cassius's were open – but dazed. He

222

hadn't spotted Seth so near in the churning water. Seth reached straight for his holster. But his heart sank when its shredded remains peeled away in his hand. The pistol was gone. Must have been ripped away inside the vortex. He felt around for the assault rifle strap, but it was gone too. He groaned. So much for his 21st-century advantage. His only surviving weapons were the two curved knives he'd shoved into the front pockets of his combats just before they'd left. He could feel their hard outlines as he moved. He pulled one out, then swam to Eva's side to prise her out of Cassius's grasp.

Cassius's fingers tightened like a vice.

'*Have I got something you want, slave?*' he suddenly snarled, rearing forward, his face screwed up against the torrential rain.

Seth instantly slashed his knife across Cassius's grip. For a moment Cassius stared in dazed confusion as the blood oozed across his fingers. Then, gurgling with pain, he released his hold, granting Seth the moment he needed to drag Eva away. But Cassius had woken up now, and with a furious bellow he pushed through the water after them. Seth instantly twisted his body round and managed to land a kick to Cassius's jaw. Along with the churning water, this was enough to momentarily deflect the Roman, giving Seth just enough time to get clear of his orbit. Without a backwards glance, Seth began ploughing for the shore, his precious cargo held tight in his arms.

44

Surveillance

Embankment, London

Nick's eyes were fixed on the turbulent water, watching for movement. He was crouched against the bridge railings, under the temporary shelter he'd constructed with a sheet of broken perspex and a mangled car door. It offered reasonable camouflage, but was barely big enough to protect the four of them from the rain. He looked briefly across at his companions. Samuel rested in a corner, while Matt did his best to bind Jake's bleeding arm with a strip he'd torn from Jake's shirt. Satisfied, Nick resumed his river watch. Although he no longer had his torch, the lightning was keeping his field of vision fairly well lit. After that horrifying human upchuck, he'd been trying to monitor the forty or so Romans spewed on to the surface. Some of them had made it to the riverbank, and were now sprawled under a couple of benches. The rest were still lying motionless on the water. Already dead? Dying?

He had no idea whether Cassius or the elite guard were among the survivors, but the number of lifeless bodies bobbing on the river had Nick feeling cautiously optimistic.

No. Optimistic wasn't the right word . . . not with Eva

missing. And he was having a real problem coming up with a plausible explanation for her continued absence – apart from the obvious one. And whichever way he looked at it, he felt responsible. Seth had trusted him to get Eva to safety. And he'd failed.

He scanned the water again. Where the hell was Seth now anyway? He'd die too if he stayed in that water any longer. And then Nick would have another damn life on his conscience.

He ran a hand furiously through his wet hair. He was getting sick of staring at his list of mistakes. He just wanted them corrected: Eva out of the vortex and Seth out of the water. And preferably himself back at City Police HQ in 2013.

'Hey, man, what's going on down there?' murmured Samuel, nudging Nick back to his rain-drenched present.

Nick shifted his eyes along the river to the point Samuel indicated, and saw a flurry of movement. 'Looks like a couple more of them have been spewed out.'

He squinted through the driving rain to try and make out what was going on. If only he hadn't lost his damned binoculars. For the hundredth time he cursed his missing backpack. They now had no night vision or communications equipment, no GPS, no spare ammo, no medical supplies and no food. He patted down his pockets. All he had left was a loaded, six-round pistol and a knife. Even the assault rifle and shotgun were gone.

Just as well so many of the Romans had gone too.

As he stared despondently out to the river a dazzling streak of lightning suddenly lit the scene and Nick got a snapshot moment of absolute clarity: Seth was dragging a body towards them.

Nick jumped to his feet and, bracing himself against the

wind as he stepped out from the shelter, waded down the rain-drenched steps to the river's edge.

He stared in awe at Seth pounding through the freezing, churning water as though he were scoring laps in a heated pool. Where the hell did the guy get his stamina?

As soon as he could reach him, Nick hauled Seth and his limp cargo on to the bank. 'Christ! You found her,' he gulped.

'Sh-sh-she's got a p-p-pulse.' Seth was shivering so hard he could barely speak. 'W-w-we need to g-g-get her w-w-w-warmed up.'

'We need to get you both warmed up,' replied Nick, frowning at Eva's bluish skin. 'She needs a hospital, Seth.'

Seth was beginning to stagger. Nick looked around for some way of getting them dry, but the world was teeming with water. He had no idea where to take them.

'A-Anton . . . W-we should try to g-g-g-get to Anton's.'

Nick crouched next to Seth, straining to make sense of his words. He wondered briefly if Seth was hallucinating.

'Seth, do you think you can make it up to the bridge?'

Seth lay panting on the riverbank, his eyes closed, his mouth slack with exhaustion. He barely registered Nick's words; his body was reaching out for oblivion. But some deep instinct refused to grant him release. His arms twitched and the chill weight he was clutching suddenly reminded him of his purpose. His eyes blinked open and his brain switched back on.

'C-Cassius,' he choked, 'C-Cassius m-made it.'

'Shit,' muttered Nick, as he helped pull Seth to his feet.

Seth tightened his hold on Eva and lurched slowly, purposefully, across the slick swirling bank towards the steps. When he finally reached the top he sank against the railings.

'Who's Anton, Seth?'

Someone kept repeating those words. He knew they were significant, but he couldn't think why. He groaned and turned his face away.

'Seth, can you hear me?' Someone was shaking his shoulder. 'Seth, who is Anton?'

He frowned. 'D-d-doctor,' he muttered.

'Do you know how to get to him?'

Seth drifted off again.

'Seth?' hissed a more familiar voice. Matthias? 'Do you know how to find Anton?'

Yes. That was definitely Matthias's voice.

'Seth, stay with us. Think, man. Eva needs a doctor. Can you find Anton?'

Seth's eyes blinked back open. He had to get Eva to Anton's clinic. Where the hell was it?

'T-t-trying to r-r-remember. N-n-not far. N-need a car, M-Matt.'

'A car?' Matt frowned dubiously. He glanced up. There were mangled vehicle parts abandoned all along the bridge, though just ahead was a road where a few strange-looking cars battled valiantly through the terrifying weather. But how was he supposed to get hold of one?

'Hey, I'll give it a go,' offered Nick, pulling himself to his feet. 'Maybe try and hitch a ride?'

Seth leaned out a hand to stop him. 'N-n-no – m-m-must be M-M-Matt . . . T-time a-a-amplification.'

Matt didn't want to admit it, but he understood what Seth was saying. He would have much more chance of convincing someone to give them a ride than Nick would, because his time was so much further back than Nick's. He nodded half-heartedly, though looking at the bedraggled pair, he'd need a huge heap of time-amp charisma to get them inside someone's car. Seth would be much better at doing it. Seth could persuade anyone to do anything. Even without time-amp help, even half dead, Seth radiated charisma.

Matt's eyes flicked towards Eva. Her skin was white and her lips were blue. He didn't dare take her pulse. It would be a miracle if she still had one.

'Seth,' he urged, shaking him back to consciousness. 'Do you think you can make it to the road?'

Seth tensed, trying to gain control of his now-shuddering limbs.

'For Eva,' Matt added.

Seth's eyes sprang instantly open and they were scorching. Clutching Eva tight against his body, he tried to stand up, but his legs wouldn't hold him.

'Here, Seth,' murmured Nick. 'Lean on me.'

Matt strode ahead, praying that Seth's doctor, Anton, wasn't just a figment of some hypothermic delirium. When he reached the road, he stood tentatively on the pavement, waving his arms towards the oncoming traffic.

Nobody stopped.

Matt began shouting, but his thin voice was instantly swallowed by the raging storm.

When Nick finally got Seth and Eva to the road and saw Matt's ineffectual efforts, he knew the guy was never going to succeed.

'Seth,' he urged, shaking him. 'You're going to have to do your thing, man.'

Seth lifted his head and tried to focus. His eyes immediately rested on Eva, and he jolted awake, then shakily headed for the road, still clutching her in his arms.

'Christ, man,' yelled Nick, suddenly realizing that Seth was walking straight into the oncoming traffic. 'Not the middle of the road! You'll get yourself kill–'

Fortunately, the auto-breaking function on the car hurtling towards them had not been compromised by the storm. It screeched to a stop, but spun a full 180 degrees on the glistening road before skidding to a standstill.

'What the fu–' yelled the passenger, as he opened his door and stormed out. Seth stumbled towards him, raised his head and stared straight into the man's eyes.

'Oh my God,' gabbled the man. 'You both need a doctor! Get in the car and I'll take you straight to –'

'Anton Trepov's clinic,' choked Seth, fixing the man with his piercing gaze.

The car owner programmed the nav-com, while Nick helped Seth and Eva inside. Matt was just climbing in to join them when Nick hauled him out again.

'Hey!' exploded Matt.

'I need you here,' said Nick firmly. 'We've got a bunch of Romans to deal with.'

Matt snorted, deeply resenting Nick for assuming authority and coming between him and his friend. But he reluctantly shut the car door and followed Nick away.

'So what's the plan?' he shouted belligerently.

'You tell me!' yelled Nick. 'There are now just four of us to kill whatever's left of Cassius's whole bloody army and nothing to do it with but six wet bullets and a couple of knives.'

45
Search

Parallon

'What can possibly have gone wrong?' repeated Zackary for the hundredth time. He was pacing his library on a relentless circuit between the door and the window, and for the hundredth time Lauren looked up helplessly from her tablet and wondered what she should do. He was like a man possessed.

'I'm sure they'll bring her soon,' she said soothingly. 'Seth gave the same order to every single one of his men. Someone will have found her.'

'Then why the hell isn't she here?' snapped Zackary. 'The plan was unequivocal.'

'Things change,' murmured Lauren wearily. 'War doesn't always go exactly to plan.'

Zackary chose to ignore that remark. He ran his hands furiously through his hair, hating his helplessness; hating this feeling of dread. Nobody got him worked up the way Eva did. The kid was killing him. Or was it the sickening knot of fear that had taken up residence in his gut?

Why the hell did he care about her so much? How had he

allowed himself to get emotionally involved? It was something he never did. His detachment defined him. Until now.

'I can't do this any more,' he hissed finally, pacing towards the door. 'I'm going out to look for her.'

'Zackary, that's crazy!' argued Lauren, jumping up and grabbing his arm. 'There's a war on! You'll –'

'Just stay here,' he snapped, shaking her off. 'If they bring her back, for Christ's sake keep her here till I return. Get her drunk, lock her in my lab, do anything to stop her leaving. This is about the only place in Parallon she'll be safe.'

Lauren rolled her eyes. How did that girl get everyone running around after her? Zackary had been so much easier to live with before she turned up. He'd even started to let her in a little. And though she was sure his feelings for Eva were one hundred per cent paternal, she still felt a rush of jealousy at the intensity of his affection.

Stop being ridiculous, she told herself firmly. Her own worries were far greater than a missing teenage girl. She had the generators going twenty-four seven, but the wormhole readings she'd taken an hour ago were reflecting no predicted improvement. In fact, the negative density seemed to be escalating. Unless she'd miscalculated, somehow. She was going to have to recalibrate the generators and check them again. She didn't think she'd made a mistake, but it was possible the calibrator was registering a coding error. So she was deeply grateful for some Zack-free space to slip out and reassess the situation.

She watched from the window until he'd disappeared from sight, then gathered up her instruments and headed out of the door, briefly glancing up at the shimmering green-tinged sky and wondering anxiously about the unusual breeze dancing around her shoulders.

As Zackary slipped silently through the deserted shadowy street, the one thought that kept him sane was the profoundly comforting certainty that Eva couldn't die. So long as she was somewhere in Parallon, she would be alive. And he would eventually find her.

He heard a distant rumbling sound and pressed himself nervously against the wall beside him. But when a light rain began to fall, and more thunderous rumblings accompanied it, he stared up at the greenish sky in bewilderment. In all the time he had lived in Parallon, it had never rained. What did it mean?

His stomach lurched uneasily, but he had more pressing concerns, so he carefully stepped forward, peering through the rain for any sign of patrolling guards. He didn't think he'd seen one in hours. That had to be a good sign . . . surely? He wasn't going to take any reckless chances though, so he continued to move cautiously, staying close to the buildings, only crossing open roads after meticulous checking.

When he finally approached the arena, he listened for the sounds of battle. But there were none: no clashing of weapons or roars of attack. Just moaning cries.

Cautiously he crept through the unguarded entrance and stood gaping at the sight before him. The arena had been transformed. Above him was now a domed roof and, instead of sand, the arena was floored with glistening marble. Writhing, broken bodies lay on mattresses in neat rows – some wearing torn rebel battledress, some in bloodstained Roman livery. Moving between them, apparently unconcerned about the colour or style of uniform, were Parallon inhabitants, intent on cleaning and bandaging wounds and offering food and water.

Zackary stood in fearful disbelief. Roman rule didn't permit independent gatherings of more than two people. All group activities were ruthlessly monitored. So why weren't guards breaking this up? The scene was absolutely forbidden; the participants doomed to public floggings.

He looked around wildly. There were no guards at all. His brain could barely compute what his eyes reported. Not for one moment had he considered the possibility that Seth's army had any hope of defeating the Romans. Even now he refused to draw an optimistic conclusion from the evidence before him. The Romans were simply regrouping. The regime would recover. Parallon would no doubt be enslaved again before sundown.

Zackary knew that there was no way Eva would be lying in this makeshift hospital unless Seth was right beside her. His army would never have abandoned her. Nonetheless, he did a bed-by-bed inventory just to be sure.

After exhausting his search of the arena itself, Zackary forced himself to search the antechambers, and when he could put it off no longer, the grim basement holding area.

He was not a man of great empathy, but even he was shaken by the appalling conditions down there. Had Cassius's gladiators really been living like this? And if so, what would his prisons be like? Zackary shuddered at the thought, especially when he considered the possibility that if Eva wasn't here, there was a good chance that she may have been taken to one. He knew there was a prison wing at the palace . . . the heavily guarded palace. Cassius's ultimate lair.

Did he honestly have the courage to try and breach that? Even for Eva?

46

Betrayal

Embankment, London

April AD 2045

As he stared down at the river, Nick's eyes were smarting from the effort of trying to pick out human movement against the raging chaos of the storm. His body still ached from the battering it had received in the vortex, while the icy chill from his drenched clothing seeped into his skin. He craved sleep. The desire to curl up on the ground and shut his eyes became so strong at times that he had to bite his arm to keep himself from drifting off. Occasionally he glanced enviously across the makeshift camp towards Matt, Samuel and Jake, who lay huddled together in blissful oblivion, their chests rising and falling in slow, easy harmony.

But it never occurred to him to ask one of them to take over the watch from him. He had too many reasons not to trust these men. There was only one man he would trust with his life right now, and he was currently God-knows-where trying to save the life of a girl he cared about way too much. But Nick couldn't really blame him. There was clearly something special about that girl. And dangerous. So dangerous that she'd managed to trigger a whole damn war.

Sighing deeply, Nick resumed his watch. Hours ago the sun had pushed its feeble way through the raging darkness, gradually revealing the extent of the storm's destruction. The river was awash with debris, its bank littered with broken billboards, sheets of metal, shards of glass and pulped wood and paper.

But Nick's only focus was on assessing the enemy. He had counted twenty-seven Romans through the vortex. A number had lain motionless in the water, then disappeared from sight, presumably sucked back into the swirl. He was pretty sure no more than seventeen had made it to the riverbank, and several of them were in pretty bad shape. At least four lay exposed and inert on the ground, unable to crawl towards shelter. Those with the strength had made straight for the protected space under the bridge, the exact site he would have headed for in their position.

Although there'd been no sign of any newcomers for several hours, he kept his eyes darting between the water and the bank, determined not to miss any additional arrivals.

He glanced down at his sleeping team again and calculated their odds. Until Seth returned, they were four against maybe twelve or thirteen. Of the four of them, Matthias was certainly unreliable – his performance up at the road had shown him to be neither courageous nor resourceful. And Samuel and Jake, though potentially capable, were criminals and therefore intrinsically untrustworthy. Eva may have had faith in them, but Nick certainly didn't.

And, of course, between them they possessed virtually no weapons.

Conversely, the Romans were trained soldiers, and though they had probably lost most of their armoury, as fighting machines they would still be pretty damned indomitable – especially with Cassius at the helm.

'So, what's the plan?' yawned Jake, pulling himself up and stretching luxuriously. Nick turned to answer, and found three sets of eyes gazing expectantly towards him. He stared impassively back at them. He'd been constructing and discarding plans from the moment they'd arrived. Initially he'd favoured the idea of attacking the Romans before they had a chance to recover and regroup, but without Seth it would be suicidal. The only viable plan was to sit this thing out till Seth returned. However, he saw absolutely no point in sharing that information.

'First mission of the day is to get hold of some breakfast,' he announced decisively.

'I like the way you think!' smirked Jake, rubbing his hands together appreciatively.

'I don't mind going on a food foray,' volunteered Matthias.

Nick's eyes narrowed at the speed of the offer, perplexed by Matt's sudden cooperativeness. Was he up to something?

'Where were you planning to go?'

'I used to know a café in this area – you never know, it may still be there.'

'And how will you pay?'

'Trust me,' grinned Matt. 'I may not have Seth's powers of persuasion, but I should be able to blag us some breakfast without resorting to actual money. Any requests?'

'Oh, man! I'd kill for sausage and eggs,' groaned Jake.

'I'll do my best,' said Matt, dropping to a crouch and edging

237

out of the hideout. 'Just make sure no Roman follows me there,' he added, flicking his eyes towards the river.

Six hours later, Matthias still hadn't returned. Nick's brain was working overtime. He'd kept a tireless vigil on Matt's pathway to the road, and was certain nobody had followed him. Was it possible Matt had walked into a Roman ambush? If so, it meant Cassius's men weren't all camped under the bridge, as he'd believed.

But with so few troops, would Cassius really divert a valuable proportion of them into some random outpost for hours, on the off-chance one of Seth's party would come along? That would seem like a crazy strategy – unless he'd somehow miscalculated their number.

No. He could stake his life that no more than thirteen Romans made it through intact.

Which meant that he had to consider the other nagging explanation: betrayal.

He didn't trust Matthias. Clare, Georgia and Winston had made it clear that Matt had betrayed them all in order to curry favour with the Romans. Which meant the guy could potentially be on some sort of double-cross. He could be with Cassius right now, exposing their location and vulnerabilities . . .

Nick snorted in frustration. Why the hell would a guy as intelligent as Seth trust someone as treacherous as Matthias, and then bring him along on such a sensitive mission? He knew they went way back – kids together or something, according to Georgia. But Seth wasn't a fool. He surely knew how brothers could turn on brothers.

He gazed out at the pelting rain, wondering why he'd allowed himself to become embroiled in this mess. But he knew the answer. Despite everything, he trusted the plan. And Seth. And he had some deep down, completely unaccountable faith that Seth would return and that the plan would work. He just prayed Matt didn't get the chance to sabotage it first.

47

Treatment

London

I was hot. *Really* hot. But motionless at last. Thank God I wasn't being hurled around any more.

'She's waking up, doctor.'

Doctor?

I opened my eyes in panic . . . and gaped. Where the hell was I? It looked like a hospital, but way too techy. More like a sci-fi lab. Unfamiliar machines and monitors lined the walls.

'Hey, there!' smiled a woman in a white tunic, looking across from the screen she'd been speaking into.

A moment later she was replacing what appeared to be an empty bag of blood for a full one, and attaching it to a tube. A tube that was disappearing into my arm.

Great.

'Just one more unit to go,' she beamed, unclipping a tablet from her belt and typing something into it. 'Can I just confirm your name, honey?'

I swallowed. My throat felt really sore.

'No need to talk just yet,' she said quickly. 'I just need to check your name is – er – Eva Koretsky?'

I nodded. So today I was Eva.

'And you are seventeen?'

I nodded impatiently. 'Where am I?' I croaked.

God, that hurt. I should have taken her advice.

'The ATEC Unit,' she murmured, as she checked some sort of monitor on my chest. 'Good. Your stats are improving. Quite a hammering you took there, girl. We've been dealing with hurricane injuries all night, but I have to say, yours were –'

Hurricane? What hurric–

'*Eva!*'

My eyes flashed to the door. I'd just heard the most distracting voice in the world.

'Seth!' I choked.

He was standing in the doorway dressed completely in white, grinning from ear to ear. Instead of grinning back, which is what my brain wanted my mouth to do, I found my eyes filling with tears and my lips trembling.

'Oh, baby,' he whispered, bounding to the bed. He leaned over me, placed a gentle hand on either side of my face, and tenderly kissed me.

'Excuse me,' scolded the woman. 'This is a hos–'

'Seth, will you stop upsetting my staff!' smirked a guy now striding through the door behind him. He was also dressed in white. 'Thanks, Nadia, I'll take it from here.'

Nadia huffed and I glanced at her. She was hovering, her eyes fixed on Seth like he was an ice cream she wanted to lick. And I was suddenly gripped by an irrationally possessive fury. Like the tears, the depth of my reaction confused me so much that I completely failed to notice that the stranger in white had moved over to my bedside.

'Hello, Eva. I'm Anton Trepov, your doctor this evening,' he smiled.

I opened my mouth to say 'hi', but he put a warning finger over my lips. 'No. I don't want you to talk for a while. I just spent nearly an hour lazonning your throat injury, and it needs time to heal.' His eyes flicked to mine. 'Strange laceration to pick up in a hurricane,' he added, his eyebrows raised sceptically.

I bit my lip and glanced at Seth, who shook his head slightly.

'Also an odd coincidence that the last time I saw Seth, he'd just got himself caught and injured by another one of our hurricanes.'

I looked questioningly at Seth. I felt the space between us opening up again – the stuff I didn't know about him beginning to swamp the stuff I did.

Sensing my discomfort, Seth reached over and took my hand. 'Luckily the storm seems to be settling,' he murmured, clearly intent on changing the subject. 'So Eva and I will be able to leave you in peace.'

'Peace is hardly something I would associate with you, Seth,' snorted Anton. 'In fact, the last time you turned up, you left us in complete chaos . . .'

Seth went rigid and stared down at our interlocked hands.

'It's no exaggeration to say that things have been off-kilter ever since.'

'What?' gasped Seth, his face white.

'Don't play the innocent, Seth. You must have known breaking into Zack's lab and whisking Lauren off would open a whole can of worms! I mean – we all knew she had the hots for you, but Zack and Engelmann were not happy about your sudden disappearance. They've even got a PI scouring the country for you both. And poor Rana was devastated.

'I honestly thought the next time I set eyes on you would be in the morgue – because everyone was out for your blood . . .'

'My blood,' echoed Seth humourlessly.

'And then when Zack disappeared, I couldn't help wondering if you'd had something to do with that – given the storm trail you left in your wake.'

Seth was frowning down at our joined hands as though they held the answer to the universe. Then he sighed deeply and stared hard into Anton's eyes.

'Thanks for all you've done for Eva and me, Anton. We really appreciate it. But now we need to get going. How long will Eva's transfusion take to finish?' He glanced at the tube in my arm.

Anton's glassy stare shifted briefly across to the emptying bag of blood. 'No more than seven minutes, but Eva needs to rest here overnight.'

Seth nodded slowly and watched the bag for a few moments. Then he swallowed and turned to me. I gasped as soon as I saw his expression.

'No, Seth!' I croaked urgently. 'You can't leave me. I'm going with y–'

'You mustn't talk,' they both yelled in unison. If the situation hadn't been so grim I might have laughed.

'Anton,' announced Seth deliberately. 'I need a word with Eva.'

Anton immediately stood up and walked out of the room, closing the door quietly behind him. Seth had just done his mind-zap thing and I hated it. I warily watched him as he moved across to the window and stood gazing out at the black sky, absently running a finger along the lines of rain patterning the glass. At last he turned to face me and cleared his throat.

'Eva, I want you to stay with Anton. You're safe here. He will take care of you until I can come ba–'

'No!' I cried. 'You can't keep doing this!'

Frowning, he strode over to the bed and put his fingers over my mouth. 'Please, Eva! You've got to rest your voice. Anton –'

'*Seth!*' I rasped, pushing him away. '*Stop!*'

Before he got a chance to respond, I was unwinding the bandage and tugging the needle from my arm.

'No, Eva!' he gasped, trying to stop me, but I was already pulling myself off the bed and standing shakily in front of him.

'Seth,' I whispered, 'you can't keep leaving me. I just can't handle it any more.'

My tough stance was unfortunately completely marred by the break in my voice and the sudden unwelcome arrival of tears.

'I have to –' he hissed.

I put a finger over his mouth, and ploughed on. 'I love you, Seth. And I need to be with you – wherever that is.'

'But, Eva, we're in the middle of a war –'

'I'm through with being safely tucked away. I need to be beside you. If that means I'll be put in danger, then so be it. I'd rather die beside you today than live forever without you. And I can't wait around wondering if you'll ever come back to me any more.'

'I've always come back for you.'

I shook my head, remembering the months I had waited for

him at St Mag's. 'No, Seth. You haven't. And you never tell me anything. I need to know what's going on.'

I dropped my hand from his face and clutched on to the fabric of his white tunic, staring fiercely into his clear blue eyes.

'What do you want to know?' he asked huskily.

I swallowed hard. Was he really going to finally talk to me?

'Where are we? When did you come here before? Did the Romans follow us? Is Cassius –'

'OK, OK!' he smiled, covering my mouth with his hand. I tried to bite his fingers in an attempt to get free, but his other arm grabbed me by the waist and pulled me tight against his body. Suddenly his mouth was on mine and he was kissing me so fiercely that I forgot my frustration and melted into him, throwing my arms round his neck, burying my hands into his curling hair. And it was like we couldn't get close enough to each other. Our bodies slammed together, our mouths opened to each other, our shared breath coming in hot, panting gasps. I just wanted to taste him, inhale him, consume him, live inside him. He groaned, his hands tangling in my hair, his lips moving in a frenzy across my face, along my eyelids, down the side of my neck, gently across my healing throat, along my shoulders.

'Eva!' he panted. 'I can't lose you.'

'Then don't leave me,' I gasped.

'Do you think I want to leave you?' he moaned. 'It kills me to.'

'Then don't. Stay here with me.'

He sat down on the bed and pulled me down on to his lap. 'I can't stay here, Eva,' he whispered. 'I have to get back to the river.'

'Wh–'

'Shhh, Eva,' he murmured, gently touching his fingers to my lips. 'If you behave, and sit here quietly, I'll try and answer the questions you just fired at me. But first I'm going to get that nurse back to finish the blood transfusion.'

Seth's powers of persuasion were – as ever – consummate, and a few minutes later I was attached once more to a bag of blood, and we were alone again.

Seth settled himself on to the bed beside me and quietly began to speak.

'Nick, Matthias and those two guards of Cassius's you somehow persuaded –'

'Samuel and Jake?' I smiled. 'They aren't Cassius's guards any more.'

'Eva!' he groaned crossly, skimming his fingers across my throat. 'You mustn't talk!'

I rolled my eyes.

'Anyway,' he continued, 'the four of them survived the vortex. Most of our weapons, unfortunately, weren't so lucky.'

'And . . . Cassius?'

Seth's eyes darkened. 'He made it,' he exhaled reluctantly, suddenly reaching out and enclosing my wrist with his fingers. 'So did quite a number of his soldiers – I don't know how many yet.'

'Where are they?'

'As far as I know they are still by the river. I doubt they would have got far in this hurricane. Nick has set up a camp on the bridge. The only advantage of this weather is that we're virtually the only human beings crazy enough to be outside. Conditions are a bit better now, but it's night, so as long as we finish this

246

before daylight tomorrow, we shouldn't need to involve anyone else from this time.'

'Apart from Anton and the nurses.'

He nodded uncomfortably.

I frowned at him. 'So where are we?'

'London, obviously, but not as close to my intended date as I had hoped – maybe a year out. I guess 2044 or 2045.'

'How long have we been here?'

'In this clinic? About twelve hours. It was just getting light when we got here.'

'Why were you here before, Seth?'

He chewed distractedly on the corner of his thumb and stared out the window.

I waited.

'Zackary sent me,' he said finally, his eyes flicking anxiously to mine. 'The night I left you at St Mag's; the night of our – er – disagreement.' He took a deep, shuddering breath. 'Zackary came for me, and told me how unstable the vortex had become, and that I was the only person who could help.'

'But what could *you* do?' I knew my gladiator had skills, but I didn't think frontier astrophysics was one of them.

'There was a physicist working in the field that Zackary knew . . . his mentor, Louis Engelmann. Zack wanted me to talk to him. Well, to be honest, he expected me to infect Engelmann and take him back to Parallon,' Seth snarled. 'Fortunately, the guy was too old to have responded to the virus.'

'So you took Lauren instead?' I murmured.

Seth dropped my hand and pulled away from me. 'I thought you knew me better than that, Eva!' He stood by the bed, rubbing his temples. 'I would *never* take anyone across to

Parallon intentionally. Lauren was a complete accident. Zackary –'

'Seth, Zack –'

'– knows a hell of a lot more about Parallon than you think,' hissed Seth. 'While I was here last time, I got into his computer –'

'You found the Parallon prototype?' I prompted.

'How did you know?'

So I was right. The Parallon prototype existed before Ambrose ever went to Parallon.

'I snuck into his Parallon lab,' I smiled, acknowledging our paired duplicity. 'I needed to try and work out the physics of the vortex. Lauren is only treating the symptoms – and they're just getting worse. Somebody has to try and find out the cause.'

'So what have you found out?'

'Not much. The Parallon file is carefully encrypted and so fragmented it's taking me a while to piece together, especially as you've had both Ambrose and Lauren watching me like hawks.'

Before Seth could respond, Anton had stepped back into the room. 'Didn't I make myself clear?' he scolded, striding over to the drip stand. 'Eva's supposed to be resting her voice! Good. The transfusion is finished,' he added, pulling on a pair of latex gloves. 'I can relieve you of this cannula.'

He deftly unstrapped me and I flexed my arm gratefully.

'Thank you,' I whispered.

'Anton,' said Seth, his authoritative tone instantly causing Anton to lift his eyes. 'Eva's clothes got wrecked. Do you have any she could use?'

Anton's whole posture straightened. 'I'm sure Nadia will be able to find some,' he answered robotically.

'And I could do with something more suitable for outdoors?' Seth added in the same tone, glancing down at his white scrubs.

'Of course,' responded Anton, moving swiftly out to the corridor.

'Seth, I hate it when you do that!' I hissed.

'It's quick and requires no explanation,' he shrugged. 'The less Anton asks, the less I have to lie. And we can't afford to impact on him any more than we already have –'

'Time anomalies?' I murmured.

Seth nodded. 'The last visit was – oh, hell, *Rana*? What are *you* doing here?'

Rana. The girl Anton mentioned earlier. The girl who was *devastated* when Seth left.

I blinked as an olive-skinned woman came bursting into the room, making a beeline for Seth. But just before she reached him she suddenly stopped dead in her tracks.

Seth glanced at me apologetically. I couldn't tell whether it was because of the mind control he'd clearly just used on her, or because of the way she was looking at him like she owned him.

I leaned my head against the pillows and shut my eyes. I really didn't have the energy for this. But the light touch I felt on my hand forced me to open my eyes again. Seth was standing beside me, lightly stroking one of my fingers. I looked down and saw the silver love ring he'd reinstated there at the arena. Glancing up at his face, I read the silent reminder in his eyes. He was mine. I was his. Nothing – nobody – was going to come between us.

I felt my shoulders relax as my anger and jealousy melted away.

'So what brings you here, Rana?' Seth asked.

'Anton v-commed me,' she blurted. 'I needed to see you, Seth. Y-you left so suddenly –'

'I'm sorry, Rana, I had to go.'

'W-with Lauren?'

Seth's eyes flicked anxiously to mine again, but I just shook my head. I was done with the jealous girlfriend thing.

'Yes, Lauren came with me,' he murmured. 'Thanks for dropping by, Rana, but Eva and I really need to get going now . . . And so do you.'

Rana blinked and nodded vaguely. 'OK. It was good to see you, Seth. Say hi to Lauren for me,' she added mechanically, and walked out of the room.

'Ah well,' I sighed. 'At least I don't have to fight a duel for you, now.'

Seth snorted and shot me a rueful look. 'Damn Anton for calling her,' he muttered. 'I wonder where the hell he's got to?'

He didn't have to wonder long, because a few moments later Anton arrived with two piles of clothes. 'Hope you're planning to go somewhere nice,' he smiled, depositing them on the bed. 'Eva, I must urge you to reconsider leaving tonight. Seth has a tendency to underestimate healing times.'

'I'll be fine, Anton. Thank you so much for –'

'Enough!' he sighed, holding up his hands. 'Please, at least do me the small courtesy of resting your voice!'

'OK,' I mouthed, dramatically rolling my eyes and grinning.

'Much better,' he smiled. 'Now, Nadia will be leaving for the day in about fifteen minutes and she's offered to give you both a lift if you need one.'

'We have to meet some friends on the embankment,'

answered Seth. 'So if it's not too much trouble a lift there would be really helpful.'

'No problem, that's virtually on her way home.'

'Thanks again for everything, Anton,' smiled Seth, shaking his hand.

'Goodbye, Seth. Next time you plan on a visit, please choose a time when I'm on holiday. Oh, and maybe check the weather forecast first.'

Laughing, Seth closed the door behind him. Then he strode back over to the bed and began sifting through the clothes Anton had left. Almost immediately he groaned.

'What's wrong?' I whispered, crawling across the bed to see.

Seth held up a tailored black dinner jacket and trousers, a crisp white dress shirt, a black bow tie and a pair of highly polished black leather shoes.

'I've now got to go off and fight a war with no weapons, wearing a tuxedo,' he growled.

I tried to stifle my laugh, but then I spotted what I'd been given . . . a sheer, short red lace cocktail dress, a soft black cashmere stole and a pair of scarlet killer heels.

I held up the shoes in shock. I never wore heels. Ever.

'No way!' I pronounced hotly.

'No choice, baby,' Seth sighed. 'The vortex ripped all your clothes to shreds. Come here . . . I'll help you put them on,' he added with a smirk.

A few minutes later we were standing in that stark hospital room staring at each other. There may have been a war on, there may have been a vicious psychopath determined to kill us, but the sight of Seth in his suit eclipsed all other thought.

'Wow!' I breathed.

He just blinked back at me, swallowing, his eyes dark and his fists clenched.

'You're staying here,' he said finally.

'What?'

'If you're anywhere near me wearing that dress, I won't be able to focus, and I can't afford –'

'I'll stay out of your way,' I assured him. 'I need to be near you, Seth, but I promise not to be a distraction.'

'You're always a distraction,' he murmured, reaching out for me and pulling me into his arms.

'So are you,' I smiled, tangling my hands in his hair and pulling his head down to kiss him.

'Oh, Eva,' he groaned, grabbing my face between his hands and deepening the kiss.

I clung to him, willing time to stop now. We'd had so few perfect moments together, and this was about as perfect as it got. After all the uncertainties, the jealousies and the insecurities, we'd somehow managed to cheat time and death, and won this tiny moment of bliss.

But time didn't grant many favours. And when Seth finally pulled his lips from mine, I knew that our perfect moment was over.

48

Comfort

Embankment, London

April AD *2045*

Someone was rudely shaking his shoulder. 'Hey!' growled Matthias crossly.

'Sorry, man,' shrugged the young barista. 'It's just that I need to lock up.'

Matt blinked up at him, trying to decipher the sentence. It wasn't until he smelt that distinctive aroma that he realized where he was.

The coffee bar. Elena's coffee bar.

He glanced around appreciatively. It had changed a lot since her time, of course. But it was still here. Warm and inviting.

He looked down at his hands. Clutched between his fingers was the crumpled bag of muffins he was supposed to be taking back to Nick and the others for breakfast.

'How long have I been asleep?' he gulped.

'About nine hours,' answered the barista, wiping down Matt's table.

'Zeus!' breathed Matt, staring out of the rain-spattered

window. Instead of the greenish storm-soiled daylight he'd arrived in, the world was now matt black outside.

How was he going to explain his absence to damn Nick-the-boss-Mullard?

Moments later, he was standing motionless under the shop awning, listening to the barista locking the door behind him, and running through possible excuses for his delay.

He got lost?

For nine hours! Unlikely. The Thames wasn't an easy landmark to lose.

Concussed by some flying debris?

Yes – that might work. It was vaguely plausible and a little heroic. A good solution.

Smiling into the bag of muffins, he decided that he could probably do with one more to fortify him for the walk back to the river.

49

Reconnaissance

Embankment, London

April AD *2045*

It was completely dark now, which meant Nick could put it off no longer. It was time to recce the Roman camp. He had hoped to wait until Seth returned – he could definitely use a decent soldier to cover him – but if Matthias had betrayed them he needed to find out sooner rather than later.

The wind was finally beginning to drop, so the flying missiles were few and small, and although it was still pelting with rain, making visibility poor, it would at least give him good cover.

Nick had endured hours of endless curses and complaints about hunger from Samuel and Jake. But, fortunately, their fear of ambush prevented either of them from leaving the safety of the camp to do anything about it. Instead they lay back and slept the afternoon away. Nick watched them ruefully: they weren't exactly the dedicated, loyal team he would have wished for, but at least they were finally quiet. So it was with some reluctance that he finally shook them awake. They were predictably tetchy.

'The bloody Greek still not back?' spat Jake. 'I'm dying of starvation here!'

Nick shrugged and shook his head. He wasn't going to share his fears.

'No sign of Eva and Seth?' asked Samuel.

'Nope,' he sighed.

'She was pretty banged up,' growled Sam. 'Jeez, I hope she pulled through.'

Nick glanced across at him and rolled his eyes. Clearly another Eva fan.

'We're going to have to proceed without them,' Nick said deliberately.

'No way,' responded Jake. 'We don't stand a chance against that number of Romans.'

'I'm going on a quick reconnaissance. I want to find out exactly how many we're up against.'

'No, man! You can't leave us here alone. You're the only one with a gun,' snarled Jake.

Nick briefly considered handing the pistol over, but the six bullets were too precious to risk in the hands of an ex-Belmarsh inmate.

'I need to know how many Romans there are,' said Nick quietly. 'And then we can make our plan.'

'You can go as soon as Seth gets back.'

'So you'd rather just sit here and wait for the Romans to attack?'

'They haven't so far.'

'They are bound to send a scout soon. I think you two should spread out, while I go down.'

'Or,' muttered Jake, 'we could jump in the river and head back to Parallon.'

'Don't you want to be rid of the Romans?' snarled Nick. 'Because if you jump into the water, you can bet your life they will jump straight in behind you, and our only opportunity will be lost.'

Jake glared at Nick through narrowed eyes.

Nick ignored him and continued. 'So – here's what we're going to do . . .'

He was just handing each of them a knife from their pitiful cache of weapons, when they heard a distinct movement outside.

They froze.

'Christ,' muttered Nick. This was it. They'd been out-manoeuvred, and were caught like rats in a trap. He pulled out his gun, trained it in the direction of the sound, and prepared to fire.

50

Defence

Embankment, London

April AD 2045

Seth twined his fingers round mine as soon as Nadia's weird little driverless car deposited us by the river and disappeared into the rain-swept night. But his action wasn't a brief display of affection. He was depositing a small knife in my hand.

'Managed to salvage that from the remains of your clothes,' he said. 'Do you remember what I told you about defending yourself?'

I nodded. 'Don't try to kill. Go for somewhere unexpected – eyes . . . er . . .'

'Crook of arm, back of knee, groin . . . and then run,' he filled in.

'In these shoes?' I grinned.

'They're the first thing you get rid of,' he said, his face deadly serious. 'Then you jump straight into the river and head back to Parallon. I'll meet you there.'

I clung to him, knowing that the scenario he was painting was far from certain.

'What if –'

He covered my lips with a finger. 'First we need to try and hook up with Nick,' he said, pointing to the bridge. 'I've no idea whether he's managed to hold his position, but I should think he'll have done his best to wait for me before trying to take on Cassius's army.'

'Cassius's whole army made it?' I croaked.

'No baby, twenty soldiers, maximum.'

'And there are only six of us,' I gulped.

'Five,' Seth corrected. 'You're not fighting.' His eyes were hard as they swept around, constantly assessing. 'Cassius currently has the numerical advantage, but with any luck he'll have been waiting for nightfall.'

'Why?'

'Better cover for a surprise attack. Our camp is on the bridge – difficult to reach in daylight without being spotted. But hopefully he won't want to risk an attack on the bridge at night either.'

'Why not?'

We walked in silence for a moment or two.

'Our attack in the arena unnerved him. He knows we are a small number, but has no idea what firepower we have, or our destructive range. I think he'd prefer to wait for us to attack him.'

'You can't be serious?'

'Don't forget, he has a taste for ambush, Eva.'

I shuddered, remembering our failed escape from Londinium.

'So presumably attacking him is exactly what we *won't* do?'

Seth kissed the top of my head. 'No – I think we should do precisely what he expects.'

'But –'

'At a time when he least expects it.'

'And when will he least expect it?'

'When he's given up waiting and is rethinking his strategy.'

'But that could take weeks.'

'No, it will happen tonight.'

I shook my head. 'Why on earth would he give up so quickly?'

'He's trapped down there. None of his men can leave their camp without being seen. They will be wet, cold, hungry, possibly mutinous . . .' As he talked, Seth dropped down on one knee and caked his hands in sludgy mud from the gutter, which he began smearing all over his white shirt.

'You're assuming too much, Seth,' I whispered, watching as his shirt gradually became indistinguishable from the dark jacket. 'How can you compete with twenty Roman soldiers? Even if you –'

'Just trust me, baby,' he murmured.

'Seth, I –'

'Shhh, Eva,' he breathed in my ear, suddenly pulling me tight into his body and pointing to a pile of windblown detritus shoved up against some railings on the bridge. 'Nick's camp,' he mouthed. 'We can't assume it hasn't been breached.'

He began edging us forward. We'd almost made it when my heel caught on a broken piece of wood and I stumbled. Seth caught me before I crashed to the ground, but I'd clearly just blown our silent approach.

Seth instantly pulled me down into the shadow of a large sheet of corrugated metal. His whole body had changed shape – it now completely tented me as he leaned forward with the tautness of a predator, a knife extending from his hand. We crouched in frozen silence waiting for the inevitable response.

Lightly touching my face, Seth nodded towards a corner of a perspex sheet. I swallowed hard.

Pointing straight at us was the barrel of a gun.

But instead of moving away, Seth was sheathing his knife.

'They can't see us here.'

'How do you know?'

'If it's one of Cassius's men, he would have taken a shot. If it's Nick, and he could see it was us, he would have holstered the gun. I think it's probably Nick, but we can't take the chance.'

Kneeling down in front of me, Seth took off my stupid shoes, and shoved them in his jacket pockets. 'Watch where you tread,' he mouthed, pointing to all the rubbish and broken bits of glass on the ground. I nodded as he gently got to his feet. 'Stay right behind me,' he whispered.

When we were close, Seth gestured for me to drop down behind what looked like the misshapen remains of a warehouse door, handed me my shoes, and then crept like a cat towards the little hideout. A second later he disappeared from view.

My heart pounded as I peered blindly into the darkness. 'Please let him be OK,' I silently chanted, not daring to take my eyes off the point ahead where I'd last seen him.

I didn't have to wait for long, because a few moments later his head popped out and he beckoned me over. I slipped on my shoes, flung myself towards his outstretched arms and allowed myself to be pulled inside.

It was even darker inside than out. 'Seth?' I gasped nervously.

I felt Seth fumbling around, and the next moment a torch beam lit up the tiny hideout and I was looking into Nick Mullard's grinning face.

'Bloody hell, I'd almost given up on you two!' he said.

'Sorry, man,' muttered Seth, slapping him across the shoulders.

'Eva!' Nick smiled warmly, reaching over and lightly touching my shoulder. 'Y-you look – er – good!' he added, his glance suddenly pausing on my crazy outfit.

I rolled my eyes at his ironic observation. 'I know, right! It was falling over the stupid shoes that nearly got me shot! Hey! Samuel and Jake! Good to see you!'

'Livia!' grinned Samuel, reaching over to pull me into a hug. Suddenly Seth's entire body was wedged between us.

'Hey, man! W-we're cool!' stammered Samuel, backing away.

Seth glowered around the hideout. 'Where's Matthias?' he barked.

'Good question,' Nick snapped back. 'Spilling our secrets to Cassius, no doubt.'

'What's that supposed to mean?' demanded Seth.

'Only that he went off to pick up some breakfast about ten hours ago and never came back.'

'Why the hell would you assume treachery?' Seth snarled.

'Why the hell wouldn't I? You do know he allied himself with the Romans in Parallon, don't you? So forgive me if I don't find his track record exactly encouraging . . . And if by some remote chance he was ambushed, how long do you honestly think he would hold out against Cassius's torture?'

For a moment Seth stared at Nick in silence, his jaw tense. Finally he murmured, 'I don't think Matt would betray us. Something else must have happened.'

I glanced anxiously between them. The air was thick with hostility. Not exactly the perfect vibe for an alliance.

Finally, Nick's posture relaxed. He shrugged and said, 'I was just on my way to recce the Roman camp.'

'Are they stationed under the bridge?' asked Seth tightly.

'Pretty certain that's where they are.'

'Do you have a head count?'

'Twelve or thirteen I think, though I don't know if they are operating as a team yet.'

'They will be . . . Damn. I'd hoped to play a waiting game with Cassius, but we can't gamble on Matt's loyalty,' sighed Seth.

Nick nodded, a look of relief washing over his features.

'We need to act fast,' continued Seth. 'Preempt any attack Cassius might be planning.'

'Strike blind?' gasped Nick.

'We don't have time for reconnaissance, and I'm prepared to go on your head count. I'd also stake my life you're right about them sheltering under the bridge. It's where I'd go in their position. Good cover along with protection from the weather.'

'But there are only five of us –' began Jake.

'Four,' corrected Nick, pointedly glancing in my direction. 'Eva's not a soldier.'

Would anyone ever let me forget?

'So how the hell are four of us going to take out thirteen Romans?' growled Jake.

'We split up,' said Nick quietly.

Seth cocked his head. 'I'm listening,' he murmured.

'We've managed to lose most of our weapons, but I still have a handgun with six bullets. I'm a bit out of practice, but with any luck I should be able to take out a Roman with each round, from a safe distance. Seven to four in close combat are much better odds.'

'Still nearly two to one,' I muttered nervously.

'I've survived worse,' said Nick.

'So have I,' murmured Seth.

'Well, I'm glad you're both so confident,' snapped Jake. 'I've seen those sadistic bastards at close quarters. They're insane. And what makes you think they won't use guns themselves?'

'If they had guns, I think they'd have already attacked,' responded Nick. 'They know they have the numerical advantage. The fact that they're waiting until dark means they're banking on close combat.'

Seth stepped out of the hideout, crouched by the railings and peered down at the riverbank below. I squeezed out of the shelter to join him. He absently pulled me into his side and kissed the top of my head, his gaze staying focused on the bank. He was in planning mode. I stared silently out at the water, picturing the forthcoming scene, and my stomach churned with anxiety. I was desperate to improve our odds.

'Seth,' I whispered suddenly. 'Are those canoes?' I pointed across the bridge towards a windswept pile.

'Looks like the remains of a boat-hire booth,' he murmured.

'If we could find something intact, could Nick approach their camp via the river?' I suggested tentatively. 'He could take them completely by surprise.'

Seth didn't respond instantly, but continued to stare out at the booth. Then he began nodding slowly. 'Could work,' he said simply.

*

Ten minutes later, Nick and Seth were hauling a reasonably undamaged canoe into the churning river. As soon as Seth had convinced himself the boat was watertight, Nick climbed in.

Holding the canoe tight against the bank, Seth said, 'Eva, do you think you'd be strong enough to paddle this canoe alone?'

'Sure!' I answered, delighted that I was finally being trusted to do something.

'OK then,' he frowned, staring dubiously at the turbulent water. 'Here's the plan. Sam, Jake and I will position ourselves near their camp. Hopefully before we have to go into close combat, Nick, you'll shoot as many Romans as you can from your position on the river. If they have some sort of visible patrol, you can pick them off one by one. If they're sitting tight under cover, we'll draw them out for you.'

'How will you do that, Seth?' I asked huskily.

'I'll think of something,' he shrugged dismissively. 'Eva, you'll be sitting really low in the boat behind Nick, while he fires from the river. When we go into hand-to-hand, you'll need to pull round on the canoe so Nick can join us. As soon as he's disembarked, Eva, you'll paddle back to the other side of the river. I'll come and pick you up from the boat booth the moment we're done with the Romans.'

I nodded and glanced up at him. I was just about to get into the canoe behind Nick when Seth pulled me towards him and kissed me hard. 'Eva, please stay low in the boat. The Romans could use bows or javelins.'

'I'll stay low as long as you stay careful,' I whispered, trying not to show him how scared for him I was.

'I'm always careful,' he murmured into my hair. 'But if – if

I don't make it back to you before light, head straight back to Parallon.'

Holding hard on to his hands, I pulled away to look into his eyes. 'You *will* make it back to me,' I whispered through gritted teeth. 'You will.'

51

Ambush

Embankment, London

April AD *2045*

Seth leaned over the bridge trying to watch Nick and Eva with pragmatic detachment as they paddled away from the bank. The canoe was by far the safest place for Eva right now. He hated putting her into the care of another man, but Nick was the only other person he trusted to protect her.

Sighing deeply, he forced himself to turn away from the receding boat and jogged quietly back towards the camp to round up the others. They needed to get in position.

Moments later he was creeping down the steps on the Roman side of the river. Pausing near the bottom, he placed himself deep in the shadows. Then he gestured for Sam and Jake to move to their posts: Sam near the top of the steps; Jake on the bridge.

From his new vantage point, Seth could just make out the barely disguised Roman camp tucked hard against the wall below the bridge. While Nick had made sure their shelter on the bridge looked like a random windblown collection of debris, the Romans hadn't bothered much with camouflage. They'd constructed a fairly comprehensive shelter, concentrating on wind and rain protection, using what appeared to be a couple of bent car doors, an advertising billboard and the splintered bow of a large rowing boat.

Seth couldn't see inside, but the interior was probably five times the size of Nick's hideout: certainly an adequate space for thirteen soldiers.

He glanced up and down the bank. Would Cassius be this overt, though – all his men piled into one obvious shelter? It all felt too easy. The perfect bait for an ambush.

So was there anyone in the shelter or was it some sort of decoy? A trap? He wasn't planning to go anywhere near it. Not yet. He'd wait. Eventually somebody would have to move.

His eyes scanned the water. There was so much cloud and rain in the starless sky that he could barely make anything out. The canoe was completely invisible to him. Which, thankfully, meant it would also be invisible to the Romans. And the noise of the rain and wind covered any sound the paddles might be making, so Nick and Eva's approach should be well masked. Seth prayed Nick would position the boat somewhere distant enough to keep Eva well out of harm's way. Cassius was unlikely to have considered the river itself as a combat location because he had no access to any boats on his side of the river. And Seth was sure that Nick wouldn't have missed any Romans crossing the bridge.

There was just enough light for Seth to be able to make out faint movements – the flutter of loose paper on the billboard, the swirl on the surface of the water as the wind and rain disturbed it. But the Roman camp remained resolutely still.

Had they abandoned it? Were they waiting somewhere else?

It was time to find out. Nick and Eva would be freezing out there, so he didn't want to delay any longer.

He signalled to Samuel on the steps above him. Sam nodded and crept up a couple of steps so that he could signal to Jake on the bridge.

A few moments later, a roof tile crashed on to the riverbank path, a little way along from the Roman camp. Seth tiptoed to the foot of the steps to listen out for any response. He instantly caught the urgent buzz of voices coming from inside the Roman shelter. Then a soldier emerged, armed with a shield and short sword. He began moving stealthily along the bank towards the place the tile had landed, but had barely managed ten paces when a shot cracked the air, and Seth watched with relief as the soldier fell.

There was a moment's stillness and then a second Roman emerged from the shelter to cautiously investigate. Seth smiled. This was pure luck. A 21st-century soldier, familiar with snipers, wouldn't be so stupid. A few seconds later, the soldier met exactly the same fate as his predecessor, and landed heavily on the ground nearby.

Two down. Four bullets left.

Before Seth had a chance to wonder if there were any men still in the shelter, one of the bent car doors that fronted it scraped sideways. Two soldiers slipped out and started running along the bank downstream – the opposite direction from the shooting.

Seth was just worrying whether Nick would be in range to target them, when two more shots rang out. One soldier fell. The other clutched his arm.

Three down. Ten to go. Two bullets left.

Seth glanced up towards Samuel, who nodded and gestured towards Jake. Seconds later Seth had Sam and Jake crouched behind him.

Nick and Eva watched from the river as the three of them moved into position. Nick was still feeling furious with himself for letting his fourth bullet go wide, but Eva was more concerned about a movement she'd just seen upstream of the two dead Romans.

'Over there,' she breathed, touching Nick lightly on the shoulder. His eyes followed the direction of her hand. Four Romans were creeping in the direction of the camp, towards Seth, Sam and Jake.

'And there,' she hissed urgently, touching his other shoulder. Nick turned his head. Another group of soldiers was also quietly on the move. They had fanned out, and were heading towards the same place.

'Shit,' muttered Nick.

'Do you think they've seen Seth?' Eva murmured.

Nick shrugged. He needed to get over there fast. Seth didn't stand a chance otherwise. 'Eva, I need you to paddle really steadily into the bank. I'm going to try and take the last two shots as we go.'

Nick quietly pulled his paddle into the canoe and squinted through the sights of his pistol. He couldn't afford to miss, so he wanted to wait until he was good and close.

Alone, Eva struggled to manage the boat. The water was choppy, the wind was strong, and paddling on her own was much more difficult than she'd expected. Nick had obviously been pulling much harder than she had, and it was all she could to stop the boat being drawn downstream by the fierce tide.

'God, I'm so sorry, Nick,' she gasped, struggling to improve her stroke.

Nick's mounting irritation at their slow progress instantly morphed into remedial action. Clicking on the safety, he holstered the gun and picked up his paddle, pulling them swiftly towards the shore. When they were no more than ten metres from the bank he stowed his paddle again, and gestured for her to keep the boat steady. A group of five Romans were about to reach Seth from his left, and what looked like four soldiers were approaching from the right. Nick cursed, then lifted his gun and aimed.

An instant later a Roman soldier had fallen to the ground. But now the others knew exactly where the shot had been fired from.

'Eva, get down!' hissed Nick, as a knife suddenly flew through the air towards them. Narrowly missing her chest, it embedded itself into the hull of the canoe. Nick reached out and heaved the knife from the wood, swiftly pocketing it. It was impossible to use the paddles from their prone positions on the floor of the canoe, and the tide was pulling them quickly downstream, but Nick started using his arms to try to steer the boat towards the bank. Eva quickly followed suit.

Seth cursed wildly when he caught sight of the knife being thrown towards the boat. He knew then that he had to deflect the Romans from their current course before Eva got hurt. Arming himself with a knife in each hand, Seth nodded to Sam and Jake, then charged.

The Romans were so focused on the river that the attack from behind took them completely by surprise. Seth managed to take down two soldiers in that first roaring charge, but now the entire troop turned on him.

Samuel stood in frozen shock as he witnessed the gladiator in action. He had never seen anything like it. Seth moved so fast, deflecting, ducking, dancing. Despite heavy, focused thrusts, not one sword made contact with him, not one man could get near enough to pin him down. Even when two of them tried to coordinate their moves by forcing him towards the wall, he feinted and, deftly kicking out a leg, swept them consecutively off their feet. When they were floundering on the ground, Jake rushed in, and had just managed to stab one in the neck when the other rolled over.

'Jake!' yelled Samuel, but his cry was too late. He watched in horror as a Roman sword buried itself deep into Jake's back. Jake's gurgled cry was thin; his death almost instant.

Samuel cowered into the wall. He wanted to go to his friend, haul him out of the fray, but fear kept him pinned to the spot. He wasn't a soldier and though, as a kid, he'd been a bit of a street fighter, he had no idea how to defend himself against the hefty weapons these Romans swung with such precision. The flick knife he held between his sweaty fingers looked like a flimsy child's toy compared to the weighty power of the weapons he was witnessing in action here.

Seth now faced four Romans, all wielding swords. Sam peered at the tangle of heaving bodies before him, and shuddered when he recognized among them two faces he'd hoped never to see again: Otho and Rufus.

Cassius's elite guard were vicious opponents, but so far Seth was holding his own. Sam could only marvel at his courage, speed and stamina. The spectacle was extraordinary. But Seth was tiring. He was dealing with too many, and had to fight defensively, so he was unable to bring the number attacking him down. How long could he single-handedly hold all four off, Sam wondered, staring guiltily down at the knife curled loosely in his hand.

With a sudden resolve Samuel took a deep breath and threw himself into the brawl. He'd just managed a small triumphant nick in the arm of an attacking Roman, when he heard Seth roar. Before he'd had a moment to register its meaning, he felt the full weight of a sword come down hard into his chest. An instant later the ground rose up to meet him, and the world turned black.

52

Impasse

Embankment, London

April AD 2045

'Eva, take the canoe back to the other side of the river and wait for us there,' instructed Nick as the boat bumped against the bank and he jumped out. From my curled-up position on the bottom of the canoe, I obediently started paddling my hands furiously to turn the canoe round. But some instinct made me lift my head and check out the state of play on the riverside.

The storm had brought the water level up so high that the normally towering bank was no more than a couple of feet above the waterline. Which meant I had a perfect view of the battle.

God, no! My throat closed up in horror. Seth was fighting alone. Surrounded by Romans. I tried to count them. It looked like four or five.

How the hell could I turn the boat round after seeing that? There was no way. I had to do something to help.

I crouched back down in the canoe to think, but because the water flow was so strong I immediately began drifting downstream. I started paddling with my hands to try and counteract the pull, but without Nick's powerful strokes I was having no impact whatsoever. Unless I could use a paddle I would be arriving in the sea in no time. I sneaked another look over the side of the boat. I'd already drifted quite a long way from the fight, but I could just make out Nick creeping towards Seth and the Romans.

Nobody seemed to be looking in my direction, so I sat up, grabbed my paddle and began pulling for all I was worth towards the bank.

It took me about five times longer than it would have taken Nick, and my arms and shoulders were shaking with the effort by the time the canoe finally nudged the bank.

Grabbing on to the concrete edge, I began hauling myself out, when a sudden swell of water pulled the boat from under me, leaving me dangling with my feet in the freezing river. Breathlessly, I heaved my sopping body on to the bank and turned to haul the canoe up after me, but it was already bobbing away on the furious tide. I had lost my only means of escape.

My great heroic rescue mission had begun really well.

Keep it together, I told myself, stumbling to my feet. I gasped out in pain and looked down. Perfect. I had just slammed my bare foot on to a pile of broken glass. Could I be any worse at this?

The riverbank was literally covered in litter of every kind. Squatting down for a few moments, I wiped the blood away, and started limping my way through the debris to the bridge. I'd drifted so far downstream that I'd cleared a small bend in the river, which meant I could no longer see the part of the bank where Seth and the Romans were fighting.

'Please be OK, Seth,' I chanted with every painful step until I finally rounded the bend.

'Oh God,' I groaned, when I took in the scene. Seth was fighting off two massive Romans. And not just any two Romans – he was facing Otho and Rufus. They had forced him into a corner. Seth had obviously managed to get in a few swipes – they were both bleeding – but his only weapon was a hunting knife, and they were using heavy swords. He was ducking and diving, and though I couldn't see any sign of blood on him, everything about the way they were attacking him boasted strength and toughness. They would never give up.

Nick was fighting close by, also with a knife. He, too, was battling defensively, and seemed to be moving uncharacteristically clumsily.

'Damn,' I breathed. He was injured and carefully shielding his left side. And the way the Roman was deliberately targeting him there told me how vulnerable he was right now. I looked around frantically for Samuel and Jake, but could see no sign of either of them.

If I could distract just one of the elite guard for even a moment, it would buy Seth the time he needed to deal with the other one. Then maybe he could help Nick.

But how could I distract them? I had a small knife, but if I were to get close enough to use it effectively, I'd freak Seth out, which was the last thing I wanted to do. I could try and throw the knife, but I'd never even chucked a dart at a board, so the chances of the knife hitting anything were zero. I could probably manage to hit a target with something bigger . . . blunter . . . like a rock. Yep – a rock would be awesome. I looked around for one and couldn't even find a brick. The only vaguely portable thing I could see was a splintered plank of wood. Obviously I couldn't throw it, but maybe I could swing it.

I heaved the piece of wood off the ground as quietly as I could and started sprinting towards the fight. I only had one chance to get this right, so I needed to be fast and accurate.

Seconds later I was smashing it as hard as I could into the back of Otho's skull.

And he went down.

I couldn't believe it.

Otho was down!

I stood in frozen shock for a second, and then just as Rufus turned on me, Seth buried the hunting knife in his gut.

'*Eva, get out of here, now!*' he yelled, catapulting himself round in response to a pained grunt from Nick.

Nick was now sprawled on the ground, his adversary standing over him, poised to strike with his heavy sword. But Seth dived straight for him, slicing through the tendons of his sword arm with his curved knife, provoking a roar of pain. The Roman's sword clanked uselessly to the ground. Seth stood panting over him, then dropped to one knee and sliced through his throat.

'Seth?' I whispered, as he got slowly to his feet. He stared at me for a moment, swaying slightly. Then he surveyed the ground around him, frowning. The three Romans lay prone at his feet, but he wasn't looking at them. His eyes were scanning around us feverishly.

'Where are the others?' he rasped.

'What others?'

'The rest of the dead!' Seth began to dash wildly along the riverbank. I moved to follow him, when suddenly I was jolted from my feet as a hand clasped tight round my ankle and jerked me backwards. I screamed as I began to lose my balance, and the sight of Otho's cold grey eyes underneath me did nothing to improve my stability.

'Get your damned hands off her,' snarled Seth, leaping across Otho's body, his curved knife instantly slicing through Otho's hand, then plunging into his chest.

As blood spurted from the wound, I instinctively jumped back . . . into a rock-solid body and pair of steely arms.

'You just can't stay away from me, can you, my sweet?' crowed the familiar voice at my back.

I closed my eyes.

'Cassius!' spat Seth from his crouched position on the ground. His voice was furious, but his eyes were totally focused on the large knife Cassius was holding against my chest.

'Familiar feeling of powerlessness, *slave*?' smirked Cassius.

Seth's eyes flicked between the knife and Cassius's face.

Cassius was right. The scene was sickeningly familiar: the three of us, the knife, the river. The only difference this time was that Seth had killed all Cassius's guards. And he hadn't been mutilated by Cassius's knife. He started to move carefully towards us.

'I wouldn't get any closer if I were you,' said Cassius very quietly. 'Not unless you are happy to see my knife slip.'

'What do you want, Cassius?'

'I think you know what I want, Leontis,' he snarled. 'And if you and your whore would just stay dead, we wouldn't be here now discussing it.'

'Sorry for messing with your plans, Cassius,' I hissed.

'Shut up, bitch,' he muttered, dragging my head back hard with a brutal tug on my hair. I gasped with pain.

'Now if you'll excuse me,' he went on imperiously, 'I wish to take my wife back to Parallon.'

'I can't let you do that,' stated Seth, moving into his path.

'Well, perhaps you'd prefer to watch her die here first?'

Seth jerked instinctively forward, but Cassius tightened his grip on me and pushed the knife blade deliberately through the flimsy lace of my dress. I flinched as it ripped the skin underneath.

I stared into Seth's wild eyes, hating the helpless rage burning there. 'Don't let him win, Seth,' I cried. 'We can't let him go back there.'

The tip of Cassius's knife instantly pushed against my chest again. I could feel blood seeping through the fabric, and I closed my eyes against the pain. Then I heard two simultaneous sounds. A gun shot and Seth's ferocious roar.

And I was falling.

53

Bodies

Embankment, London

April AD 2045

'Eva!' Seth's arms were round me, his breath hot against my cheek. 'It's over, baby!'

He was pulling me off the ground and untangling me from the monstrous weight of Cassius Malchus's body. I clung to Seth's shoulders as he hauled me to my feet. From the safety of his arms, I looked down at the man who had terrified me for so long. Blood gushed from a bullet wound just above one eye.

'B-but h-how?' I began, and then, hearing a movement behind me, turned to see Nick limping towards us, his gun still in his hand.

'Couldn't afford to mess that one up,' he smiled tightly. 'It was my last bullet.' His eyes flickered uneasily to Seth, who was shaking his head.

'That was a hell of a dicey shot for a rusty marksman, Mullard,' he muttered, pulling me hard into his body. 'If that bullet had gone wide –'

'I was too close to miss,' interrupted Nick. 'I wouldn't have taken the shot if there'd been any risk.'

Seth's fingers tightened against my arm. Finally he nodded slowly. 'Thanks, man,' he said huskily. 'I owe you.'

'We all owe you,' I added. Nick shrugged, and started heading over to check on Cassius's body, but his movements were awkward and he stumbled.

'Nick!' I gasped. 'Are you OK?'

He looked down dismissively at the blood seeping through his shirt. 'Just a flesh wound,' he answered. 'I'll be fine.'

The three of us stared down in silence at the body of Cassius Malchus: the man who had single-handedly destroyed so much in our lives.

'I can't believe he's finally dead,' I whispered, shaking slightly.

Seth's arms wrapped round my shoulders, and he pulled me into his rock-solid warmth. I closed my eyes and clung to him, the sudden sheer bliss of the moment almost taking my breath away.

'Christ!' gasped Nick, breaking through my euphoria. 'What the hell –?'

Seth and I jerked instantly back to the present . . . to the body lying on the ground below us . . . the body that was disappearing before our eyes.

'*No!*' I breathed, reaching for Seth's hand. But Seth had pulled away. He was desperately scouring the riverbank, picking up swords and shields and empty tunics. It didn't take a genius to work out what he was discovering . . . *All* the bodies had disappeared.

'Oh God!' I groaned. 'Do you think they're –'

'– back in Parallon?' growled Seth, shaking his head in confusion.

'I don't get it,' I murmured. 'Professor Ambrose was always

adamant that as soon as you left Parallon, your body would resume its previous physical vulnerabilities . . .'

'He was right about that,' muttered Nick, wincing as he touched the skin under his shirt. 'No instant healing here.'

'Yeah,' agreed Seth. 'If it hadn't been for Anton, I don't think Eva would have survived the vortex.'

'But Cassius clearly isn't dead,' I pressed.

'OK, then, we'd better get back to Parallon,' sighed Seth.

'What about Sam and Jake?' I asked.

Seth shook his head sadly. 'If Cassius is there, then that's where we'll find Sam and Jake . . . They fought bravely, Eva.'

'And Matthias?' I whispered.

Seth and Nick exchanged glances. 'Who knows what has become of Matthias,' said Seth quietly.

54

Wrong Side of the War

Embankment, London

April AD *2045*

By the time Matthias made it back to the bridge with his slightly stale provisions, the hideout was completely empty. He peered around nervously. Had Cassius attacked? He couldn't help feeling guiltily relieved that he'd managed to avoid that particular event. He definitely didn't want to face Cassius again – especially from the wrong side of a war.

Unsure quite what to do next, he decided to settle in and wait. He was just folding himself into a corner, when his buttock landed on something hard and sharp. Yelping with pain, he pulled the offending item out from underneath him, and stared at it in bewilderment. What in the name of Apollo was a high-heeled woman's shoe doing in the hideout? He felt along the ground, and found its partner. Holding both shoes in his hands, he stared at them contemplatively, trying to decipher this clue. A *pair* of shoes was much less random than a single one. They had to have been taken off in the hideout. And the only woman likely to be sheltering in the hideout was Eva. And if she had been here, Seth must have been too.

His heart began to race. *Seth had come back*. So what had happened to them? Matt looked around again, and came to the conclusion that if the Romans had attacked there was no way in hell that the shelter would still be standing, with a pair of shoes tucked inside.

Which could only mean that Seth had gone on to the offensive. Matt whistled through his teeth. There were so many Romans – would Seth really risk it? He suddenly felt a little guiltier about his absence. Not that Seth would have put him in any combat situation. Seth knew how much he hated fighting. But maybe he should have been here.

Zeus, Seth could have been injured. Of course he should have been here. It was his job to take care of Seth. Wherever he went.

Matt remembered how Nick had sat watching the riverbank. He had obviously believed the Romans were camped down there. Perhaps that's where they'd all gone?

He peered over the bridge railings. It was still raining hard, so it was difficult to see through the falling water in the dark, but he thought he could just make out some moving shapes. He kept himself tucked well down, and wondered what to do. If Seth was there, Matt ached to join him, but he really didn't want to go down and get caught by Cassius.

As his eyes squinted through the darkness, he began to make sense of what he was looking at. Three people. Two of them seemed to be wearing party clothes. One of them was definitely a girl . . . with long dark hair. No question who she was. Especially when Matt realized who she was attached to. By Hades, it was good to see Seth again.

Without another thought, he began bounding down the steps towards them. They seemed to be heading straight for the river.

Were they going back to Parallon already? He'd arrived just in time.

'*Seth!*' he bellowed. But the rain and the wind and the roar of the churning water completely swallowed up his voice.

They were definitely heading for the vortex. He knew the spot as well as Seth did. Desperate to reach them before they jumped, Matt battled his hardest against the wind, and pushed his legs until they shook, but by the time he reached the riverbank they had already disappeared into the churning murky water.

55

Curfew

St Mag's, London

13 February AD 2014

'Is the Crisp ever going to ease up on this damn curfew!' moaned Sadie, banging her fists on the desk and stomping across to her window to peer out at the swirling rain.

Astrid lifted her eyes and shook her head. 'Nah, he'll never let us out in this weather. It's a force-twelve hurricane out there.' Then she returned to playing the same four-bar riff she'd been repeating for the past two hours.

'*Astrid, for God's sake stop playing that song!*' yelled Sadie.

Astrid's hand stilled. 'Sorry,' she muttered. What the hell was wrong with her? Why had she got so fixated on the last song Eva sang? 'Must be this damn guitar!' she mumbled, pulling herself off Sadie's bed and propping the instrument against the wall.

Sadie glanced across at the bashed-up old acoustic. 'Have you had that since Eva . . . ?'

'Yep,' she said. 'Hid it when they came for all her stuff.'

'Figures,' nodded Sadie. 'I'm surprised she didn't take it with her, when she left,' she added pointedly. 'It was her dad's, you know.'

Astrid ignored the comment and ambled over to the window to join Sadie. 'Jeez, it's a miracle that bench is still standing!'

'It's bolted down,' responded Sadie. 'I think just about everything in the school is now.'

'Yeah, Crispin has definitely got a bit OCD since we lost the biology lab roof.'

'Him and the rest of the world,' muttered Sadie. 'Mind you, we still get a hell of a lot of junk blowing through. I had to move a damn tumble dryer from the bottom of the art room stairs last week!'

'Do you think it was still working? Everything I own is damp.'

Sadie shook her head. 'Nah. Door was missing.'

'Harry and me were just walking across to the drama studio last week and somebody's bloody barbecue hit the wall a few metres from the main entrance!'

'Oooh, don't talk to me about barbecues. I'm starving.'

'God, I could kill for a burger.'

'Won't find anywhere open.'

'Try telling that to Ruby and Omar.'

'Why would I talk to them?'

'They skipped out to McD's this afternoon.'

'Are they totally *insane*?'

'Not insane. Mean. They refused to take orders. And I only asked them to bring me back some nuggets.'

'Christ – the wind is picking up, maybe we should move away from the window?' suggested Astrid. 'I know the glass is reinforced and all, but the rattling is beginning to freak me out.'

'Yeah, you're probab– Shit, talk of the devil – there they are! Ruby and Omar! The Crisp will do his nut if he sees the – *Oh my God! Get out of the way!*' screamed Sadie, hammering desperately against the window.

But neither Omar nor Ruby could hear her. They couldn't hear anything above the wind and rain, and they were so busy trying to fight their way through the storm that they weren't looking up. So they didn't see the mangled child's scooter hurtling through the air towards them.

The handlebars struck Ruby on the side of her head. She didn't even have time to look stunned. She just fell like a stone to the ground.

Astrid and Sadie watched in horrified silence as Omar dropped to his knees beside her. He was shouting. Screaming. Thumping her chest. But Ruby remained resolutely still, her blood blending with the spilled chocolate shake, until the rain swept it mercilessly away.

56

Torn Apart

Parallon

I heard a low moan and twitched, sending pain signals darting all over my body. When a second, louder moan forced its way through the fuzzy blur in my head, I wondered vaguely why it sounded like it was coming from inside me. There was no doubt about the third moan. Appalled, I swallowed hard and tried to turn the sound into a cough. Bad idea. That just sent the pain signals haywire.

'Hell,' I croaked.

'Feels like it,' groaned a voice nearby.

I gingerly opened my eyes and turned my head.

'Nick.' It wasn't really a question. More a confirmation. So he didn't bother to answer. My last coherent thought as I blinked at his bloody, bruised face was that he looked wrecked.

The next time I opened my eyes I was being dragged along the ground. I came to with a start, and instantly began struggling against the grip under my arms.

'Eva, calm down! You're not helping!' muttered an exasperated voice . . . another voice I knew.

'Professor Ambrose?'

'Sshhh!' he hissed. 'We can talk once I've got you inside.'

I squinted around me, trying to make sense of the environment. It was hard to see anything clearly through the pounding rain.

Rain. My heart sank. It never rained in Parallon. Which could only mean we were still in London. But what was Ambrose doing here? And why were there so many shimmering Roman buildings? And . . . where was Seth?

I suddenly slammed my feet down, forcing Ambrose to an instant stop.

'What the –?' he exploded.

'Where is he?' I gasped, shaking myself out of the professor's grip and pulling myself to my feet. My grogginess had suddenly completely dissipated.

'Who?'

'*Seth!*' I cried, gazing frantically around me. 'Where's Seth?'

Ambrose clasped my shoulders to stop me pulling away. 'He's not here yet.'

'He has to be!' I gulped. 'We were together. Nick made it back, I saw him.'

'Nick's the soldier who was sprawled on the ground beside you?'

'Yes – is he at your house?'

'No, I imagine he's exactly where I left him. I'm not in the habit of picking up waifs and strays.'

'*Waifs and strays?*' I exploded. 'Nick's the man who put a bullet in Cassius's skull and saved my life!' I pulled free of Ambrose and broke into a run.

'Eva!' grunted Ambrose, chasing after me. But I was faster. After a couple of minutes I skidded to a stop next to the motionless body of Nick Mullard. Though his clothes were completely ripped apart, his face was no longer bloody and bruised. I crouched down next to him. He was breathing steadily.

'Hey!' I whispered, shaking him lightly on the shoulder. 'How're you doing?'

I saw the lump of his Adam's apple move. Then his narrowed eyes blinked up at me. 'Hey, Eva,' he smiled.

I exhaled in relief. He was fine.

'Another hero for your collection?' muttered Ambrose behind me.

'Definitely another hero,' I smirked, catching Nick's eye. He laughed and started pulling himself up. I grabbed his elbow to help him.

'Professor Ambrose, meet Nick Mull– Are you OK?' I asked as Nick stumbled momentarily.

'I'm good,' he answered, steadying himself and glancing down at his newly healed body in bemusement. Then he looked around, and his bemusement turned to confusion. 'Where are we, Eva?'

'Parallon.'

'But –' He was staring at the sky. The swirling rain.

'Looks like the weather followed us.' He was shaking his head. 'I can't believe we actually made it back through that hellhole . . . Seth already here?' he added, squinting towards the river.

I felt the blood drain from my head. Seth. Where was he?

My legs began to shake, but I forced them to carry me back to the river's edge. Crouching down, I stared desperately into the water. 'Please, Seth. Come back to me,' I whispered into its murky depths. The only movement was the pattern of rain pounding its surface. I stared blindly down for several minutes until the silence of his absence became unbearable.

'I'm going back in,' I muttered decisively. 'I have to find him.'

Pulling myself to my feet, I began searching my mind for the best destination. 2044? 2045? Where would he be? I didn't allow myself to consider even the smallest possibility that he was lost in the vortex. All my thoughts were centred on getting the destination date right.

Bad time for procrastination. Should have just gone for a date and jumped. Because by the time I'd decided on 2045, I'd been grabbed from behind.

'Eva, are you crazy?' shouted Ambrose.

'Where the hell were you planning to go?' Nick had suddenly added his weight to the arrest team.

'Back to London. Seth must be stuck there . . .'

Wrenching out of Ambrose's grip might have been possible – he wasn't that strong and was reasonably distractable – but Nick was another matter. Extricating myself from his iron grip was totally out of the question. But I continued to try.

'Seth will find his way back! I guarantee it,' he assured me. 'And if he gets here and finds I've let you jump back into the vortex, he'll crucify me.'

I gave up struggling pointlessly against their combined grip and stood in defeat, gazing down at the water below, willing Seth to appear.

57

Care

'*Just tell me how long we've been gone, Ambrose!*' Nick's furious voice hammered through my numbness.

I looked up. We were sitting at the table in the library. Ambrose was fussing around us while Lauren sipped from a glass of red wine.

There was a bowl of vegetable soup in front of me. How long had that been there? The room was unnervingly silent, Nick's question hanging unanswered in the air.

'Days? Months?' he hissed. 'For Christ's sake, man, there's a lot at stake here.'

'I'll answer your question when you've answered mine,' snapped the professor.

I sighed. 'Professor, what's the problem?'

'We had a plan,' Ambrose said through gritted teeth. 'You were supposed to bring Eva back here.'

'I'm here now!' I said wearily. 'Please, Professor Ambrose, just answer Nick's question.'

Ambrose rolled his eyes. 'You were gone five days,' he finally conceded.

'And what's been happening here?' asked Nick.

Zackary shrugged. 'Nothing,' he answered. 'No marching feet. No guards. No soldiers. No screams from the arena. The streets are deserted. Everyone's gone into hiding.'

'And Cassius?' Nick asked pointedly. 'Any sign of him over the last few days?'

Ambrose frowned. 'I thought Eva said you shot him.'

Nick shrugged non-committally.

'There's been no sign of anyone,' said Lauren.

'I think we'd probably know about it if Cassius was here,' Ambrose added impatiently.

Nick got to his feet. 'OK, then. I'd better go out and make sure.'

I bit my lip. 'Be careful, Nick!' I whispered.

'Always,' he grinned, touching my shoulder and heading for the door. 'Eat the soup, Eva!' he called over his shoulder. 'It's pretty good.'

I took a spoonful of the soup and picked at the roll next to it. Then I drifted again . . .

'Eva, please!'

I frowned and jerked back to the room. I was now on one of the sofas, a cold, undrunk mug of coffee in my hands; Lauren's face looming in front of me.

'The vortex, Eva. How stable was it?'

What could I say? Wild? Anarchic? Bone-crushing? Terrifying?

'What the hell do you think, Lauren?' I hissed. 'Seth hasn't come back . . . Doesn't that tell you everything? And if that fact isn't eloquent enough, it looks like the "disruptions" you predicted are under way. London was being torn apart by storms . . . and I've come back to rain in Parallon. Has that ever happened before, Professor?'

Ambrose shook his head. 'But it may have nothing whatsoever to do with the vortex –'

'Professor!' I choked. 'Why are you doing this? You're a genius scientist for God's sake! How can you deny the obvious?'

He shrugged. 'A scientist doesn't jump to obvious conclusions. There are alternative explanations for the weather –'

'Whatever explanations you want to come up with for the weather, Zackary,' interrupted Lauren, 'there is absolutely no doubt that the vortex is dangerously volatile.'

'As long as nobody uses it again, I'm sure you can keep it reasonably stable, Lauren,' said Ambrose firmly.

'Professor, you know as well as we do that the vortex is out of control,' I argued. 'Lauren can't fix it. It's going to blow. This rain – this is just a shadow of what Earth is enduring. And the vortex has to be the cause.'

He lifted his eyes to me, and his face looked suddenly haggard. 'What do you want from me, Eva?' he asked huskily.

'Your help, Professor. It's time.'

'How can I help? I am not an astrophysicist!'

'The virtual Parallon prototype on your computer –'

'What the hell do you know about that?'

'Not enough. But I'm pretty sure once I've pieced together the encrypted fragments I will know a great deal more.'

'Eva, stay with the subject!' cried Lauren. 'We're talking about an unstable wormhole here, not some virtual computer game.'

'Let me speak, Lauren,' I persisted. 'Professor, I think the virus, your Parallon simulations, the memory work – they are all connected –'

'Oh, for Christ's sake, Eva, grow up!' exploded Lauren. 'See what you've done, Zackary! You've given this kid the licence to speak with the adults like she knows something! But this is real bloody life! Not some game we're playing! We don't need to bring in irrelevant –'

'*Nothing* is irrelevant!' I shouted. 'Ambrose's Parallon simulation has screens of code for the streets, the buildings, the sky, the river . . . and somewhere – somewhere there will be the code for the vortex. Which I would say is relevant. It's all relevant. *Everything* is connected! That's the whole point – and the professor knows it! It's time to blow open all these secrets and half-truths. They're going to get everyone killed! We've got to –'

My rousing speech was cut off in its prime by the sound of the front door closing downstairs.

Seth?

Please God let it be him.

I dashed towards the stairs, but Ambrose was right behind me, shoving a hand over my mouth and pulling me back.

'What do you think you're doing, Eva?' he hissed in my ear.

I froze and allowed him to drag me against the wall behind the door. I glanced across the room and saw Lauren crouched beneath the table. Strange how fast I'd forgotten the fear of living under Roman rule.

We listened, our breaths held, to the quiet footsteps on the stairs . . . the pause at the library door. Then the slow turn of the handle.

'Anybody home?'

Not the voice I was longing to hear.

'Nick!' I breathed, slipping quickly out from Ambrose's hold and doing my best to rearrange my features into a welcoming smile.

Nick's eyes flashed between the three of us. 'Something happen?' he asked.

'We're just a little jumpy,' answered Lauren, pulling herself to her feet. 'Did you find anything out?'

Nick paced over to the window and stared into the darkness.

'No sign of Cassius,' he said finally.

I swallowed, my fists tight balls at my sides. 'Where did you go, Nick?' I asked.

'The arena, the forum, the palace . . .'

'The *palace*?' I gasped.

'It's just a building now, Eva,' he said gently. 'A deserted building. I went through it room by room.'

'*Every* room?' I whispered.

He nodded. 'I even did a bit of *redecorating* while I was there.'

My eyes closed. Cassius's torture chambers were gone.

'And you really saw no sign of him?'

'Cassius is not in Parallon,' Nick confirmed. 'And I couldn't see any of his elite guard.'

'So what happened to Seth's brilliant plan if you're still looking for Cassius and his guards?' asked Ambrose.

'The plan worked fine,' I growled.

'Well, then I'm guessing your friend Nick, here, can't be such a great shot.'

'Actually, Nick's shot on Cassius was fatal,' I hissed.

Ambrose narrowed his eyes at me. 'So what are you saying, Eva?'

'I'm saying that Seth and Nick killed all the Romans who followed us to London . . . and every single corpse disappeared.'

Ambrose blinked. 'But – but that's not possible.'

I shrugged.

Ambrose shook his head. 'I've been experimenting for years. As soon as we travel back through the vortex we reclaim *all* our physical frailties . . . we bleed . . . we age. I am living proof –'

'Well,' interrupted Lauren impatiently, 'if Cassius isn't *here*, then where the hell is he?'

The moment Lauren framed the question, some connection in my brain suddenly snapped into place. I knew exactly where Cassius was.

'He's in Londinium,' I breathed with cold certainty.

I glanced away from Nick's mystified expression to look at Ambrose and waited for him to put the pieces together. I knew he'd figure it out, it was just a matter of time. And a few moments later he shook his head and hissed out a breath.

'Of course!' he nodded, giving me one of his proffy 'commendable-effort' smiles. 'Eva's absolutely right.'

'B-but –' spluttered Nick, 'h-how would you know that, Eva?'

'Because Cassius isn't the only one to be killed outside time.'

58

Revelation

Ambrose's House, Parallon

'I think you're going to have to give our friends a little more explanation than that, Eva,' suggested Ambrose as he strode across to the kitchen. 'Coffee anyone?'

'Sounds good,' answered Lauren, rubbing her temples and sitting on one of the sofas.

'Let's all sit,' said Nick, leading me across to the other sofa.

I curled into the cushions and glanced nervously around. Nick and Lauren were politely waiting for me to share my revelation. I cleared my throat. 'I was sixteen when I was infected with the virus.'

'That was last year, was it?' asked Nick.

'I guess,' I smiled wearily. 'Though time doesn't seem quite so linear to me any more. It *was* last year, but a lot more than a year has passed in my life since then.'

'How did you get the virus?' asked Lauren.

I glanced over to the kitchen where Ambrose was pottering about noisily.

'Professor Ambrose came to our school and . . . infected me . . .'

'Intentionally?' growled Nick, his face darkening.

I hesitated and shrugged non-comittally. 'Anyway, I got very sick very fast. I woke up briefly in an ambulance, and then considerably later in a hospital bed . . . recovered. I was told that my survival was some kind of miracle, that only hours before I had lapsed into total organ failure and had flatlined for just under a minute. The haematologist had been ready to call time of death and was frankly bewildered by my complete recovery.

'But it wasn't complete. Not only did my body fail to heal properly, my mind was plagued with strange hallucinations.

'Then S-Seth . . .' I swallowed hard, and forced myself to continue. 'Then Seth turned up at St Mag's and recognized me. He helped me understand that my weird visions were actually memories of another life – a life in Londinium, which I'd shared with him. But neither of us could figure out how my two lives connected. I was Eva, but I had also been Livia.'

I glanced up as Ambrose clattered a tray of coffee and biscuits on to the low table between us.

'But you now remember arriving in Parallon the first time, don't you, Eva?' he prompted.

I nodded. 'I think I've sorted out more or less all my memories now, and pieced it all together. When the professor first gave me the virus I died, like everyone else who gets infected. And like everyone else, I arrived in Parallon. I lived here in this house, then travelled with the prof through the vortex to Londinium, where he introduced us to the Romans as Ambrosius and Livia. Not long after he left me with Flavia and Domitus, I met Seth . . .' I stopped speaking as my throat seized up again.

Nick put a cup of coffee between my hands and wrapped his fingers round mine. 'Drink this,' he murmured gently.

I swallowed the coffee and stared down at my cup for a moment.

'The last thing I was supposed to do was fall for a gladiator – that definitely wasn't the plan. I couldn't even begin to imagine how furious you'd be, Professor. Not to mention Domitus and Flavia. And their fury was nothing compared to Cassius's. But how could I have predicted Cassius's terrifying obsession with me? When he proposed marriage, I knew I should have tried to escape, but by that point I – I couldn't leave Seth. Then somehow they all found out about Seth and me, and I was taken to Cassius's palace, imprisoned and f-forced to m-marry him.'

'Christ, Eva –' began Nick.

I put up my hand to stop him; I had to get through this. 'When Cassius took me, Seth should have abandoned me. Cassius was horrifically powerful and – well, you've all seen what he's like – he ruled Londinium exactly the same way as he ruled here . . . but Seth was crazy fearless. He worked out a plan for us to run away together. We were to take a boat from the Thamesis dock at midnight. But someone betrayed us. We were ambushed . . .'

I clenched my fists as I relived that ghastly night. 'Cassius started with Seth. He got his guards to h-hold him down, then kicked him and slashed him over and over with his long curved knife until Seth was barely conscious. Then he turned the knife on me.' I unconsciously touched my neck. 'I don't remember what happened after he c-cut my throat.'

'You don't remember what happened to you?' asked Lauren.

I shook my head.

'Did you ask Seth?'

I nodded. 'He told me I died. He told me he crawled over to die next to me, but assumed they had taken my body . . .'

'So you think you disappeared –' Nick prompted.

'Yep, that's exactly what I think. I'm pretty sure that when I died in Londinium, I disappeared from there and returned to my own time . . . to my dead body in that hospital bed. I became the miracle the haemotologist couldn't understand . . . the girl who died and came back to life.'

'So you think Cassius has now returned to his own death-bed?' said Nick.

'I do.'

'Do you have any idea how Cassius would have got the virus in the first place?' asked Lauren.

I blinked . . . Good question . . . Only a time-traveller could have infected him . . .

'*Oh God!*' I choked as the final piece of the puzzle suddenly slotted into place. 'It was *me*. I gave the virus to Cassius . . . and Seth! *I'm* responsible for both of their deaths!'

'No, Eva,' snarled Ambrose. 'You can't take responsibility for Cass–'

'I was his wife,' I whispered, not daring to look at any of them. 'Not a day went past when he – he didn't make me bleed.' I swallowed. 'Or it could have been the knife he used on Seth and me the night he killed us both . . . It would have been covered with my blood . . .'

'But Cassius didn't die that night, Eva,' said Ambrose gently. 'When you failed to come home I went back to Londinium to look for you. By the time I arrived you'd been missing for months. And Cassius was still alive.'

My head jolted up. 'He didn't have the virus, then?'

'He was clearly dying . . . and the symptoms were extremely similar . . .' said Ambrose. 'But apparently he'd been sick for weeks.'

'So Seth was right,' I muttered.

'About what?'

'The age correlation. Cassius was out of the optimum age range. When Seth took his blood samples at St Mag's he found that most of the teachers were totally immune to the virus, but a few just needed a longer incubation period. Just our luck that Cassius turned out to be one of those.'

'Well, thank God he's out of the picture now,' sighed Nick.

I nodded slowly, then stared deliberately down at my hands. I kept my eyes fixed down because otherwise I knew that Nick would be able to read the fear in them. Cassius *wasn't* out of the picture and he never would be. Not until he was finally, truly dead.

I was bone weary but sleep was the last thing on my mind when I eventually headed up to my room. I had spent hours gazing out of the window at the river, praying for Seth to emerge from the water and make it home. I needed him so much. And I needed to talk to him. There was too much going on in my head – I couldn't compartmentalize it. What was my priority? Ambrose's lab? Cassius?

My brain told me that I should be trying to fix the vortex. But my gut told me that Ambrose and Lauren would do everything in their power to prevent me doing any coherent work on it. I'd stupidly admitted to Ambrose that I'd hacked into his computer, so he would already have changed all his access codes. It could take me days to get back in.

In the end I decided that my best option was honesty. I would tell him what I knew, what I feared, and what I would have done if he'd let me. And hope to God he did it himself. Then I wrote it all down in a letter.

A goodbye letter.

I didn't tell him where I was going. The last thing I wanted was for anyone to try to follow me. I had enough on my conscience.

I left the house just before dawn. As I headed towards the river, the rain hammered horizontally against my body. This did not bode well for the state of the vortex. But I didn't fear the vortex any more. I didn't fear Londinium. Or Cassius. Because I didn't fear death. I'd confronted it too many times now. It held no secrets. My only fear was failing the people I cared about, and being condemned to exist in a world without the one person who made me whole and happy.

As soon as I'd fought my way through the storm to the swollen river's bank, I replaced my jeans and hoodie with an ornate roman dress and cloak. Then I added a strong leather belt with two holstered knives – one long and curved to rival Cassius's, and a smaller dagger that could be more easily hidden. Hopefully at least one of the knives would survive the vortex and keep me company on this final quest.

As I stood by the water's edge, I allowed my mind to drift momentarily to Seth, his perfect, beautiful face lit by that strange and compelling blend of tenderness and heat. I closed my eyes and pictured another life – a life we could have spent together. Not in Londinium, where Cassius would have torn us apart . . . not at St Mag's, where illness, stupid jealousies and insecurities constantly tormented us . . . but here in Parallon . . . a free Parallon, where we could have laughed and learned and loved forever. But we'd been doomed from the start, two star-crossed lovers, always separated by time and space. There was never a perfect world for us, just a handful of snatched moments, filled with impossible promises and hope.

I swallowed hard, swiped away the tears that were stupidly gathering, and pushed all sappy, unhelpful thoughts away. I had one last job to do.

59

Rescue

London

Seth jerked into consciousness when his body slammed hard against stone. Groaning with pain, his mouth was suddenly filled with churning, bitter water . . . river water.

Surfacing, he forced his eyes open and squinted against the torrential rain and watery grey light. As his brain slowly began to function, his unease grew. He could make out tall, angular buildings. Rectangular squares of electric light. What had happened? Why was he still in London? He should be in Parallon. How had he failed to get back there? And . . . and . . . where was Eva?

His eyes frantically scanned the choppy water. He was totally alone. Had the vortex just spewed him straight back into 2045? He noticed that the river was no longer running below the bank; it was spilling out on to the path, creating a weird wonderland of semi-concealed objects – benches with no legs, half-submerged sculptures. But there was the bridge, still standing proud above the higher water.

The churning waves surged and Seth was once more thrust against the submerged river wall. This time he clung to it and rolled on to the watery bank. He sat, half submerged in freezing water, dazed from the vortex ordeal, and tried to make sense of the deluged world he now surveyed.

A part of him knew he needed to return to the vortex and try to find his way back to Parallon and – gods willing – Eva. But the totally exhausted, aching, bleeding part of him needed time to recover. So he waded along the bank to a half-submerged bench and lay down.

'Seth? *Seth, brother!*'

Seth twitched back to consciousness. Someone was shaking him hard, which neither his flayed skin nor his aching limbs appreciated.

'Aggh!' he moaned.

'Seth, open your eyes, man! We've got to get out of this weather.'

He blinked awake. 'Matt?'

Matt was shivering against the bitter wind, and trying to pull Seth off the bench. 'Y-you've g-got to m-move!'

Seth tried to sit up and focus on what Matt was saying, but an icy gust nearly forced him back down again. He'd just about dragged himself to his feet, when a bicycle flew past his head and landed in the water a few metres away.

'Zeus!' he gasped. 'The hurricane's starting up again.'

Matt didn't answer. He'd begun wading towards the bridge. 'Move, Seth!' he shouted.

Crouching against the howling wind, Seth followed Matt up the rain-slicked steps. When they arrived on the bridge, he stared in bewilderment. This wasn't 2045 as he'd initially thought. The skyline was wrong. The half-drowned abandoned cars were wrong.

'Matt – any idea where we are?' he shouted. But the wind swallowed the question and he didn't bother trying to repeat it as Matt was entirely engaged in trying to stay upright. When it became obvious that he was about to lose the battle, Seth grabbed Matt's shoulder and hauled him forward, pulling him into the shelter of a doorway.

'I think we may have landed in Eva's time,' gasped Seth, squinting against the flailing wind and rain.

Matt gazed around. 'D-do you think she's h-here too?'

Seth froze in horror, his eyes widening. 'Zeus!' he cried, staring wildly towards the river. 'She can't survive her own time.'

'Sh-she knows th-that, Seth,' shivered Matt. 'She'd head back into the vortex.'

Seth shook his head. The vortex was so confusing and agonizing that Eva could be tempted out of it. 'She may have headed for St Mag's,' he said wearily. When he'd landed in his own time, his weak legs had carried him straight to the place he knew best. 'Please hold on, baby,' he whispered, as he began pushing through the storm to find her.

60

Tremor

St Mag's, London

14 March AD *2014*

Astrid sat in the middle of her bedroom floor, shoulders swaying to the pounding rhythm of Livid Turkey blasting at full volume from her pride-and-joy JBL speakers. Strewn chaotically around her, vibrating in solidarity, were her clothes, books and instruments. Despite the two open suitcases, she wasn't packing. She was staring blankly at her bass guitar, wondering what had happened to her life.

Just a few short months ago her world was totally rocking, and her only worry was whether Theo was going to sign the Astronauts to his record label before or after the school summer holiday.

Now – *everything* sucked. Eva was gone. Ruby was dead. The whole world had slipped off-kilter.

She closed her eyes and leaned her head against the wall, determined to let the music blank out her fear. There was something so soothing about the heavy bass lines vibrating through the floor . . . actually, shuddering through the floor . . . no – *rocking* through the floor.

Her eyes widened. Oh shit. It wasn't the speakers making her suitcases bounce. Everything was moving . . . sliding across the parquet . . . her books . . . her guitars . . . her laptop. She was jumping up to catch the coffee mug as it ricocheted off her desk when a crash and the sound of breaking glass down the hall made her freeze. Grabbing on to the desk, she gazed around the room, watching as her clock and lamp smashed off her bedside table on to the floor.

She held her breath, counting slowly in her head until the vibrations began to still.

Seventy-four.

Longer than last time.

She cautiously let go of the desk and moved over to her iPod to turn off the music.

Which meant she could now hear the wild rattling of her window frames.

'Bloody wind,' she sighed, standing up and walking over to the clattering window. 'Please do your best to keep the damned weather out for one last night, would you?' she muttered, moving over to haul the heavy-duty curtains shut. She headed back to the only visible bit of floor in her room.

'Stupid damn climate,' she hissed, throwing a pair of high-tops into a case.

The climate was now sitting right at the top of Astrid's Suck list. If it didn't improve soon, London would be entirely under water. Not just London. The whole of the UK was flooded. And you'd have to be deaf, blind *and* living underground not to know that the nightmare was spreading across the world. Even countries known for their completely stable climates were now being rocked by tsunamis, hurricanes, devastating storms . . . and earthquakes.

Astrid had got so sick of flipping TV channels to avoid the news or the succession of doom-mongers urging people to escape the final Armageddon and head for the mountains, that she'd thrown her coffee cup at the common-room TV last week and smashed the screen. It had almost been worth the five days in detention.

Until yesterday, Dr Crispin had remained adamant that St Mag's was one of the safest places in Europe to be. London didn't sit on any fault lines, and the school had been built on a hill. The building had withstood Thames flooding and storms for five hundred years.

But now even the Crisp had caved and given the word to evacuate. The clamour of anxious parents, the rising water levels and the shutting down of transport systems had finally shaken his resolve.

'What a wuss!' muttered Astrid, chucking a couple of philosophy books into a suitcase.

Her bedroom door suddenly crashed open. '*Astrid!*' gasped Sadie, rushing in. 'Guess who just –'

Before Astrid even had time to stand up, Rob and a scrum of his housemates were tumbling into her room.

When they finally separated, Astrid paled.

'Seth?' she breathed, watching in shocked silence as they dragged him, Matthias and about fifteen gallons of rain and river water across her floor.

Then her voice returned. 'For Christ's sake, guys! The last thing my guitars need is a damn bath! Harry! Get some towels!'

'Astrid,' hissed Rob, moving close to her ear, 'we'd better call that damn woman.'

Astrid chewed her lip uneasily. 'You mean Jennifer Linden?'

He nodded. 'Direct order if you remember – the moment Wonderboy returned.'

61

Choices

Jen was in a foul mood when Rob met her at the school gates. It had taken her well over two hours to wade her way through the only high-ground route to get there, and she was tired, hungry and soaking wet. It was clear Rob's mood wasn't much better.

'About time!' he grumbled. 'Seth may have arrived half dead, but it's not been easy keeping that bastard contained in Astrid's room.'

'Wow, you've got it bad,' snorted Jen.

'What?' sniffed Rob defensively.

'You're gonna have to get over her, Rob. She's not coming back . . .'

'Well, what's *he* doing here, then?'

Jen frowned. 'Good question . . . Haven't you asked him?'

Rob was silent.

'Jesus, Rob! When are you going to get it into your skull that Seth and Eva –'

'Whatever,' snapped Rob, furiously marching ahead of her towards Astrid's door.

'Well, do me a favour,' hissed Jen, moving up behind him and grabbing his shoulder, 'just try and keep a lid on that testosterone fest going on in there, and let me do my job. I need answers that only Seth can give me.'

Rob knocked on Astrid's door, which instantly triggered a thunderous cacophony of shouting, banging and swearing.

'OK, we're good to go,' puffed Astrid, opening the door a few moments later.

Jen gingerly peeked her head inside and saw six teenage guys in a writhing scrum on the ground.

'What the —?' hissed Jen.

The pile suddenly erupted and Seth emerged from the middle, sending the boys around him flying. As soon as he was clear, he made straight for the door, saying, 'Happy, Astrid? I waited as requested. She's seen me. Now I'm leaving.'

Jen immediately stood in front of the door, blocking his path. 'Seth,' she groaned. 'It's taken me forever to get here. I've had no lunch . . . and I'm way too weak to beg. So please, just give me *five minutes* of your time!'

Seth moved her gently out of his way and opened the door. 'Sorry, I don't have five minutes —'

'*Please*, Seth. Eva wanted me to talk to you.'

Seth blinked. 'You know Eva?' he rasped.

Jen had played her only card and, thank God, it had been the ace. She'd witnessed Seth's desperate anguish when he'd found Eva dying in a pool of blood, but she hadn't been certain about the depth of his devotion until this moment, where the mere mention of her name had completely deflected him from his course.

'Is there some place we could talk?' she murmured, her eyes darting across at the wrapt audience now literally gaping at them.

Seth's instincts were warring. He needed to get back to the vortex, but how could he refuse to fulfil any wish of Eva's? He couldn't. So releasing a slow breath, he lifted his chin and fixed his clear blue gaze first on Rob, then Sadie, then all of Rob's friends. Their expressions seamlessly shifted from enthralled to serene, as one by one they started filing from the room. But just as Rob was stepping through the door, Astrid lunged forward and dragged him back in.

'I have no idea what you just did to them, Seth,' she hissed defiantly, 'but Rob deserves to be included. He was there that night at the Underworld. He loves Eva too.'

Rob slumped against the wall in dazed confusion. Seth glowered. He definitely didn't need reminding about Rob's feelings for Eva.

'What the hell was that, Seth?' breathed Jen, trying to get her mouth to close. 'Some kind of hypnosis?'

Matthias, who lay sprawled across Astrid's bed, barked a quick laugh. 'Zeus, Sethos! Even with one foot in Hades, you can control an entire room. Not bad.'

'Won't last long,' responded Seth wearily. Collapsing into a chair, he lifted his face to Jen and gazed at her through narrowed eyes. 'I've seen you before. With Nick Mullard . . . at one of Eva's gigs. You were watching her.'

Jen nodded. 'I was also there the night Cassius –'

Seth's eyes suddenly flared with such a fierce and terrifying rage that Jen couldn't finish the sentence. She cowered against the door frame and didn't dare move until his posture eased and his breathing settled.

'So, what do you want from me?' Seth asked finally.

'Where do I begin?' Jen murmured. 'So many questions . . . OK . . . *Nick* . . . What happened to him after he disappeared? I-I –' Jen started gulping and couldn't bring herself to say any more.

'You and Nick – were t-together?' asked Seth in surprise.

Jen nodded. 'Is – is he . . . alive?'

Seth's eyes tightened. 'I hope so.'

'D-did he make it to P-Parallon?' Jen's face was a mask of tension.

'Who told you about Parallon?' whispered Seth.

'Eva.'

Seth inhaled sharply. Eva had told Jennifer Linden about Parallon. She had also wanted to tell Mullard. Seth would never forget the terrible outcome of that argument. There was so much he and Eva hadn't yet spoken about. So many words left to say. His chest ached at the thought that they might never get the chance now.

'So – did Nick survive the virus?' persisted Jen.

'Yes,' said Seth. 'He made it to Parallon.'

'Parallon? What the hell are you two talking about?' demanded Astrid.

'C-can you take me to him, Seth?' continued Jen, totally ignoring Astrid's interruption.

Seth shook his head.

'Why not?'

'Because there's only one way to get to Parallon, Jennifer.'

'I know there is. And I want to take that way.'

Seth shook his head again. 'You don't know what you're saying – what you're asking.'

'Of course I do. And the trade is worth it.'

'You couldn't be more wrong, Jennifer. Parallon is no paradise. I don't even know if Nick is there.'

'What do you mean? You said he made it . . .'

'He did. But we had to leave . . . We were on our way back there and we got separated. I lost him . . . I lost Eva –'

'You didn't lose her, Seth,' snarled Rob. 'You killed her!'

'Rob, keep up!' snapped Jen. 'I know you've just had your brain zapped, but try and remember what you saw. Eva didn't just die in Camden. She disappeared. She went somewhere else.'

Seth ran his hands through his hair. 'I have to try and get back there –'

'Take me with you, Seth. *Please!* I can't stay here any more. Look around you! This world is turning into a kind of hell . . . And I know for a fact it's only going to get worse,' she added quietly.

'W-what do you mean?' asked Astrid.

Jen's face twisted as though she was struggling with herself. Finally she let out a shaky breath. 'I work in a newsroom, and every meteorologist, geologist and seismologist is saying the same thing . . .'

'W-what are they saying?'

'That the cranks have got it right. We *are* heading for some Wrath-of-God-type Armageddon.'

'What the hell's that supposed to mean?' snorted Rob.

'OK – let me try to explain this simply. We. Are. All. Going. To. Die,' snapped Jen.

'Huh! So glad to finally meet a journalist who doesn't sensationalize the facts!' Rob said with a sneer.

'I wish to God I was exaggerating,' she whispered. 'Nobody understands why it started happening. But everyone agrees that it *is* . . . some weird global butterfly effect . . .'

'The so-called butterfly effect is *theoretical*, Jen! It only exists on paper,' hissed Rob.

Jen sighed. 'It stopped being theoretical when a random, monumental series of electromagnetic charges triggered a whole kinetic sequence of natural fracking events . . .'

'Fracking isn't a natural event,' contradicted Astrid.

Jen was impressed. These St Mag's kids weren't stupid. 'True. Normally. But –'

'But – what? Some crazy fracker miscalculated his charge, and triggered the end of the world? I'm sorry, Jen, but I can't –'

Jen laughed humourlessly. 'No, Astrid. I know I said *butterfly effect*, but we're talking about the kind of power surge that burns up planets – enough power to reverberate across the entire Earth's core.'

'So all those earthquakes and typhoons . . .'

'Yep – not to mention volcanoes. They've just begun a mass evacuation of Wyoming because of an earthquake swarm at Yellowstone. It looks like the volcano is about to blow . . .'

'Yellowstone?' gulped Astrid. 'But that's a *supervolcano*!'

Jen shrugged. 'When something screws around with tectonic plates . . .'

'*Christ!* But wouldn't that mean *mass extinction*?'

For several moments the only sound was the wind beating

furiously against the window. Seth moved wearily across the room, sat down on the edge of Astrid's bed and put his head in his hands.

'Why haven't we all heard about this, then?' whispered Rob. 'Why only you? You're lying, Jen. That's what journalists do, they lie –'

'I wish I was lying,' exhaled Jen. 'The reason you haven't been told the truth – and believe me as a news reporter I think this sucks – is because we've had an international press embargo, a gagging order . . . Newspapers, radio stations, TV companies all guaranteed instant shutdown if this news leaks.'

'But *why*? We have a right to know.'

'You're a bright kid, Rob. Just think about it for three seconds: think mass panics – people are still being relatively civilized about the food shortages, the transport chaos, the evacuations. But imagine what will happen once they know the truth. We'll have total chaos. And what would be the point in telling everyone? We can't do anything to stop it. When the world is either submerged, burning up or split apart, even the handful of survivors will probably end up starving to death. Nobody is going to make it.'

Matt, Astrid and Rob stared at her in horror. Seth alone sat in frozen recognition of the truth . . . the world was on the brink of destruction and he himself was ultimately responsible. If he hadn't been monumentally careless and allowed Matthias to follow him into the vortex that one time, it would have never reached this level of instability. And Seth had no doubt that this current global disaster was entirely the result of the unstable vortex.

Matt slid across the bed towards Seth and slapped him across the back. 'Seth, man, tell this woman she's talking like a crazy person!'

Seth flinched. 'Are you *ever* going to be able to see, Matt?' he asked wearily in Greek. 'You're not a boy any more, yet you've somehow failed to become a man.'

'W-what is that supposed to mean?'

'Do you really have to ask?'

'Don't you dare patronize me, Leontis! Yes, I want to know what you mean by that statement. Because when I last looked – with both eyes working pretty efficiently – I was in fact most definitely a man.'

Seth stared back at him. 'Would a *man* be able to look in the mirror after abandoning and betraying his friends? Would a *man* avoid conflict at any cost? Would a *man* welcome his enemy into his house and let him piss on his food? Would a *man* desert his outnumbered brothers in their fight for survival? Would a *man* with two eyes in his head not be able to see what everyone else sees? These people here are enduring this catastrophe because *we* allowed the vortex to be breached: you and me, Matthias. This is *our* fault.'

'*We* didn't do this; the Romans did.'

'Who opened the door to the Romans? Who showed them the way?'

'I don't see the point of this, Seth,' grumbled Matthias. 'You always over-think everything. You'd take responsibility for the sins of the whole damn world –'

'*Well, somebody has to!*' shouted Seth, looking around helplessly.

'OK then, if Jennifer's right, maybe we *should* take her back to Parallon. Maybe we should take the whole school. Hell, we could take the whole damn city.'

Seth went rigid. Matthias was suggesting systematic genocide.

'Hey, you two!' exploded Astrid. 'Out of the loop here! I'd really appreciate a bit of English right now.'

Seth and Matt sat silently staring at each other for a few more seconds and then turned to face the others.

'So what was that all about?' snapped Jen. 'I heard my name mentioned.'

Matthias glanced at Seth defiantly and said, 'I was just arguing your case.'

'About what?'

'About taking you to Parallon.'

Jennifer looked at Seth. 'What's your problem with it, Seth?'

Seth shook his head in disbelief.

'He's just a little squeamish,' sniffed Matthias dismissively.

'*Squeamish?*' bellowed Seth. 'Surprisingly, *yes*! I am a little squeamish about *killing* you, Jen.'

'Oh, please, Seth. Nothing comes more naturally to you than killing!' argued Matthias.

Seth stared at Matthias as though he was seeing him for the first time. Then he took a deep breath and began speaking as though he were teaching a small child. 'Yes – I was forced to injure, maim and kill people day after day in the arena. If I hadn't killed them, they would have killed me. That was survival. But not one day has passed since then that I have not begged their souls for forgiveness. Their blood will be on my hands for eternity.'

'Oh, come on, Seth! You've spent the last few months in Parallon training a whole army to maim and kill efficiently!'

'*In order to survive!* As a gladiator and a soldier you do what you must. But don't ask me to kill innocent people.'

'Even if killing them is the only way they can survive?'

Seth moved over to the rattling window and stared out at the horizontal pelting rain. Then he leaned his forehead against the glass and smashed his fist against the wooden frame.

Jen moved over and put a hand on his shoulder. 'When Eva was dying, you saved her. You took her to Parallon. Now we are dying, Seth. Won't you save us?'

62

Suicide Mission

Parallon

'Where is she?' roared Ambrose as he stormed through his house, waving a piece of paper in his hand.

'Where is *wh*o?' snarled Nick, slamming out of his room. He'd had about all he could take of Ambrose's histrionics.

'*Eva*, you fool! She's gone!' Ambrose bellowed.

Nick paled. '*What?*'

'She left in the night,' sighed Ambrose, running a hand impatiently through his already dishevelled hair.

'You sure she wasn't taken?' asked Lauren, pulling on a robe and joining the men in the kitchen.

'She left a note. Anyway, the security cameras recorded her walking out alone.'

'How long ago?' asked Nick.

'Three hours, twenty-three minutes.'

Nick ran down the stairs, opened the front door furiously and stared out at the rain. 'Did she say where she was going?'

Ambrose shook his head. 'She didn't need to,' he murmured from the top of the stairs.

Nick blinked at Ambrose. 'I've no idea what you mean.'

'She's gone after Cassius, of course,' Ambrose spat.

'Why would she do that? She herself worked out he's safely back in Londinium.'

'*Safely* is a surprisingly ambiguous word when used in conjunction with Cassius,' mocked Ambrose.

'But how could he do any real harm?'

'By becoming immortal again, obviously. Which is exactly what would happen if he managed to acquire the virus.'

'Who could infect him in Londinium?'

Ambrose shrugged. 'He was infected for several months before he died – who knows who he managed to pass the virus on to during that time.'

'Christ,' sighed Nick. 'And Eva worked this out.'

'She also has a ridiculous and completely erroneous sense of responsibility.'

'And it's going to get her killed,' groaned Nick. 'Or worse. For God's sake – she of all people knows that where Cassius is concerned, death at his hands would be the least of her worries.'

Ambrose started pacing the room.

'And has she factored in that Cassius won't have returned to Londinium alone?' persisted Nick. 'All the Romans we were fighting disappeared too. Which means his elite guard will have joined him. Eva doesn't stand a hope in hell of getting out of there alive. She's untrained, probably unarmed, and half the size of any of them. It's a bloody *suicide* mission!'

Ambrose stared at Nick and nodded. 'I think she knows that,' he said quietly. 'It's all that damned gladiator's fault!'

'How the hell is this *Seth's* fault?'

'Because he didn't manage to get his ass back here.'

Nick glared at Ambrose.'Well, *I* did,' he hissed, looking down at his scanty sleepwear and exchanging the boxer shorts for a roman tunic, a long heavy cloak and sandals. Then he armed himself with two holstered pistols: a Glock and a SIG, along with a beltful of ammunition.

'Hopefully I'll manage to make it through the vortex with at least one of these babies,' he muttered as he strode purposefully through the front door.

Zackary stood at the top of the stairs, spitting expletives. That girl was killing him. She was the only person in the world who made him feel like an idiot. And *he* was supposed to be the teacher. The wise one. The mentor. His fist tightened, crumpling the note in his hand.

'What is that?' asked Lauren softly behind him.

'Nothing,' he croaked.

'Show me.'

He shook his head, but his fingers loosened on the paper.

She pulled it from his hand, smoothed it out and read it.

'Is it true?' she whispered finally.

Ambrose shrugged.

'So she's right about the vortex?'

'Yes, Lauren, she's right about the vortex. She's right about everything. She's always bloody right.'

'And are you going to do what she asks?'

'Of course I am,' he said finally. 'Though it's probably too late.'

He walked wearily down the stairs to his lab and started keying in the new door-entry code. 'This whole damn vortex is my mess to clean up. It was my damned transmuted virus . . . my infected program . . . my very own cosmic catastrophe.'

Lauren stood gazing at the closed lab door for a few more minutes, then slipped out of the house.

The least she could do was try to buy everyone some time. She moved swiftly through the rain to the generators and programmed them to maximum emission.

63

Blood

'Seth, for God's sake don't take any more!' gulped Astrid.

Seth glanced up as he started to fill the twelfth syringe with his blood.

'Where'd you find them all, Seth?' Jen asked.

'All what?'

'The *syringes*! You look like a junkie.'

'Medical block and biology lab. I only managed to scrape together about twenty of them.'

'Any more and you'd be needing a transfusion! So – are lessons in taking blood part of the curriculum in Parallon, then?' Rob asked, staring at the deep red liquid as it slowly filled the barrel of the syringe.

'I just watched the nurses when Eva was in hospital.' Seth winced as he accidentally jerked the needle while capping the filled barrel.

'I'm not exactly crazy about needles,' Astrid muttered.

Seth stared at her. 'Astrid, you don't have to do this,' he said gently. 'None of you do. My blood is the most toxic substance on this Earth. You probably shouldn't come anywhere near it.'

Astrid bit her lip and gazed at him, trying to realign her whole world order: she was struggling to get the hang of this inverted world where poison was a gift; where you healed people by destroying them; where death meant life. Distractedly, she pulled aside the curtain. The rain pelted relentlessly outside, and the howling wind was throwing anything not nailed down across the quad . . . She could see planks of wood, a punctured ball, flowerpots . . . all smashing around like a gang of delinquent kids with nowhere to go. Did *she* have somewhere to go? Did this strange other world really exist? Was Eva truly there?

Her stomach clenched. God, she missed Eva. She loved Sadie, and Rob was a good mate . . . but Eva . . . Eva had brought her own weird, unbearable light to St Mag's. Way too much for some people: she was just too bright, too beautiful, too challenging. And she made you work so damn hard for her attention. *Never* gave out . . . except when she sang. But when she did sing, she shared her soul. And for Astrid that was enough . . . that was everything. She unconsciously began humming one of Eva's songs – until she heard Seth's sharp intake of breath. He was standing frozen before her, his face turned away, a syringe full of blood vibrating in his trembling hand.

'I have to get back,' he croaked, moving swiftly towards the door.

'*Stop!*' cried Jen, grabbing his sleeve. 'You've got to help us first!'

Seth shook her off. 'I've done what you asked. There's my blood. Take it, do what you like with it and let me go.'

'But we need you, Seth. Please help us with this.'

He stared at Jen's desperate face, then heaved a deep breath. 'OK,' he agreed finally. 'I'll help you.'

'Thank you,' she whispered. 'So how do we do it?'

'Pretty straightforward, really,' he said, carefully placing the filled syringe barrels on to Astrid's desk and unsealing another empty one. 'I suggest we divide these samples between us and spread the virus as broadly and exhaustively as possible.'

'Can we start with our families?' asked Rob.

Seth fixed his eyes on Rob, and hesitated for a moment before speaking. 'Depends how old they are.'

Rob frowned. 'What's that supposed to mean?'

'The virus doesn't work well on people much over twenty-eight . . . or under thirteen. There are a few exceptions, but they normally seem to need a long incubation and I don't think we have any time to play with here.'

Rob stared at him. 'You m-mean . . . we can't bring our parents?'

Seth shook his head sadly. 'I'm sorry, Rob.'

'I don't believe you!'

'Rob, I don't have time to argue with you, or to show you my pages of research, so you're going to have to trust me. We haven't got enough virus for you to waste on people with immunity. And if you ignore me and infect them anyway, I promise you they won't thank you. Nobody will thank you for making them endure the virus symptoms for month after month.'

Astrid swallowed as she thought about her father in Amsterdam. She would probably be there right now if the airlines hadn't abandoned all flights. He was the only family she had. How could she leave without him?

Seth saw the horror in their eyes and said gently, 'None of you have to choose this course. You could stay here and take a chance that Jen is wrong . . . that the world will recover. But . . . I need to tell you that I'm fairly certain Jen is right. The meteorologists are right. Parallon is probably your only chance.'

'How can we abandon our families?' croaked Rob.

Seth rubbed the back of his neck for a few moments and then began speaking. 'In the spring of my fourteenth year, the Romans came to Corinth: dark, ominous shadows annexing our waters and invading our land. Exactly a week before they arrived, my mother had a terrible dream: a premonition. Every day she begged me to leave, to take my younger siblings and run. She wanted her children to live. Unfortunately, we all dismissed her warning.

'Even as they marched up the hill to our house, she tried to push me out of the back door – desperate for me to escape. But, of course, I wasn't going to abandon my family. I stood beside my father and fought. An entire cohort came into our village that day. We were no match for four hundred soldiers, although I did manage to kill three of the bastards. As punishment they made me watch while they burned our houses and slaughtered every single person I loved. Even my baby brother.'

'Oh God,' breathed Jen.

'But as the Roman soldier raised his sword above my mother's body, she turned her head towards me, her eyes on fire, and cried, "Live for us, Sethos."'

The room was silent as they all stared in horror at Seth's

unfocused eyes as he relived the scene. Then he swallowed and gazed at them. 'I think your parents would want you to survive,' he said quietly.

The last thing Jen needed to do was think about her family, so she moved briskly towards Astrid's desk. 'How many people can we treat with one syringe?' she asked, reaching out to pick one up.

'Don't touch it yet,' snapped Seth, dashing across the room and pushing her fingers away. 'I haven't cleaned the surfaces or sealed them properly.'

Jen frowned.

'It'll take one microscopic drop of that to infect you, Jennifer,' he hissed. 'If you succumb to the virus now, you'll get sick almost immediately and won't have a chance to infect anybody else. I still have to fill the last eight syringes with Matthias's blood.'

'You're kidding, Seth!' groaned Matt.

Seth ignored him and continued. 'We need you all to live long enough to spread this. As soon as the twenty syringes are filled, we divide them between us and split up. How many people do you think you might know in the target age range, Jen?'

'Hmmm – I guess I could easily find a hundred or so at the newsroom. With friends and family– maybe three hundred.'

'I reckon each syringe could get at least three hundred people to Parallon, maybe more. A single infected blood cell should be able to annihilate a healthy body within seven hours. So by this evening we could have six thousand evacuees into Parallon. Not many on the scale of things – but . . .'

'Better than nothing,' nodded Jen. She watched, mesmerized,

as Seth tightened a band round Matt's bicep and started drawing blood from his arm.

'Hey, careful there! That hurts!' Matthias complained.

'Just remember this was your idea, Matt,' snapped Seth, capping the first barrel and attaching a second.

Nobody said much as Seth methodically filled the final eight containers, carefully capped each barrel, meticulously cleaned any traces of blood from the surfaces and sealed them one by one into a plastic bag. Then he handed them out.

'Right – I think we can get going now,' he said finally. 'Start with people you care about. A tiny scratch with the contaminated needle is all they'll need, so you can probably infect most people without drawing too much attention. Avoid getting caught at all costs. Explanations will either cause panic or distrust. Just try to make sure they're somewhere reasonably comfortable when you infect them. Fever onset is pretty fast.

'As soon as you've run out of friends and family, move on to strangers. But remember we could be stuck with anyone you bring for eternity, so try to avoid any obviously vicious bastards. We've already had our fill of them. Inject yourself last. When you're ready, get a sick bowl if you can and get into bed. It will be the worst couple of hours of your life . . . but when it's over you'll be in Parallon. Your family, friends and colleagues will probably get there before you.'

'Shall we divide up geographical areas?' suggested Jen. 'That way we won't duplicate.'

'Yeah, good idea,' agreed Seth, watching as Jen took out her phone and selected a map app.

'Try and go for well-populated places – schools, shopping centres, cinemas . . . It'll be easier to operate unnoticed if you're in a crowd, and you'll get the chance to hit a lot of people very quickly.'

'That shouldn't be a problem,' said Jen. 'With the evacuation, people are either congregating or gone . . . I've got a list of evacuation points here,' she added, scrolling through her emails. 'They'd be as good a place as any to start.'

Half an hour later Seth, Matthias, Astrid, Rob and Jen stood sheltering under the oldest of the St Mag's arches gazing into the school quad for possibly the last time. Each held a backpack containing four syringes.

Astrid was going to start at St Mag's, then head off to Camden. Rob was determined to head home. He insisted he wasn't going to try and infect his parents or his little sister, just his older brother who'd recently been sent home from university. As his town was on a hill, it was one of the official evacuation centres, so he figured he could cover the train stations, the shopping centre, library and sports building at the same time. Matthias was headed for Soho – the cinemas, clubs and restaurants – while Seth was going to trawl London universities and schools that hadn't yet evacuated.

Seth cursed the water on the streets for slowing his pace as he raced through the storm to the first school on his list. He needed to get this operation finished as fast as possible so that he could get back to the vortex. He hated the idea of sending such a huge influx of people into such an uncertain world. He had no idea what kind of Parallon they faced. Had another Roman despot emerged to take Cassius's place? Had the Parallon citizens drifted back to their former acquiescence?

He was also horribly aware that even if he were to jump into the water right now his journey back would be deeply unpredictable. At best, he faced injury, a great deal of pain and a lengthy time delay. At worst – he faced death.

But he couldn't allow himself to consider that possibility. Because somewhere between this world and that, Eva waited for him. And he was going to make damn sure that he returned to her.

64

Retribution

Londinium

AD 153

Pain. Pain everywhere.

So I wasn't dead, then.

A pair of large brown eyes blinked down at me. I tried to focus. There was a face swimming above me.

'*Tune valida es?*'

A child's voice – speaking in a familiar language . . . *Latin*.

My heart started to pound. I no longer felt pleasure when I heard Latin. Even lisped by a child, even when all he was asking was if I was all right, the sounds of the words filled me with a profound dread . . . until I suddenly remembered this was a horror I had actively sought. Londinium. I'd come here with a purpose; a single purpose: to kill Cassius Malchus. And against all odds, the turbulent vortex had delivered me. Assuming I had arrived in the right timeframe.

I tried to sit up. Yep. I was definitely still living. The young boy was staring at my torn tunic and ripped skin. I had to tell him I was OK. '*Maxime: valida sum,*' I winced.

The child clapped his hands, then grabbed my arm and started trying to haul me up. A part of me wanted to resist and stay resting on the ground, but he was making such an effort, and the wind looked like it might literally blow him away, so I took a deep breath, gathered all my strength and dragged myself to my feet.

I tried to take stock. I'd arrived on a wild, stormy evening, which had to mean the vortex's volatility had spread right across time.

'It isn't safe here,' the boy gasped out in Latin as he started trying to pull me away from the river.

Was he talking about the weather or Cassius's guards? A blinding flash of lightning and simultaneous clap of thunder prevented any further conversation, so I just allowed him to lead me quickly through rain-flooded streets until we finally arrived at an imposing white marble villa.

'Come,' he beckoned, pulling me through the arched entrance.

As soon as we were in the atrium, a broad-hipped house-slave rushed over to the boy, berating him for his delay, and wrapped him in a coarse towel. The boy snorted furiously, and told her to leave him alone and get help for his guest.

The moment her eyes turned from her charge to me, her face paled and she threw herself to her knees.

'Jupiter preserve us!' she gasped hoarsely, and began muttering frantic incantations. When her eyes finally lifted to mine she whispered huskily, 'W-what *are* you?'

What the hell was that supposed to mean?

'G-Giulia?' stammered the little boy. 'What's wrong?'

'On your knees, Marcus!' she hissed to the boy, who was

looking as bewildered as I felt. Frowning, he stumbled to the floor.

'Have you crossed the River Styx to claim retribution?' the slave woman whispered weakly. 'Or . . . or are you a . . . god?'

I gaped at her, trying to make sense of her words. But there was probably only one way I was going to find out.

'Look at me,' I said softly. Her eyes instantly gazed up to mine, and I suddenly felt a surge of power . . . the time-amp power I had never attempted to channel before.

'Who do you think I am, and why do you think I am here?' I asked in Latin.

'Y-you are the Lady Livia, returned to this land t-to . . . to seek retribution for your death and the slaughter of your maidens, Vibia and Sabina.'

'Vibia and Sabina are dead?' I gasped.

She nodded. 'V-Vibia was my friend.'

'Cassius killed them?' I gulped.

Her shoulders stiffened. 'V-Vibia met with an *accident*,' she hissed. 'But she had confided in me. I knew about the letters she carried between you and the gladiator. I begged her to stop. *Nobody* crosses Cassius and lives.'

'And Sabina? Did she also meet with an accident?' I whispered.

'Sabina was . . . c-crucified.'

'For helping me?' I swallowed.

Her eyes held mine as she nodded. 'Sabina knew what she was doing. Even *loyal* slaves do not live long in Cassius's palace.'

'Oh God,' I sobbed.

'When you disappeared and Cassius sent out no search parties – we all assumed . . .'

337

'That he had killed me?' I finished the sentence.

'But you live!' she breathed in wonder.

'*Not for much longer*,' I muttered under my breath. I had no doubts. Getting out alive wasn't part of the deal. But if I could rid both worlds of Cassius permanently it would be worth it. I'd be righting my own wrong. I was to blame for Cassius's arrival in Parallon. It was for me to make sure he never got to return.

Suddenly a heavy hand clamped on the boy's shoulder.

'Marcus, what are you doing in here?' a man growled. 'You were due in my study at sundown.'

'S-sorry, Father,' gulped the boy. 'I g-got caught in the rain.'

'And who is this?' the man continued belligerently.

I lifted my head to face him.

I was suddenly staring into the eyes of a broad, heavily scarred man. As soon as he caught sight of my face he flung himself backwards. 'L-Lady Livia!' he panted. 'B-but I watched you d-die!'

I swallowed. If he was there when Cassius cut my throat, he had to be one of his guards. I held him with my eyes. 'You were there that night?'

His eyes glazed and he nodded.

'How long ago was it?'

'Four months past.'

'And what did you see?'

'I watched you bleed to death . . . then . . .' he swallowed hard, 'nothing else.'

'Nothing?' I persisted. His discomfort was palpable. 'Tell me. What else did you see?'

'It was dark. Chaotic. A cohort of soldiers arrived . . .'

'*Tell me!*' I commanded.

'I thought . . . I think I s-saw you . . . d-disappear . . .'

He suddenly threw himself to the ground. 'Forgive me, lady. Have mercy on my soul. That night I finally recognized what you really were. Until then I believed you were a siren – some sort of witch . . . the way you conquered Cassius. His infatuation with you consumed him. As soon as he set eyes on you, every single one of his household whores disgusted him. And his loathing for that gladiator knew no bounds.'

I blanched as the guilt ratcheted up. Cassius's hatred for Seth was also my fault.

'But that night by the river I knew you would return to seek vengeance,' he breathed. 'I tried to warn Cassius . . .'

'You were expecting me?'

'The gods never let us go unpunished.'

The gods? He also believed I was a *god*?

Suddenly the child, Marcus, grabbed my soaking cloak. 'L-Lady Livia, please spare my father,' he gasped.

I looked down at the kid in shock. 'I am not here to hurt your father!'

He jumped up and clung to me. 'Thank you!' he gulped.

'Giulia,' hissed Marcus's father to the slave woman still prostrate on the ground. 'Find suitable clothing for our guest and order the cooks to prepare a feast in her honour.'

'I'd be grateful for some dry garments and some water to clean my injuries, but no feast,' I said quickly.

'Lady, you cannot visit my house without tasting my food.'

'Some bread and fruit would be welcome.'

'I shall immediately make a sacrifice in your honour, lady,' he continued, jumping to his feet.

'*No!*' I interrupted. I hated that stuff. 'No sacrifice –'

'We *will* sacrifice,' he insisted. 'You are not the only god we have angered.'

I cocked my head.

'Jupiter's wrath knows no bounds,' he muttered bitterly, his hand sweeping towards the small glazed window being battered by the storm.

I gazed out. Yeah, the Jupiter theory was probably a whole lot easier to stick with than the alternative. I exhaled shakily.

'Is there something else I can do for you, lady?' he murmured in response to my unease.

I dragged my thoughts away from the vortex and back to this room. Staring into his eyes, I said, 'I am visiting Cassius's palace tonight. I will be forever in your debt if you could spare me two strong guards.'

'I can do better than that,' he answered. 'I will accompany you myself.'

65
Guilt

London

14 March AD 2014

Seth flashed his mesmerizing smile at the college receptionist and handed back his visitor badge. She tilted her head flirtatiously. 'You can't be leaving already?'

He nodded. 'All done here, thank you. The college is cleared for evacuation.'

'Oh! B-but I can't let you go . . . er – out into that nasty weather yet . . . ahem . . . not without having a cup of tea . . . and a slice of cake. I've just put the kettle on.'

'That's very hospitable of you, but I am on rather a tight schedule,' smiled Seth, pressing the glass entrance doors. They were locked. 'Would you please release the security bolt,' he demanded, looking directly into her eyes.

Her expression glazed over. 'Of course, I'm sorry.' There was an audible buzz and click as the lock released. 'We're so grateful for your time. It is such an honour to receive an official visit from the evacuation committee. You must all be so busy.'

'No problem,' said Seth with a wave as he strode out of the building.

He didn't duck away from the rain or shield himself from the ravaging wind as most people did. He strode purposefully out into the storm and began moving quickly towards his final destination. The river.

He had just emptied his last syringe. The blood had gone even further than he'd predicted – he reckoned he'd probably managed to infect four to five hundred students with a single barrel . . . which meant between them they had the potential for saving ten thousand lives. If killing people with an agonizing virus could be considered 'saving'. And if ten thousand refugees were about to arrive in Parallon, somebody had better be there to welcome them.

He was well off the campus, but he glanced around quickly just to make sure nobody was following him. Years of slavery and Roman rule had embedded the kind of paranoia that would take an eternity to lift. But apart from the occasional ambulance and army truck, the streets were empty. Not many people wanted to be battered by this kind of weather. When he hit City Road, he crossed quickly over, dumped his now-empty bag into a bin, and ratcheted his purposeful stride up to a sprint. He had practically reached the riverbank when he heard a cry behind him.

'Seth, wait!'

Craning his head round, he squinted through the rain. Matthias was dashing towards him, his bag flapping on his shoulder.

Seth paused and waited tensely for him to catch up.

'Are you done already, Seth?' Matt gasped, doubling over and panting hard.

Seth nodded and looked at Matt's bag. 'You?'

Matt glanced up uneasily. 'Er yes.'

Seth's eyes narrowed. 'Have you still got some blood left, Matthias?'

'Not really . . .'

Seth grabbed his bag and tore it open. Two untouched syringes chinked together in the bottom. He stared at his friend in shock. 'Why would you lie, Matt?'

Matt shrugged. '*Your* target group was clearly much easier than mine. I bet if you tried finding people of the right age in all the Soho shops and cinemas like I had to, you'd have been struggling too. And it's virtually impossible to infect anybody without them noticing. So I can only assume you must have cheated.'

Seth gaped in disbelief. 'What are you saying, Matt? That I threw full syringes away? Or that I injected babies?'

'Well, how did you get through all that blood, then?'

'By going into classrooms and lecture halls and passing along row after row of students. As long as I managed to make eye contact, I could move pretty efficiently. And, believe me, if I still had blood left in my bag, I would be in another school doing exactly the same thing until I ran out. So no, Matthias,' he concluded, 'I didn't cheat.'

'Well, I've had enough of this,' growled Matt. 'I'm cold, hungry and wet, and I want to go home.'

'Zeus, Matt, give me your damn bag! *I'll* finish your job for you.'

'No, Seth! Let's go back! We've already infected plenty of people. We can forget about the rest . . . *What the –?*'

Matt stared at Seth in alarm. The ground had started to vibrate.

'Get down,' hissed Seth, pushing his friend to the pavement. 'It's probably just another tremor.'

'We've got to get back to Parallon, Seth!' cried Matt, trying to crawl towards the river.

'In the name of Apollo, Matt, just calm down. It's already passing. You're fine.'

When the last vibration stopped, Seth counted to thirty, then got back to his feet and hauled Matt up. As soon as he was upright, Matthias started tugging Seth towards the river. But Seth remained rigidly immobile.

'We need to get back to Parallon right now,' urged Matt. 'It's not safe here. We've done all we can. We owe these people nothing . . .'

'I don't think *you*, in all honesty, can say that,' accused Seth.

'What is this, Seth? Are you judging me for a change? Whatever I do, you're never satisfied! It'll never be enough!' gulped Matt furiously.

'Matt –'

'We were happy once, Seth. Do you remember? You and me . . .'

'We weren't happy, Matthias. We were slaves, fighting to survive each day.'

'I was happy,' breathed Matt. 'Until *she* arrived and ruined everything.'

'Eva?'

'Eva . . . Livia, whatever the witch is currently calling herself.'

344

Seth didn't often lose control. He had trained himself hard. But he did have one trigger. And Matt had just hit it. His fist shot out and landed hard against Matt's jaw. Matthias flew backwards and fell heavily on the ground.

Seth stood over him, breathing hard. 'Don't ever talk about the girl I love like that again,' he hissed. And picking up Matt's bag, he strode back into town.

Matthias gazed after him dejectedly. He hated Eva for coming between them. He hated Seth for choosing her. But he couldn't hate Seth with any real conviction because he loved him too much. He'd loved him for so long . . . probably since that terrible sea journey from Corinth, when the Romans had dragged them from their village. It was Seth who had kept Matt alive. Literally. When sickness, grief, hunger and despair had nearly killed him, Seth had washed him, watched over him, told him stories, stolen food for him and promised to protect him. And he kept that promise. Ferociously. Even at fourteen he'd had the strength and courage of a lion. No wonder the damn Romans had dragged him off to fight in the arena. But Seth had been so much more than his physical protector. He had been his friend: transforming those months of stench and whippings and broken raw skin and hatred from a living hell into a place of comfort.

He couldn't return to the river without Seth.

Instead, he crawled into a bus shelter by the side of the road and crouched in a corner to wait for him to return. It was completely dark by the time he caught sight of the weary figure jogging slowly towards him. And Matthias was feeling sick with guilt and remorse. He had let Seth down yet again, and there was nobody whose respect he craved more desperately.

345

He waited until Seth had passed by, then slipped silently behind him. He knew how acute Seth's senses were, but the rain was pounding and his friend was clearly exhausted, so Matt managed to follow him without being detected.

Their progress was slowed once they moved on to the riverside. The torrential water had risen higher and was now thigh deep on the bank. But Seth ploughed relentlessly forward, his entire body focused on reaching that point on the bank where he could re-enter the vortex.

Matthias could tell the moment his friend's thoughts shifted to the journey ahead. He watched the transition as Seth crossed into the same meditative state he always used to access before a fight in the arena. Matt had loved watching him prepare; loved the taut concentration, the slow, deep breaths that swelled his chest. And this preparation was not so different. Except this time Seth was readying his body and mind to face a far wilder enemy than any he met at the arena.

He knew he could move a little closer now. He could tell Seth's entire consciousness was engaged in the process. He smiled as Seth's lips began to move. That meant he was ready. Seth was framing his intention: his destination.

But the shape of the word looked wrong. That wasn't 'Parallon' his lips were murmuring.

'Damn!' hissed Matthias, as realization dawned.

Seth's destination word was *Eva*.

66

God

Londinium

AD 153

It was official. Apparently I was now a god: a fiery, vengeful god, seeking retribution. And though I was nothing like a god it probably suited my purpose to play the role. Mostly because it meant I was no longer bleeding and shivering in a ripped, soaking dress. I was well-fed, bathed, salved, oiled and resplendent in a heavily jewelled gown and cloak. It was time to leave for Cassius's palace.

My little rescuer, Marcus, stood sheltering under the portico waiting to say goodbye. I knelt down to give him a brief hug. He reached out and touched the new knife slung at my belt. It glittered with rubies.

'Did father give you his hunting knife?' he whispered in awe.

'He did because I lost my own. But don't worry, I will return it to him,' I smiled.

'It was *his* father's. And *his* father's before him. It is ancient. And carries charms that will protect you just as they protected my father's ancestors,' he whispered.

'I am honoured, then,' I murmured, touching the hilt reverently. 'Goodbye, Marcus. Thank you for taking care of me.'

'I will remember you in my prayers and sacrifices,' he announced.

'I'd like that,' I whispered, as I turned reluctantly away.

Waiting in the doorway were Marcus's father, Atilius, and two heavily armed soldiers. As soon as I joined them, we began moving through the flooded streets – my army of four: three temporarily bewitched soldiers and one messed-up girl doing her best to look like a kick-ass god in the hope that she might finally manage to get something right. When you are a god, you don't cower in doorways or flinch every time you hear a noise. You have to walk proud and tall. And I did my damnedest to walk as proud and tall as Juno herself.

It wasn't far to Cassius's palace, but as soon as it loomed into view, I was stalled by a sickening memory of another night when I'd been flanked by soldiers. But that time they were dragging me, twisting my roped arms and oblivious to my screams of fear and pain. It was the night I was hauled from Seth's side to become Cassius's prisoner-wife. My heart began to pound.

Pull yourself together, Eva. You are not that frightened girl any more. You are powerful and strong.

I forced myself to push away the fear by concentrating on the pattern of rain as it smashed against the wing of one of Cassius's huge gilt eagles. It stood arrogantly defiant, of course, just as I intended to do . . . I lifted my chin and was proceeding haughtily towards the entrance portico when my eyes flicked on to an unfamiliar shape in the paved entrance courtyard. My feet moved involuntarily towards it. Blurred by the haze of rain, it looked remarkably like a crucifix. I blinked in surprise. Had Cassius had some sort of religious conversion? I moved closer, then recoiled in horror when I realized that tied to the beams of the rough wooden cross, ruthlessly battered by rain and wind, were the pitiful remains of a body.

My stomach heaved and my mouth flooded with saliva.

Gods do not vomit, gods do not vomit I frantically chanted in my head. *It isn't my handmaid, Sabrina. It isn't Sabrina.*

But I knew it was. From the fragments of clothing still clinging to the gnawed bones, it could only be her. I swallowed and swallowed but my stomach refused to stop roiling. Through watering eyes I glanced at my escort, then hurtled towards the ornamental rose bushes flanking the path, where I threw up the entire remains of Atilius's hospitality. When there was nothing left to hurl, I stood dry heaving and shaking until Atilius strode up behind me.

My cover was so blown. Who was seriously going to believe in a god that puked?

He was staring down at me, frowning, clearly reassessing his entire value system. I had to do something to drag him back to team Eva. Fast. Wiping my mouth on the back of my hand, and wishing this was Parallon so that I could create a damn pack of gum, I looked into his eyes. That weird surge of energy heated through me as I told him he hadn't just seen me throw my guts up. I had simply been admiring Cassius's roses.

I made sure to thoroughly time-amp his guards with the same lame conviction, and then the four of us moved over to the ostentatious palace entrance. God, how I loathed this place. Especially when I took in the six heavily armed guards lining the doorway.

They were staring impassively in our direction until they saw my face. Then they blanched.

'L-Lady Livia?' one of them stammered, his eyes fixed on my throat.

So he had also been present the night Cassius sliced his knife through it.

'Yes, I am the Lady Livia,' I answered in Latin. 'Now take me to your master.'

After glancing at the others for affirmation, he turned and drew back the huge bolt across the outer wooden door, and led us inside.

This whole resurrection deal really rocked.

'Y-you have come to join Cassius at the feast?'

'Feast?' I frowned, momentarily losing my godlike swagger.

'Feast of celebration.'

'Oh? I thought the master was sick,' I said, as we followed the guard through the showy atrium.

'Oh, he was. Gravely sick. And then exactly three weeks ago, on the night the physicians agreed he would be drawing his last breath, he suddenly woke up, refreshed.'

I swallowed. This was disastrous news; a mega miscalculation. I had banked on catching Cassius before he got round to his magical recovery . . . Still sick and weak would have made him much easier to deal with, especially as I would have had a high chance of finding him alone. People in Londinium avoided sickbeds, fearful as they were of contagion. Now I not only faced hundreds of drunk and loyal Romans, I was also going to have to deal with Cassius at almost full strength. And more worrying still was the possibility that he'd woken up with memories of Parallon. He may even already be on a mission to get himself re-infected in order to get back there. I wasn't sure exactly how much he'd learned about the virus, but he'd read through Seth's notebooks, so he knew enough.

My only hope was that he'd woken up like I did: dazed, bewildered and with only fractured memories of his afterlife. He'd only been restored for three weeks, after all. As long as I got to him before his memories were complete, there was still a chance I could pull it off. I needed to keep everyone well time-amped, especially team Eva. Then I had to somehow get Cassius alone . . . at a celebratory feast.

Easy. Not. I'd experienced first-hand how many people turned up to Cassius's celebrations.

'I will take you straight to the banqueting hall,' announced the guard leading us. 'I believe they are about to begin the entertainment.'

Moments later we halted in front of the two sentries guarding the hall's ornately carved double doors. Again, the instant the guards recognized me, shock and fear transformed their features and their shaking hands moved swiftly to swing the doors open. Adrenalin spiked through me, but I lifted my chin, told myself I was a god and prepared to move forward.

I could have done without the musical announcement. A nice incognito entrance was all I asked, but as soon as I entered the room, three musicians put auloi to their lips and blew.

All sounds in the hall stopped. All eyes turned to me. But one pair inexorably found mine. The sadistic black eyes of Cassius. And they were like burning coals. They destroyed whatever they touched. And the moment they found their mark, they lasered right to the core of me, cauterizing all fantasies of gods and courage and victory, leaving only aching fear behind.

He was lying across his couch, his hand poised above the platter of delicacies a crouching slave held out to him. Without taking his eyes from mine, he slowly sat up, his lip curling slightly as he clapped his hands, sending the banquet-slaves scrambling away.

My legs were beginning to shake and my hands had dampened with sweat. I twitched my palms to wipe them against my dress, and my right hand brushed against something cold, metallic: the rubied knife. I swallowed hard as a fleeting image of Marcus's trusting face flashed across my mind. If I failed here, his father would die. His mother would die. He would die. I would be taking his entire household down with me.

With a supreme effort of will I dragged my eyes from the locked hold Cassius had on them, and glanced quickly around the hall: hundreds of inebriated diners lolling on couches gazed at me expectantly; and at least sixty soldiers and guards lined the walls. But more worrying than any of them were the three men standing proud, tall and lethal behind Cassius's couch: Otho, Pontius and Rufus – Cassius's elite guard.

How had I managed to airbrush them out of my projection? My eyes flicked across their faces as I tried to calculate whether they too were in their resurrected states. The slight smirk on Pontius's lips told me everything I needed to know.

How had I managed to get my timing so wrong? To be confronted by all four of them post-Parallon was disastrous. And they looked so damned healthy. Why? Why the hell hadn't they woken up like I had – sick and weak? Had their ages protected them?

Now any fantasies of playing a wrathful god with them were

completely off the agenda . . . How much did they remember of Parallon? Were they already burning with the desire to reclaim their immortality?

I swore. Every profanity I knew. But silently. I had to get my brain in gear.

I soon regretted that impulse, because the moment I started thinking, another horrible realization struck me. If Cassius and the elite guard were resurrected, it was highly likely that several of the other guards lining the walls were too. All the 'disappeared' Roman soldiers we'd fought on the riverbank with Nick Mullard would be resurrected. And the only way to safeguard Parallon from them was to kill them as well.

Oh God! Where the hell was my brain when I jumped into the water to come here? I couldn't believe how stupid I'd been.

Think Eva, think!

OK . . . On the plus side: I had three guards at my back, a lucky knife and the time-amp factor.

On the minus side: I faced Cassius Malchus, his elite guard and a roomful of hostile soldiers. Not only would they all want me dead, but at least four of them possibly knew that swimming around in my blood was a fast-track ticket to get them straight back to Parallon.

I was so screwed.

67

Tsunami

Jen had managed to get through one and a half syringes, and was just about to head out of the newsroom when a third tremor shuddered through the building. She didn't bother throwing herself on the floor as she'd done before. Instead she clung to her desk to wait it out.

But even before the tremors had subsided, Amanda, her boss, came dashing through the newsroom.

'*Get out of here, everyone!*' she yelled '*Get out!* Drive into the mountains – get as far away from London as you can.'

'What's going on?' Jen demanded.

'*Tsunami!*' screamed Amanda. 'A massive tsunami. Get going! *Now!*'

'*A tsunami here?*' gasped one of the researchers Jen had infected seconds earlier.

'W-when's it due to hit?' shouted Hugo from his desk on the other side of the room.

'Sometime tonight! *Get the hell out, for Christ's sake! Everyone! Go!*'

Jen looked frantically around the room. She'd managed to infect most of them, but would the virus hit in time? She looked down at her bag. She still had two and a half barrels of blood to get rid of. But she'd never get herself injected in time if she didn't move now. As she ran along the corridor and sprinted down the stairs, she pulled her phone from her pocket.

'Astrid!' she croaked.

'Hey, Jen! Nearly finished three,' whispered Astrid. 'But these damn tremors have slowed things down a bit. I've just stepped into a little goth shop with loads of people rammed inside – so can we talk later?'

'Forget them, Astrid. Just sort *yourself* out, right now!' shouted Jen.

'What the hell's going on?'

'We're totally out of time. I mean – *totally.* Tell Rob. Just do it, Astrid. Find a place and do it now . . . Gotta go. Good luck, girl.'

'Jeez. You too, Jen,' croaked Astrid. 'And . . . hey – fingers crossed we get to meet on the other side.'

68

Cross

Londinium

AD 153

Nick was choking. Water filled his lungs. His body was boneless. Thrown, hurled, torn apart. Falling. Crashing.

He groaned. 'Stop spinning!' he muttered as the hard surface his cheek was pressed against twisted beneath him. He didn't dare open his eyes. He'd only fall off whatever was bucking below him. Instead he listened to his own breaths. Pants. Rattling in his chest. Something hard was digging into his hip. He twisted his body slightly. Tried to shift into a more comfortable position.

At last the motion beneath him seemed to be slowing. He hazarded another slight movement . . . a finger twitch. And another . . . Then he felt mud. Water. Gravel.

He opened his eyes. Didn't make much difference. Darkness all around him. And rain. And wind.

He cautiously turned his head a little. Water all about. He pulled himself on to an elbow. God, that hurt. He peered out into the darkness. Feeble moonlight. No stars. No shimmer.

Not Parallon then.

But no tower blocks. No rectangles of comforting electric light. No cars. No sirens. He could see the swirling wild water of the river a few metres away. It had clearly risen enough to have started leaking on to the bank – which was where he now seemed to be sprawled.

So where was he?

Could he have actually made it to Londinium?

Nick hauled himself painfully to his feet and checked his injuries. No broken bones, thank God, just a couple of cracked ribs. Both elbows and one shoulder had the skin ripped off, and there was a deep gash across his thigh, and one down his neck. Apart from that – he was in pretty good shape. The ammo belt was gone, as was the SIG. But by some miracle his Glock had survived the journey with its loaded magazine in place. So he had sixteen rounds: sixteen bullets to get himself and Eva safely out of here.

If she was here at all . . . If she'd made it through the vortex . . . If things hadn't already gone bad for her.

No negative thoughts. He needed to get this manoeuvre underway.

Nick pulled his dripping cloak round his shoulders and started running. It was raining and there was so little moonlight it was difficult to see, but he found the roads were laid out on exactly the same grid as they were in Parallon, so he skirted close to the buildings until he hit the forum. In Parallon, the forum was the centre from which all roads radiated, so he figured it was as good a place as any to start. If there were any ordinary people about, this was where he'd find them. But the weather was so bad, the only people roaming the streets seemed to be soldiers. And there was no way he was going to chat to one of them.

He was beginning to consider desperate measures, like knocking on a door, when he spotted a woman scurrying from the temple, her cloak pulled well over her head to protect her from the howling wind and rain. Nick skirted round her, then doubled back to block her path. The moment she stumbled to a stop and her eyes met his, he gave her his biggest smile and framed a single-word question: 'Cassius?'

It was a gamble. He had no idea how well known the bastard was here. But it seemed likely that Cassius had been playing pretty heavy power games long before he brought them all to Parallon.

The mere mention of Cassius's name froze the woman into a pose of such abject fear that Nick knew without a doubt that he had his man. She waved her hand towards the towering, palatial building dominating the skyline, and then scuttled quickly out of sight.

Nick started moving towards the building; its white marble facade loomed eerily through the murky sheet of rain. As he approached he couldn't miss the familiar pair of golden eagles flanking the imposing front doorway. The slimeball clearly liked his birds of prey, thought Nick, as he crouched on the borders of the palace.

He'd expected the place to be guarded – but he wasn't expecting a whole damn battalion. As he soundlessly skirted the palace he counted fifty-six pairs of guards posted around the perimeter. All patrolling their own five-metre allocation. The guy was seriously paranoid.

Nick moved cautiously back towards the main entrance, glad

for the constant battering rain to mask any hint of sound his movements made. But no amount of rain could mask that putrid smell drifting towards him. Glancing around, he suddenly spotted the gruesome source: a decomposed corpse hanging off a wooden crucifix. Nick exhaled hard and tried to swallow. What kind of man kept a rotting body right next to his front door? As if he needed any more confirmation, Nick Mullard knew in that instant that Cassius Malchus was completely insane.

69

Vengeance

Londinium

AD 153

Eva, you can do this!

We were hopelessly outnumbered and outclassed. Every brain cell told me there was no way we could win, but I had to convince myself that it was possible. Or I was just going to curl up and wait for Cassius to end it. Again. I had come too far for that.

Of course I knew it was going to end here one way or another. I would never make it back to Parallon. I'd always known that. But I had to kill Cassius first. And I was going to have to use every particle of time-amp power to persuade Atilius and his men to kill the elite guard.

My fingers curled round the hilt of the knife as I stood in that doorway facing my enemies. I closed my eyes for a moment. I couldn't allow Cassius's gaze to derail me. I had to use everything I had. And all I had at this moment was a ruby knife and my virus-enhanced will.

I took a deep breath and straightened my back. Turning to Atilius and his guards, I looked them straight in the eye, but instead of blasting them with time-amp, I decided to simply speak the truth . . . and prayed my Latin would keep up.

'That man, your procurator, Cassius Malchus, has wronged me, you, Londinium, Rome, and so many others that his sins cannot be counted. He is driven only by his lust for power, and to that end he has tortured, killed and robbed without compunction or shame. By allowing him to live we are condemning countless more human lives to be blighted by his cruelty. It is time to end this.'

'We are behind you, lady,' murmured Atilius.

Cassius was still staring at me, his face impassive. How much did he remember? It was impossible to tell. But with his head slightly cocked to one side and his fingers steepled under his chin, he didn't look as though he thought I was an avenging god. Unfortunately. His elite guard stood behind him with their arms folded across their chests. They didn't look cowed by my god status either. They didn't even bother resting their hands on their swords. Clearly none of them saw me as a threat, so I decided to play on that assumption.

Smiling broadly, my eyes fixed on Cassius, I began to move forward.

'I have come back for you, husband mine.'

The blasting surge of power sizzled through my veins. Cassius's eyes remained locked on mine, but as the force crackled between us I began to feel his confusion. The slight furrow of his brow and the small tic in his jaw said it all. Cassius's composure wasn't absolute.

Seizing my moment, I gazed around the room, blasting every pair of eyes looking in my direction with the same high-voltage charge. I could feel their submission as their wills bent to mine.

'She has come for vengeance,' someone whispered.

'The gods be praised,' breathed another.

'The gods walk among us.'

People started throwing themselves on to their knees, prostrating themselves.

Wow! This was kind of awesome! Why the hell didn't I know about this the last time I was in Londinium? Could have saved myself a hell of a lot of grief.

I had reached Cassius's couch.

'Remember me, Cassius?' I breathed.

'Livia,' he whispered. 'You came back to me.'

'Now, why do you think a girl would come back to her husband after he cut her throat, Cassius?' I murmured, as my fingers grazed the knife under my cloak.

Cassius smiled uncertainly up at me, his brows furrowing,

I knew this was my moment. I would never have a better one. I clutched the knife handle, unsheathed it and an instant later the point was pressed into his chest. He stared down at it in bewildered shock.

In all my fantasies about this moment, he was never vulnerable. Never human. He was the monster who tortured me. The monster who'd abused, beaten and killed Seth . . . and Sabina . . . and Vibia, and God knew who else. But that monster wasn't sitting here. All I saw was a confused, unguarded, blood-muscle-and-bone human being.

And my hand stilled.

I had never plunged a knife into anyone before. I'd seen Seth do it. In the arena. And it was bloody and gory and sickening. But he had been fighting then. For his life. It was kill or be killed. I tried to tell myself that I was doing the same. But I wasn't fighting for my life. This was an assassination. A cold, hard kill to get rid of a cold, hard killer . . . For all human beings . . . For Parallon . . . For the world.

So why the hell wasn't the knife burying itself into his chest? Why was it still in my hand?

'Lady Livia,' hissed a voice behind me. Atilius. My wingman. Urging me to act.

I glanced round at him, and in that moment the spell I'd been casting on the room broke.

Cassius jumped to his feet. His elite guard pushed forward. The knife clattered to the ground and my arms were dragged behind me.

Damn. This had never happened when I played Ace Warrior in my bedroom. I seriously sucked at the real thing.

I lifted my head. Cassius no longer looked lost and bewildered. The monster was back in charge. And, of course, now, staring into his cruel, arrogant eyes, I wouldn't have a problem plunging a knife in his heart. Except that the knife was lying on the floor, and he was telling me that it was time to die again.

'No,' I snarled, releasing the full force of the time-amp. He staggered backwards, straight into the armoured bodies of his elite guard.

I stared at them one by one. 'Hold him,' I hissed.

I could see them struggling against my power. I could sense their compulsion to bend to my will fighting with their hatred of me. Maybe it thinned out when I tried to zap more than one person at a time. I really could have done with a chance to experiment with it. They were holding Cassius, but I could tell my will alone wasn't going to last long.

I had to be fast.

Keeping my eyes firmly on them all, and concentrating all my effort on controlling them, I bent my knees as my hand flailed around on the ground, searching for the elusive lucky knife. When all I managed to touch was a lump of bread and something squashed and congealed, I considered telling Marcus not to set too much store by his damn family heirloom. It certainly wasn't exactly living up to expectations right now. Holding eye contact, I shifted a little to my right, hoping that the knife would now be within reach. I was just extending my fingers further along the cool, mosaic floor when a rumbling tremor started rocking the ground.

What the hell?

Goblets and trays shuddered off low tables and crashed to the floor around us. Women started shrieking like they were in some lame disaster movie. I decided that this might be the perfect opportunity to drop my eyes for a moment to see if I could get a quick glimpse of the ruby knife. I caught a momentary flash of red, then the tremors were vibrating it further under Cassius's couch.

Suddenly it wasn't just the floor. The whole building had started to shake. People began throwing themselves to the ground. Flaming torches were being tossed from their fixtures on the wall. One landed in the intricately coiled hair of a woman, who started screaming her lungs out. Oh God, now her dress was on fire. This was no longer a lame parody of a disaster movie.

'*Fountain!*' I yelled across the rocking room towards the flaming woman. '*Atrium!*' I pointed wildly in the direction she needed to take, but she just carried on screaming, oblivious. I looked across at Cassius. No longer time-amped, he and his elite guards were staggering through the hordes of people to get to the door. As I started moving to follow them, my sandalled toe stubbed on something hard and sharp. I looked down. Maybe Marcus's grandfather knew what he was talking about after all. The ruby knife was sliding around my feet. I bent down and grabbed it, then continued my slow pilgrimage towards the door. The room was a cacophony of screams, bodies, smoke and flickering flames. The fallen torches had managed to light small fires round the hall . . . fires that were spreading across wall drapes, through clothing and table coverings.

I carefully picked my way through the melee, and had nearly reached the door when a servant whose tunic had just caught fire, brushed past me. For a moment it looked as though the flames would catch, but luckily my cloak was still damp from the rain.

I didn't have time to mess about. I had to find Atilius, and reach Cassius before he got away. But there was a lot of smoke in the hall. So much that my eyes were watering and it was getting impossible to see anything. And the screams and the coughing and the crashing of pillars and furniture were so loud that I couldn't hear anything either. Despite the chaos of sound and sight I still knew where the door was. That was my goal . . . my finish line.

If I can make it to the door I can get to Cassius . . . If I can make it to the door I can get to Cassius . . .

The floor rocked again. Hard. I crouched, clinging to it,

wheezing through the smoke, praying the rocking would end. I needed to get into the air . . . but the tremors continued – and I couldn't wait any more. I couldn't breathe any more. It was too hot and there was no air and . . .

Suddenly all thought and breath was pushed out of my body as a heavy weight landed hard and fast on my back.

'*Jesus, Eva! You're on fire!*'

70

Clash

Londinium

AD 153

Nick tore off the flaming cloak Eva was wearing and hurled it away from her. Her dress had also started to smoulder, so he rolled her on to her back, pressed his body over hers and tried to stifle the flames with his weight.

'Nick,' she gasped, squinting up at him. 'What the h-hell are you d-doing here?'

'Saving your ass,' he coughed, grabbing her hand and pulling her roughly to her feet.

When they made it through the chaotic furnace of the banqueting hall to the atrium, Nick glanced up at the open sky with a kind of joy. The rain was cool and torrential, instantly salving their burning skin. But it wasn't safe here. They had to get clear of the falling building and there were still at least two corridors to cross before they made it to the front doors.

'We can't stop yet,' he rasped, hauling her ever forward.

'My dress . . .' she suddenly choked, stumbling behind him. He looked back.

'Damn!' He hadn't managed to kill the fire. The hem was shooting bright flames behind her.

His eyes darted towards the corridor. The flames were climbing up her dress too fast for him to get her outside in time. She could read it in his eyes. Instantly she pulled her hand from his, grabbed the knife from her waist and thrust it into the fabric of the dress, then twisted it until it ripped the lower half of her dress away. Throwing it as far as she could, she reached for his hand. As soon as he felt her fingers he pulled her forward again. They were close to the doorway – he could almost feel the thrash of the rain on his skin when an almighty shudder shook the building and the columns holding up the vestibule ahead of them came crashing to the ground.

Eva hauled him back just as a huge chunk of marble landed in his path.

'This way,' she shouted, dragging him back towards the collapsing atrium.

'No! We'll get trapped that way!' he panted, trying to turn her round. But she was gasping and coughing and shaking her head, refusing to be deflected.

Nick froze and pulled his fingers free. No. He couldn't follow. Eva's choice of direction felt so wrong.

'Trust me, Nick,' she pleaded.

There were so few people he trusted. Why would he put faith in this inexperienced girl?

'Nick, please! We've got to move!'

And for some inexplicable reason he allowed her to drag him further into the depths of the crashing nightmare, to fight their way through the flow of screaming people heading towards them. They were the only ones moving contraflow, Nick observed ruefully, as they crawled and stumbled between scattered fires, across fallen pillars, broken chunks of marble and overturned tables. When the earth trembled again, they flattened themselves to the ashy, littered floor, and held their breaths until the movement subsided.

Nick wasn't sure what he heard first, the voices or the rain. 'Christ,' he breathed, suddenly feeling the breeze of fresh wet air on his face.'You knew where you were going.'

Eva turned and covered his lips with a finger. 'Cassius,' she mouthed, nodding her head towards the large garden they were about to reach. Cassius was standing there with all three elite guards. They were speaking Latin so Nick had no idea what they were saying.

'Planning where to go,' Eva murmured. 'Cassius has a house a few miles north of here in Verulamium.'

Nick peered around carefully. It looked like the rest of Cassius's guards had fled. This couldn't be a better time. He quickly reached for his Glock, and it was only then that he realized how burnt his hands were. How could he have not noticed the pain till now? There was barely any skin left on his right hand. As he tried to curl his fingers round the grip he let out an involuntary hiss of pain, making Eva turn her head.

'Jeez, Nick!' she winced.

'You're going to have to pull the gun out for me,' he rasped. 'And then we'll have to take teamwork to a whole new level.'

71

Team

Londinium

AD 153

'Now,' Nick breathed, as soon as I had the gun in my hands. 'Very carefully take hold of the magazine in your right ha– *Stop!*'

I nearly jumped out of my skin.

'Don't touch the trigger.'

'Keep your hair on!' I hissed, repositioning the offending finger.

'Damn – it looks like they might be on the move,' murmured Nick. 'This had better be real quick.' He carefully rested his hands over mine. 'I'll be adjusting your position with my left hand. Don't squeeze the trigger until I give you the signal. There's a round already in the chamber and fifteen in the magazine. That's all the ammo we've got. Which should be fine. There are only four of them. And we're at pretty close range.'

'Except that I've never shot a gun before.'

'Yep,' he swallowed. 'Except for that.'

I took the gun from Nick and held it as he showed me, my

right hand on the grip, with my index finger gently resting on the centre of the trigger. He made me wrap my left hand firmly round my right in the hope that it would increase my stability. Then I had to crouch down, pressing back against his chest so he could lean his head on my shoulder and use the sights on top of the barrel. I held the gun out, while he lightly guided my hands with his. He was doing the aiming and I was pulling the trigger. That was the theory anyway.

Our first shot missed everybody. I wasn't surprised. Not just because the ground chose that moment to do one of its little rumbles, but also because when the bullet discharged, the recoil gave me such a shock, I nearly dropped the damn gun. Fortunately, the sound of the gunshot was completely masked by the crash of falling masonry so Cassius and his crew remained oblivious.

'Deep breath, Eva,' murmured Nick in my ear, as he edged the gun slightly higher and we took aim for our second shot.

'Ready? Fire!'

I pulled the trigger slowly as he'd directed and this time held the gun as still as I could to counteract the recoil.

I stared. Pontius was down. Definitely down. But the others were looking straight in our direction.

'Focus, Eva. Deep breath. Fire!'

God! Nick had moved the gun. I squeezed the trigger. The bullet whizzed past Otho's ear.

'Fire, Eva!'

I pulled the trigger. I saw it. The bullet hole. Right above his eye. Blood.

'Two down. Fire!' hissed Nick.

I pulled the trigger. No one went down, and they were both heading this way.

'*Move!*' ordered Nick. We ran at a crouch back into the palace, until Nick suddenly swerved across me and pushed us both behind a pile of rubble. While I leaned back trying to recover, he edged forward and peered through a tiny gap. Using his left hand, he shifted bits of plaster and stone and worked the hole bigger. He gestured with his head, and I pushed the gun through the hole. It made a neat resting post. Nick carefully repositioned us again.

Cassius and Rufus were heading our way. We were waiting for them. As soon as they were in striking distance, Nick squinted through the sights and shifted the gun slightly. 'Ready?' he breathed.

I nodded into his chest.

'Fire.'

Cassius stumbled. Was he shot?

'Eva, focus! Now! Fire!'

'Christ!' I breathed. Rufus no longer had a face. I felt myself retching.

Then Cassius, who had disappeared from view momentarily, suddenly loomed into our sightlines. He was charging towards us.

'Get down, Eva!' hissed Nick, as he rose on to his knees, grabbed the Glock from me and, holding it in his injured left hand, started pumping bullets at Cassius. But they were flying wild. One hit the corner of Cassius's thigh, one grazed his elbow, but Cassius was almost on top of us, bearing straight down on Nick. I heard the crunch of bone smashing, and a small exhalation. Nick stopped moving.

'*Nooooo!*' I yelled, as Cassius straddled Nick and pulled the knife from his belt. I hurled myself towards him. Holding my ruby knife between both hands, I plunged it hard into his back. As far as it would go.

Cassius reeled forward, straight on to Nick's limp body. Roaring with pain and fury, he hoisted himself back up and whirled round to grab me.

Why the hell wasn't he dead?

I darted out of his reach, but the heavy tug on my hair told me I hadn't moved quickly enough. He began reeling me in with one hand, while the other now swung his large curved knife. I felt the hot slash as it dragged across my shoulder. Without thinking, I pulled my knees to my chest and kicked the hand holding the knife with all my strength. The knife clattered across the floor, but I couldn't reach for it because his other hand still held fast to my hair.

'Livia – when are you going to learn?' he snarled. 'I am your nemesis. You will never defeat me!'

I stared back at him. Hating him. Hating his cruelty. His endless tyranny. And above all his arrogance. He was in pain, I could see it. But his pleasure at seeing me trapped again dominated his features. Before I could spit out a response, his free hand suddenly reached towards the blood oozing from my shoulder, his eyes glinting with intention. But it wasn't until his fingers rammed hard into the aching wound and raked through the blood that my hate-filled brain jumped to attention. *He knew about the virus.*

In desperation my eyes flicked once more to his unreachable knife. It was definitely out of range . . . but Nick's gun wasn't. It lay loose in his burnt hand. I slid my fingers along the floor, grabbed the gun, aimed, and squeezed the trigger.

Would have been a perfect kill.

Only the magazine was empty.

My heart sank.

It was over.

I sobbed in fury and despair as Cassius deliberately stroked my blood into his grazed elbow. Then I caught sight of Nick's hand edging towards Cassius's knife on the floor between us. But his movements were too jerky and dazed. He wasn't going to reach it before Cassius spotted him.

I had to finish this.

Relying on Cassius's momentary distraction with my blood, I chopped down with my knuckles on Cassius's hold of my hair. He snarled with pain, which gave me my moment to jerk sharply out of his grip. Then I stretched for the knife, grabbed it and thrust it with all my might into his throat.

Blood literally gushed everywhere, all over me, all over Nick, all over Cassius, and for a second Cassius's face wore an expression of confused disbelief. Then his eyes rolled up and his body slumped to the ground.

'Check for a pulse, Eva,' rasped Nick weakly.

I shakily knelt on the ground and picked up Cassius's wrist. I held it until the faint uneven beat finally stopped.

Cassius was dead.

No fanfare. No rousing music. Just rumbling earth, distant screams and relentless rain.

'I need to make sure . . .' I whispered.

Nick understood. I had to wait with the body. There had been too many unfinished endings between Cassius and me to be able to walk away now. He'd taken my blood. Was he going to escape death again? Or would his age slow the virus enough?

I moved to crouch next to Nick. Wordlessly, he covered my shaking hands with his bleeding burnt ones, and together we watched; sitting a kind of undeserved vigil for the man who had savagely and systematically destroyed the lives of so many.

But in the end the body was just a body. It bled out and stiffened. It didn't transform and it didn't vanish.

We'd beaten the virus. Cassius's iron grip on life was finally over.

'OK, Nick, let's get the hell out of here, before the whole place blows.'

I heard an ominous crack above me. Which was the only reason I glanced up and saw Pontius barrelling towards us.

'*Look out!*' I screamed.

72

Sacrifice

Londinium

AD 153

The moment Seth surfaced, gasping for air, he knew something was wrong. The tyrannical thrashings of the vortex hadn't ended. The whole world was churning. He could see water. He could see land. But the divisions were indistinct.

'Brother!' gasped a faint voice nearby.

He turned his head. 'Matthias?' he croaked.

Matt looked bad. Really bad. It was a dark night but Seth couldn't mistake the gaunt paleness of his friend.

'Seth. This . . . this . . .' Matt closed his eyes.

'Matt?' Seth rasped, swimming towards him. Zeus, the vortex had drained him this time. Both legs were ripped to pieces, but instead of grinding pain, his body felt strangely numb . . . sluggish . . . powerless.

Matt didn't look any better at close quarters. In that condition, there was no way he was going to survive the vortex again, so Seth started wearily hauling him on to the bank.

'Sethos . . . m-my brother . . . we can't . . .' murmured Matt, as he lay gasping on the waterlogged ground.

Seth dragged himself on to the bank and crouched beside him. He tried to pay attention to what Matt was saying, but it was hard to concentrate because Matt's body seemed to be drifting in and out of focus. Even his own hands seemed strangely translucent.

Translucent.

Seth's blood froze. 'It can't be . . .' he choked. 'Not our own time?' He gazed in confusion towards the city. It couldn't be Londinium. It bore no relation to the grimly ordered Roman city he'd lived in. This place was a scene of devastation.

Suddenly his entire body jerked. His brain tried to assimilate the strange rocking sensation beneath him. It felt familiar. Not the vortex. Not that kind of wild, thrashing tumbling. This reminded him of somewhere else . . . London. The London he had just left. The rocking earth . . . the shaking buildings . . . Seth stared around him. Temples, columns, walls, cornices – all were crashing down. He could hear screaming . . . see flames . . . hundreds of staggering people heading blindly in different directions.

He stared, trying to get his fuzzy brain to make connections. Another earthquake? Earthquakes across time . . . So this was the scenario Lauren had been working against. She'd seen it coming – the end of the world.

Seth helplessly watched the terrified figures. It made no difference whether it was AD 152 or 2014, the fear was the same.

'We have to leave,' he said, pulling Matt back towards the water.

'Can't we just rest a moment, Seth?'

Seth nodded wearily. He could use a moment's rest too. Laying himself down on the bank beside Matt, he watched the horror unfold. Then suddenly, in the distance, silhouetted against the flames of burning buildings – he saw her. The girl he would know anywhere. His girl. His perfect Livia . . . His beautiful Eva . . . But she was stumbling, dragging a body behind her, crawling, falling . . .

The moment he saw her on the ground he pulled himself to his feet and took a step forward. 'Get up, baby,' he breathed. 'Get up!'

But she didn't get up.

'Eva!' he moaned, forcing his body upright and forward, his eyes fixed on her. She wasn't moving at all. Her body was limp, just another scrap of matter on the rocking, vibrating ground.

'Come on, Eva! Move, baby,' he begged, as he staggered towards her, willing her upright with every fibre of his being. But he had no power over her. She remained motionless. Oblivious.

He had to get to her. He tried to run, but his legs felt so heavy.

'Just one foot in front of the other,' he told himself. 'One foot in front of the other. Not hard. Do it. Push. One. Two. Left. Right.'

Edging forward, he kept his eyes only on her, terrified that if he lost his focus for even a moment she would disappear forever. 'Please get up, baby!' his mind screamed. 'I need you to get up!'

He couldn't feel his feet. He glanced down. Translucent. He could see the ground through them. His arms were just as insubstantial. How the hell was he going to get her to the river?

He couldn't lift her. Probably couldn't even touch her. Would she even be able to see him? Hear him?

She had to.

He squinted towards the shape of her body curled on the ground. Still too far to reach. 'Eva! Get up!' he bellowed with his mind. But his mind had even less power than his body.

'*Seth!*' He heard the plaintive wail of his friend behind him. 'Don't leave me!'

'Get back to the vortex, Matt!' he yelled. 'I'll join you as soon as I can.'

By the time he had made it to Eva's side he could barely breathe. He crouched down next to her, gasping.

'*Eva!*' he shouted. His voice was barely a sigh. He reached out to touch her, his hand so ephemeral – a mere whispered shape. But as his fingers ran desperately over her hair, she flinched. He did it again.

'*Eva!*' he screamed.

Her eyes opened. Her head lifted. 'Seth?' she breathed.

'I'm here, baby,' he cried, greedily raking his eyes all over her. She was so pale. White. And scorched. Covered in soot and dust and blood. He scoured her body for injury. Her fingers were bloody, one hand curled round an ornate knife. And it looked like she was bleeding profusely from a shoulder wound.

'You need to get up, sweetheart,' he urged. 'You need to get back to the vortex . . . *Please*, baby.'

She shook her head. 'Y-you're dead, Seth. You're never coming back to me,' she choked, tears tracking through the sooty grime on her face.

'Eva, look at me. Look at me, baby.'

She blinked, trying to clear her vision, one hand impatiently wiping the tears from her eyes. 'Seth?' she whispered, reaching out. 'I can feel you! Are you a ghost?'

'Come back with me, Eva. I can't be in Parallon without you,' he gasped.

'B-but I c-can't move any more,' she choked, trying to pull herself to her knees.

'Yes you can,' he shouted. 'You must!'

She nodded and took a deep breath. Then turned to the crumpled, bleeding body beside her. 'Nick!' she whispered, staring down despairingly at the motionless body.

'He's breathing, Eva. Shake him!' yelled Seth. 'Slap him.'

Eva was blinking towards Seth again. Squinting. 'Seth, you're fading out.'

He nodded.

'Oh my God!' she gasped, her eyes suddenly widening in realization. 'We're in Londinium. Your own time! You'll get trapped here. You have to get back to the vortex!' She was choking with anxiety. '*Please, Seth! Move!*' she screamed huskily.

'Not without you!' he said, but even he could barely hear himself.

'*Nick!*' Eva screamed, beating her fists against his chest. 'Wake up, damn you!'

Nick groaned. The fight with Pontius had been bloody and brutal, and he'd nearly lost it. Would have, if it hadn't been for Eva and Atilius's lucky knife.

'Please, Nick,' she sobbed.

Nick coughed. Blood spattered over his lips. He cracked open his eyes. They were bloodshot and dazed.

'Please, Nick,' Eva begged. 'We need to get to the river.'

He closed his eyes for a moment, then took a deep breath and heaved himself forward. He coughed again and crouched, panting. But he didn't lie down. He ground his teeth and pushed himself forward.

Eva reached out a hand, but he shook his head, motioning her to move.

'Seth?' she gasped tentatively, her eyes darting around in panic. 'Are you still with us?'

'I'm here.'

She smiled. She could barely see him, but it didn't matter. She could feel his warmth beside her. She knew he was there.

'Please stay with me,' she whispered, as she stumbled and crawled towards the water.

'Always,' his faraway voice murmured beside her.

'Nearly there,' panted Nick, clutching on to the ground as a particularly big tremor suddenly shook the earth beneath them. Their progress had been painfully slow. Not just because every movement was excruciating, but also because the journey was so unstable: skirting obstacles or avoiding falling marble required deep concentration. As she helped Nick forward, Eva's lungs felt raw, she could barely swallow and the pain of every movement tortured each step, but she had just one conscious need: to stay with Seth. And if that meant endlessly scraping one knee after another along the harsh, trembling earth towards the river, then that's what she would do. That single purpose defined her. It allowed her to relinquish her hold on everything else. She no longer heard the screams of broken people. She no longer felt her battered body, the driving rain or the buildings crashing around her.

But neither did she notice that the warm shadow staggering beside her had finally collapsed. Seth's prodigious strength had found its end point. And as he lay watching the girl he had loved forever stumble further and further away from him, he silently wept his grief and loss.

73

Shadow

Londinium

AD 153

The riverbank was just ahead. We'd made it, though I was panting so hard I thought I might throw up. Vomiting in the vortex was probably not to be recommended.

I lifted my head to check Nick was still conscious enough to make the jump.

'Hey,' he smiled weakly. 'You ready?'

I nodded, then turned to reach for Seth. I felt a chill. I couldn't see him. At all. I held my breath . . . froze stock-still, listening for his voice, his breath . . . anything.

'Seth?' I choked.

Nothing.

Please, God. Please let him be there.

I shut my eyes, trying to sense the warmth that I'd been sure was beside me. '*Seth?*' I screamed. 'Where are you?'

No answer.

'He was here, Nick! *Right here!* W-where h-has h-he g-gone?'

Nick blinked into the darkness. 'I don't know, Eva.'

'I can't leave without him. I'm going back to look for him.'

'Eva, don't be crazy. If you go back there you'll die.'

'I *cannot* leave,' I sobbed. 'Not without Seth. You – you go. I'll follow l-later.'

'Eva. There is no later. Look out there. You have to come now! *Please!*'

He tugged on my arm, but I shook him off. 'I'm sorry, Nick – but S-Seth . . . he's my everything . . . I-I can't live an eternity without him.'

Nick was shaking his head. 'Eva, Seth wouldn't want –'

I put a hand over his mouth and hugged him. 'Thank you!' I gulped. 'Th-thank you for coming for me, Nick. I-I would have totally screwed the Cassius thing without you. P-Parallon should be saf–'

I never got to finish that sentence because I suddenly noticed what looked like a massive shadow coming towards us on the river behind Nick's head.

'*Oh my God!*' I gasped.

Nick instantly turned to look and choked out his own strangled cry. 'Christ! It's a bloody tsunami!'

Before I had a chance to react to the huge wall of water rolling towards us, Nick had hoisted me by the arm and hurled me into the swirling river underneath it.

74

Scream

Vortex

Seth . . .

My mind wailed his name in one endless scream as my body spiralled downwards. Images of crashing buildings, a flashing ruby knife, a towering wall of water and pain-filled eyes flitted through my brain, until the agony of lashing waves and burning lungs drove everything away.

And then . . . blackness . . . emptiness.

And peace.

75

Mirror

Jen groaned and opened her eyes, then blinked in confusion. She seemed to be lying on the floor staring up at a shimmering fluorescent strip light. Gingerly, she turned her head and bashed her nose against the porcelain base of a toilet . . . a toilet that had obviously seen better days.

She closed her eyes for a second, her brain trying to play catch-up, then inhaled sharply as memories suddenly flooded back. Vomit. Toilet cubicle. Channel 7 newsroom. This is where she'd fled to inject herself with the virus.

She sat up and stared at the stained, cracked seat with dismay. Clearly she hadn't made it to the magical kingdom. Damn it. She was still stuck in bloody London. Unlocking her cubicle door, she moved across to the sinks. Everything was exactly as it should be. Same faulty soap dispenser. Same chipped, smeary mirror. She peered at herself and ignored the slight shimmer around the edges of the mirror as she smoothed down her hair. The fluorescent lighting was probably on the blink again. Then she checked out her crumpled skirt and shirt. They were covered in sweat and what looked distinctly like dried puke. Slamming the faulty soap dispenser, she pushed the taps on full and began furiously dabbing at the stains. Without soap it was useless, and now she was soaking wet as well. She closed her eyes and leaned her head against the mirror.

'Dear God!' she hissed in frustration. 'A clean shirt! That's all I ask! How the hell can I go back out there looking like this?'

She glanced down at her clothes in despair . . . then gasped. She was now wearing her favourite blue silk cami. Was she dreaming or had some miraculous event just taken place?

She cast her eyes upwards in awe. 'Er – could I just request one more teeny favour?' she coughed tentatively. 'L-like maybe – some help with the skirt too?'

Her mouth fell open as her skirt instantly transformed into the cute pencil skirt she usually wore with the cami top. Wow! Since when did God answer all her fashion prayers? Her eyes continued down to the massive rubber boots on her feet. Which unfortunately triggered another memory. Flood . . . Earthquake . . . Tsunami.

Heart thudding, she threw open the washroom door and ran along the corridor to the newroom.

Monitor screens flickered with light, and the buzz of computer terminals and printers and scanners still filled the room. But there were no people at the desks.

Of course there weren't. They'd all evacuated.

She rushed to the window. It was raining, but she could see no sign of the tsunami. Maybe it had been a false alarm?

She headed for the stairs rather than the lifts and started galloping down the three flights, until one of her rubber boots slipped and had her catapulting towards the metal banister.

'Aggh!' she yelped, as her forehead collided with steel.

'Useless damn boots!' she spat, pulling them both off and hurling them at the wall.

She could feel blood dripping into her eye. She dabbed nervously at the gash. She needed a tissue – where was her bag? The toilets probably. Damn – she could really do with something to mop –

Jen swallowed. Her fingers now curled round a clean tissue.

'This must be some alcohol-fuelled dream,' she told herself. 'That did not just happen.'

Pulling herself to her feet, she headed back to the toilets to look for her bag. Yep – on the floor in the cubicle. Grabbing it, she moved across to the mirror to inspect her cut. Not too bad. Should clean up fine. Adding a few drops of water to the tissue, she lifted her eyes to the mirror again.

'What the –?' she gurgled. The skin on her forehead was literally knitting back together.

'Christ,' she breathed, suddenly laughing. 'I did it! I bloody well made it to Parallon!'

76

Triggers

Parallon

Nick opened his eyes to find himself flying through the air on a great arc of water. The sudden shock of it was so intense he couldn't even scream. All he could do was wait until gravity brought him down. He tried to make sense of where he was . . . Some place between water and sky . . . London? Londinium? . . . Parallon?

The ground was hurtling towards him. He heard a scream behind him . . . and then he landed hard.

When he next woke up he was stretched out on one of the sofas in Zackary's library. Eva was curled up on the opposite sofa, her eyes closed. Zackary himself was perched on the arm by her head, gently running his fingers through her hair.

Nick pulled himself up on one elbow. 'Is she OK?' he asked huskily.

Zackary lifted his head and his face creased into a rare smile. 'She will be. Thank you for bringing our girl back,' he said quietly.

Nick slumped again, and exhaled slowly. '*She's* not going to thank me.'

Zackary frowned. 'Why not?'

'She found Seth there. And then lost him again.'

'Seth was in Londinium?'

Nick nodded. 'Kind of . . . in a shadowy sort of way.'

Zackary nodded. 'He of all people knew the risks . . . What the hell was he doing there?'

'I guess he was there for Eva. Why else?' sighed Nick, standing stiffly and walking towards the window. 'Any Roman soldiers patrolling out there?' he asked, peering down at the rainy street outside.

'The Romans have been gone for weeks. The rebuild has already started.'

'How long were we away?'

'Four very long months.'

Nick nodded wearily. So Parallon was finally free.

'And Earth? What's happening there? The weather . . . the tsunami . . .'

Zackary took a deep breath and shook his head. 'We've been working on nothing else since you left. Eva's last orders.'

'Eva's ordering *you* around? Yeah, right!' snorted Nick.

'Oh, you'd be surprised. This girl isn't just a pretty face, you know.' Zack smiled down at her.

'I know that,' agreed Nick. 'She saved my life in Londinium.'

'Yours isn't the only life she saved.'

'What do you mean?'

'Enough conversation for one day, I think. Please don't start confusing me with a sociable person, Nick,' he said drily. 'That would be most unwise.'

Nick barked out a laugh and rubbed a hand over his face. 'You know what, Zackary, seeing as you're obviously done with the big *Welcome back thanks for getting rid of Cassius* ceremony, I think I'd like to take a walk round. Get a feel for this free new world.'

Zackary smiled but didn't move. He was still staring at the sleeping girl on the sofa.

'Don't expect her to wake up happy to be here, Ambrose,' Nick sighed. 'I forced her back.'

Zackary nodded. 'It's going to take her a while to get over the gladiator.'

'A little longer than a while, I think,' muttered Nick, heading for the stairs.

When he emerged on to the wet street, he was unsure where he wanted to go. His entire experience of Parallon had been as a prisoner – either in the palace the Romans had commandeered from Matthias, or the arena. Nothing would induce him to go anywhere near the arena, so he found himself walking towards Matt's old home.

It wasn't until he was approaching the large roman portico that he realized the music he'd been catching thin snatches of was very familiar.

What the hell? *Livid Turkey?*

Memories flooded back, memories of a former life . . . *Standing with Jen tucked in front of him at that gig; their bodies swaying; the pair of them screaming out lyrics; laughing that they both knew all the words.* He was stunned by the powerful cocktail of images and deep longing the music triggered. When the song finished he found he was standing completely still, staring at a string of purple and gold balloons bobbing from the marble cornice above the front doors. Before he could stop himself, he walked hesitantly up to them, pushed the balloons out of the way and stepped inside.

'*Nick!*' screeched Georgia, careering into him and wrapping her arms round his waist. 'I didn't think we'd ever see you again! Oh my God, everyone, Nick's back!'

Nick stood in bewildered shock as Clare, Elena, Winston, Tamara and Emerson came rushing through the huge crowd of revellers towards him.

'Oh, man, it's good to see you,' grinned Winston, slapping him on the back.

'Where have you been?' squeaked Georgia. 'Some weirdo said you and Seth led the magister into the river – like the pied piper or something!'

'Or something,' shrugged Nick, smiling tightly.

'So – is Seth here too?' asked Clare, skipping to the door excitedly. She gazed down the path, then turned expectantly to Nick.

His jaw tightened. 'No, Clare. I'm sorry. Seth – he . . . he didn't make it.'

'W-what do you mean?'

Nick swallowed. *What the hell did she think he meant?*

'You mean he didn't make it to the party, right?' she persisted. 'You can't mean anything else . . .'

Nick shook his head and turned away. He couldn't do this. He couldn't lie to Clare. But what could he possibly tell her? Not the truth. The vortex was still classified information. In any case, he didn't want to talk about Seth.

Suddenly the idea of a party was unbearable. 'Look, I'm really tired, guys. It was so good to see you – we'll catch up soon.'

'Wait, Nick,' pleaded Clare. 'Please. You only just got here, don't leave yet –'

Nick shook her off and strode blindly out of the door . . . straight into the path of Jennifer Linden.

'*Nick!*' she gasped, gazing up at him in wonder.

He stood in frozen shock. 'J-Jen?'

'I've been looking for you. Everywhere . . .' she whispered. 'For weeks and weeks.'

He blinked, flailing for the right thing to say . . . to think . . . to feel. 'I-I didn't know you were here.'

'Hey,' she grinned. 'You know I'll go anywhere with Livid Turkey on the playlist!'

He smiled tentatively and nodded. 'Yeah,' he said quietly. 'Me too!'

77

Guests

Parallon

'Eva, you've been staring at that screen for eight straight hours and I've promised Lauren that we'd both go and drink tea and eat lemon drizzle cake with her.'

'You go, Professor. I'd like to keep going with this. I think I'm close . . .'

'Please, Eva. You have to eat. Since you got back from Londinium you've done nothing but –'

'Nothing but what?' I snapped. 'Mope around? Or try to save the world?'

'Saving the world is of course a very commendable objective, Eva, but – I know Seth was –'

'Enough!' I hissed. He had just spoken the unmentionable name. 'I'll come upstairs and eat some damn lemon drizzle cake – but I'm heading straight back here afterwards.'

'Deal,' he muttered, pulling me out of the chair, through the door and up the stairs.

I glanced at his tense face, and gave his arm a small squeeze.

'Thank you,' I whispered.

'Thank Lauren. It's her cake,' he smiled.

'Not for the cake,' I snorted. 'For putting up with me,' I added quietly. Ambrose had been forcing me to get up and face each day. He'd encouraged me to work. To sleep. To eat. In his own quiet, sarcastic way, he was helping me survive.

We'd just about made it into the library when there was a heavy knocking at the front door.

Ambrose's eyes shot warily to mine. The instant frisson of fear was still my first instinct. But the Romans had gone, we were confident of that now. And Ambrose's glance definitely wasn't fear. It was unease. He wasn't exactly Mr Sociable . . . but I was about a hundred times worse. So I just shrugged and continued towards the library, clearly indicating that there was no way I was going to answer the door. It turned out Ambrose's sense of social responsibility was more acute than mine. Sighing, he turned back and headed downstairs. I glanced over at Lauren, who was sitting in front of a tea tray, but instead of joining her, I hovered on the landing, listening out for Ambrose's rude dispatch of the unwelcome caller.

'Hey, Zackary!'

Oh God. It was Nick. I hadn't been able to face him since we got back from Londinium. And fortunately I hadn't really had to, because he had moved back into Matt's old house.

'Nick.' Good. There was a cool finality about Ambrose's one-word greeting.

Awkward pause.

'Er – how's she doing?'

'Same. I'll tell her you came by.' I heard the door creak. Ambrose was clearly trying to shut it.

'Zackary!' persisted Nick. 'I've brought some of Eva's friends to see her.'

'What friends?'

Could Ambrose sound more suspicious? He had reason to. I had no friends.

'I think they may help her, Zack,' Nick said stubbornly.

'I very much doubt that,' snapped Ambrose.

Silence. I listened for the door slam. But all I heard was a heavy sigh.

'I suppose you'd better come in.'

What? No way! Did he just say *come in*?

I probably had about ten seconds to get to my room before they made it up the stairs.

'*Eva!*' barked Ambrose, catching me just as I was clicking my bedroom door shut. He threw it straight open. 'You have visitors.'

'Professor, please —' I begged.

'I'm sorry, Eva,' he said gently. 'They —'

Before he could finish his sentence a black and silver whirlwind was bounding through the door and I was suddenly being ambushed by a pair of scarily familiar arms.

'A-*Astrid?*' I gasped when she finally released me for an oxygen break. 'What the hell are you doing here?'

'Jeez, it's *so* good to see you, babe!' she grinned, holding me at arm's length. 'Doesn't Eva look great?' she called, turning back to the doorway.

Which is when I noticed she hadn't come alone. My mouth went dry. Not only was Nick Mullard standing uneasily on the threshold, but trying to push through behind him were Rob, Sadie and . . . *Jennifer Linden*!

Here . . . at Ambrose's house.

In Parallon.

I staggered backwards until my shoulders hit the bedroom wall. I leaned against it gratefully, staring at them all in disbelief.

Nobody spoke.

'Er – tea, anyone?' asked Ambrose, easing his way through the awkward gaggle.

Nick cleared his throat. 'Tea sounds great. Shall we go and sit down?' Moving purposefully towards me, he pressed a hand into the small of my back and propelled me into the library where Lauren was nonchalantly slicing cake.

Nick gently pressed me on to one of the sofas, then sat down on the one opposite. Astrid flung herself down beside me, and Rob perched himself on the arm of the sofa on my other side, grabbing my hand into both of his and squeezing it tight. I fought every instinct to pull it free again.

'Room for another Astronaut on that sofa?' grinned Sadie, shoving Astrid along so she could sit down next to her. My eyes flicked around the room, but stopped on Jennifer Linden, because she was eyeing me warily for some reason. The moment our eyes met, she pointedly squeezed herself closer to Nick and placed her hand proprietorially on to his thigh. I smiled, glad that someone at least had got her happy ending.

'Milk?' offered Ambrose, passing a jug round. Wow. He was pulling out all the sociability stops. I glanced up at him, expecting the usual Ambrose smirk, but his expression was kind of anxious.

'So, finally the Astronauts are back together!' chanted Astrid, throwing her arm round my neck and pulling me towards her. 'Are *we* going to rock this place!'

Rob did an enthusiastic air punch, but I just stared at my mug of tea. I wished I could have joined in, but their enthusiasm made me feel about a hundred and fifty years old.

I was also becoming seriously uneasy about the huge unanswered question burning in the air. No amount of tea, cake and rock-band hype could deflect it.

How the hell had they ended up in Parallon?

'Eva,' said Nick quietly.

I tried really hard to bring myself to look at him. It wasn't that I blamed him for pulling me back through the vortex. In his place I would probably have done the same. But I just couldn't forgive him. Any more than I could forgive myself for failing to stop him doing it.

'Eva,' he repeated, 'there's stuff I think you need to hear.'

I closed my eyes and shook my head.

'Look at me, Eva,' he commanded.

I opened my eyes and leaned back against the sofa.

Unexpectedly, it was Jen who started talking.

'Eva, has anyone told you about what's been happening back home?'

Reluctantly, I shifted my gaze to her. Since I'd got back from Londinium I'd been living like a recluse. Sleeping, eating, trying to find and fix the vortex coding. That was about it for me. Basic conversation was way too demanding, even with Lauren and Ambrose – so whenever they were talking I literally zoned out.

But personal space clearly wasn't an option with Jennifer Linden, and within a few minutes I found out that the horror I had been working night and day at trying to prevent had happened. The Londinium tsunami we had escaped was a symptom of a global catastrophe across time itself.

My eyes darted towards Ambrose. How much did he know?

His eyes glanced guiltily back at me.

Oh my God.

I felt sick. 'How bad was it when you left?' I asked nervously.

Jen stared at me. 'It-it's probably all over now . . .'

I just sat there. Our *world*? Our whole damn world was over?

'When Seth arrived –'

'*Seth?*' I jerked out of my seat, a moment of impossible hope suddenly filling me. Had Seth somehow made it out of Londinium to London?

'Eva, sit down, sweetheart,' urged Nick quietly. 'Seth would have been in London *before* – before we saw him in Londinium.'

'Seth and Matt were trying to get back to Parallon,' continued Jen smoothly. 'They arrived in London by mistake. Seth thought you might be there, so he came to search for you. When he realized you weren't, he tried to head straight back to the river. We literally had to hold him down.'

'Why would you do that?' I choked.

'Because I had to persuade him to use the virus to bring us here before the whole damn planet imploded.'

'No!' I protested vehemently. 'Seth would never give people the virus willingly.'

'He gave it to you when you were dying, Eva. I watched him,' said Jen quietly. 'He saved your life. And I begged him to do the same for us.'

My control was slipping. My hands had begun to shake, and my lip was doing that horrible twitching thing, so I shoved my plate on the coffee table, pulled my hand free from Rob's and stood. 'Thanks for telling me this,' I croaked. 'I'm – I'm really glad you all made it.'

Turning quickly to Astrid, I gave her shoulder a little squeeze, then fled to my room. As soon as my door was safely shut I lay on my bed and sobbed . . . Sobbed for the world that I hadn't managed to protect and for the boy who was always saving everyone else – but couldn't save himself.

78

Channelling

Parallon

I sat up. A soft blanket shifted from my shoulders. Someone had covered me up. I must have fallen asleep. I blinked around my room. It was dark. My eyes felt heavy, and my throat was swollen. Too much crying. But there was so much to cry for. Seth. Earth. The vortex . . .

I jumped off the bed, sudden realization crashing through me. If the vortex had already destroyed Earth, Parallon would be next. There was no time to wallow in misery. I had to get back to Ambrose's lab.

Two hours later I was still sat at Ambrose's computer scrolling down endless lines of code . . . And then I saw it flashing on the screen before me. The corrupt coding sequence I'd been chasing since the beginning.

'*Got you!*' I gasped.

'Got who?' murmured a voice at the door.

I jumped. 'Ambrose! You scared the crap out of me!'

'What the hell are you doing here, Eva? It's four a.m. You can't completely bury yourself in work, you know!'

'Yeah, right! You of all people –'

He shook his head, but pulled a chair up next to me. I smiled tightly. It was one of the things we had in common. Channelling. Channelling everything into work.

'By the way . . . I never really thanked you,' I said quietly.

'For what?'

'For reading my note. And –'

'For working my nuts off piecing together the Parallon fragments while you disappeared on your little suicide mission to Londinium?'

I nodded.

'Didn't manage to find the corrupt sequence though, did I?' he said bitterly.

'No, but I think I may just have –'

'You're kidding!' He moved his chair closer and started peering at the highlighted line of code on the screen. 'But it's nowhere near the river files.'

'That's why we didn't find it earlier,' I muttered, scrolling through all the adjacent lines of code to confirm it was the only faulty fragment.

'So have you tried overwriting the sequence?' he asked excitedly.

'That's what I was just about to do when you arrived.' My fingers flew over the keys. 'For some reason every time I punch in the correct code, it reverts.'

'We need to reboot,' Ambrose said decisively, deactivating the power source.

After the third failed attempt we both stared at the screen in frustration.

'You don't suppose Lauren's electromagnetic ramping could be impacting on the rewrite?' he mused.

'It's possible. I think we're definitely talking reciprocal energy transfer of some kind.'

I stared at the screen for a few more moments, considering the physics of that notion. 'Professor –'

'My name is *Zack*.'

'Yeah, yeah. OK – *Zackary* – how did you originally upload the digital memories?'

'Electrodes.'

'So when S-Seth got that direct download of your memories . . .'

Ambrose's eyes flicked anxiously to mine at the mention of Seth's name. I gritted my teeth. He was right – it had cost me. But this was too big to let my own personal junk get in the way.

He cleared his throat. 'Touch . . . Seth touched the screen.'

'Right. So you were nowhere near. Have you done any direct down or uploads since Seth?'

Ambrose shook his head.

'I think maybe you should, *Zackary*.'

Ambrose's eyes flew to my face, his mouth turning up at the corners. I assumed he was smiling because I was finally calling him by his first name. But I was wrong.

'Damn it, Eva, that's not your worst idea ever . . .'

From Ambrose this was *high* praise.

'But the vortex was never in my original upload. I didn't programme the vortex in at all. It would never have occurred to me to include a corridor between the two worlds because as far as I was concerned, one was physical and the other was virtual. I saw no possible connection between them – they were on different existential planes. It wasn't until the virus transmuted the virtual world that the vortex emerged – like some weird cosmic side-effect; a spontaneous umbilicus.'

'But it was when *you* – the progenitor – got infected with the virus that Parallon erupted into being?'

Zackary nodded again. 'Yep. Our very own big bang.'

'So maybe we should try rebooting that way. A kind of clean reinstall.'

Zackary sat in frozen silence for a few moments, then reached a hand up and touched my cheek. 'I sure picked right when I chose you, didn't I?' he said huskily.

'Hey, Prof,' I answered lightly, 'save the speeches. It probably won't work.'

'Let's find out, shall we?' He smiled tensely, stretching his arms above his head and flexing his fingers.

'Right now?' I whispered, suddenly terrified. What he was about to do was huge. Unpredictable. Desperate.

'No time like the present,' he shrugged. 'Shove over!'

A few moments later he had prepared the data store for transmission. Then he closed his eyes.

My heart was crashing against my ribcage as I watched his fingers stretch towards the screen. Just as he was about to make contact, I grabbed his other hand and clung to it with both of mine.

If he was going down, I was going down with him.

79

Reset

Parallon

Lauren jerked instantly awake when she heard the scream.

Heart pounding, she sat up in bed, trying to orientate herself.

Had she imagined it?

She knew she hadn't. She also knew without a doubt that it was Eva she'd heard. Eva had been waking up screaming every night since she'd returned from Londinium.

But this scream was different. One solitary vocal stab in the air. And then silence.

'She's probably gone back to sleep,' Lauren mumbled to herself.

But something felt weird. Wrong.

She threw back the covers and tiptoed to the landing. Eva's bedroom door was open. Peering inside, it was immediately obvious that Eva wasn't there.

Lauren moved across the landing to the library. It was dark. And empty. So was Ambrose's bedroom.

A shiver of fear ran through her body. Where were they?

Lauren did a cursory check of the bathrooms and the kitchen, then arming herself with a carving knife, started moving towards the stairs. Her hand had just touched the banister when she felt a deep tremor in the floor. As a native Californian, she immediately recognized the sensation. Earthquake. Instinctively, she dropped to her knees and clung to the banisters for support. Then gasped. Something strange was happening to the banister. She could have sworn she saw the wood momentarily pixelate.

Lauren rubbed her eyes. Was she still asleep – or was her eyesight going? Taking a deep breath, she forced her gaze downstairs . . . the distance would exercise the optic muscles. Good. Vision restored. She was just beginning to breathe normally when it happened again – the entire stairwell suddenly shifted into a pixelated mosaic. Then righted itself again. Her heart raced. Was this it? Was this the reason Eva had screamed . . . The meltdown they'd been doing everything in their power to prevent had finally started?

She pulled herself to her feet. She was not going to cower helplessly on the floor any longer. If the world was about to end, she was at least going to make sure she wasn't sitting alone on the bloody landing.

'Eva?' she called, as she dashed down the stairs. 'Are you OK?'

The door to the lab was open.

Zack's lab door was never open.

But it wasn't the open door that caused her eyes to widen in shock and her breath to hitch. It was the sight of Ambrose lying prone on the floor. And Eva lying lifelessly beside him.

80

Call

Parallon

We're sitting on a huge checked picnic rug in our meadow. Seth and me. Delicious foods are spread out between us: soft, pungent cheeses, fresh, fragrant bread and plump, juicy strawberries, all shimmering in the bright sunlight. We have slipped off our shoes, and my bare feet stroke sensuously through the cool blades of grass, forcing daisy heads to rise up between my toes like fairy jewellery. Almost imperceptibly I'm aware that instead of grass it is Seth's hand skimming my toes. He is right beside me; warming me, enclosing me. His other hand holds a perfect scarlet strawberry. He touches it to my lips. Then laughs. We are both laughing as he bites from his side and I bite from mine. We meet in the middle. I start licking the juice from his lips, but before I can finish his tongue has darted forward and is licking mine.

And then I hear a cough. Professor Ambrose is there. Smirking at us. So is Lauren . . . and Astrid, Sadie and Rob . . . as well as half of St Mag's. Then I notice Jennifer Linden, Nick Mullard, Elena, Georgia and Clare. All picnicking. All laughing.

I watch them in bewilderment. What are they doing in our meadow? I turn to Seth to ask him, and he's disappeared.

'Seth?' I call. But I know then he hasn't slipped away. He is gone.

'Seth!' I scream into the trees. But the trees simply rustle in response. Rustle and sway as the wind grows and the sky darkens. I look around frantically. I am alone. Everyone has gone. The sky is nearly black, and now the storm begins. Swirling vicious rain and wild savage winds transform seamlessly into huge black birds with heavy wings and polished hooked beaks. They fill the entire sky with their screams of fury, and then they fly down to claw at my face, my arms, my legs.

But I refuse to leave the meadow.

'I'm waiting for him! I shout at the birds. I'm not giving up! I will never give up again!'

And then I hear his voice. Calling me . . . from a long way away. Miles and miles and miles. His voice is so faint. A whisper on the wind.

'Eva!'

It sounds like a prayer.

'I'm coming, Seth,' I gasp, running through the rain-beaten grass towards him. But the grass begins growing round my feet. Growing and twisting round my ankles like vines, stalling me, pulling me, holding me fast.

I look up through the rain and I am in a twisted forest, where snakes curl round branches and bright predatory eyes stare from dark corners . . . but I tear my body from the writhing vines, stumble towards his voice . . . past Cassius's palace . . . past St Magdalene's School and Ambrose's house . . . until I reach the river. The feeble glow of moonlight shimmers on the turbulent, churning surface, but no amount of turbulence can

*drown out the fierce desperation in his voice as it perpetually
calls my name . . .*

I gasped awake. Panting.

'Oh, thank God, Eva! You're OK!'

'Lauren?' I gulped, blinking at her in surprise. What was she
doing here? My head was full of Seth.

And then I took in the scene . . . Ambrose's lab . . . Ambrose
lying on the floor next to me, groaning.

'Professor!' I choked, shaking his shoulders, tears filling my
eyes. He suddenly looked so frail. My professor. And I was to
blame. The whole upload had been my idea. Had the power
transfer killed him?

'He's coming round, Eva,' said Lauren.

'Professor!' I cried. His hand twitched. I wrapped my fingers
round it.

'Seth,' Ambrose croaked, his eyes fluttering open. 'Go find
him, Eva.'

'You heard his voice too?' I gasped.

'Go!' Ambrose repeated, pulling himself up on his elbows.

I stumbled to my feet and swayed for a moment. Then I
looked uncertainly at Ambrose.

'Will you be OK?' I whispered. But even as I asked, I could
hear Seth's voice in my head, urging me to the river.

'Eva, you don't have much time,' insisted Ambrose, pulling
himself to his feet and leaning on Lauren. 'Just go! I'll be right
behind you.'

Lauren stared between us in bewilderment as I threw open
the front door and ran out into the rain.

*

The closer I got to the river, the stronger Seth's voice seemed to grow, until at last I stood on the bank gazing down into a churning, writhing cauldron of water. Its wildness reminded me of London, of Londinium and of my psychotic nightmare. The Parallon river never roared and swirled like this, as though a hurricane was twisting beneath it. My pulse raced, fear and the vestiges of my dream blending nightmare with reality; making it difficult to distinguish between them. And I could still hear his voice:

'*Eva! I'll find you. Don't give up on me!*'

Crazily, I found myself answering. 'I'm here, Seth! Can you hear me? Please come home to me!'

'*Eva!*'

He sounded so far away, just like in my dream. I stared down at the maelstrom below, listening desperately. But now all I could hear was the churning water, the howling wind and the hammering rain.

'I think it may be crunch time, Eva.'

I turned sharply. Ambrose was beside me, his face pale and haggard. Lauren wasn't far behind.

'The reset came too late?' I croaked.

'Possibly.'

'W-will Parallon implode . . . like Earth?'

'Fifty-fifty, I'd say. If the negative density does a diametric shift . . .' He tailed off. 'The truth is, Eva, I really don't know. I-I don't feel like I know anything any more.'

'And Seth?'

He shook his head. 'I-I just don't know.'

I had never heard him sound so lost. So humble. Professor Zackary Ambrose – master of the universe, gifted, ruthless scientist, imperious teacher and accidental creator of Parallon – was finally admitting weakness. If only Seth was here to witness this momentous event. It was probably the closest Ambrose would ever get to acknowledging his responsibility for the scientific catastrophe that had ricocheted down the vortex and destroyed the world.

One man. One lab. One rat.

I reached out and squeezed his hand, because despite his sins, I loved the man. And, anyway, who was I to talk about sins? My hands had blood on them too . . . So much blood . . . So much loss . . . Yet so much love. I glanced up at Ambrose. His mouth twitched into his nearest approximation of a smile, as his eyes squinted against the storm raging around us.

And then . . . it came again. Seth's voice. And I knew what I had to do.

'Zackary, I'm going to find him,' I whispered, brushing my fingers along his sleeve. Before he could try to stop me, I moved to the water's edge and jumped.

81

Faith

Vortex

The moment my body hit the water I felt the pull. Only instead of dragging me down as it had always done before, the water was spinning round me like a whirlpool, in fast concentric circles – turning me and twisting me until I couldn't think or breathe or see.

But Seth's voice stayed with me . . . soothing, anchoring, reaching for me.

'I'm here!' my mind answered. 'I'm right here, Seth.'

There was a burst of pressure. My lungs felt as though they were exploding, and then I was scalding in a searing, terrible heat.

'Seth!' I screamed.

And suddenly I felt him: the whisper of him at first; the whisper of his presence . . . cooling the water . . . entering it like some palliative current vibrating against my skin. I could feel him. His energy. It was all around me . . . engulfing me, filling me, completing me, growing from a whisper to something vital and strong. We were tangled, coiled, knotted together, indelibly and permanently joined in a constant, endless spinning motion . . . holding each other, comforting each other, exchanging dark for light, cold for warmth, past for future, me for him and him for me . . .

'What the hell?' Ambrose's voice . . . breaking through the dizzying motion, dragging me back, tugging at me.

I was lying on a hard surface, sunlight on my eyelids, warmth all around me . . . and a faint stirring beside me, across my stomach, over my legs.

That scent. The scent I would know anywhere.

I opened my eyes –

Two startlingly blue eyes blinked back at me.

I couldn't speak.

I had to be dreaming.

My eyes explored his face greedily. A fading bruise over his brow. Wet, messy dark hair, curling against his temple, down his neck.

And those lips – opening, spreading into the most beautiful smile.

'Seth!' I breathed, touching his cheek. 'Please be real.'

He stared back at me, pulling me tightly into his arms. 'I thought I'd lost you,' he choked into my hair.

I was shaking. Crying. Kissing him. Touching him. Clinging to him. Praying this wasn't a dream. Or that if it was, I would never wake up.

'Hey,' he murmured, touching his thumb under my lashes and wiping away the tears. 'Please don't cry, baby.'

'Then stop leaving me!' I sobbed, clutching on to his soaking shirt.

A moment of agony crossed his face, and then he closed his

eyes and held me hard to his chest and murmured, 'Never again, Eva. I can't ever lose you again.'

Suddenly his lips were pressed against mine, and my heart was beating furiously as his fingers tightened in my hair, closing any possible space between us.

'Ahem! Would it be too much to ask you two to come back to the house now? Some of us have had very little sleep.'

Ambrose's sarky face glaring down at us instantly dispelled my 'perfect dream' theory.

I giggled and rolled my eyes. 'Aw. Prof. Cut me some slack here. The love of my life just came back from the dead.'

Seth stilled beside me.

'Seth?' I reached up and touched his face.

'I should be dead,' he whispered.

'No, baby,' I choked.

'I wasn't supposed to survive, Eva. It was over. I couldn't stay with you . . .'

My chest heaved at the memory of finding Seth gone.

'But why, Seth? Why didn't you stay beside me?'

'I was out of time,' he said sadly. 'I couldn't make it back to the river – I didn't have the strength – it was all used up. Maybe the battles. Maybe the vortex . . . I said goodbye to you . . . But then Matthias came back for me.'

'Matt was there?' I gasped.

Seth nodded. 'He shouldn't have been. We shouldn't have been. Not in Londinium. It was my fault. I was focusing on your name in the vortex. Using it to find you. And we ended up in Londinium because that's where you were. I'd felt you, Eva, so I could never have turned back. But I told Matthias to return to the vortex – and – instead – he came after me . . .'

'And took you back to the river?'

Seth frowned, staring sightlessly ahead, trying to remember.

'I couldn't walk, I was barely conscious . . . just aware that Matthias was talking to me . . . supporting me . . . telling me that we would soon be home – and I would find you. And then he wasn't talking any more, he was gasping, shouting. And I opened my eyes and I – I thought I saw a wall of water!'

'You did. The tsunami,' I nodded, remembering the terrifying sight.

'Matthias was stumbling. He didn't have the strength or speed to carry us both to the vortex before the wave hit.

' "Put me down, brother," I told him. "You have to jump now."

'But Matt shook his head and said, "After carrying you all this way? No, Seth. You're not going to rob me of my one worthy act . . . Now, go find your love." And before my barely conscious mind had worked out what he meant, I was thrust in the air and plunging into the river. He'd used up every atom of energy and strength he had left to send me into the vortex.'

I saw how hard it was for Seth to bear the gift that Matt had given.

'He loved you, Seth.'

Seth nodded. 'We'd stood side by side for so long, Eva. He was my brother: despite his weakness, I always loved him. Yet in all the time we knew each other, he had never shown me how truly strong he could be.'

'Because you were always the strong one.'

'But that final act of friendship was . . .' His voice broke.

'. . . worthy of a hero,' I whispered, wrapping his hand in mine.

Seth nodded, his jaw taut with pain.

'*Eva, Seth! I think we need to move!*' shouted Ambrose, staring wildly at the river and pushing Lauren behind him.

'Oh God!' I gasped as I stared in horrified wonder at the whirlpool exploding through the water and pushing up into the sky.

Seth grabbed my arm and practically hurled me towards the road. Then he doubled back and dragged Ambrose and Lauren with him.

When we had reached a safe distance, we stood and watched. This was no tsunami. It was a spiral of swirling energy pushing the water high into the sky, creating a breathtaking spinning prism of revolving light. The ground all around us vibrated with the sheer power of the vortex. Buildings shook, pavings fractured, and just when I feared the earth would crack under the pressure, the water started to subside, gradually descending until at last it flattened out.

'Is that it?' I whispered.

Ambrose shook his head. 'I don't think so.'

We continued to watch as the vortex began to reverse, descending into the river, creating a deep and infinite tunnel of swirling water.

'This is the break moment,' murmured Ambrose. 'This is where we find out whether our wormhole is going to collapse – or transform . . .'

'Transform into a –' I swallowed.

Black hole.

Two small words.

Too big to say out loud.

Ambrose shrugged. 'Fifty-fifty. Not such bad odds.'

Fifty per cent chance we'd survive sounded OK. Fifty per cent chance Parallon would cease to exist, not so much.

I swallowed, grabbed Seth's hand and said, 'Whatever happens . . . I'll love you forever.'

He pulled me tightly into his chest. 'I'm going to hold you to that, baby!'

82

Afterlife

Parallon

'*Eva!*' Groan.

'Hey! Ground control to Major Koretsky!'

A heavily ringed hand was waving in front of my face.

I blinked back into focus. Café. Parallon.

'OK! OK! Stop flapping, Astrid. You're gonna knock over my cappuccino,' I complained.

'Where does she *go*?' Astrid snorted to the table at large.

'Your guess is as good as mine,' shrugged Rob.

'Disney World? Stadium gig with Livid Turkey?' offered Sadie.

I rolled my eyes. How could they still be so normal? Just weeks ago we narrowly escaped total black-hole annihilation, yet here we were still acting like a bunch of kids.

'So you're OK with this, Eva?'

'Er – with what?' I asked tentatively.

'The Astronauts gig!' snorted Astrid.

'I guess,' I hedged. 'You really sure Parallon is ready for us?' I asked, looking around the café dubiously.

'Of course! Everyone needs to rock. We'll blow this place apart!'

'Good to see the Astrid brand of humility's still intact!' I grinned.

'Er – putting a rock god and "humility" in the same sentence is an oxymoron, Koretsky. And I know you're not a moron!'

I laughed. 'Not sure you're right there, Astrid. I've been known to be monumentally stupid . . .'

'Hey, who's calling my girl stupid?'

I looked up. And there he was: my very own Greek god. Grinning at me, rivulets of sweat trickling down his neck and seeping through his running vest.

Without even registering the impulse, I was out of my chair and in his arms.

'Hey, I'm covered in sweat!' he protested, wrapping his arms round me and kissing me hungrily. Even covered in sweat he felt good. Tasted good. He moaned into my mouth.

'Guys! You're over-sharing again!' groaned Astrid, throwing half a doughnut at us.

'Let me go and get showered,' Seth murmured in my ear. 'Then you're coming out with me.'

I stepped back to look at him. 'Oh, I am, am I?'

'No question!' he answered, his eyes sparkling.

'And where exactly are you planning to take me?'

'Surprise,' he smirked, kissing the top of my head. Before I had a chance to argue he was jogging through the tables towards the exit.

'Aw, Seth!' I whined after him. 'You know I hate surprises!'

He didn't stop stop moving, but I could see his shoulders shaking with laughter.

'What's up?' I frowned, when I turned back to our table and noticed that my band crew were warily watching a couple of

419

girls sat near the exit. Despite their cleaned-up appearance I immediately recognized them from the arena dungeon: Georgia and Elena. I followed their gaze. They were literally gawping at Seth like he was a tub of Ben and Jerry's.

And then I saw a third girl. The one who'd obviously tipped over her chair in her haste to run after him.

I recognized her too: Clare – the girl who'd 'hated me forever'.

She had clearly managed to intercept Seth's departure, and the two of them were now talking animatedly. Seth was shoving his hands through his hair and frowning uneasily as one of her hands fluttered flirtatiously against his shoulder. His gaze flicked to mine. Clare caught the look and her eyes narrowed dangerously.

'Awkward moment alert,' Astrid murmured under her breath, as Seth suddenly started striding over to our table, with Clare still hanging on to him.

Georgia and Elena also seemed to be watching the scene play out with rapt interest. My eyes nervously scanned the rest of the café. Damn. When we'd started our band meeting there'd only been a couple of tables occupied; now the place was rammed. Apart from a load of St Mag's kids having a food fight, it looked like we were the chosen diversion for everyone else. And – typically – that *everyone else* roll call included Nick and Jen, who were sitting at a corner table unashamedly watching us. To be honest, Nick looked pretty uncomfortable, but Jen seemed to be thoroughly smirking. Did she get off on other people's pain, or was it just mine?

'I'm not doing this,' I muttered, standing up to leave. 'OK if we take a rain check on the rest of the meeting?'

Astrid's hand shot out and grabbed my wrist. 'Eva, just see it through, babe.'

I rolled my eyes and turned to face Seth and Clare as they approached our table.

As soon as he reached me, Seth gently disengaged from her and pulled me towards him, running his lips across the top of my hair.

'Sorry to interrupt your meeting again, baby, but this won't take long,' he breathed into my ear.

'I hope this isn't the surprise you had planned,' I murmured back.

He chuckled. 'Trust me, I didn't see this one coming either.' He gave my neck a quick nuzzle, then cleared his throat.

'Clare,' he smiled. 'I don't think you've been formally introduced to my girlfriend, E–'

'We've met,' she hissed icily.

'That's great!' smiled Seth. 'So now that Eva's here to stay, I'm hoping you can make her welcome and we can all be friends.'

Yeah, she looked totally stoked by that idea. Not.

Seth glanced at me, and I did my best I'm-a-really-forgiving-and-unpossessive-girlfriend impression. Astrid's smirk suggested I may not have quite pulled it off.

'Right, well, I have an urgent appointment with my shower, and then a surprise date with my girl,' grinned Seth, turning round and heading away. 'So I'll see you guys soon,' he called over his shoulder.

We all stared after him.

Clare stood in front of me, her shoulders taut, her fists clenched, and her eyes burning into me bitterly. I didn't move, just shrugged slightly, licked my dry lips and waited for whatever it was she was planning to dish out. I'd been here before. It was familiar ground – fighting for Seth. So I couldn't blame Clare. Not really. I mean – he was kind of worth fighting for.

And then I saw it in her eyes. A sudden deflation. An acknowledgement that it was over. She looked defeated. Her shoulders slumped and her head dropped.

Instinctively, I reached out a hand and touched her shoulder. 'I'm sorry, Clare,' I whispered.

She nodded sadly. 'Yeah . . . well – er – I guess I'd better get back . . .' she mumbled, turning to leave.

I glanced at our table and winced at their unashamed gawping. But I couldn't help noticing that Rob seemed pretty fascinated by the pattern on Clare's shirt.

'Er, maybe catch you later, Clare?' he called after her, as she headed back to her friends. She didn't turn, but she lifted a hand in a vague suggestion of a wave.

Astrid instantly dug an elbow into Rob's ribs and cackled. 'See something you like there, bro?' she sniggered.

'Cork it, Rettfar,' he snorted. 'Now if the drama's over, can we get back to this damn band meeting?'

'Sure,' said Astrid. 'Where were we?'

'About to sort out the set list and publicity,' prompted Sadie.

'Set list? Publicity?' I frowned. 'We only start on that stuff when we have a definite gig date . . .' I reminded them. And then I saw their faces. 'What did I miss?' I groaned.

'Tomorrow night, sweets!' grinned Sadie. 'We've been booked to play here at the café. Man, it's going to be a blast!'

I rolled my eyes. I knew it would have to happen some time. They needed to play and Parallon deserved some music and fun.

'Fine,' I sighed, submitting to the volley of shoulder punches and enthusiastic whoops from the crew.

We'd just finished sorting out which songs we'd do, as well as planning some cool flyer designs, when the most delicious scent of showered, body-washed Seth crept up behind me. It took all my willpower not to moan out loud.

He put his hands over my eyes and whispered huskily: 'Ready for your surprise, Eva?'

'Are we done here, guys?' I grinned, shoving the set list in my pocket and jumping to my feet.

'Just get out of here,' groaned Astrid, waving me off.

'Catch you on stage tomorrow, then!' I laughed, grabbing Seth's hand and following him out.

83

Forever

Parallon

We walked hand in hand, quietly enjoying the strange new hybrid streets. Parallon was evolving. A few buildings remained Roman, but most had reverted to the mixed architecture of my first visit. A couple of people had wanted to build a completely new Parallon; a totally fresh start. But that idea hadn't gone down well. Probably because it sounded too much like what the Romans had done.

There was a determined air of optimism in Parallon now. Though so many had arrived bewildered and shell-shocked during that last great influx, Seth had done everything he could to induct and welcome them. Since the vortex had imploded, we knew there could be no more arrivals. Parallon was a contained world. Complete. So we had to try and put our guilt behind us, and look for ways to make sure that the stability would never be breached again.

I squeezed Seth's hand and smiled up at him. He grinned down and swung our arms as we continued to walk. I was just beginning to wonder where exactly he was taking me, when the 1920s facade we were passing abruptly ended, and I was staring up at the Temple of Jupiter. My heart lurched.

Seth let go of my hand and tucked me closer in to his body as he steered me round to the back of the temple. And there it was: our meadow – the place that had haunted my dreams and nightmares.

We made our way to the oak tree, our exact spot. Seth created a heavy wool cloak, a perfect replica of the one he'd borrowed that day in Londinium, and laid it on to the grass. He waited until I sat down and then dropped down beside me, pulling me so that we were lying face to face.

'How much do you remember about the last time we were here, Liv – Eva?'

I smiled, reaching out to brush back a lock of hair that had fallen across his forehead. 'You haven't called me Livia in a while, Seth,' I whispered tentatively.

'Blame this place! But I think I've more or less got used to calling you Eva now,' he smiled.

I took a deep breath. 'It hurt you, didn't it – finding out who I was,' I whispered.

He picked up one of my hands and played distractedly with my fingers. 'I thought it did . . . Finding out that Livia wasn't the girl I'd thought she was . . . Until I realized that what really hurt was the fear.'

'Fear?'

'If your name was false, how could I trust your words? That fear nearly killed me . . .' His breath caught as he spoke, and the pain I'd caused him made my whole body ache. I pressed myself into his chest, and laid my hand across his heart.

'But then I remembered the way you looked at me in the arena, and in that wretched blue sickroom, and the forum, and this meadow . . .' He picked a daisy and twirled it round in his fingers. 'And I knew that it didn't make any difference what you called yourself, or where you came from. Because I was entirely yours. And whatever name you used, I still trusted that you were mine.'

'I am yours. Forever!' I murmured into his chest.

He wrapped his arms tight round me, then pulled his head back so we were nose to nose. Slowly lifting my right hand, he tenderly kissed the ring he had given me and whispered, 'So, Eva, I was wondering, given that we're a forever kind of thing . . . if maybe – er – you would . . . marry me?'

I gasped, blinking at him in surprise.

Wow! Marry?

I had never imagined myself marrying.

Seth was watching me, his expression suddenly uncertain.

'Shall I tell you what I told Clare, when she attacked me this afternoon?' he asked, kissing my fingers one by one.

I tried to swallow. It made a kind of gulping sound. He ignored it.

'I told her I loved you so much that I was lost without you. I told her you owned me and there will never be anyone else. You know that's true, don't you?'

I nodded and cleared my throat. 'I feel the same way.'

'So do you trust me, baby? Do you trust us? Can you trust in tomorrow? In forever?'

He was watching me with his clear blue eyes.

I touched a finger to his lips. They parted slightly and I could feel his warm breath tickling my skin. I smiled, it felt so right.

'Yes,' I whispered.

'Is that a yes you trust me; or a yes you'll marry me?' he asked quietly.

'It's a yes to everything,' I giggled, throwing myself on top of him and kissing him all over.

I could feel the deep vibrations of his laughter through my whole body, and as I wound myself round him and laughed along with him, it was impossible to distinguish who was shaking who, who was kissing who or who was touching who.

We stayed locked together in that meadow: breathing together; moving together and loving each other until the stars came out. At least I'm pretty sure the stars came out. I completely forgot to check.

Acknowledgements

I can hardly believe the journey is over. It's not going to be easy to say goodbye to Eva and Seth after all we've been through together. Although that might sound like a self-indulgent author conceit, it's true – the characters in the Parallon books have literally become like real friends to me.

And they aren't the only friends I've made during this epic process.

My two extraordinary editors have not only nurtured these books on to the shelves, but have become valued friends in the process. It was to Shannon Cullen I tentatively showed the first draft of *Fever*, and it was her faith, care, commitment and imagination that breathed life into the series. Anthea Townsend joined us for *Delirium* and then took over while Shannon went off to create something even bigger and better than a book series – her fabulous baby, Mattie! Anthea was given the unenviable task of making sure I finished the trilogy properly . . . and what an exceptionally insightful voice she's been.

I was thrilled to have Karen Whitlock for the copy-edit after her stellar contribution to *Delirium*. She is both keenly observant and thoughtful, and once again every comment and suggestion has been invaluable. I owe a whole heap of gratitude to the wonderful Samantha Mackintosh, for meticulously coordinating the copy-edit and proofing, for her empathetic troubleshooting, and for generally throwing her angel dust around.

As an illustrator myself, the book jacket designs were hugely important to me – and that level of commitment is never going to be very appealing to a designer! But Katy Evans stalwartly circumvented my OCD tendencies and produced this third beautiful cover.

Continued thanks must go to the rights team: Zosia Knopp, Jessica Adams, Camilla Borthwick, Joanna Lawrie, Susanne Evans and Josephine Blaquiere, who have all worked so tirelessly with our world publishers over the last three years. I am so grateful to them.

And then there are my indomitable experts.

It is not always the most comfortable experience handing over a manuscript to authorities in subject areas that you are woefully under-equipped to write about. They have every right to be patronizing or appalled, but I am glad to say each one offered comments with thoughtfulness, generosity, imagination and an astonishing absence of scorn!

Thank you again Andy Mylne for ploughing your way through yet another entire book, rewriting my Latin and checking for classical errors. I promise the next book I write will have no gladiators, magisters or ancient languages!

Thank you Tom Adair, a very altruistic internet friend I made during the writing of this book. He is a forensic scientist, who freely offers his expertise to writers needing to know important facts like how long a crucified body takes to decompose!

Thank you again Duncan McNeil, my generous IT adviser,

who managed not to wince too noticeably at my futuristic projections and once more offered important insights into the future digital world. Thanks to physicist Kevin Walsh for (amongst other invaluable suggestions) gently pointing out my inadequate understanding of Einstein's Postulates. I'll do my best to keep astrophysics out of my next book!

Although I am the least physically courageous person you could meet, courage – both physical and moral – is probably the quality I admire most. And courage is a recurring theme in the trilogy. As *Afterlife* progressed, I realized that the particular brand of heroism I was exploring required consultation with someone who genuinely understood it. I am honoured to have been able to speak to military expert Lieutenant Colonel Dominic Biddick. Dom is the real deal – the kind of soldier Nick and Seth are modelled on. Not only was his help invaluable, many of his comments gave a unique insight into a life of real personal sacrifice and tough choices.

My sister Caroline (the doctor) has continued to be one of my most valued readers – and of course a major source of medical information. This time, instead of getting into trouble with *hypo* and *hyper*tension, I managed to stumble over my *hypo*thermia symptoms. So just make sure if you ever fall into the river, get a fever or have blood pressure problems, you see her rather than me!

Thank you my lovely Addison for starting to read the book before I'd finished and then demanding instalments so voraciously I was forced to work faster! And thank you so much for all your fantastic work on the website. Thank you Max for tirelessly talking vortex, digital glitches and time travel with me. Your contribution has been immense. And finally – as unsentimentally as I can – I want to thank you, Chris: for putting up with a distracted wife; for allowing me to talk Parallon and plot variations until you glazed over; and for sticking your head in the lion's mouth to make uncomfortable (but crucial) suggestions. Your patience, support and kindness have been boundless. I simply couldn't have done any of it without you.

TWO WORLDS.
TWO MILLENNIA.
ONE LOVE.

COLLECT ALL THREE BOOKS IN
THE **PARALLON** TRILOGY!

PRAISE FOR THE SERIES:

'Full of twists, immaculately researched, it is very exciting and unpredictable'
Independent on Sunday

'It's a great ride with evocative settings and intense emotion'
SFX

'Completely addictive and if I could have read it in one sitting
I would have done ... an excellent and compulsive read which has
left me wanting more' goodreads.com

WWW.FEVERBOOK.CO.UK

FEVER

Two worlds. Two millennia. One love.

'Full of twists ... exciting and unpredictable' *Independent*

www.parallonbooks.com

www.deeshulman.com

'Absolutely brilliant book. This series just gets better and better ... A very clever read, while being thrilling, romantic and original' goodreads.com

www.parallonbooks.com
www.deeshulman.com